TERMINAL VELOCITY

Vassily Petrov swore as the stealth suddenly lost altitude and precipitously nosed down. He tried to emergency restart, but both his engines were now dead. His altimeter line, white numbers flashing on the right upper portion of his main screen, showed he was dropping like a stone with the fierce storm swirling around him, pelting the cockpit canopy windows with hailstones.

Petrov tried to restart one final time. His engines briefly caught, but then died of infectious flameout. Now, he knew, there was but one option left: He had to land the plane dead-stick, on the desert, with all the risks to which such an emergency landing would expose him. The choice was as clear as it was Draconian—crash-land or simply crash. There was no longer any in-between for Shadow One.

SHADOW DOWN

David Alexander

BERKLEY BOOKS, NEW YORK

SHADOW DOWN

A Berkley Book / published by arrangement with
the author

PRINTING HISTORY
Berkley edition / February 2000

For information address:
The Berkley Publishing Group, a division of Penguin Putnam Inc.,
375 Hudson Street, New York, New York 10014.

The Penguin Putnam Inc. World Wide Web site address is
http://www.penguinputnam.com

ISBN: 0-425-17305-4

BERKLEY®
Berkley Books are published by The Berkley Publishing Group,
a division of Penguin Putnam Inc.,
375 Hudson Street, New York, New York 10014.
BERKLEY and the "B" logo
are trademarks belonging to Penguin Putnam Inc.

PRINTED IN THE UNITED STATES OF AMERICA

10 9 8 7 6 5 4 3 2 1

Acknowledgments

A number of good people helped with research on this purely imaginary work, though none of them would like to be identified by name. They would prefer to inhabit the realms of the imagination, where gremlins and gnomes, but also spooks and moles, live, work, and play. To these imaginary friends, my genuine thanks.

For the unsung war heroes in my family: my great-grandfather, infantryman; my uncle, bomber crewman; and most of all my father, secret saboteur of Hitler's deadliest "victory" weapon.

For heaven is parted from thee, and the earth
Knows thee not . . .

—John Keats

Nothing is true. Everything is permissible.

—Hassan i Sabah

For we wrestle not against flesh and blood, but against principalities, against powers, against the rulers of the darkness of this world, against spiritual wickedness in high places.

—Ephesians

Author's Introduction

The scenarios described in this novel take place in the very near future, where the paths of current events and future technological, political, and military challenges converge. Yet the concept on which the novel is based has interested me for a long time.

When I was a kid, the nuclear submarine *Thresher* disappeared on her maiden voyage. For months, nobody had a clue about her fate. The idea that this complex piece of big-ticket military hardware could simply vanish into the depths of the ocean with all her crew aboard captured my youthful imagination. To me it was a real-life *Flying Dutchman*. As the years passed, the revelations concerning our country's covert actions in the *Thresher* incident, and in connection with Soviet submarines, began to leak out of secret files. These, too, went into the mental hopper.

In the late eighties the concept that the then just-rolled-out stealth fighter might also be lost one day and become the subject of a rescue operation, in this case a clandestine mission on the ground, took form. But publishers scoffed at the notion that this could ever happen to the then newly minted superplane, invisible to radar and thus invulnerable to attack.

I remember sitting across the desk from one editor at a paperback house in New York's Chelsea district, an editor then known for his acumen regarding military and action thrillers, who spontaneously began shaking his head and clenching his fists as I pitched my concept. His body language declared loudly that my ridiculous idea was turning him off. Funny that he now seems to have vanished from the publishing scene like a human *Thresher*.

As it turned out, about six months after I began working on *Shadow Down* for Berkley, and ten years after I first began pitching the book to editors, my dumb idea turned into the six o'clock news when an F-117A stealth was downed over Bujanovici by what—at this writing—was presumably a low-altitude SAM strike. The rescue mission, proclaimed by the media as a humanitarian effort to save a downed airman, but likely as much intended to retrieve or destroy classified components of the F-117A, also became reality. Judging by the experiences of many downed fighter pilots in the Persian Gulf, the rescued pilot was fortunate indeed to have been in the cockpit of a stealth, instead of an F-16, F-4, or virtually any other aircraft in the USAF inventory when "whatever-it-was" brought him down over Yugoslavia.

Since even real events have their gray areas, especially those concerning military actions, it should come as no surprise to readers if in the course of this book they find I have taken occasional liberties in treating doctrine, technologies, politics, weapons systems, and other elements of the plot.

I've striven at all times to base characters and events as closely on real-world situations as possible. But I've also made various exceptions to this rule because I've found that whenever life imitates fiction, the closer it comes the more interesting it gets. Yet when fiction imitates life, the opposite is generally the case. This is also why, as Zarathustra was once said to have spake, any resemblance to persons living, dead, or otherwise, is purely and completely coincidental, and everything in this novel is totally a work of the imagination. That, and absolutely nothing more.

DA
March 1999

Book One

Low Observable

One
The Votrin Algorithm

Like daggers in flight, two black-hulled aircraft cleaved the predawn darkness. They showed no lights as they crossed into the mountainous northeastern tier of Iran from the low-lying steppes of Azerbaijan and began to climb and turn their way through the high, rocky passes.

Each plane carried a single missile in its conformal weapons bay. It was all the mission would require. One missile, one kill. After being a dream since the days of Douhet's World War I theories on airpower, after showing itself possible at Ninh Binh Bridge in North Vietnam, and then becoming accomplished fact in the Desert Wind air campaign, it had established itself as air combat doctrine.

But the missiles that would be launched when the stealth aircraft reached their pinch-off coordinates were unlike rounds fired from any planes that had been part of the Gulf air tasking order. They were far more sophisticated than the LGBs that, their targets painted by invisible laser radiation from emitters on the undersides of

F-117As, were seen on bomb camera footage wreaking surgically precise destruction on targets in Baghdad, Kosovo, and other enemy bastions.

In fact, the rounds nestled in the belly of each aircraft were not even bombs at all—smart, dumb, laser-guided, or otherwise. They were true fire-and-forget weapons. Deployed from extreme standoff range, they would autonomously find their way to their targets and trigger their high-explosive conventional warheads once in place.

The missiles, called JASSMs, were closer in lineage to the Tomahawk cruise missiles that were launched from ships, submarines, and bomber aircraft in the Gulf. The joint air-to-surface standoff missiles were air-breathing predators, steel-skinned sharks with silicon intelligence, uplinked to global positioning satellites, capable of flying a low-trajectory path to their targets inside Iran.

They had been programmed with three-dimensional data from a KH-14 photoreconnaissance satellite orbiting one hundred miles above the Middle East some thirty-six hours before. When released, and after a brief booster stage burn, the JASSMs' ramjet turbofan engines would ignite and their navigational systems would place them on increasingly serpentine flight vectors toward their targets across the arid desert of Iran.

The stealth planes that flew the mission were also unlike any flown before in combat, but for somewhat different reasons. In design, they were similar to the F-117A stealth fighter and, like the F-117, deliberately misnamed because neither plane would ever intentionally engage in a dogfight, and was therefore no true fighter.

The subsonic stealth aircraft, depending on a sophisticated inertial navigation system linked to an onboard computer processor array to keep the plane stable, and incapable of anything like the rolls, turns, wingovers, and other high g-loading maneuvers of true fighter jets like the F-22 or MiG-29, would not last a minute against an airborne interceptor aircraft that had it in his sights. It was a ghost plane, flying under cover of darkness only, destined never to see combat by the light of day.

The two planes that crossed into Iran this night at four hundred twelve hours, Greenwich mean (or "zulu") time, precisely according to the timetable prepared by the mission commander, were not F-117s, however. They were not even part of the United States Air Force inventory.

Though similar in appearance to the F-117, the planes had rolled off the assembly line at the Mikoyan-Gurevich plant at Krasnovodsk, C.I.S., on February 19, 2002, where they were emblazoned with the red star of the Russian air force on their rear stabilizer fins.

The stealth aircraft were MiG multirole fighters, designated MFI-19 by the former Soviets, dubbed "Eclipse" by NATO, and each single-seat plane was flown by a Russian pilot. Their mission, however, was a joint undertaking by the air arms of both the United States and the former Soviets against a common threat. Its objective was to destroy the nuclear warfighting capability of the Islamic Republic of Iran.

Four hundred feet beneath the sand desert of western Kuwait, Brigadier General John "Stick" Yarwood of the U.S. Air Force sipped coffee from a porcelain mug that bore the image of a cartoon character from a prime-time television comedy show. The coffee tasted like a sock boiled in sweat. The incongruous thought that this is what Yarwood's own nerves would taste like right now if they were brewed in a twenty-dollar electric coffeemaker flashed through the general's mind.

Yarwood glanced at his wristwatch. Four hundred twenty hours, zulu. He'd been up without sleep for the preceding nineteen straight hours. He needed some sack time, but that would have to wait awhile yet. Not until the targets had been destroyed and both planes were back in their hangar would Yarwood permit himself some downtime.

Yarwood stopped his pacing and cast a look toward the operation's joint commander, General Mikhael Korniyenko of the Voiska Protivovozdushnoi Oborony, or C.I.S. Air Defense Force. Korniyenko was scanning the center display panel of a three-screen array on the wall that faced the two-tiered command and control pit—the battle cab. The mission's ground support personnel went about their duties below. The commanders and their staffs oversaw everything from the upper level.

The command, control, communications, computing, and intelligence—C-4I in military jargon—center was still under construction. It was one of the concessions the U.S. had made in order to mount the operation. Kuwait was the ideal place from which to launch a strike on targets across the Persian Gulf. But it had cost. The base, as well as a sizable arms package including tanks, planes, and mechanized artillery, was part of the price paid the tiny but avaricious oil sheikhdom.

If the operation succeeded, the expense would be cheap. Yarwood well knew the risk it was designed to eliminate. Iran had emerged as the biggest winner in the late twentieth century's Mideast power sweepstakes. Quietly, with exquisite patience, the revolutionary government in Tehran had played both Eastern and Western power blocks against the EEC and reaped a harvest of military hardware and weapons technology for their pains.

The U.S., wishing to continue the thaw in relations that had come about following the election of the moderate Rasulali to the Iranian presidency, had rewarded Iran with fighter aircraft and computer technology. The Iranians had paid court to the Russians as well—more accurately paid them large sums of money—and in return gained important nuclear reactor and ballistic missile expertise. As long as Iran continued to overtly snub Iraq and make friendly overtures to its distant suitors in Washington and Moscow, it continued to harvest a bumper crop of war machinery. East and West both believed for a time that the Iranians would be content to savor their toys and leave it at that. Both were wrong. By the late nineties, Iran had made rumblings about taking over swathes of Azerbaijani territory toward creating a Persian superstate.

In 1998, Iran had mobilized its forces along its shared northeastern border with Afghanistan, and sent secret shock waves through the intelligence communities of both the Americans and Russians. Iran had not only mobilized its land army, it had placed its nuclear forces on standby alert as well. Overhead surveillance satellites tasked by the CIA's National Photographic Interpretation Office, under the Directorate of Science and Technology, had shown beyond doubt that Iranian MRBMs—medium range ballistic missiles—were aimed northward. HUMINT or human intelligence resources revealed that Iran's Strategic Rocketry Forces had its collective finger on the figurative launch button.

These revelations were nothing new to the Israelis, who, by way of their national intelligence agency, the Mossad, had warned Central Intelligence for years about the burgeoning threat of Iran's nuclear weapons capability and her growing will to use those weapons of mass destruction. But Mossad's warnings about Iran were ignored, much as Israel's own nuclear weapons program had been ignored some thirty years before.

It was only now, when the Israelis, claiming that Iran was on the verge of launching a major regional power bid and would not hesitate to strike at Israel in the process, threatened to mount an attack of their own, that the U.S. had finally been moved to act.

On June 7, 1981, the Israelis had launched a daring mission to destroy SAAD-17, an Iraqi nuclear reactor then under construction outside Baghdad, with a sortie of F-16 fighters. The planes demolished the plant in under two minutes before sweeping back across the Jordanian border. The international complications caused by the raid threatened to undo U.S. policy in the Mideast because, for one thing, the Israelis had been secretly provided sophisticated KH-11 satellite imagery by Washington which was used to target the strike. A strike by Israel today against Iran, even if successful, would have far more ominous consequences. Nor could the U.S., given its new détente with Iran, risk even indirect involvement.

The solution came with the downing of an Aeroflot commercial jet by terrorists financed by Iran. That was the straw that broke the camel's back, or more accurately, angered the bear. At the U.S.-C.I.S. summit in 2001 held directly after the accession to the presidency of former General Dimitri Pavlovich Grigorenko, the strike plan was broached. Grigorenko, an ex–military officer and Afghan war veteran, approved the plan. It would give his forces a chance to outshine the Americans for once, even if only a select few would ever know of it—and none beyond a handful ever would.

Furthermore, there was a legalistic pretext that appealed to the Russians—the obscure 1926 Tehran Agreement, signed by Reza Shah Pahlavi, father of the shah of the same name deposed in Iran's 1979 Islamic Revolution, which permitted the U.S.S.R. to enter Iran should, according to the wording of the document, "circumstances develop which constitute a danger to Russia." Until now, the Russian-Iranian treaty had never been invoked since its signing, with one near exception.

In 1981, the Soviet Union, looking on as Iraqi forces penetrated into Iran during the Iran-Iraq War, had concentrated fifty mobile divisions in the Caucasus and Afghanistan near the Iranian border, poised to cross into Iran had the Iraqi penetration continued and Iran found itself in serious danger of defeat. Then the Soviets were prepared to move with or without Iran's consent, invoking the terms of the 1926 treaty.

Events never required this move, but neither had the Russians lost their keen interest in a region which Leonid Brezhnev had described in a 1977 speech given in Mogadishu, Somalia, as "one of the great treasure houses on which the West depends." Strategically, Iran's importance remained as great to the C.I.S. as it had been to the Soviet Union that preceded it. The buildup of Iranian nuclear forces was a development that the Russians would never tolerate for long.

The surgical interdiction operation would have to be conducted in total secrecy, and be completely deniable. Russian stealth aircraft carrying American cruise missile technology would serve the purpose. The planes would launch from a point hundreds of kilometers distant from their targets, and the missiles would never be seen until they exploded. Iran would know the truth, of course, but it could never prove it had been hit by a peacetime air strike. Tehran would have been sent a message it could understand in no uncertain terms.

Flying time–on–station on a broad circular track high over the southeastern quadrant of Saudi Arabia, a USAF E3-A Airborne Warning and Control System or AWACS aircraft scanned the airspace out to a distance of 320 klicks with its suite of computer-linked air defense radars. The thirty-foot-diameter parabolic rotodome situated on double struts atop the forward fuselage revolved continually, providing coverage deep into Iran via the newly upgraded RSIP radar suite to which the antenna was linked.

Over a thousand miles to the northeast, across the low mountain chains that formed a natural barrier between Iran and Khazakhstan in the Urals, a plane with a silhouette remarkably like AWACS's and an identical purpose, an A-50 Mainstay, was flying an almost identical circular track across the still-dark skies.

Both surveillance aircraft were linked by secure military satellite relay to the C4I center in Kuwait, where the coded telemetry from their computer-enhanced radars was viewable separately on the two flat-panel side screens, or as a composite on the larger central screen of the command post.

The tactical picture showed that the airspace surrounding the projected track of the Shadows was free of fighter aircraft. Eavesdropping on Iranian communications also indicated that enemy ground tracking radars had picked up no hint of the impending strike. The large screen also displayed the projected track of the stealth aircraft, which, though invisible to radar, were not quite as invisible as most would believe.

On the other side of the vast ar-Rub' al-Khali or "empty quarter" of the Saudi Arabian desert, others were monitoring events. They, too, knew the truth about stealth, and had known from the first. In the C4I center, part of a DUF or deep underground facility buried in a remote corner of the Negev desert, communications specialists attached to the Directorate of Signals Intelligence of the Zahal or Israel Defense Forces, also studied the imagery on their own screens.

Officially kept out of the loop, the Israelis knew about the coordinated strikes anyway, just as they knew about the Votrin Algorithm, the so-called antistealth algorithm that formed the nucleus of a sophisticated computer program that made antistealth radar possible.

The Americans had their own version of the algorithm. They had possessed it from day-one, because stealth had never been intended to blind friendly eyes, only becloud the vision of the enemy. The myth of stealth's near invisibility to foe and friend alike has been, and still is, one of the most effective disinformation operations of the United States government, and one that has had willing accomplices in global defense establishments, which see it in their interests to perpetuate the long-standing myth.

Because of the disinformation surrounding the capabilities of stealth, few outside of a select group of warplanners have ever asked this question: What military force commanded by sane individuals would ever build a sophisticated weapons system that they did not have the power to detect and destroy should it ever fall into unfriendly hands?

The Americans had designed stealth, and had simultaneously designed the capability to defeat stealth. This capability was one of the most closely held secrets of the United States government—so closely held that there was a termination order applicable to anyone attempting to reveal it, one that had been used on at least two occasions, as far as the Mossad knew, and maybe more.

The counterstealth secret was U.S. property—until Votrin came along in 1989. The Russian mathematician had led a group working for the Soviets during the Gorbachev era tasked with finding a way to defeat stealth. Acting on the fact that stealth does not make planes invisible, but only reduces their radar cross section, or RCS, to a fraction of its actual size, Votrin devised his algorithm. It could be used to computer-enhance radar images and show where stealth was located in the skies.

The Votrin Algorithm wasn't as good as its American counterpart, but it was good enough to make at least the initial "angular stealth" aircraft designs visible to the right radars—and they had to be powerful enough radars to begin with, linked to powerful enough mainframe computers. If you had these, then you could see stealth. It was that simple.

The system wasn't as effective against later upgrades of stealth, and useless against the more advanced "curved stealth" of the American B-2 bomber, nor did it work against the new active electronic measures that the Americans had begun incorporating into their upgraded stealth after the Gulf War. But against the original angular stealth of the F-117A, it worked well enough to paint a usable picture.

The Israelis had been working on the Votrin Algorithm for over a decade, enhancing it and the computer-linked radar systems necessary to make it work. Votrin himself had been found dead in a Brussels apartment block in 1999 where he had lived since after escaping the Soviet Union following the fall of the Berlin Wall and the end of the Cold War. The official explanation had been death by natural causes, a heart attack suffered in an open-cage elevator rising between the fourth and fifth floors of the building. The Israelis put a different spin on it. They called it a KGB *mokri dela* operation, a "wet job" by Department K of Line S, the Komitet Gosudarstvennoy Besopastnosti's efficient assassinations directorate.

But whatever had killed Votrin, his work lived on. The Israelis retained a full set of his technical papers giving the essential parameters of the antistealthing process. The problem was, at least for them, that the Iranians had it, too. The Russians themselves had sold them the basics of the system, and their own petrodollars had financed the rest from the best of the brains of the expatriate Russian scientists who fled their homeland in the wake of the Cold War.

Against the American Block-III upgrade of the F-117A that was still under wraps at Nellis Air Force Base in Nevada, far from prying eyes, Iran's Votrin-enhanced radar would be nearly useless. But against the more primitive stealth of the Russian clone of the U.S. jet, the Eclipse, it was an enhancement that would increase the stealth's RCS by as much as 35 percent. That could make all the difference in the world, the Israelis knew, as they continued to cast probing beams of electrons at the equivocal night skies above the Middle East.

Two

Of Sales Reps, Radars, and Stealth

In the cockpit of the stealth plane code-named Shadow One that was now flying its programmed "black line" toward the nuclear reactor at Kasjhan, there was little for Vassily Petrov to do except detachedly observe. On autopilot, the plane practically flew itself, its inertial navigation system taking bearings from the array of GPS satellites overhead and matching these against onboard sensor data.

Protracted inactivity changed Petrov's focus, and his attention began to wander. His mind cast back to the two-month training period that had preceded the mission. Preparations had taken place in strictest secrecy. The joint U.S.-Russian team had been based at Vnukovo, a military rocket base at Kapustin Yar, in a remote section of the Urals. It had been agreed that Russian pilots would fly the mission in Russian planes, but the Americans had brought along their own personnel, including technicians and pilots who had flown actual missions in stealth aircraft during the Gulf War and in Yugoslavia.

Captain Chuck Covington had been one of those pilots. Covington had taken part in the opening sorties of the Desert Wind air campaign. The destruction of an Iraqi chemical weapons plant with laser-guided bombs had been his baptism by fire. Petrov had found a friend in Covington, and the American stealth driver had added personal details concerning his combat flights to those in his regular briefings.

Covington described the terror of his flight over the night skies of Baghdad, a city that glowed in the distance with an orange radiance like live coals on a barbecue grill, due to the density of antiaircraft fire flung at the skies. The streams of triple-A were so thick, the pilot said, that they blended into glowing sheets. As he approached the Iraqi capital, the acrid stench of cordite that had slowly seeped into the Nighthawk's cabin had become a choking cloud. Covington was convinced that he would die.

"They fired more bullets than I thought were ever made in the history of the world," Covington had told the Russian. "The only way I can describe it is if you turn a room into the world's biggest popcorn popper—with popcorn going off all over the place—and try to walk from one end to the other without getting hit by a piece of popcorn. That's what it was like."

"But then how did you succeed in not getting hit?" Petrov had asked the American pilot.

"By thinking, 'they're not going to hit me,' over and over again, like some kind of mantra," Covington had replied, "and just keeping on moving."

Then Covington told about the elation of hitting the target, seeing it blow sky-high in a mushrooming pillar of flame and heat, and realizing that he could not be seen by the enemy, that he was invisible and therefore untouchable.

Tonight, Petrov's flight presented none of the tension and terrors that Covington had described. The view through the cockpit windows of Shadow One was of a sky jet black and crystal clear, flecked with the countless ice chips of blue, white, and yellow stars.

There was darkness below, too, occasionally broken by the flash of headlights from vehicular traffic on one of the tributary roads crisscrossing the desert floor. Produce and consumer goods from Haifa, Amman, Cairo, Tehran, Damascus, and places far removed from the Mideast were trucked to commercial centers in Iran at all hours, just as they were in the C.I.S., Europe, or the U.S.A.

Although the stealth flashed through the sky at a velocity approaching the speed of sound, there was virtually no sense of physical motion for its pilot. Unless he chose to look out the cockpit windows, Petrov's only impression of movement was a purely psychological one, produced by the muffled roar of the plane's twin turbofan engines, and the color visuals on the multimode display screen at the center of the console, which showed a pictorial representation of the plane's flight path on a moving map display.

The plane's avionics suite was in large part a product of French technology. It had been designed and built by the French aerospace firm, Aerospatiale, in a deal that had mated French expertise in electronics miniaturization with Russian breakthroughs in high-power radars. The Phazotron Zhuk-PH system in Shadow One incorporated a stealthy synthetic-aperture laser-radar, or ladar, moving-target identification, and terrain-avoidance modes.

The result of the collaboration was a rate of cockpit miniaturization that was unprecedented in Russian aircraft design. The breakthroughs meant that for the first time Russian aircraft could begin to approach some of the sophistication that had put American military aircraft light-years ahead of them for so long, and even exceed it in certain realms.

Unlike true fighter aircraft, or the F-117A Nighthawk, for that matter, the Eclipse did not have a heads-up display or HUD, which overlaid the pilot's line of sight through the cockpit window with navigational references, target acquisition data, and other pictorials. The Eclipse didn't need a HUD. Though called "multimode," it was neither an air-superiority nor an air-dominance fighter. It flew one mission and one mission only—that of a silent, unseen platform for air-to-ground ordnance of various kinds. That was it.

Instead of a HUD, the plane's console was divided into a complex of three 9.7-inch active matrix color screens, with smaller dedicated displays for target information and navigation data at either side. The left and right screens gave configurable air-combat imaging and radar readouts. The center display was a multimode monitor linked to a RISC processor-based CPU that integrated all the data the pilot would need into a comprehensive whole. Right now the multimode screen showed Petrov a green-and-pink trough that undulated and curved toward a distant horizon line.

The trough represented the plane's trajectory, with distance and altitude, in klicks and degrees, marked off by black intersecting lines. To either side of the winding, snaking flight path was a representation of terrain out to a distance of one hundred klicks, and on this terrain field were pictorials that showed waypoints, terrain features, and threats, each color-coded according to their threat priority.

Petrov's most immediate concern as the plane flew past the first of its three waypoints were the two threat balloons—balloonlike wire grid representations in glowing orange—about fifty klicks ahead, representing SAM sites. The orange color indicated threat-rich environments with overlapping radar coverage, to be avoided at all costs.

Each of those SAM installations was equipped with a battery of surface-to-air missiles. The latest intel had shown a mix of SA-6 "Gainful" low-to-medium altitude missiles and the much newer 90Zh6 upgrade of the Soviet SA-10 "Grumble," which could reach high into a fighter's altitude envelope. A typical Iranian battery, he knew, would be made up of two or three launchers sitting atop tracked armored vehicles. Each mobile launcher was a self-contained unit including tracking and guidance radars and up to four missiles ready for deployment on pneumatic-actuated launch pylons.

The SA-10 upgrade in particular had a number of improvements that worried Petrov. Among them was its new 64N6 long-range, 3-D phased-array surveillance radar that bore the NATO code designator "Tombstone."

Unlike other SA variants, the 90Zh6 utilized two separate system components. The transporter-erector-launchers, or TELs, which fired the new 48N6 missiles, were carried on the trailers of the 54K6 command modules, which contained the radar and were mounted on a heavy MAZ-543 truck. About the same length as the earlier 5V55 series, the 48N6 was a much fatter missile, carrying more fuel and giving it greater range than previous versions.

The 64N6 radar upgrade, which was good enough to allow the SA-10 to engage tactical ballistic missiles at medium altitudes, was linked to a new-generation fire control computer with multiple scan modes enabling the simultaneous engagement of six targets with up to two missiles per target. All things being equal, the 64N6 radar stood a minuscule—but genuine—chance of detecting Shadow One in flight.

In an electronically cluttered environment such as a multiple sortie attack would create, the small, pigeon-sized radar cross section that the stealth returned to probing radar lobes might never be detected. But in an empty skyfield, in an electronically sterile environment, there was a chance of radar engagement, however small. The SAMs would have a hard time acquiring the target, but they had formidable range, and even a lucky near miss might prove fatal because of the blast radius of the missiles' high explosive fragmentation warheads.

As the threat balloons grew larger on the Eclipse's multimode screen, Petrov's thoughts turned in other directions. It was pointless to worry, and besides, the envelopes of the balloons were far from the perimeter of his projected flight path. Many kilometers separated those deadly missile launchers from his plane, and as he approached them, he knew INS would decrease the aircraft's ceiling to further maximize his low observability. Terrain-following radar would take over then, the stealth would dip low and hug the contours of the desert. Amid the ground clutter of reflected radar side lobes, it would be hidden from detection.

He would never be seen. Under cover of the night, he would ghost right past those SAMs.

Still many kilometers from the black arrow streaking toward it, Petrov's intended target lay exposed on the flat tableland midway between the Dasht-e-Kavir desert and Iran's capital, Tehran. The venting stacks of the nuclear power plant at Kasjhan now were cold and silent. Ordinarily the stacks vented nonradioactive waste steam produced by the plant's three-hundred-megawatt reactor into the night air. But tonight the French-built plant operated on only a skeleton staff, as it had been doing for the past two weeks.

The plant was undergoing a periodic downtime during which its spent uranium fuel rods were replaced and routine maintenance and inspection were conducted. The air strike had been calculated to coincide with the final week of these maintenance procedures, when the facility would remain functionally idle and understaffed. Apart from reducing the loss of human life and other collateral damage, this also significantly lessened the hazards of the explosive release of radioactive contaminants into the atmosphere as a result of the missile strike.

None of the estimated annual ten kilograms of plutonium produced by the plant would be found on-site. HUMINT, or human intelligence assets, had confirmed that all the plutonium had been transported to the Iranian Nuclear Technology Center some five hundred kilometers to the southwest, not far from the Isfahan processing complex, which included a uranium hexafluoride plant using high-speed centrifuges to enrich uranium into weapons-grade material.

Isfahan, too, was on the night's air tasking order. As

Petrov flew his heading toward Kasjhan, his fellow pilot Lavrenti Samsonov flew the other stealth aircraft in the direction of Isfahan, where another JASSM would be launched to destroy the facility. Both the CIA and KGB's estimates placed the amount of bomb-grade plutonium at the facility in the vicinity of thirty pounds. While the amount of enriched uranium already processed was not precisely known at the time of the raid, the available plutonium was estimated to be enough fissionable material to make ten Hiroshima-size bombs, or single warheads of about one megaton each. In the scale of the Mideast target set, that was easily enough for Armageddon.

The Isfahan site was a windowless four-story concrete building on the surface, and a five-story underground complex directly below where the plutonium was processed, stored, milled, and machined into warheads. Estimates placed the number of operational warhcads in Iran's nuclear arsenal at somewhere between ten and fifteen. Were the reactor at Kasjhan not destroyed, the number could rise to twenty or more within a matter of months. Coupled with Iran's growing arsenal of medium-range Shihab-3 ballistic missiles, each with an approximate two-thousand-kilometer range—enough to threaten the flanks of Central Europe—the nukes presented a major regional power shift in the making, one that threatened both East and West.

The strike on Isfahan posed no danger of triggering a nuclear detonation. On the contrary, the explosives stored at the complex would help cook off the plutonium and prevent it from forming fissionable critical masses. The danger of the explosions releasing a toxic, radioactive cloud was there, but the risk was deemed acceptable. The plutonium was stored on the lowest level of the plant and would be buried beneath tons of concrete rubble.

The blast would, in effect, entomb the plutonium underground.

Or so it was hoped.

• • •

At the al-Rash'd ground radar station, all was quiet. The lonely outpost in the arid desert landscape was a node of the Iranian air defense system garrisoned by a small contingent attached to the Iranian 21st Signal Corps, headquartered at Mehrebad Air Force Base near Tabriz.

The personnel assigned to al-Rash'd included radar operators and technicians, missile crew for the single SA-10 launch system, and a mechanized detachment of Warsaw Pact BRDM-2 and BTR-70 APCs, heavy trucks and Jeeps from the 2nd Regional Command of the Iranian People's Army that provided security. Apart from the two monthly deliveries of food and the contraband, including forbidden liquor, purchased from Bedouin traders that regularly sold to the base, the duty was tedious, and personnel usually rotated out as soon as possible.

Tonight, at four hundred twelve hours, life at the remote desert station was no exception to the general rule of monotonous drudgery. Apart from the scopeman monitoring the radar display in the station's control room and the sentries walking their posts around the fence surrounding the installation, no one was awake.

Izmir Albrouny, whose surname was Turkish, reflecting his family's southward immigration after World War I, was twenty-six and had trained as a radar operator at the Iranian military academy in Tehran. Because Albrouny had showed himself to be skillful at his job, he had been selected to train on the new, Valkyr-II digital pulse Doppler radars that had been built by the German firm of Oberlikon under a contract with the Iranian military.

The Valkyr-II radar was linked to a Siemens mainframe computer system running SNA-Unix that could process the radar returns at ultrahigh speed, comb and filter the returns, and display the data on the high-definition color screen. The system also incorporated Votrin algorithms under a feature Oberlikon called its "advanced antistealthing" feature set.

Oberlikon had demonstrated its new radar at the Defense Services Asia Exhibition in Kuala Lumpur, Malaysia, in the spring of 2001, at the IDEX arms trade show in Abu Dhabi, UAE, the following summer, and then at the Paris Air Show at Le Bourget Airport. Its sales representatives at these and other global arms bazaars had aggressively marketed the enhanced radars, and their efforts had not been in vain. Oberlikon sales reps in the firm's Bonn headquarters had set up appointments with a number of interested buyers representing the military branches of their respective governments.

Later that season, the Iranian government had clinched a multimillion-dollar deal with Oberlikon to retrofit their French-made radar system with the VK-II upgrade package. The enhancements in the retrofit would make the Iranian air-defense system the best in the region, barring that of the Israelis, which was built by a consortium including Oberlikon, the Israeli firm IAE, and the U.S.-based McDonnell Douglas Military Electronics Division. The retrofit of the Iranian system was only partially complete, which was another reason for the timing of the strike mission flown by the Shadows.

Nevertheless, the retrofit was more complete than intelligence available to the U.S.-Russian coalition had indicated. The radar defense node at al-Rash'd was not listed as among those scheduled to receive the Valkyr-II upgrade until the fall. The Israeli military intelligence agency, AMAN, had confirmed this through intelligence from a highly placed informant in the Iranian military, but though true at the time the intel was received, it had been rendered false by a step-up in the pace of the retrofit program.

The net result was that tonight, as Vassily Petrov cleared the first SAM site along his flight path and approached the second to his right, the presence of his aircraft was picked up by the air defense radar node at al-Rash'd and seen by Albrouny at precisely four hundred fifteen hours, while Shadow One was passing thirteen kilometers to the east at an altitude of ten thousand feet and a sub-Mach speed of seven hundred miles per hour.

The radar contact did not register as a blip, nor was the radar scope that Albrouny watched a round, green screen dominated by a moving sweep hand of white electronic snow. Albrouny's screen was a large, modern computer monitor equipped with a keyboard and mouse that showed a full-color digital relief map of the roughly two hundred klicks of territory covered by the radar node.

The view from the screen was the airspace looking down from an imaginary point above the earth. Instead of the blips of yesterday's technology, symbols and lines indicating the type of threats and vectors of approach flashed into being on the screen, and slid across the map as radar tracked them.

At four hundred fifteen hours, zulu, Albrouny was surprised to see an icon he knew only from training exercises appear on the extreme left of the screen. The symbol was a yellow triangle with the approximate speed and heading of the aircraft it represented listed beneath it as it crossed the map.

"*Madergenduh!*—motherfucker!" Albrouny muttered in Farsi as it appeared. He knew the yellow delta icon stood for a radar contact with a stealth aircraft.

A split second later the contact disappeared from the screen, but then reappeared in under a minute, already many kilometers from the point of the first sighting. Then it disappeared and was not seen again.

Since the new radar system was equipped with several advanced, computer-aided options, Albrouny used them to the fullest. While he waited for the contact to reappear, the scopeman clicked on the histogram button on the toolbar atop his screen. This feature enabled operators to replay, then analyze, recent contact data that was stored in computer memory.

Albrouny found the first and then the second stealth contacts, playing each back in slow motion in a window superimposed over the main digital map, which continued to show real-time radar returns. He next ordered the system to display the lobes and ellipses of the recorded contacts and to analyze their signatures against a library of aircraft radar signatures stored in the system's extensive database.

The results of the analysis gave Albrouny a textual and pictorial match on several points of convergence between the actual contact and the statistics the database contained about low-observable aircraft.

The pictorials were good, but not conclusive. The bottom line for Albrouny was that he'd maybe had an actual stealth contact, but it might just as well have been atmospherics, a glitch in the software, an electronic hiccup, or a radar lobe bouncing off a natural object with a radar cross section small enough to fool the system into thinking it had seen a stealth. A cluster of hailstones in the midst of a *shamal,* or severe storm, could account for this. Other things could, too.

Still, there it had been. Albrouny pondered awhile as he continued to process and analyze the contact data, displaying lines of bearing, estimated speed, and other information.

Did he want to wake "the Beast" from his slumbers and risk his commanding officer's legendary wrath? This was the question. Albrouny knew very well that he had replaced a radar officer who had dared to disturb Major Kuraytem while he was enjoying the company of one of the women smuggled into the base from the regional capital, Semnan, and had paid for his indiscretion with a hasty transfer to the hard-duty garrisons in contentious Kurdish strongholds in the mountainous region north near Tabriz.

Staring at the screen, Albrouny rhythmically drummed his fingers on the edges of the computer keyboard. Finally, he picked up the phone beside his console, taking a chance on rousing the base commander from his nightly drunken sleep, and hoping that tonight the major slept by himself.

Three
Ghosts in the Machine

Vassily Petrov heard a warbling, two-note chime announcing that the stealth had reached its final waypoint, in this case its initial point for ordnance release, or IP. The IP is generally keyed to a prominent terrain feature. Here the landmark was part of a system of deep culverts with steep, poured concrete sides, lying athwart the north-south axis of the Tehran to Isfahan highway approximately ninety-six klicks from the target site.

The glowing blue triangle indicating the boundaries of the zone that overlaid the plane's position on the flight path display echoed this new situational development. Though Petrov's left scope showed a thermal imaging view of the landscape, enhanced with pseudocolor to bring out contrast, he straightened in his seat and glanced directly out Shadow One's cockpit window at the terrain below.

Now Petrov could just discern the unlighted four-lane strip of blacktop highway some two thousand meters below the plane, with the steeply inclined concrete walls of the culvert a few hundred meters directly ahead. The twin headlight beams of a big lorry barreling down the highway toward the culvert lit the way for him.

Petrov armed the stealth's missile launch system as he checked the kilometers-to-go readout at the top of his main scope that counted down the distance to the ordnance release point. The estimated time of arrival at the heart of his launch envelope was also projected on the multimode display: six minutes.

Shattered by the sound of the IP warning tones, forgotten as he went through his checklist of procedures, Petrov's broken reverie was now replaced by an all-over alertness fed by the rush of adrenaline that coursed through his veins. Suddenly all the implications of the mission, of where he was and what he was about to do, stood out in stark definition. This was combat, not an exercise. He was soon to launch a live round on an actual target.

An unexplainable fear swept over him, the ancient fear expressed in tales of letting the genie out of the bottle, and of taboos about crossing thresholds, that have always been attended by a sense of deep foreboding. The human who first picked up a burning stick must have known this fear, and the human after him who saw the sharp point the fire had formed and then fashioned an arrow, surely also experienced it. On and on through the ages that fear had become familiar to those who had crossed thresholds in peace and in war.

Vassily Petrov was just another in a long line, stretching backward and forward to vanishing points in a dark infinity, who was destined to know it. Covington, his American briefer, had certainly known it, too. Petrov wondered if his own fear was greater than Covington's. Did the absence of the sound and fury of war that the American Nighthawk driver had experienced over Iraqi airspace during Desert Wind make a difference? Or was it simply the primordial psychological fear of threshold crossing that brought it on?

Petrov would have to think about this later. For the moment he was a pilot, not a philosopher, and he had a job to do.

As Shadow One's icon neared the center of the glowing green box depicted on the screen, Petrov continued the missile arming and prelaunch procedures, first initializing the computer link to the JASSM's onboard processor that interrogated its multiple systems, including the missile's ring laser gyroscope, which took positional readings and backed up data from GPS.

Only when all systems read in the affirmative did Petrov open the conformal carriage bay doors and lower the JASSM down from the belly of the stealth. Then, in the heart of his launch envelope, he hit the pickle button on his joystick and held it down, a signal to Shadow One's battle management computer system to take over the remaining launch procedures that were to vector the missile in on its target.

The plane lurched as the JASSM's chemical booster stage ignited, thrusting the stub-winged, snub-nosed robot bomb from beneath the black abdomen of the aircraft. The rocket's exhaust whooshed out in a steaming, smoke-gushing contrail as the departing JASSM quickly outstripped the plane. Seconds later the booster stage burned out and the missile's air-breathing ramjet propulsion system took over, hurling the JASSM into the night at supersonic speeds.

Petrov felt the plane lighten as the fifteen-hundred-pound tube of metal, computer hardware, and high-explosive warhead separated, and sideslipped left. Coming off the vector, Petrov saw the missile's jet exhaust flare on his right as the bird disappeared into the darkness. It was soon visible only as an arrow-shaped red pictorial gliding down the wire-grid flight track on the central multimode cockpit screen.

Petrov kept his eye on the right visual display unit showing nose-camera TI video from the missile as it flew its course. Headers on the video feed displayed GMT, elapsed time, and the presence of an active lock on GPS satellites, which augmented the JASSM's terrain contour matching or TERCOM and digital scene matching correlator or DSMAC programming to enhance the accuracy of delivery on the target.

The nose-camera video showed a colorized image of moving terrain features slashed in half by the ruler-straight vertical line of a highway below. An eerily glowing rectangular object, like some luminescent deep-sea shrimp caught in the glare of diving lights, slid past on the highway before being lost to view. The object, Petrov knew, was a truck whose path JASSM had just overflown less than fifty feet below it.

Until the missile struck its target, or until a failure of the plan warranted its premature detonation or retargeting, Petrov would scan his TI nose-camera screen to track the JASSM's progress. During the approximate six minutes until the missile reached its delivery point, Petrov would loiter near his IP, ready to take any of several actions. When the TI image registered a kill, he would turn, burn, and head back to his RV or rendezvous point across the Iran-C.I.S. border with an Ilyushin-78 Midas fuelbird.

The next few minutes were the most unnerving of Petrov's career as a military pilot. Though he'd practiced the launch procedure many times in flight simulations, doing it for real was an entirely different experience. The eerily soundless moving imagery on the TI screen continued to depict the ghost landscape passing beneath the JASSM, terrain features looming larger, then smaller, as the missile executed dips and turns on its preprogrammed flight trajectory that would make it nearly invisible to radar by losing its signature in the ground clutter.

Trucks and other vehicles continued to appear in the final minutes before delivery, eerie spectral forms that passed soundlessly beneath the hurtling cruise that had looped back to confuse ground detection radars and followed the rift of a wadi for several kilometers, then popped up again and flew a course along a lateral road. This was not surprising—as in the Gulf War, roads were used as reference points for the missile's homing system because they were easy to follow and led unerringly to the assigned targets.

And then, in the final sixty seconds of flight, Petrov began picking up the target itself on his feed.

The venting stack and dome of the main reactor building were clearly visible, as were the four outbuildings placed on a circular access road that serviced it and the vehicles in the parking area outside.

Suddenly the view shifted as the JASSM, which had been paralleling the road on a low trajectory at nearly twice the speed of sound, shot upward to commence its terminal engagement phase.

Now Petrov was looking downward at the gaping mouth of the venting stack, lit with a ring of small, flashing red aircraft warning lights, and the broad, stressed concrete cupola of the main reactor dome beside it.

Two more seconds passed. Suddenly the image of the dome filled the entire screen. Now there came a bright flash of obliterating whiteness and the missile's nose-camera feed snowed to a maelstrom of electronic noise.

Petrov stared at the now empty display for a second more, aware that he was soaked with sweat, then switched it over to standby mode. Banking sharply, he turned Shadow One around and reset the plane's inertial navigation system for the return track of the covert flight. The first boom of the multiple explosions at Kasjhan reached him a full minute after the actual destruction took place.

The explosion that reduced the Kasjhan nuclear reactor to a charred and melted mass of heat-fused wreckage and killed five staff members who were on duty on the night watch at the plant, was thorough and all-consuming.

The incendiary system the JASSM used was an FAE or fuel-air explosive, recently developed to utilize a payload of jellied explosive that filled most of the one-ton missile. The FAEs deployed in the Gulf were monsters, but the technology had matured to the point where a lot more bang could be had for a lot less buck and took up considerably less volume using heavy-density, jelled incendiary sources.

The JASSM's terminal velocity had propelled it downward into the center of the reactor dome, where its hardened-steel penetrator head punched a hole in the twelve-foot-thick steel-and-concrete vault. Milliseconds later, now inside the reactor building, the FAE warhead detonated in two coordinated phases.

First, a cluster of very fast electronic switches akin to the kryton switches that trigger nuclear explosions, fired a ring of small plastique charges that air-dispersed the jelled explosive in a spherical cloud. Milliseconds after that, the main charge aft of the primary charge detonated, igniting the fuel cloud, which exploded in a fierce chain reaction equivalent in power to a one-kiloton nuclear blast.

Many kilometers to the south, at almost the same time, the nuclear weapons processing plant at Isfahan was subjected to a similar cataclysm from the second coordinated JASSM strike. In this case, the presence of a full night shift on duty resulted in many more human casualties, most of them buried under thousands of tons of the same concrete-and-steel wreckage that sealed off the plant's plutonium reserves forever. Apparently in Isfahan's case, the intelligence estimates had been somewhat faulty.

Vassily Petrov heard the second, and louder boom of the final explosion as he swung Shadow One in a broad circle and headed back toward the mountainous borderland. This time the noise was accompanied by a shock wave, riding a bubble of supercompressed air, that buffeted the plane and resulted in a momentary warning of imminent engine flameout on his console gauges. The brief loss of power gave Petrov a queasy feeling in the pit of his stomach.

But then, seconds later, the crisis was past and he was vectoring along his return flight path, all systems now back to normal. Except for one development, the flight back was identical in all respects to the flight in. Now the night sky was less black, less clear outside his cockpit windows; a film of dust seemed to hang in the atmosphere.

In a moment Petrov understood the reason for this. He was flying into a desert storm, but one of nature's own this time. What the inhabitants of the region called a *shamal* was blowing up, a tempest of sand, wind, rain, and sometimes even pelting bullets of ice, that could become very bad at times.

There it was again. Another group of radar returns classified as a stealth contact by the Valkyr-II system. This time it held for a moment longer. And now, to top it all, the track was approaching the station.

Albrouny had roused the Beast from his lair, and now Kuraytem was standing over his shoulder, watching the screen, too. The major, looking unkempt in his hastily donned olive-drab fatigues, was rocking a bit and he reeked of hashish smoke and the chewed stimulant called *naswar,* but his attention was focused on the screen and he was not shouting.

Then, just as before, the contact disappeared from the scope. Yet this time Albrouny was told to keep his eye on the display. The base's SA-10 missile battery was activated, too, just in case the contact turned out to have been real.

Suddenly it was back again. Major Kuraytem grabbed the phone beside him and punched a three-key internal number. He was immediately connected to the SAM battery outside.

"Sergeant, I want your crew to put radar on coordinates delta-nine-zero-seven. You are to synchronize fire control with my instructions."

Kuraytem continued issuing orders to the Grumble crew. To Albrouny, he now seemed as sober as a mullah at morning muezzin, and shouting just as loud.

"Sir, I have another contact on my scope," Albrouny told the major. "It's the stealth again." The scopeman read off the new coordinates, which Kuraytem relayed to the SAM crew. Seconds later they had launched a missile.

• • •

The situation had changed again, changed for the worse. Petrov realized he was now in serious trouble. The *shamal* was buffeting Shadow One with incredible force, freezing rain and blinding sand pelting the aircraft's thin metal skin. He pulled back on the throttle, gaining altitude, pushing the plane above the worst of the weather, but using up precious fuel reserves in the process.

Petrov's tactical situation had also deteriorated by this point. The plane's Zhuk-PH threat-fingerprinting ladar popped a SAM symbol onto his field of view, simultaneously shrieking out tones of warning. The missile was vectoring in his direction, the round's active radar seeker head emitting a telltale electronic signature. Intellectually, Petrov knew there was no chance that the missile could achieve a terminal guidance lock on Shadow One, but his gut instincts flew in the face of reason. Again, he throttled back, clawing higher to move out of the path projected on his main screen.

To his surprise the missile changed course and began to close. Petrov took further evasive action, now flying down into the center of the storm. The missile continued to close but suddenly became erratic. Petrov didn't know it, but on the radar screen back at al-Rash'd, the stealth pictorial had also disappeared from the map display.

The SA-10 warhead was moving at Mach 2.5, almost three times Shadow One's velocity. Its trajectory brought it close enough to the plane so that when it exploded, a mixture of circumstances ensured that the concussion wave caught the aircraft on its leading edge.

The combination of the *shamal* and the warhead's adaptive detonation feature was enough to cause a flame-out of the stealth's left engine. The warhead's onboard processor used a best-guess approach to direct the fragments of detonation in the direction of the contact as opposed to the conventional spraying of blast fragments in all directions. In this case, the warhead guessed right.

Petrov swore as the stealth suddenly lost altitude and precipitously nosed down. He tried to emergency restart, but both his engines were now dead. His altimeter line, white numbers flashing on the right upper portion of his main screen, showed he was dropping like a stone with the fierce storm swirling around him, pelting the cockpit canopy windows with hailstones, some the size of moth-balls.

Petrov cursed and tried to restart one final time. His engines briefly caught, but then died of infectious flame-out. Now, he knew, there was but one option left: He had to land the plane dead-stick, on the desert, with all the risks to which such an emergency landing would expose him. However, the choice was as clear as it was Draconian—crash-land or simply crash. There was no longer any in-between for Shadow One.

Four
A Sea of Brown Sugar

"Missile detonation, sir," Albrouny informed Major Kuraytem. "Near the last radar contact with the bogie."

"I can see that for myself," the major replied dourly.

Kuraytem picked up the phone and was answered by a crisp: "Armored brigade headquarters, Lieutenant Gosaj speaking."

"It is possible that an enemy fighter aircraft has been damaged or destroyed by a SAM strike," Kuraytem told the lieutenant, measuring his words. "I want you to put everything you have into a search for wreckage."

Kuraytem read off the grid coordinates of the likely wreckage scatter zone from the digital radar's map display.

"Yes, Major," Gosaj replied. "Is there anything else I should know about the aircraft?"

Kuraytem considered for a few moments, then said, "Nothing else. Except I want to be informed the moment you find anything, no matter what. Understood?"

"Yes, sir," Gosaj replied, and rang off. He, too, paused a few seconds to reflect on what he had just been told. To order up a mechanized search detachment in the middle of one of the worst winter storms to hit the region in years meant that something big indeed was up. He'd have to keep his eyes open and his wits about him.

Picking up the handset, Lieutenant Gosaj punched in four numbers, soon dictating a series of instructions of his own.

Few alternatives remained. With all thrust gone, Petrov had only his inertial navigation system to stabilize the aircraft via movements of wing flaps and tail rudder. The Eclipse, like the American F-117 Nighthawk stealth fighter, was a hard plane to control even with all systems functioning normally. Under the present circumstances, it was like flying an iceberg over Yellowstone Park. But for three very sound reasons there was no possibility of Petrov ejecting.

The first was that the plane was cruising too low to the ground for his ejector seat's chute to reliably open, the second was the howling hell of ice and sand that surrounded the plane, and the third was that Petrov could not be certain that pulling the hazard-striped ejection lever beneath his seat would not simply result in detonating a large explosive charge that would blow him and the plane into a cloud of fragments.

The last consideration was the same one that Francis Gary Powers had faced almost forty years before in a U-2 spy plane some twenty-five thousand meters above the Soviet Union, and had resulted in the same decision Petrov now made—not to pull the ejection lever but instead land the plane if he were able.

Petrov could only succeed in this by attempting an instrument landing. The view from the cockpit was a dark, swirling chaos, punctuated by the steady rat-a-tat of hailstones drumming against wings, fuselage, and canopy windows. The only reliable picture Petrov had of the environment outside the plane came from its thermal imaging screen. He kept his eyes fixed on that. *Thank God I still have electrons,* he thought.

The TI sensors linked to the screen looked downward through the storm, revealing the flat desert floor below in shades of black, white, and polychrome. Petrov could see a mountain range off in the distance and surmised that he had enough taxiing room to land the plane. But the resolution was by no means sharp enough to tell him if any small boulders, shallow wadis, thorn trees, or other hazards that could snap his nose gear lay in the plane's line of approach.

Buffeted by the storm's intensifying fury, the aircraft violently lurched and pitched, and the stick bucked in his hand, so he could hardly hold it. Petrov continued to scan the TI screen. He was searching for a highway. It would be a far safer place to touch down than open desert. Time was running out, though, and he was pushing the envelope. Shadow One was losing altitude fast. He had to start his approach now. He'd be hitting the desert crust one way or another damned soon. Whether he did it landing or colliding was up to him.

Petrov lowered the landing gear, and angled Shadow One's nose down into the weather. It was not easy. Apart from the wind that was trying to flip the plane over the way a cat savages a mouse in its claws, the plane was still doing better than four hundred miles per hour. With its angular fuselage design, the Eclipse was an inherently unstable aircraft. This was why it needed a fly-by-wire flight control system. Without it, the plane was the aerodynamic equivalent of a fallen leaf caught in a strong wind, albeit a leaf equipped with ailerons and tail rudder. *And I have no engines,* he thought.

Within seconds, after the nose and aft landing gears extended and locked into position, Petrov had dropped another two hundred meters through a dangerous, swirling soup of sand, rain, and ice. He could see the ground jumping up at him in the TI scope, and though the altimeter showed he had cut his descent rate in half, he was still moving forward at tremendous speed.

In a heartbeat his nose gear dug into the desert crust. The stealth rolled along the flat surface of the Dasht like a bullet on wheels. Petrov ejected his braking chute and felt it deploy out the plane's rear with a bone-crunching lurch. The chute caught the wind with a savage jolt and the plane skewed to the right. It was still moving at better than a hundred miles per hour, and going sideways in the bargain.

Suddenly Petrov felt an even greater jolt, and the plane's nose pitched over. The horizon tilted crazily as the plane seesawed, its tail section flung in the air. The forward landing gear had struck a boulder, he at first surmised. But as his world was stood on end, Petrov realized the truth: he'd rolled right into a wadi.

Petrov's next sight was of sand being dumped over his canopy windows, as though a malevolent giant were shoveling great heaps of it onto a tiny black insect that had fallen by his feet and howling with laughter while burying his victim. Petrov had the perverse sense that he was sinking in a dry, granular sea, a sea, it seemed to him, that was made of dark brown sugar.

•

By seven hundred hours the *shamal* had largely petered out, leaving the desert floor encrusted with a thin film of ice and piled with heaps of sand where no dunes had existed scant hours before. In the lead APC of the armored detachment that was already many klicks from its base, Lieutenant Gosaj scrutinized the desert through high-power binoculars.

The *shamal*, he realized, had also obliterated all traces of anything that might have rolled, walked, fallen into, or sunk beneath the area overnight.

Just the same, Gosaj had another twenty kilometers' worth of vacant desert to cover before he could report back that he had found nothing. After that, helicopters would take advantage of the more suitable flying conditions now prevailing in which to conduct a thorough search by air.

Expecting to find nothing, Gosaj continued to peer through his binoculars as the tracked vehicle lumbered forward, followed by a GAZ heavy transport truck carrying a detachment of Iranian regulars in case there was trouble.

It was going to be a real son of a bitch. Both men could sense it in their guts. The American air-force general and his Russian PVO counterpart had seen enough missions to know when things had gone sour, and this one had just curdled like day-old cream. The initial jubilation following the successful strikes on the two targets was followed by a tense wait for the planes to return.

Only one of them had come back so far. Samsonov had made his run, turned around, and flown a course back across the Iran-Azeril border to rendezvous Shadow Two with a waiting fuelbird.

After tanking up, Samsonov had been escorted to the staging base by two MiG-29s. Directly on landing he had been debriefed.

But Petrov had never made it home across the border. Shadow One had not been sighted by any of the MiG fighter patrols sent out to scan the border for the MFI's return. There had been overhead surveillance by a KH-14 photoreconnaissance satellite, but this had showed only the possibility that the plane had been shot down.

Maybe it would return after all. For now, though, the plane was missing. Lost was a better way of putting it.

Petrov couldn't bring himself to do what he had been ordered to do. He had received clear instructions: if he made a forced landing and the stealth was still intact, he was to trigger a special demolition charge that would blow up the plane and then attempt to escape on foot.

Supposedly Petrov would have five minutes between activating the demo charge and the explosion to get clear of the blast zone. But Petrov entertained lingering doubts about this. He reasoned that on a mission as secret as his had been, it might have been deemed prudent to obliterate all traces of the aircraft, including the pilot. Twice Petrov had steeled himself to activate the destruct sequence, but both times he'd faltered and held back.

Petrov came to the conclusion that he was neither brave nor patriotic nor suicidal enough to execute his orders.

He then decided on a different approach.

Daylight found him crouched against the lip of the wadi in which the plane had crashed, shivering in the bitter morning cold as he set up the portable satcom unit he had been provided in case he'd had to eject and needed to be rescued. Petrov understood that the command center would be listening on all emergency frequencies. The satcom rig used an advanced signal hopping, spread spectrum transmission mode that would make the call harder to detect and impossible to eavesdrop on even if detected, although any form of transmission posed a risk.

Petrov had climbed up the side of the shallow wadi and peered over its edge. Beyond lay an empty expanse of desert, the sky above vacant of any man-made object. Either the Iranians hadn't seen him go down, or if they had, they were not yet within visual range of his aircraft.

With no reason to hide, he ascended the sloping embankment to the level of the desert floor and took stock of his situation.

The plane appeared intact from this vantage point, but that could be deceiving. All he could see of Shadow One was the top half of the peaked fuselage and the projecting two thirds of its canted wings. The flat underside of the plane was buried under a few hundred kilos of windblown desert sand that had been funneled down around it by the *shamal*. Thankfully, the wadi had been shallow, or he'd never have gotten out.

Petrov was willing to bet that Shadow One's nose gear had been damaged during the last few seconds of landing; in which case, even if he could restart the engines, it would make getting airborne again highly problematic to say the least.

Still, with a little help it might be possible. If a rescue team could be gotten in somehow . . .

Petrov let the thought trail off without troubling to complete it in his mind. It was all academic, and no doubt wishful thinking. He had his orders, and he should have followed them to the letter. And yet . . . let any of the bastards sitting on their padded rears across the border find themselves in his position, Petrov had no doubt that they would think twice about blowing up the plane. Fuck them, he thought. Let them cut him a second set of orders. He wanted to live.

Breaking open the gray metal container, he extracted the satcom unit. The unit was far smaller than previous units he'd seen, roughly the same size as the original cellular phones designed for cars, which it closely resembled, with a large rectangular base and separate handset. In fact, the unit's main difference from old-style bag phones was in the shape and size of its antenna, which was a mini–satellite antenna like those found in commercial satellite television systems.

Once Petrov had unpacked and set up the antenna, which unfurled like an umbrella, it went through a scanning procedure that aligned its beam with a Russian communications satellite in low earth orbit or LEO and executed an electronic handshake protocol that established the secure uplink. The Cyrillic letters on the unit's small monochrome LCD display told Petrov he was ready to transmit.

General Korniyenko's phone buzzed.

"Sir, we have just received a satcom transmission from Major Petrov," the voice of one of the communications technicians working in the pit below the installation's upper, tactical level announced. "Would you like to be patched through?"

"Yes, at once," he replied.

Korniyenko motioned to Yarwood, whose translator listened in on the conversation despite Yarwood's textbook-fluent knowledge of conversational Russian.

Seconds later Petrov was in touch with the general.

"Greetings, Vassily Ivanevich. What is your situation?" asked Korniyenko, addressing Petrov by his patronymic in informal fashion, a sign the pilot took to indicate that the general did not suspect the true and serious nature of events.

"Not good, sir," Petrov replied guardedly, aware that he was sure to provoke the general's wrath before long. "The plane lost power. It might have been due to a near miss by a homing missile, the effects of last night's severe weather, or both, but the upshot is that I was forced to land the aircraft."

"You have not destroyed it, then?" the general asked, and Petrov could not fail to note the new edge of suspicion that had crept into his voice.

Petrov took a deep breath. "No, sir, I have not," he replied. "The plane does not appear badly damaged. It may even be flyable. But it is partially covered with windblown sand as a result of the emergency landing during the storm. I believed it was my duty to try to contact you before carrying out the destruct order."

Korniyenko thought over what Petrov had just told him. His first impulse was to threaten the pilot with court-martial for insubordination, for his orders had been unmistakable and not subject to interpretation. In the old days this is what he would have done, at the top of his voice. But these were new times, and Korniyenko tempered his reply accordingly.

"Say your position and then destroy the plane," he spoke into the handset. "A search-and-rescue mission will be flown out tonight. A team is waiting on standby. At hourly intervals from nightfall on, listen for instructions on emergency channel number three. We will get you out. But you must destroy the plane at once. Is this understood?"

"Understood, sir," Petrov replied. "I will do so immediately."

"Very good," the general replied. "We will see each other later. Now do as ordered, Major." There was no mistaking the general's intention in these last words, nor, Petrov noted, was the patronymic being used anymore. He had been addressed in the businesslike form of "Major." So be it then. An order was an order.

The satcom unit's LCD display showed that the uplink had been terminated. Petrov saw no other choice. Whether or not he died as a result of triggering the destruct sequence, he was duty-bound to do it. In any case, he would rather die carrying out orders than return home in disgrace and branded permanently as a coward. There would be no point in living such a life. He would forfeit his career and military benefits. His life, in effect, would be as much over that way as if he'd been blown up with the stealth.

Petrov stowed away the satcom rig and got his survival kit and gear out of the downed plane's cockpit. He reached in again and pressed the arm button for the detonation charge.

All at once hell broke loose.

A sudden staccato burst of automatic fire made Petrov start reflexively. He thought at first he'd been hit. But he felt himself and discovered with relief that he was unharmed.

When the pilot looked up he saw a heavily armed Mil-24 Hind-F attack helicopter hovering overhead, its fuselage painted in a desert camouflage pattern of grays and browns. A wisp of smoke curled from the four-barrel rotary cannon beneath its cockpit that had fired the 12.7-mm warning salvo.

For a brief instant Petrov incongruously thought that a Russian rescue party had somehow reached him. But that moment flashed past him as quickly as it had arrived.

Right chopper, wrong army, he thought. The helicopter bore the green-white-red insignia of the Pasdaran Air Corps, and Petrov could now see a pillarlike cloud of dust trailing behind tiny black specks on the horizon that he knew was surely a mechanized armor column following on with additional troops. Although he didn't understand the commands, in Farsi, being barked at him by the amplified voice of the helo's pilot, he was well enough aware of their connotations.

Petrov raised his hands high over his head.

Many kilometers away, his superior officer was mouthing the Russian word for traitor, sotto voce, out of earshot of his American colleague.

Major Kuraytem heard Lieutenant Gosaj's distant voice over the radio set's speaker. Static and interference played their usual tricks with reception, but even so there was no mistaking the excitement that had seized hold of Gosaj.

"Sir! Excellent news," he declared. "We have discovered a plane intact. It appears to be a highly advanced aircraft, possibly experimental—a stealth aircraft even, perhaps."

"The Americans have attacked us?" Kuraytem asked, perplexed at his subordinate's talk of stealth aircraft. Who else but the Americans flew them?

"No, sir, I don't believe it is the Americans."

"Then who?"

"Shuravi," Gosaj replied.

Kuraytem was stunned. Gosaj had just used the Farsi word for "Russians."

"Explain," Kuraytem ordered.

"Sir," Gosaj answered, "the plane bears no markings or other insignia of nationality we can see. And it is partially buried in sand. However, the instrumentation markings are in Cyrillic characters and the pilot appears to speak only Russian." He paused. "What are my instructions?"

Kuraytem thought a moment. "The pilot has been captured and he is alive, you say?"

"Yes, sir," Gosaj answered. "The pilot is alive and apparently uninjured."

"Very well," Kuraytem answered. "You are to guard the crash site pending the arrival of reinforcements. Until then you are to let nothing come between your men and the plane, is this understood?"

"Completely understood, Major," Gosaj answered crisply.

"As to the pilot of the plane, he is to be placed onboard one of the two Hinds under armed guard and immediately flown back to base. The other helo is to remain with your detachment. I will issue the appropriate orders."

"Very good, sir," Gosaj said, and replaced the radio handset as the conversation ended.

Within a matter of minutes Petrov had been searched for weapons. Then, with his wrists cable-tied behind his back, he was pushed into the open side hatch of the low-hovering Mi-24.

As Gosaj watched the helicopter rise to its cruising altitude of nine meters and chug off to the west, trailing faint brown contrails from its port and starboard engine exhaust vents, Major Kuraytem was already thinking about his next posting—to the military academy in Tehran if things worked out right. After this coup he would be promoted, he would make certain of that. Then it would be good-bye to this lonely desert hellhole.

"I shall be in my quarters," the major told the radar operator. "Keep me posted, Albrouny. And good work."

"Thank you, sir," Albrouny replied, and smartly saluted.

Major Kuraytem returned the salute and left the command center. It was time for a shower and shave, and maybe even a pinch of *naswar* to celebrate his good fortune, and the still better things yet to come, thanks to the ill-starred adventurism of his country's foes.

Five
Stratagems of Power

The president's ten A.M. briefing in the Oval Office was not what he'd anticipated. Travis Claymore had received the reports of the downing of Shadow One via the morning's National Intelligence Estimate sheet from the CIA, which he normally skimmed at his six A.M. breakfast.

This morning the intel briefing was accompanied by Critic-coded cables from Defense and the Pentagon. All concerned the joint U.S.-C.I.S. mission inside Iran and the loss, and presumed capture, by Sepah-e-Pasdaran or Iranian Revolutionary Guard forces, of the Russian stealth plane.

By nine o'clock Claymore was at his desk in the Oval Office, with his planned weekend getaway to Camp David canceled and fresh intelligence reports littering his desktop. By nine forty-five the president had placed and received a half-dozen phone calls, concluding with a twenty-minute-long conversation between himself and Russian President Grigorenko.

Claymore had sounded the Russian leader on his country's plans, aware that in the seven-hour time lag between Washington and Moscow there would have been time for Grigorenko and his staff to explore several options. Specifically, he wanted to know if the Soviets were considering an operation to retake the plane.

"Yes, candidly we are considering such an alternative," Grigorenko had told Claymore. "I'm sure you will agree that the possession of the aircraft by Iran poses grave risks to regional and world security."

"I do agree," Claymore had replied. "No question. But I have to tell you, Dimitri, that from the information I have available, I have my doubts about the wisdom of a military option. First of all, we don't really know yet what the Iranians will do with the plane. For example, there's a question in my mind about whether they'll just take the plane apart and reverse-engineer or go for a deal. In my opinion we should try a little old-fashioned horse trading first."

"We don't think this is likely," Grigorenko returned, trying to remember that the U.S. president, like most Americans, could be at times extremely naive concerning global political realities. "We have committed an act of aggression against them, indeed an act of war. We have set their cherished nuclear weapons program back a decade. It seems unlikely that they will have any inclination to bargain."

Claymore paused a moment to gesture to his secretary in acknowledgment that the chairman of the Joint Chiefs had just arrived for their scheduled ten A.M. meeting.

"Sorry, Dimitri. You still there?"

"Right here, Mr. President."

"Glad to hear it, partner," the president replied. "Now, I hear what you're saying, and it makes sense. But the way I look at this problem is, 'Well, hot damn. They got the plane.' We've got to accept that. But we have other things they might want to trade for it."

"Such as what?" Grigorenko asked. "Oil? Iran is awash in crude. Wheat? They have more than sufficient staples.

Technology? They have stolen plenty of it and have bought the rest. Weapons? This, they might want. But do we wish to offer them weapons after we have gone to such extreme lengths to take their weapons away?"

"Well, now let's back up, here, Dimitri," suggested Claymore. "In fact, there may be an option in there you've missed. It's an open secret that the Iranians have been negotiating major arms upgrade packages with the U.S. and C.I.S. both. Now, we have warned them repeatedly about repercussions concerning nuclear proliferation. On the other hand, we have always been willing to provide arms for legitimate defense needs."

"And you are suggesting that things can go back to normal if they return the plane? Just like that?"

"That's an oversimplification, but essentially that's exactly what I'm saying. Look, Iran knew damn well that their possession of nuclear missiles capable of hitting Tel Aviv, let alone Belgrade, Bonn, or Kiev, would not be tolerated. So they took a gamble. Well, they lost. My position is that we've gone and hit them with the stick, so why not dangle the carrot before giving them another whack in the teeth?"

Grigorenko considered the American leader's words a moment. "Your point is well taken, Mr. President," he replied. "I will bring it up at a meeting of my cabinet later today. But I must tell you in all frankness that I do not think a political solution will find acceptance in Russian legislative circles. Unlike your country, Russia is not blessed with a secure southern border. Iran is behind guerrilla factions in Afghanistan and insurrection in the Caucasus. Imagine Mexico, armed and belligerent, and you will appreciate the threat as we do. However, I will look into this."

"Thanks, Dimitri," replied Claymore. "I know we can work this out advantageously."

"Good-bye, Mr. President."

When Claymore hung up the phone it was already ten minutes past the briefing hour. He punched a button on his intercom and told his secretary to send in the chairman of the JCS as well as the secretary of defense and national security advisor, who also waited outside in the Oval Office's anteroom.

In his Moscow office, President Dimitri Grigorenko, looking and feeling considerably more tired than Claymore at the end of a long day, also had a visitor cooling his heels outside. He did not plan to discuss any horse trades, though, no matter what he had told his opposite number in the White House. Politically, the Americans drank Pepsi—his drink was Stoli Kristall.

The sprawling farm occupied hundreds of cultivated acres in the north of the scrub desert Israelis call the Negev. Craggy mountains, looking for all the world like immense mud pies left by the Creator to bake in the searing desert sun, loomed in the near distance. Yet where the tractor rolled along at its snail's pace, near the terminus of an irrigation pipeline that sprayed jets of cool water across a field of vine-ripening tomatoes, the air was pleasant, and the farmer sitting in the shade of the tractor's sunroof could gaze over his well-tended crops with justly earned satisfaction.

The farmer had only returned to the land in the past few decades, working it as he had once done as a much younger man on the *moshav,* or community farm, where his family had settled a year or two after the Russian Revolution of 1917. Former IDF general and minister of defense during the Begin government's second term, Assaf Gilad had been out of politics for the last two years, and out of the military for at least a decade. To all intents and purposes, he was a farmer now, and the farm was his home, his *bayit shehu bayit,* as the Israeli saying went.

But Gilad had more than tomatoes on his mind as he sat on his tractor and ruminated. Farming was in his blood, it was true, but so were the soldier's calling and Israeli politics. Gilad had lost his taste for neither of the three. In recent months he had become as determined to regain his lost place at the helm of Israel's ship of state as he was to bring in the winter's bumper harvest of, in the Old Testament phrases, the fruit of the vine and the bread of the earth.

As to the military, the old-boy network in the Israeli Defense Forces is stronger than many of its foreign counterparts. Gilad had current contacts with Israeli military intelligence, known by its acronym, AMAN—strong ones—and he made sure to keep them strong. His contacts did him favors and he returned those favors. It was the unofficial way of accomplishing certain things in Israel, as everywhere else, though here more especially so.

What Gilad had recently learned through one of these contacts could be his ticket back into the center of regional and global events, he believed. A Russian stealth aircraft had gone missing. The plane had been tracked covertly as it entered Iranian airspace, but it had never returned. Human intelligence—HUMINT—sources in Iran confirmed that the plane and its pilot had both been captured intact. The Zahal could not officially conduct a mission to retrieve the stealth, were that even an option, but Gilad might be able to do so—unofficially.

If so, he would be able to pile up many favors owed him, including placing the current Israeli prime minister deeply in his debt. Israel would never overtly acknowledge the technological windfall that possession of the Soviet stealth plane would afford it, just as it had never overtly acknowledged its massive nuclear weapons development program over the decades. But Israel would covet such stealth technology and make good use of it both in its regional fight for survival and in its global fight to gain economic markets with high-end military technology.

If anyone knew this, and was in a position to exploit this knowledge, it was he, for Gilad had been one of the prime movers behind the now defunct Lavi project of the 1980s. The Lavi was to have been Israel's home-built advanced technology fighter plane, a jet optimized for the high-endurance and long-range bombing missions that Israeli military needs dictated. Apart from its combat role, however, the Lavi could have also be used as a potent political weapon.

The U.S. had been using its fighters for just that purpose for decades, postponing, reassessing, and even embargoing fighter sales to Israel every time Israel did something that ran contrary to the United States' Mideast policy. This was a potent form of pressure on Israel to conform to U.S. wishes, but it could work the same for Israel against other countries should Israel sell them the Lavi, tying them to future upgrades and supplies of spares.

The Lavi had proven too costly to build in the end, but there had been a raft of high-technology subsystems developed for it that Israel had successfully and profitably marketed to other countries' defense establishments. Now, with a Soviet stealth fighter in Israel's possession, the potential gains could prove enormous. The windfall in stealth technology, advanced radars, avionics, and other subsystems would alone guarantee tremendous strides in Israel's defense sector. But even more than that, Gilad thought he saw the key to a revival of the Lavi project, or even something far beyond it, in the capture of the stealth.

Gilad brought the tractor's slow creep to a stop and switched the ignition off. Glancing across the tomato field at the flat mud cake of Mount Haran in the middle distance, he unclipped the satcom phone from his belt. The phone was the best in the world, as secure as state-of-the-art electronics could make it. It needed to be, considering the number at the headquarters of Israel's elite Nahal Brigade which he dialed and would erase from the phone's memory as soon as the call had been completed. Most of Israel's commando forces were drawn from the Nahal. Like the Lavi project, it, too, was a unit Gilad had helped found.

A few seconds later Gilad heard a clipped voice answer.

"In Tel Aviv," Gilad said, "the beach umbrellas are opening on Dizengoff Street."

He paused and waited for the expected reply.

• • •

The television news special was headed by veteran newsanchor Scott Dunnelsford, whose deadpan delivery style was familiar to millions of American TV viewers. The report, which ran a week after the strike on the Kasjhan and Isfahan nuclear facilities, delved into the theories concerning what actually took place.

"Now from foreign correspondent Bradley Pearsall, who reports live from Tehran," Dunnelsford said. "Brad, you've been in Tehran for two days, what have you found out?"

"Well, Scott, for one thing the Iranians are not saying much. Though theories abound concerning a secret mission involving the United States in bombing the reactor complex at Kasjhan and the nuclear facility at Isfahan, this is no replay of the 1979 storming of the embassy. The Iranians are keeping mum and their new détente with the U.S. is holding steady."

"Now, you say U.S. involvement in the bombings, just what do you mean by that?"

"By involvement, Scott, I mean that the United States might at least have some complicity in the bombings, meaning again, that if not actually sending U.S. planes to strike the facilities, it might have contributed targeting data to some other country."

"What other country? Do you know?"

"No one's saying, but the implication is that Russia might have been the nation that actually sent the planes."

"Thank you, Bradley, please keep us posted," the newsanchor concluded. "And now from our Israeli correspondent, Chaim Bar-Lev. Chaim, what's the word in Tel Aviv?"

"Well, Scott—"

"Just a moment, we'll have to interrupt, Chaim. Ambassador Marlene Dockweiler will soon be meeting with Iran's President Rasulali, and she's on live remote feed. We'll get back to you. Madame Ambassador, good evening . . ."

• • •

In Tehran's bustling Zarnegar Street, in a multistory glass-and-steel building fronted by a driveway protected by a heavy iron gate and speed bumps that is well known to the Tehranis, is located the southern military district headquarters of the Iranian Vezarat-e-Ettela'at va Amniat-e-Keshvar, or military intelligence directorate, which is more commonly known by its acronym VEVAK. From this building it is a short and, in good weather, often pleasant walk to the Presidential Palace situated only a few city blocks away, and similarly, though far more noticeably given the presence of armed soldiers, protected from unwanted intrusion.

Today, punctually at 9:15 A.M., local time, the chief of VEVAK, General Katayoon Shadrokh Choubak, met with Iran's president, Othmar Beheshti Rasulali, in the president's spacious and well-appointed fourth-floor office at the Presidential Palace.

Nominally accountable only to the Ministry of Defense, VEVAK was in fact solely under the control of the Iranian president and *faqi,* or chief religious leader, and answerable only to Rasulali and his coterie of loyal and discreet bureaucrats. So, for that matter, was the Iranian General Intelligence Directorate, otherwise known as the P-ID or Political-Ideological Directorate, or secret police. It was responsible for detecting and punishing dissent among Iranian citizens, and boasted a detachment in every police station in the country.

President Rasulali had welcomed Choubak and bidden his Uzbeki servant to pour the general a cup of *chai siah,* or Iranian-style black tea from the ornately chased silver samovar that stood on a serving table near the president's desk. The *faqi* often took *chai* at this hour, as he sat on the Louis XIV chair with red velvet back and arms carved in the shape of lions' heads that had once belonged to Iran's deposed ruler, the shah-in-shah, Reza Pahlavi. The *faqi* liked to sip his tea as he scanned his desk calendar to prepare for the day's appointments, and the tea was generously sweetened with sugar in the traditional manner he favored.

Choubak, who preferred *chai sabz,* a green Afghan-style tea more popular in the north of Iran, took a courteous sip from the china cup and then set it down on its saucer. Apart from the clinking of Delftware and the turning of the pages of the president's desk calendar, the only other sound was the hum of the ceiling fan turned high against the stuffiness of the room. Though luxuriously appointed, the windows of the *faqi*'s office were made of bulletproof glass and were never opened when the *faqi* was present, as a security precaution.

At last, Rasulali looked up and regarded Choubak. Despite his gray unkempt beard, worn in the style of the mullahs, Rasulali was as distant from the Ayatollah Khomeini in the spectrum of Iran's internal politics as Jimmy Carter had been from Richard Nixon in the U.S.'. Rasulali had run as a moderate with an agenda of political and cultural reform. The people had given him an overwhelming mandate to implement liberal change in Iranian society. This included a new détente with Iran's regional neighbors and global adversaries, including the former "Great Satan," the United States.

Iran was on the road away from isolation and pariahhood. Paradoxically, this also made her far more dangerous to the world at large. A revitalized Iran more and more saw herself as a regional military and economic power. She was as big geographically as she was rich economically, with oil revenues only surpassed regionally by Saudi Arabia's. Iran wanted to grow economically and territorially, and every step away from the religious parochialism of the past decades was a step closer to potential regional conflict.

"How is the business with the plane proceeding?" Rasulali asked his intelligence chief.

"Well, Excellency," Choubak replied. "The aircraft which, as you know, is in a secure location, is being studied by our Directorate of Technical Affairs. Its officers report important discoveries in the areas of military electronics, miniaturization, semiconductor design, and computing, to name a few."

"I understand the pilot was taken alive," Rasulali went on. "I would assume that this *Shurav* is being interrogated with respect to any additional information he can provide."

"That's correct, Excellency," Choubak answered. "For the time being it has been decided to keep the pilot at the location of the aircraft. We considered bringing him to headquarters here in Tehran, but rejected this option."

"Why is that?"

"Too risky, for one thing, and also he would probably know very little. After all, he was merely a pawn in a far larger strategic game. The pilot's greatest knowledge asset would be in operating the aircraft. We could best exploit this knowledge at our base in the Dasht-e-Kavir at which the stealth is being kept."

"Very well," Rasulali replied, and asked what steps were being taken to attend to security concerns brought about by the plane's capture.

"As you are aware, *faqi,* the military brigade controlled by VEVAK includes a rapid intervention battalion that is trained to deal with any threat that may arise. It is commanded by Colonel Farzaneh Hossein Ghazbanpour, who is an able leader. I suggest he be given any additional men and equipment he requires to carry out his task."

The president raised his teacup to his lips and sipped, his heavy-lidded eyes half closing as he reflected on what he had just heard. After a few seconds he nodded his assent, and turned his full gaze on the general.

"The American ambassador is scheduled to meet with me shortly after your departure," he said. "I want to be completely prepared."

"Understood, your excellency," Choubak said to the Iranian leader. "And you will be, *faqi.*"

Choubak decided to take another sip of his *chai.* The president was known to ask many questions, and he might be occupied with answering them for some time yet.

Dimitri Pavlovich Grigorenko sat brooding in his oak-paneled Kremlin study. He looked up, studying the mantel above the fireplace, which gave the room a comforting cheer. He had not yet decided whether he would keep the fire burning during the summer, as Nixon did and as Brezhnev also had done during his tenure as general secretary of the party. Something about the fire in the summer bespoke the character shared by those two world leaders. He was not of their stripe. He was of a new breed.

Grigorenko presided over a new Russia. He was an ex–military man, the Eisenhower of his generation. Russia would have its stealth and its new brigades of tanks. It would be militarily on parity with the West, and would compete in the lucrative global defense market.

But it would not be building up its nuclear arsenal and it would be scaling back its conventional forces. Grigorenko had vowed that he would no longer be cowed by the ancient fear of invasion. If Russia was to continue into the twenty-first century, it would have to forge stronger links with the West. From this point on there was no turning back.

Nevertheless, the stealth mission would have to be salvaged somehow. And it could be done, certainly it could be done. Grigorenko was a soldier first, foremost, and always. Eisenhower had also been a soldier and had nearly been brought down by the exposure of the U-2 spy plane flights over the Soviet Union. Grigorenko could face political difficulties over this, during a far more critical time in his country's history.

But there was a way out. Grigorenko pressed the intercom button and summoned into his office a man in paratroop uniform who had been waiting in the anteroom for some time. He regarded this man. He had known him for many years, in Afghanistan.

"Sit down, Viktor Sergeivich."

Captain Arbatov of the GRU's Spetsnaz forces removed his red beret emblazoned with the paratroops insignia and took a seat opposite the president's desk.

"You are looking well, Mr. President," he said.

"There's no need to be formal, Viktor," Grigorenko replied, "so you needn't subject me to your usual sarcasm."

"I have never uttered a sarcastic word in my life, General," he replied.

"You are a lying son of a bitch, Captain," Grigorenko said, handing one of the glasses of Stolichnaya vodka he had just poured to his visitor. *"Prosit,"* he said, and knocked it down, watching the Spetsnaz officer do the same. "Now to business," Grigorenko resumed. "Viktor, you and I have known each other for a long time, since Afghanistan."

"Before that, General," Arbatov cut in.

"*Da,* before that, I forget," Grigorenko said. "So what I am about to tell you will go no further than this room until the appropriate time, understood?"

"Perfectly, General."

"Good. Now listen carefully. We are in deep shit, my friend. You have no doubt heard rumors concerning the loss of a stealth aircraft somewhere in Iran."

"I might have heard a thing or two about this, yes," Arbatov replied.

"Since I know that your 'thing or two' probably amounts to more than I myself know, I'll skip that part of it," Grigorenko told his guest. "But I doubt if even you have heard that our political gray eminence, Yeltsin, has succeeded in circumventing my executive powers. On his own, he has managed to sell the general staff of the GRU on his independent choice to lead a raid into Iran to retake or destroy the plane."

"Who is it?"

"I cannot tell you yet," Grigorenko equivocated. "All I am willing to reveal at this point is that it's one of Potapenko's fair-haired boys. You know the kind the old *'pidar gnoinizh'* favors."

"It must be Nemekov, then," Arbatov said, nodding to himself as if in confirmation of a good guess. "In that case, God save us all. He hasn't seen a day of real combat. He's a fucking *shavski* who got lucky one fine summer day and made his reputation." Arbatov used the slang word for a major incompetent and fuckup; *shavski* literally meant a "shit-eating dog."

"But a politically connected *z'opolit,* for all of that," he added. "This ass-kisser will probably get the job no matter what you try to do. And I *am* right about Nemekov, eh, General."

"Yes, you are indeed," admitted the Russian president. "Still, there's no arguing about the operational soundness of a raid as opposed to other alternatives, wouldn't you agree?"

Arbatov smiled. "You are sounding me out, General, I, a lowly captain, on matters of such strategic importance?"

"Viktor, I am too tired to fence right now and too depressed to joke," returned Grigorenko. "I am well aware of your undeserved demotion in rank and the persecution you've suffered. I promise you I will see to righting all wrongs, once I am able. Now please answer my question."

"A colonelcy, Dimitri. That is the least I deserve. I am now the oldest captain in the Russian army, dammit!"

"You'll have it, Viktor. And a full pardon."

Arbatov nodded, sipped at his vodka, and began, "There's no question about it, Dimitri. A raid is the only possible recourse at this stage. A few men on the ground, a few light infantry vehicles—quick in, quick out. That's the way to do it."

"But surely attack helicopters—"

"Are a needless complication, and a risky one," Arbatov cut in. "Remember the dangers and complexities of the American hostage rescue mission of 1980? It was unbelievably elaborate. Each level of complexity was one more reason why it could not possibly work, one more nail in the plan's coffin."

"Quite true," said Grigorenko.

"Also," Arbatov went on, "force-on-force symmetries tend to escalate matters rather quickly. You send in helos, the opposition answers with missiles and other aircraft. The thing can snowball into a major incident if even the slightest problems arise. But with a small Spetsnaz force, there's little risk of this happening. Also, if the men are captured or killed, it's far easier to deny."

Grigorenko poured them both another glass and said,

"We are of the same mind, Viktor. That is why I want you to prepare to lead precisely the sort of commando mission you have described."

"As a colonel?" Arbatov asked.

"After the mission I'll be able to make you a damned marshal, Viktor. For now, you'll have to remain a captain. Pick your men and start training. And mind not to pass Nemekov on the way out. He's scheduled to arrive next."

"You are meeting with him, too?" the visitor from Spetsnaz asked incredulously after drinking the last of his vodka.

"*Da,* I must," Grigorenko replied. "I have not yet consolidated my position to act autonomously. Don't forget his connections. Now go—it's best your paths don't cross."

The portly, gray-haired farmer from the Negev had changed from his comfortable jeans and T-shirt to his best Savile Row suit for the meeting. His wife had assured him that he looked better than she had seen him in a long time and suggested he wear suits more often. Gilad had produced nothing concrete as yet, but this meeting was still a triumph. They, the mandarins, had come to him. Finally, after these lonely, painful years of political exile in a desert both figurative and real, the big shots from Tel Aviv had come to Assaf Gilad for help, just as they had in '68 and in '73.

Gilad was now the only one they could come to with such a problem, the *mamza'rim,* the double-crossing bastards. Gilad would be there to pull the rabbit out of the hat when nobody else could do anything but wring their hands and cry out to the heavens above.

The prime minister himself had groveled before him. Gilad had been respectful to that pompous windbag, although he had no reason to be. Who was the prime minister anyway? A nobody. A Johnny-come-lately. A rich, well-educated, Ivy League nobody from a well-to-do American family.

He should still be sitting in his posh apartment on New

York's Upper East Side, spouting his bilge before the network news cameras during every crisis involving Israel, as he did in his old days as UN ambassador. That's all he had ever been. A face and a voice. What war for Israel did he ever fight in? What blood had he ever shed for the Jewish State? None, that was the answer. Gilad had shed more than his share of his blood for Eretz Yisroel.

It had been Gilad who had been a true warrior, with the vision to see over the horizon what those putzes in the Knesset could not discern. *Wait, just wait,* Gilad said to himself. In a few weeks' time they would all learn a lesson from an old warhorse who still had a thing or two to teach them. They had chosen to brand the mark of Cain upon his forehead. What Gilad planned would remove that stain of infamy forever.

Six
Horses and Tree Heads

Anatoly, acting as spotter for the sniper squad tasked with taking down the sentries guarding the hangar, spoke into his throat mike. "Twenty degrees to your right, Leonid. Guard in the tower."

"I see him."

Anatoly was positioned on a rise that gave him a good vantage point on the hangar through the bipod-mounted image intensification scope in front of him. Cammied up and wearing black BDUs like the rest of the three squads that made up Captain Arbatov's handpicked Spetsnaz company, he was low observable in the predawn darkness.

The mission's objective was to breach the base's perimeter defenses, storm the hangar, and destroy the Eclipse stealth fighter guarded by the Iranians inside it, killing anyone and anything that stood in the way.

At three hundred forty hours, zulu, the squads had moved into position with squad one, the sniper detail and machine gunners, taking the point. Squad one's two snipers would eliminate guards on the perimeter while the two machine gunners, each equipped with a bipod-mounted RPK-74 light machine gun, set themselves up for intersecting fire lanes a hundred meters down the road leading to the base.

As Anatoly gave targeting instructions to the squad's second sniper, nicknamed "Tanker," he saw Leonid's man slump across the barrel of the machine gun high in the crow's nest of the guard tower off to his left, struck in the head by a well-placed 7.62-mm bullet from Leonid's bolt-action Dragunov SVD sniper rifle. A few moments later the lookout in the second, right-hand tower went rag-doll limp.

The two kills were followed in quick succession by volleys of sound-suppressed fire taking down more sentries walking their posts. A last pair of Iranian regulars manning a sentry booth at the main entrance were killed as one stood outside smoking a cigarette; as he fell dead, his partner in the booth rushed out and was stopped by a round from Tanker's Dragunov SVD. The attack dog he'd held on a leash was also silenced.

Once the guard and lookout detail had been dealt with, the motorized second squad moved in through breaches in the perimeter fence. Some Spetsnaz dismounted to aim RPG-18 Strela shoulder-fire missiles. The mounted troops opened up with rockets and heavy-caliber automatic fire from their assault vehicles.

The successive salvos discharged high-explosive warheads into the barracks building, the radio tower, and the motor-pool area. Helos were destroyed on the ground and stray vehicles were shot up. Before the echos of the explosions had a chance to die down, squad three, beefed up to platoon strength, punched in through the breach, taking advantage of the pandemonium to storm the hangar at the center of the enemy compound.

Led by Zil Larovich, Arbatov's second in command, the third squad mowed down the scattered opposition and soon reached the hangar. Fast armored vehicles rolled in behind them, machine guns throwing fire, cleaning up whatever was left over.

"There she is, *moj' drugoi,*" he shouted to his men. "Boris and Lev, double quick."

While the squad's gunners formed a cordon of fire around them, the team's two sappers rushed toward the aircraft. Placing the demo charges at key points between nose assembly and tail rudders of the stealth plane, they armed the charges and set a four-minute delay.

On Larovich's signal they hustled from the hangar toward the waiting main team element outside, where they took cover behind a screen of APCs.

The hangar exploded behind them with a thunderous report. A pillar of fire reared up into the black skies. In seconds it had risen fifty meters and was still climbing.

In just under twelve minutes following the snipers' opening salvos, the dismounted squads were piling into the two infantry fighting vehicles and driving hard to their preplanned LZ, where the Antonov AN-72 Coaler transport plane would be warming up.

They met no opposition on the road and were soon inside the belly of the plane, where Arbatov was waiting for them.

"Not bad," he said, checking his stopwatch. "Under twenty minutes this time." Arbatov lit a cigar and tucked the stopwatch into a pocket of his black BDU trousers. The technical staff was getting better at combat simulation, he noted. "At nine hundred hours tomorrow I'll have reviewed the video of the exercise and have my criticisms ready. I think there'll be plenty. You have about four hours to get some sleep. Pleasant dreams."

Brussels was never warm, or at least Raful Barak had never been in Brussels on a job at any time other than winter, and he had never been to Brussels for any other reason than to do a job. At one time Barak's jobs had been on company time, so to speak. These days he freelanced.

Sometimes he did jobs for Israel's Mossad, other times

for what originally had been called Sayaret Matkal, before it became AMAN, the Israeli military intelligence bureau. Still other times Barak did jobs for select individuals, those who'd stood for him as what were called *susim* or "horses" in Israeli intelligence circles—people who had helped Raful move up through the ranks and covered his ass when he got into trouble or protected him from the predations, machinations, and arcane schemes that were part of business and survival in Israel's secret intelligence establishment.

One of Barak's most influential horses had been Assaf Gilad, whom he had known since his days in the elite Egoz or special forces units. The old soldier of Israel's hard-line right political wing had used Barak's services or a number of occasions during his term as the Begin government's minister of defense, and before that while head of Unit 101's Egoz. But Barak was not on a job for Gilad at the moment.

Today, Barak's employer was Mossad's secret assassination directorate, called Komemiute, for which he'd jumped as a contract *kidon*, which translates into English as "bayonet" and which is slang for an expert skilled in what is otherwise known as wet operations or wet jobs. This jump—and to "jump" in Mossad parlance means to insert into a foreign country under false cover to do a job and then quickly extract—was one of many he routinely freelanced.

Though not especially tall, Barak stood out in a crowd due to his cadaverous face, shaven skull, and lips set in a kind of perpetual grin that resembled nothing so much as the death rictus of a corpse. The long, gaunt face he'd been born with, and the ravages of time and war, had molded deeper furrows into the hollows of his cheeks.

But the death grin was the result of a sniper's bullet that had struck Barak in the face during the war in Lebanon and resulted in permanent damage to the trigeminal, the large nerve that runs along either side of the head and controls the facial muscles. In the war's final stage, after the car-bomb assassination of Bashir Gemayel, when the

Egoz were involved in uprooting nests of PLO guerrillas from the bomb wreckage that had once been the city of Beirut, Barak had gone out to hunt down the man who had disfigured him for life.

He had found the rifleman partying in a discotheque, for even amid the rubble of war-torn Beirut the nightlife for which that city was famed had never stopped for a moment, even during the worst of the fighting between warring PLO factions and between the PLO and the Christian Phalangists. It was surreal, like something out of Poe's "Masque of the Red Death"; but there it was, a continuous party in the midst of death, bomb rubble, and daily chaos. That was Beirut in 1982.

Barak had patiently waited until his quarry had filled himself to the brim with imported French champagne and then gone off to relieve himself. Later that evening they found the rifleman with his lips and mustache cut away from his mouth, encircling his severed penis, which had been jammed between his teeth.

The woman PLO member who had been the shooter's companion for the evening, a young recruit from Weisbaden, Germany, full of revolutionary ardor, had vomited at the sight of the corpse as she caught a glimpse through the disco's open toilet door. The sight had made it impossible for her to have normal sex again; her future contacts were limited to women. Barak had left the Ka-Bar knife he'd used to do the sniper buried in the former PLO shooter's heart as a reminder of his visit. He had never felt sorry about his damaged face again.

A sharp, quick knife had been Barak's weapon of first choice from that day on, but circumstances occasionally called for other means to be used, sometimes a silenced pistol, other times poison or a bomb. Still other times it was the spike, Barak's next favorite method of dispatching his targets. On the crowded Brussels street, the target had never seen Barak approach, had never suspected that he was marked for death, or that the execution would be carried out with the swiftness and anticlimax of a twinge of heartburn.

The *kidon*'s target, a Swedish national named Uwi Sondergaad, had often contemplated his own death, the nature of his work as an international arms broker specializing in big-ticket transactions—tanks, APCs, SAM transporter/launchers, and the like—and the forged end-user certificates that rendered such transactions possible, made him naturally prone to such musings. Sondergaad had never suspected that he would go out with scarcely a whimper, though. Yet that's just what happened.

Sondergaad's offense was in providing television reporter Bradley Pearsall with secret documents he'd stolen from an office in the Israeli Bureau of Defense. Sondergaad had often used the office in which to work and the safe was not locked. He had microfilmed the copies of Israel's stealth development efforts for a series Pearsall was planning on the arms race in the Mideast in the decade following Desert Storm.

Pearsall had promised Sondergaad total anonymity, but had burned him without a second thought by revealing enough about him in his series to make the identity of his informant read like an open book to those with the right needs to know. Sondergaad's duplicity was being punished by his death not so much to protect Israeli defense secrets as to send word that another member of Israel's old-boy network, a former Mossad head whom Sondergaad's revelations had embarrassed, would not be trifled with.

The spike Barak would use was already in the hand that was hidden inside the pocket of his zipped nylon ski parka. At close range, the spike was deadlier than any bullet or explosive. Plus it had the benefit of leaving no visible marks. Even a sharpened pencil could be pressed into service as a spike weapon, providing it was properly braced against the heel of the hand when put to use—this was the now infamous "Liddy pencil trick."

The gangland killers of Murder Incorporated had favored ice picks sharpened to a razor edge, but modern synthetics had devised far better weapons. Today, spikemen could choose from an array of slim Kevlar spikes whose tips could be honed to perfection and had tensile strengths high enough to puncture the bone of the skull with effortless ease that would have made Lepke Buchalter salivate with envy.

As he followed his quarry and watched Sondergaad hail a cab, Barak savored the moment. He had dropped a letter bomb in a mailbox a short distance away. The charge was only a quarter ounce of C-4, but when it exploded it would create a sizable commotion. Barak tensed himself for the moment of the coup de grâce, the moment of supreme pleasure for him. The letter bomb exploded twenty seconds later, causing all heads to turn in the direction of the smoking mailbox across the road. Sondergaad's head was one of them.

The mailbox with its plume of smoke was the last sight Sondergaad saw on earth. The five-inch Kevlar spike in Barak's palm had already punched through the thin membrane of bone at Sondergaad's left temple and pierced the temporal lobes of his brain, cutting off his centers of balance, breathing, and blood circulation. As Sondergaad's knees began to buckle, Barak's spike was already hidden inside his head, and the small puncture wound in his temple was masked by his shock of graying hair.

Barak was already passing Sondergaad as he collapsed, a smile on his thin lips. Anonymous in muffler and woolen watch cap, he paid no attention to the sudden commotion that the corpse lying in the middle of a busy street in central Brussels produced. He was already hailing a cab on the other side of the street, on his way to the airport, bound for Tel Aviv.

Halfway around the world, within the space of the same hour, it was start of business at Fort Bragg, the commencement of another day at the United States' main training center for special forces troops, including the still officially secret Delta Force.

Bragg was still home to Delta, but the unit's facilities, like Delta itself, had changed dramatically since the early days of its formation by Colonel Charles "Chargin' Charlie" Beckwith.

One of the ways that Delta had changed was in its culture. It had begun to recruit a more laid-back type of operative, one that would have given the spit-and-polish-minded Colonel Beckwith cause for one of his well-known cussing fits. Those in the classic snake-eater-and-tree-head mold were not as popular on campus as they once had been.

However, Delta's outgoing commander, Colonel Armand Pellegrino, looked down on this trend. For one reason, Pellegrino could point to Major Peace Mitchell, who, in Pellegrino's opinion, was a disgrace to his flag, his country, his uniform, his president, and even his first name.

Mitchell once had listed his military occupational specialty as "guitarist." He had a nasty way of pronouncing the word "sir." His troop seemed to have been handpicked on the basis of how badly they had flunked their psych evals. He smiled at the wrong things. He was also too short, in Pellegrino's estimation, and he had a foul mouth. But since he was about to be transferred overseas, Pellegrino didn't give much of a damn anymore. Mitchell would soon be somebody else's headache.

"Major, I have some good news and bad news," Pellegrino told Peace as he stood in his office. "The good news is that you and your unit will not face court-martial charges for kidnapping General Swann and holding him hostage for seven days."

"Boss, that's wrong. We held him for eight days."

"You interrupt me again, Major," Pellegrino said, "and I'll put you in the stockade, is that clear?"

"Yes, boss," Mitchell replied.

"And don't call me 'boss.' It's 'sir,' got it?"

"Yes, *sir*."

"Now," the colonel continued, "I am sick and tired of you and that bunch of prima donnas you call a troop exceeding all rules of professional military conduct. The general could have pinpointed his acknowledged security leaks without such dangerous theatrics."

The colonel shifted in his seat.

"Now for the bad news," he went on, and this time he was almost grinning. "You and your troop are about to begin training for what I would characterize best as a suicide mission. Unfortunately I'll be gone by then. Maybe it'll be on *60 Minutes*."

Pellegrino pushed a set of orders and the mission plan across the desk at Peace, thinking that he would not want to be in the major's shoes at this point, because Mitchell was caught between a rock and the hard place.

Mitchell picked up the report and simply asked, "When do we start, boss?" He was smiling now, too.

The farm was remote enough to be safe from prying eyes, the ones that could cause problems, that is. Other prying eyes, in the form of recon satellites in orbit, he didn't worry too much about. They might see what was happening but they belonged either to the Americans, his own people, or maybe to the French.

The Russians didn't have a bird tasked with this region, as far as his knowledge went, and the old man's knowledge in these matters was as up-to-date as the knowledge of how his prize hybrid sheep were being bred, maybe better. As to the sheep, he had begun with a herd of Persian Blackhead, and developed a breeding program that crossbred them with the native Awasi variety, producing an entirely new strain.

Old Man Gilad's sheep, which he had named Colchis, after the fabled land in the story of the Golden Fleece, had reaped him a fortune, but this was only part of his sizable holdings. His farm had been as blessed with good fortune, with *barak*, as his political career had been cursed by ill luck, bad timing, and treacherous bedfellows, like the contemptible Begin, who had turned him out as a political scapegoat after the Sabra and Shatilla massacres of the Lebanon War days. His lemon and olive groves, his fields of wheat, corn, and barley, had made Gilad an extremely wealthy man.

He would never again want for material comforts, and he was not without friends in high places, nor did he fail to note that he had earned his place in the history books as the hero of two wars, ranking in achievement with his old mentor and sometime rival Moshe Dayan.

Still, Gilad was not content to be a name on the page of a book, a subject of schoolchildren's history classes. As long as he breathed, he thirsted to be in the spotlight, to be part of the forces shaping not only Israel and the Middle East, but the world as well. It was as much in his blood as the farm was, and although he had grown up on a *moshav,* or communal farm, with the smell of earth in his nostrils, he had known from the first that politics and fame were the two greatest loves of his life.

He would no longer be denied these. Yet there was more.

Gilad believed he had never been more needed by his country than he was today.

Now, when Israel faltered on the brink of sanctioning a full-fledged Palestinian state on its West Bank, history itself cried out for him to step forward and stretch forth his strong hand, like the patriarchs of old. His so-often-misguided people had profaned the Eternal and risked kindling His wrath. He would save them from the consequences of their wickedness.

And like the patriarchs of old, like Abraham, like Isaac, like Jacob, and like Joseph and Moses who came after them, Assaf Gilad had the means at his disposal to make his plans manifest. His sophisticated video surveillance system showed one of them arriving right now. It was Raful Barak, just back from Brussels, and now driving through the gates of the farm and up the long road that led to the main house.

As Barak walked toward Gilad's door, another elder statesman who had played a role in global political events, in a dacha many kilometers to the north and east on the birch-forested outskirts of Moscow, also prepared to receive a visitor.

Like Gilad, the ill and aging political mandarin was still well connected, though he had been out of office for the better part of the past year. And also like his Israeli contemporary, Boris Yeltsin still thirsted for power and a direct hand in the way Russia, and to a lesser extent the world beyond the *Rodina*'s borders, was run.

Indeed, Yeltsin had arranged it so that when the ex–Colonel General Grigorenko became Russia's second democratically elected president, he would be making decisions contingent on Yeltsin's advice and approval. But the wily general had outfoxed his patron and to Yeltsin's chagrin had gone off on his own, moving ahead with reforms at a pace far faster than the former Russian leader believed practical, let alone possible.

Still, Yeltsin held cards he could play. One of those concerned this recent blunder in the Iranian desert, which he knew all about through his many sources. The secret report on the crash of the stealth plane had reached him at the same instant as it reached Grigorenko, and Yeltsin had immediately made his plans based on the opportunities he deemed it presented.

"Come in, sit down, Valery Fedorovich," Yeltsin said, nodding to his servant who poured both him and his visitor a glass of aged Napoleon brandy, which Yeltsin still drank despite strict doctor's orders. "How is everything at home? Your pretty wife Elena has received the small household gift I sent?"

"It was overly kind of you, sir," the younger man said to the former president. "Far more than we deserve."

"Nonsense, it's the least I could do," Yeltsin said. "Now drink up. We must talk business before my doctors arrive for their afternoon torture session. Tell me all that you have learned since your last visit."

Yeltsin watched Valery Nemekov take a strong belt of the brandy, the way a man should drink his liquor, and set the glass on the coffee table. Yeltsin immediately filled it again, and would continue doing so throughout the conversation, as much to enable himself to enjoy the sight of good whiskey being drunk as to loosen the other man's tongue.

Nemekov still had the boyish good looks and fair hair that Yeltsin had recalled from the turbulent days of the 1991 democratic revolution. Then it had been Nemekov who had headed the *boyevaya,* the hit men of the KGB Alfa team that, under orders from the reactionary cabal headed by the accursed Kryuchkov, was to break into the Russian parliament building where Yeltsin had barricaded himself. Alfa was to assassinate him and his close associates in a hail of automatic fire and grenade shrapnel.

Kryuchkov, who had been appointed chief of the KGB under Gorbachev, and who later aligned himself with hard-liners and recidivist Communists when the reforms under glasnost and perestroika had seemed to falter, was to have assumed control of a resurgent Soviet Union in a coup d'état that would have swept Yeltsin, the new president-elect, from power. But as a moving wall of tracked armor flowed into Moscow one workday morning, and pressed toward the Kremlin to the shock of Center-bound highway commuters, the Russian *nomenklatura* had gotten the word out and the people took to the streets, erecting barricades against the tanks of August, stopping them in their tracks with often no more than their bodies as living barriers.

Yet the confrontation might still have ended with the Kryuchkov faction victorious had it not been for Nemekov's refusal to carry out the assassination directive the KGB head had given him. In the end, it had been Kryuchkov who had—at least to the outside world—committed suicide in the wake of his defeat.

Yeltsin, and many others, knew that Kryuchkov's "suicide" had been what Russians called *vyshera mera,* "up-against-the-wall time." Not without irony, this had been the same form of punishment that had been meted out to so many "enemies of the state" during the tenure of Kryuchkov's KGB leadership.

Like his own victims, Kryuchkov had been led into a

room in the basement of KGB headquarters in Moscow's sprawling old Lubyanka prison building, made to kneel in a corner with his face to the wall, and executed with a single nine-mm hollow-nose round fired from a Makarov pistol to the back of his head. Akhromeyev, Pugo, and Kruchina, the other three members of the Kryuchkov cabal, had met the same fate as their leader, first watching his brains explode in a wet red nova, then taking Kryuchkov's place against the blood-streaked wall.

Due to his courage in defying the KGB *chekisti,* the opposite fate was in store for Valery Nemekov. Yeltsin had rewarded him for his courage and promoted him to head the C.I.S.'s elite special operations unit, Vasaltnik Force G. Nevertheless, there was one problem with the young man, perhaps a grave one in light of the reason Yeltsin had summoned him to his dacha today.

Nemekov's entire fame rested on what he had not done as opposed to what he did do. With the Vasaltniki, he had proven himself inept, and had survived only because he was Yeltsin's chosen favorite and protégé, and could meet with the old man directly, virtually any time he wished. Now, however, it was a different story. Yeltsin was being eased out of his advisory position by Grigorenko. Soon enough he would be a forgotten and sick old man in full retirement, with no voice in Russian affairs, breaking wind in his dacha as he waited for the end.

The host continued to wait for Nemekov's story. The younger man began by stating what Yeltsin already surmised.

"Grigorenko has chosen Arbatov to head the mission into Iran. I have been passed over once again."

"Arbatov?" Yeltsin said, his brows crinkling in thought. "Is he not the vodka-swilling miscreant who was court-martialed for unsoldierly conduct in Afghanistan?" He thought back to his days as party chairman under Gorbachev, and the prosecution of the Afghan War, in which he had played a minor political role.

"Yes," said Nemekov. "The same one. But you should

know, since it was you who agitated for court-martial, was it not?"

"So I did," Yeltsin replied, and the memory returned from across the gulf of years. "He had killed his superior officer, a Colonel Panshin, I think it was."

"Yes, Panshin was his name."

Yeltsin's brows furrowed deeper.

"This Arbatov had been ordered to carry out a revenge attack for terrorist atrocities against our forces in the Khunduz region. He was to lead Spetsnaz into a village harboring CIA-trained Mujahideen killers and destroy their stronghold. Instead, he ended up murdering his superior officer."

"Correct, sir," Nemekov replied, drinking another glass of brandy. "Arbatov refused to obey his orders, and when the colonel drew his gun, Arbatov took it from his hands and struck him down with a single blow. The colonel never got up again."

Nemekov was somewhat drunk by now, but not drunk enough to add to his story that Arbatov, though demoted in rank from major to lowly captain, was found to have acted in self-defense at his trial and had enjoyed the support of many other officers, who by then were fed up with the cycle of atrocities that marked the later stages of the war. Arbatov's troop had been ordered to kill every man, woman, and child in the village and then raze it to the ground.

He had killed all of the Mujahideen he could locate, but refused to permit his men to execute innocents and noncombatants. Arbatov's defense became known as the Mai-Lai defense; he pleaded he would not become the Lieutenant William Calley of Afghanistan. His plea was accepted by his peers, and though Arbatov was punished, he was not executed as a traitor as Yeltsin and supreme commanding officer of Afghan forces, Army General Vladimir Potapenko, had wished. In the end Arbatov became a hero, though none who valued his career was foolish enough to admit this in public.

Yeltsin poured his guest another glass of brandy, almost

draining the bottle. "Don't worry, Valery Fedorovich, my good friend," the old man told his young protégé, "it will all be taken care of. Wait a week or two. You will see that I am still not without my helpers and supporters in many high places. Arbatov will never lead this mission, you can be sure of this. I give you my pledge that you and only you shall be the one. *Prosit!*"

Boris Yeltsin lifted his glass and drained it dry.

Seven
Bumps in the Night

The guard sullenly shoved the bowl of thin soup and the hunk of stale bread through the narrow slot in the door of Petrov's cell, stared at his charge a moment through the Judas hole above it, rammed shut the latch, and went down the hall. When the cadence of footsteps and the jingle of keys died away, Petrov left his cot and examined his supper.

The bread was a sex club for maggots and the soup looked, smelled, and tasted like it had been freshly ladled from the prison latrine. Nevertheless, Petrov wolfed down his meal with a gusto that nobody unacquainted with his predicament could be expected to fully comprehend. By now he'd learned the amazing fact that starvation held the miraculous power to transform even filth into caviar, and in his weeks of captivity the stealth driver had become no stranger to starvation.

Petrov had already spent time as the guest of several Iranian military encampments, being shuffled around like a walnut shell on a monte player's table. They had blindfolded him with each move, but they had not plugged his ears and nostrils. Petrov had heard and smelled and tasted the desert around him. He retained his pilot's sense of time, speed, and distance. He doubted if he had traveled more than a hundred klicks in any direction.

At each new stop he had been questioned about the operation of the plane. Usually the interrogation was preceded by a beating or a mock execution. The Iranians seemed either to take a perverse enjoyment in holding an unloaded pistol to his head and dry-firing the gun or to believe that after several exposures to this pretense Petrov would still think they were serious. This time there was a new wrinkle. After the *de rigueur* snap of the hammer against firing pin, Petrov was actually brought from the stockade to demonstrate some of the aircraft's instrumentation to his captors.

He had been taken under guard from his cell, frog-marched blindfolded through a compound alive with motor-pool noises, sour cooking odors, and, at one point, the sound of a television or radio playing the theme song of the universally recognized American TV show *Bonanza,* into a large and busy aircraft hangar, where his blindfold was removed. It was night, but the floodlit hangar swarmed with technicians, soldiers, and officers, their collective attention focused on the black aircraft that occupied center stage. Like the holy Ka'ba stone of some high-tech priesthood, it seemed to hold them all spellbound.

Petrov could see at a glance that some internal gear from Shadow One had been removed for examination. Modules from the rack-mounted secure communications system lay on a steel trundle table near the fuselage, where technicians with a sweep oscilloscope touched diagnostic probes to the ICs of the exposed printed circuit boards. But virtually everything else about the exterior of the plane appeared intact.

The Iranians sat Petrov down and told him they were interested in the MFI's inertial navigation system. They wanted Petrov to demonstrate how the pilot interacted with its menu-driven command interface. Would he be willing to do so?

Petrov gave them what they wanted, but volunteered nothing whatever. This was not just out of patriotic duty or a flier's *esprit de corps,* but derived from an instinct for self-preservation. Petrov reasoned that the more information he provided the Iranians and the more quickly he downloaded useful data into their brains, the less he was worth to them, and the sooner his meager rations of thin soup and maggoty bread would become a fast bullet between the eyes and an unmarked hole in the ground beyond the floodlit perimeter of some isolated desert camp.

Nevertheless, Petrov also noticed that they had fully refueled the plane, which they would want to do in order to taxi it from hangar to hangar, and in order to perform other tests on its onboard systems. When they threw him back in his cell again, Petrov decided that if it were at all possible, he would try to get back into the cockpit and fly the plane to freedom. He could sense that his days as a captive were numbered, in any case.

If death awaited him, he thought, then it was better to meet it as a soldier than as a whipped cur. He would make a run for it. This he swore.

Viktor Arbatov found himself summoned to the base commander's office from the training area in the midst of a training exercise. However, instead of his normal commanding officer, Colonel Golovsky, another officer sat behind the oaken desk.

Arbatov already sensed what was going to happen, but he saw no other choice than to play the farce out to its inevitable climax. In some regards, Russia would always be Russia, and nothing would ever change the innate love of intrigue and backstabbing that characterized everything from politics to art in the intensely and hopelessly Slavic country.

"Captain, I won't mince words with you," the newcomer began. "I am Colonel Putilin, your new commanding officer."

"What became of Colonel Golovsky?" asked Arbatov.

"He was transferred suddenly on medical leave," Putilin answered gruffly. "Anyway, this does not concern you."

"No? Then what does—sir?"

"Your record of insolence has not gone unnoticed, Captain," Putilin replied. "You would do well to adopt a more soldierly tone. It might be of help to your career—what is left of it, anyway."

When Arbatov said nothing, Putilin went on. "In any case, you have been ordered to stand down from mission training at once. You and your men are to return to your headquarters until further notice."

"Then the mission has been scrubbed?"

"No, not scrubbed, nor did I say that it had been," Putilin answered testily. "Your unit is to be replaced with one led by Major Valery Nemekov."

"Nemekov? How can this be? He is a Vasaltnik, not even Spetsnaz. He is a paratrooper trained to do grunt work. That is good soldiering, in its place, make no mistake. But we Spetsnaz are surgeons, specialists at what we do. It is ludicrous to send mere crunchies to do our kind of work."

"Guard your insolent tongue or I will personally see to it that you are court-martialed. This time you will spend the rest of your life in prison, I guarantee it. Now get out of here. You have received your orders. Obey them."

"Yes, sir," Arbatov told his glaring superior, saluting smartly, then turned on his heels and strode into the hall. But he thought to himself that if Putilin believed that this was the end of it, then that posturing little martinet was very much mistaken.

The red light atop the camera glowed, a signal for him to look up, speak in rich, cultivated tones, and show some of the expensive caps that covered his front teeth. That, and reading from the TelePrompTer, was what they paid him for.

"Thank you, Linda. I'm sure those Korean orphans will never forget the first lady's surprise visit."

Newsanchor Scott Dunnelsford faced the number-two camera, which pulled in for a close-up head shot, beaming his familiar smile to millions of dinnertime TV viewers—the same ones who had long since forgotten his failed stint as a daytime soap opera actor many years before.

"Next, the crisis in Iran heats up," he said next, his voice crisp and modulated. "Today the United Nations Security Council voted unanimously for sanctions against the United States and Commonwealth of Independent States in the wake of the destruction of two Iranian nuclear facilities.

"At a press conference earlier today, White House Press Secretary Helene Goldthwaite denied U.S. involvement in what Iran has called 'naked aggression' against its territory, instead claiming that the explosions that destroyed the two nuclear facilities were the result of accident or sabotage.

"So far there has been no comment from Russian officials on the Iranian claims. But Iranian President Othmar Beheshti Rasulali, in a speech before the Iranian parliament, has threatened military action in retaliation for the alleged attacks. Just what form this would take has not been made clear."

Camera two pulled back for a long shot while camera one dollied into position for a close-up of the female anchor. As soon as she saw the red light come on, she began reading from the TelePrompTer screen below the camera lens.

"And we'll be following that story as it continues to unfold," Linda Bailey said, the thirty thousand dollars the TV station had spent on speech instruction to remove all traces of the accent she'd grown up with in the slums of Brooklyn's Brownsville section replaced with the bland but perfect diction of a media clone.

"In Belfast, the death toll continues to rise after the explosion of a bomb at a packed rugby stadium. The Irish Republican Army has claimed credit for the bombing.

British Prime Minister Harley Peters, fresh from his courtroom defense in the number 10 Downing Street sex scandal, pledged that Britain would not take this matter lying down. In Colombia, a resurgence of narcoterrorist activity has government forces on alert . . ."

The ancient trade route known as the Silk Highway meandered through the Caucasus Mountains and down its granite flanks into the flat grasslands of Azerbaijan. From there it wended its way steadily southward, into Afghanistan and Iran. Ancient though it was, the Silk Highway followed the far more ancient tracks laid down by the Crusaders, who had trudged on foot toward Constantinople and down into the Holy Land by way of Libya and the Sudan.

In the twentieth century the route had been trodden by Gypsies and heroin smugglers, arms traders and clandestine travelers shuttling between Europe, Asia, and the countries of the Middle East.

Along the tortuous, zigzagging route, diverse peoples who were basically stateless had sprung up over the centuries—Tatars, Khazars, Uzbeks, Kurds, Sabians, Yazedis, Druze, and many others. Citizens of their respective countries mainly by decree, they were often willing to turn a blind eye, shelter fugitives, or smuggle them across their porous borders, if the price was right or other considerations were met.

Even during times of war, which came often to the region beset by the shifting winds of nationalism, dictatorship, and ever-changing political affiliations, the borders remained porous, and though the price of the bribes could drastically increase, the border guards could always be counted on to do business as usual.

To the Russian military forces, embroiled in the civil war in Afghanistan throughout most of the 1980s, this ancient road had become the latter-day equivalent of the Ho Chi Minh Trail that had bedeviled the Americans in Vietnam during the 1960s and early 1970s.

Like the Ho Chi Minh Trail, the overland mountain

route was an open channel for thousands of tons of weapons, spare parts, and ammunition for Mujahideen forces throughout the war years. Unlike it, however, there was no hope of even token bombing of the route, which stretched across a dozen countries and even more ethnic regions, and which could never be stopped at its source. With the right couriers, contraband of every kind was virtually guaranteed to reach its destination intact.

As the sun rose on a barren stretch of mountain road in a high mountain pass one fog-swept morning in late March, its rays burned through the tatters of fine, drifting mist and reflected off the dull, dust-caked chassis of a Land Rover that rolled toward a nearby Azeri town, a village of stone houses and narrow, unpaved streets called Kushtam. Inside the vehicle were Raful Barak and a squad-strength detachment of handpicked mercenaries, all of them Israeli and all of them drawn from Nahal Brigade Egoz forces loyal to Gilad.

The group's destination had been planned and mapped out during their preparations by elements of AMAN's Unit 504, which specialized in cross-border intelligence, and they bore forged papers that identified them as Turkish merchants, modern-day counterparts of ancient traders who plied the region in centuries past.

They, said their papers, had been on a buying mission for a prestigious Parisian antique dealer. The papers and cover story had been prepared by Unit 8520's Development Directorate, which specializes in false identification, counterfeit currencies, special covert weapons, and other nonstandard items and services for agents abroad. Both were flawless.

Any check on the dealer, which was what the Mossad called a *sayan,* or an unaffiliated helper, would confirm the cover. The Mossad maintained contacts with *sayanim* throughout the world who, though themselves not members of the intelligence organization, were willing to provide support for its operators. Their ranks included business people and professionals from all walks of life.

Usually these were fellow Jews, but not always.

The Egoz team did not carry arms other than a single Pakistani-made variant of the AK-47 and a few handguns, but these weapons would not attract undue concern in this rough and remote mountain country, no more than scimitars would have done in the days of the ancient caravans that had once trod this same route.

There was a full consignment of military weapons, ammunition, and special electronics, including commo and GPS awaiting delivery for Barak's team, but that would come near the end of the journey, just before they crossed over into Iran in search of the downed plane. Carried with them now were only a few rugs, seemingly purchased during their travels, but really bought in the large collectibles market of Istanbul.

As Barak rode in the front seat of the first Land Rover, he thought back on his final days at Gilad's farm, just before the team's departure. Gilad had been jubilant, more full of his old energy and confidence than Barak could remember in years. They had drunk a glass of aged French cognac, the Old Man's favorite drink, and smoked imported Cuban cigars, talking about the mission and its importance.

Apart from Gilad's messianic belief that by retrieving the secret of Russian stealth, he could somehow bring peace to the Mideast and save the world, which Barak regarded as megalomaniacal nonsense, the Old Man's plan had a far more materialistic side to it. If they could succeed in flying the plane out, or even in dismantling enough of its electronics and fuselage to bring it back to Israel, they would have struck a gold mine.

Once reverse-engineered, the Russian stealth technologies could be improved upon and sold individually to any buyer with the money to afford them. It was the old equation known to junkyard dealers—in pieces, a car was worth many times more than it was worth whole. The Mossad had become expert at this practice, and Gilad had been one of its inventors.

It was settled that Barak would be Gilad's agent in selling the technology, and they discussed ways of contracting out stealth to various countries. The Chinese, the Koreans (both North and South), and the Swedes, who wanted to enter the fighter plane market with an upgraded, first-line version of their Gripen second-line fighters, were all on the short list.

And why not? In a year or two, maybe five, the secret of stealth would be out anyway. By 2010 the Americans and the Russians would be selling stealth openly at global arms shows, the way the Americans now sold laptops, electric guitars, refrigerators, and their inane pop culture, and like the Soviets sold Kalashnikovs and vodka.

And furthermore, who really owned stealth, after all? Probably the Nazis of Hitler's Third Reich, who had invented the concept back in the early forties, Barak thought. The original stealth plane was the so-called Horton Wing, prototypes of which the Americans had found along with so much other technology amid the ruins of Nazi Germany and transported to their country for development. It was ironic how much—including helmets identical to those of the Nazi Wehrmacht, save that they were made of Kevlar instead of steel—the Americans had taken from their former enemies and made as Yankee as apple pie.

Barak's thoughts snapped back to the present. The Land Rover was now approaching the stone hill town on the dusty mountain road. Yigael, at the wheel, honked at an old man leading a flock of shaggy-pelted, long-horned goats that blocked the road. The villager stopped and smiled, revealing a set of *naswar*-stained teeth in a gaunt, unshaven, and craggily windburned face. He held out his hand in an okay sign and moved it back and forth indicating, in sign language, that he wanted a cigarette if the car was ever to pass his loudly baa-ing flock.

Colonel Farzaneh Hossein Ghazbanpour was a rarity in the Iranian army or Pasdaran. His tenure in its ranks dated from the final days of Shah Reza Pahlavi's doomed kingship.

Somehow, he had survived the worst excesses of the Khomeini years, distinguishing himself as an able field commander during the bloody eight-year-long war with Iraq, to emerge during the more moderate period that followed as a highly decorated military hero and a well-known figure to most Iranians.

Ghazbanpour was even more unusual in having received military training in the United States at the U.S. Army's Academy of the Nations, which had trained military officers of the shah's regime during the 1970s, just prior to the fall of the house of Pahlavi.

Because Ghazbanpour was an expert on air warfare, and considered a prime example of the new style of Iranian military operations and tactics, he was given command of the remote base in the Dasht-e-Kavir, the high desert in central Iran, where the captured Eclipse aircraft was being kept.

Ghazbanpour was uncertain of many things, but he was sure of one: that the Russians, or even the Americans, would mount a mission to retake the lost stealth fighter. Too much was at stake for both nations simply to leave the plane in Iranian hands and shrug their collective shoulders at the consequences. He himself, Ghazbanpour thought, would lobby for such a mission were he in the places of those who made military decisions in the U.S. and C.I.S. And since such a mission was inevitable, in Ghazbanpour's opinion, he would plan for it in advance.

The stealth plane, he decided, would make excellent bait with which to reel in his adversaries. Ghazbanpour was a student of the ancient Chinese tactician Sun Tzu. He recalled that the old General Sun had advised that in order to prevail on the battlefield, a good commander needed to first attack his enemy's strategy. Ghazbanpour would follow the sage's wise counsel. All he needed to do was to set the mousetrap and listen for the sound of a snap in the night.

Precisely at seven hundred hours on a Sunday morning, the *chekisti* invaded the barracks of Spetsnaz Group G and marched down the double row of wooden bunks. Men looked up and said nothing, for they knew better. The contingent of KGB, with a colonel at their head, proceeded to Captain Arbatov's private quarters and stopped. The major did not bother to knock. He signaled to the two men behind him who carried fire axes. They rushed forward and viciously swung them, shattering the wooden door to flinders.

The two men with axes rushed into the room but quickly regretted their haste. Arbatov sent the first man sprawling with a butt smash of the Avtomat Kalashnikova AKS to the side of his head, and impaled the second man through the arm with the compact autoweapon's fixed bayonet.

"Stop!"

It was the head *chekist* who barked the order. The Makarov pistol in his hand gave it teeth. Arbatov pulled the bayonet from the bleeding wound into which its tip had bitten deep and kicked the man against the wall in the groin to hasten his slide to the cold wooden floor.

"Drop your weapon and step forward or I shall not hesitate to shoot!"

Arbatov tossed the AKS onto his cot and stepped out into the barracks as the KGB colonel backpedaled. Arbatov saw a potentially disastrous situation in the making. The *chekisti* had chosen to beard the lion in his den. They had brought along a troop that surrounded the barracks and was inside it, but his own men would be willing to fight if he gave the order.

"What is the meaning of this?" asked Arbatov, though he already suspected what would happen and knew he could not prevent it.

"We have received reports that you are dealing heroin from your quarters, Captain," the colonel answered. "Step aside. Your quarters are to be thoroughly searched."

Arbatov said nothing. There was no point, especially now that the martinet Putilin had put in an appearance and was glaring at him with open hostility. He was to be set up and there was nothing to be done about it—at least not at the moment.

Expectedly, the major's underlings returned clutching a kilo bag of a white powdery substance.

"What is your explanation for this?" asked the *chekist*.

"My explanation is that your lackeys just planted it. Why didn't you simply shoot me and get it over with?"

The colonel pulled his lips taut in a kind of grin.

"You deny dealing dope, then?" he asked.

"Get fucked, you *chekist* scum-eater!" Arbatov cursed. "You can shove that bag of shit up your faggot's ass." A roar of laughter rose up from the barracks at this remark.

At this point Putilin stepped in. He made Arbatov's choice a simple one. Either face court-martial, and risk execution for what was a capital offense in the army of the C.I.S., or accept transfer to a punishment battalion in the Caucasus for a year of hard labor. Boris Yeltsin had made good on his pledge to Valery Nemekov, and Arbatov had been left with no cards to play. He left the barracks under armed guard.

Eight
To Each Their Own

The command center was located at the former Strategic Rocket Forces base at Kapustin Yar in the Caucasus. The large military map was secured to the broad tabletop, lit by overhead fluorescent panels. Major Valery Fedorovich Nemekov and his aging mentor, Army General Vladimir Illich Potapenko, who had pushed hard for his commanding the mission, supporting Boris Yeltsin's wishes, stood beside the map table discussing the operational planning of the impending strike.

Both were attired in stiff, new camouflage fatigues, the bottoms of their BDU trousers bloused into the tops of their high black paratroop boots. Nemekov's uniform was completed by the maroon beret of the Vasaltniki, worn at a rakish angle to complement his angular features. If clothes made the soldier, both men would have ranked as Napoleons. But soldiering took more than a good custom tailor and a pair of shiny boots.

Potapenko was a doddering throwback to the Neanderthal age of the Brezhnev political era, too well connected to be forced out of his sinecure just yet, and determined to hang on as long as possible. Privately, though, Potapenko had been planning his imminent retirement for the last several months and had already announced it to his inner circle of close confidants.

This mission, in which his young protégé would use the storehouse of warcraft the old general had passed on to him like a Zen swordsman to an ardent young samurai, would be a fitting end to his long and illustrious career.

At least in uniform, Potapenko was still an imposing presence. His six-foot-two frame gave him an august stature, and his broad chest, still looking muscular thanks to adept tailoring, was draped with at least a kilogram of shining medals and colorful campaign ribbons. They were decorations won in a host of engagements stretching back to the heyday of Soviet domination of Eastern Europe and the U.S.S.R.'s strategic involvement in the Middle East and Central America.

Potapenko had been the liaison man in Cairo for Gamal Abdul Nassar in the mid-sixties, and had helped train the Egyptian army that was to launch what soon became known as the Six Day War. A year later he had helped defeat the 1968 Prague Spring uprising in Czechoslovakia, pouring Soviet T-72 tanks, BTR assault vehicles, and other mechanized armor into the rebellious East Bloc satellite state to create a juggernaut of steel that crushed all opposition.

Today Potapenko was dressed in the camouflage fatigues of a Russian field commander, and wore only shoulder flashes as insignia of rank. He also wore a general-issue Makarov PM nine-mm automatic pistol holstered at his waist, though the only thing worth defending oneself against here were the hordes of fat blueblack bottle flies that infested the southern region of the Eurasian landmass.

An aide suddenly entered the command post staff room and handed the old campaigner a sheaf of printouts that had just been downloaded from the tactical computer system installed at the base. The lieutenant saluted smartly, the way Potapenko required his staff to salute, and promptly withdrew. Potapenko scanned the printouts, then handed them to the younger man similarly attired in fatigues who stood at his side.

"The latest reports from our forward observation team of ground agents," he told Nemekov, who skimmed through the pages while the general summarized. "Conditions on the ground are currently highly favorable. There is little chance of adverse weather, and optimum flying conditions will likely continue through the next three days." Potapenko smiled at his protégé, flashing a set of perfectly capped front teeth. "A great time for daring," the general concluded.

"The plan is sound," Nemekov told him. "That's the most important thing."

The older man turned back to the large military map on the table. Clusters of multicolored pushpins had been inserted to represent targets and waypoints, and lines of march had been drawn between the fixed coordinates. Move by move—it was there, all laid out in front of them—an inexorable progression from the landing of troops and equipment to the storming of the base and the destruction of the stolen stealth fighter-bomber. Simple, by the book, and as certain to be effective as anything could be in combat. All in all, one could not hope for a better chance at success.

Potapenko had no use for military revisionists who wanted to adopt so-called modern Western procedures and doctrine. As a young disciple of the extraordinary Marshal Zhukov, he had helped draft the warfighting manuals after the Great Patriotic War. They were as sound today as they were back then, he knew.

Potapenko pointed to the landing zone marked on the map where two all-weather Antonov transport planes would touch down, carrying sufficient Vasaltniki and equipment for a high-mobility assault force of company strength.

Such a formation would be the perfect size for an operation that called for high mobility and rapid insertion and extraction from the combat area. Also—and though he had said nothing of this to Nemekov—should things go wrong, there was an excellent chance that a force so small would be wiped out entirely, reducing political problems in its wake.

But this would not happen, he reminded himself. The plan was sound and the mission was destined to succeed.

The old general continued to smile as he fixed his clear blue eyes on the face of the younger man. "From here you must follow the timetable to the minute," he advised the major. "If you do, it will all fall into place."

The pointer moved to the first cluster of red pins, indicating the initial waypoint, a deep wadi, actually a rift, situated midway between the base and the LZ. "From landing to Wadi Kumar is twenty-six minutes. From there a scout detachment is sent. Who is its leader, I've forgotten."

"Lieutenant Trapezhnikov," Nemekov told the general, "an able leader. He served with honor in the Afghan campaign."

"Yes, I know the man, yes," Potapenko said, thinking of a young recruit in one of the Vasaltniki detachments. "Next, the main strike follows. There are no reports of new defenses being installed since our last photographic reconnaissance satellite pass."

Nemekov checked his watch. "The latest data should have been ready by now. I'll look into it."

He picked up a phone and called an aide for the satellite imagery. The aide said that he would check back. He soon came in and placed the large sheaf of acetate printouts that had just come off a color plotter on clips above a light box stationed near the main tactical map.

Nemekov and Potapenko studied the orbital photoimagery. Blown up by a factor of three, the overhead surveillance data showed a great deal of detail, comparable in quality to the U.S. Keyhole series output at low resolution. The two soldiers could clearly see that defenses at the base had not significantly changed in the last twelve hours.

Most important, there was still no armor guarding the ground approaches to the base. Either the Iranians had not yet brought in their mechanized equipment, or they were deliberately not trying to attract attention to the installation by signs of beefed-up activity.

Nevertheless, a series of photos taken the previous morning, when the angle of the sun was just right, clearly showed the sharply angled nose assembly of the stealth plane projecting from between two open hangar bay doors. The plane was apparently there, and they would soon make sure the Iranians no longer possessed what they had stolen from the former Soviets.

Potapenko was pleased at the high-grade satellite photointelligence. "Good. Nothing material has changed," he told the younger man. "I am more certain than ever that this mission will go smoothly."

Nemekov smiled. As usual, he was in complete agreement with his mentor.

Already inside Iran, and far closer to the target of the impending operation, Raful Barak was not as blandly certain of success as the two men who finalized their war plans far away across the chain of mountains to the east.

The Egoz team's photointelligence or PHOTINT was not as good as that available to the Russians. It might have been better had they had access to American overhead surveillance data from a Keyhole, Lacrosse, or one of the other half-dozen types of birds the Pentagon, NSA, and CIA had in orbit. These spy satellites could use multiple cameras, lasers, and radars, or combinations thereof, along with specially polished and movable mirrors, to produce amazingly accurate and detailed imagery of sites on the ground that no other force on earth came remotely close to having.

What the Americans could do with their satellites was incredible, which is why Gilad had lobbied the Reagan Administration years before for Keyhole satellite imagery back in the early eighties. The U.S. spysat imagery was not only good in its raw, unprocessed real-time form, but could be further enhanced by computers to produce three-dimensional graphics of target sites, accurate down to the last millimeter.

Gilad's Ministry of Defense had desperately wanted Keyhole access so it could aim Israel's then fledgling offensive nuclear missile force at targets inside the Soviet Union. The strategy had been to threaten the Soviets with nuclear first strikes if they did not keep their Arab client states on a short leash. Though Ronald Reagan amiably complied with the request, the Weinberger-controlled U.S. Defense Department had withheld access, and had made the decision stick. The president's mind, stricken by Alzheimer's, had by then deteriorated to the point where virtually all policy decisions were made by his subordinates and rubber-stamped by him.

Gilad got his Keyhole data anyway, through convicted espionage agent Jonathan Pollard's spying, and also by other, yet more secret means. The farmer in the Negev still had a back channel into the American National Security Agency today when he needed more of the satellite intelligence in which the NSA specialized.

But nobody was supposed to know about this mission, least of all the Knesset or the prime minister. Both, Barak suspected, would have heart attacks if they had the slightest inkling of what the former general was up to. Israel officially wanted no part of Russian stealth technology, nor did the long-beleaguered Jewish state want to anger the Russians, the Americans, or the Arab states, with all of whom they now had increasingly cordial diplomatic relations. This is why most of Barak's intelligence came from HUMINT rather than orbital PHOTINT sources.

Gilad's private network of *katsas,* or undercover agents on the ground, stretched from one end of the Mideast to the other. It included the east and west coasts of America and everything in between, as well as the capital cities of Europe. Gilad had worked for decades to build up this formidable private intelligence service, and he considered it his personal fiefdom, which he ruled as the laird of the manor.

The Old Man had assets on the ground that nobody could match, not Mossad or the KGB, and certainly not the CIA, which had always run the most laughably inept agents in the business, such as the clownish Aldrich Ames, and then usually sold them out in the end. It was from these assets, including the *marats* or "listeners," who picked up stray bits and pieces of useful intelligence and sold them for a price, that Barak had been able to build up a strategic picture of where Shadow One might be found and the steps necessary to retake the plane. Tonight, in the desert darkness at twenty-one hundred hours, Barak entertained nothing resembling the certainties that the two Russian soldiers held at their Azeri staging base while poring over their mission maps.

The Egoz's vehicles had already begun to fill with the rugs that the caravan of "merchants" had bought at the towns and hamlets along their route. Now Barak's men were halted at a small cooking fire lit in the desert. They might have spent the night at a Kurdish village only about fifty klicks behind them, where they had freshened their fuel reserves, but it was important that they be away from prying eyes and ears. Tonight, weapons and gear from a hidden stash site had joined their inventory.

At each stop, more than fresh gas and rugs were purchased. Fresh information from confidential sources, concerning the whereabouts of the plane, troop dispositions, the names of bribable border guards, the schedules and habits of desert patrols, was all bought and paid for by the merchants from Istanbul. At the last of the towns, Barak had also taken on two guides well versed in the roads, weather, and general conditions of the Dasht-e-Kavir, ones who knew every wadi, rock, *sabkah,* and tree in the desert by heart.

Barak had decided that he needed these guides because of his uncertainty about the target—for the moment, anyway. There seemed to be reason to believe that the plane was at a small base at al-Kabriz, where workers had seen an aircraft resembling it.

But Bedouin contacts told another story. Some had traded at a more remote, and more heavily secured, base equipped with bomb-resistant hangars. Their informant had seen nothing. But one of the soldiers had griped about the "damned black plane" he had to guard, then quickly fell silent. The Bedouin had been well paid for their information.

Barak had decided to form two reconnaissance groups, one going to the smaller base at al-Kabriz, and the other, which he would command, to the secure base at Wadi Quom. The two teams would leave as soon as preparations were finalized, and the guides would lead them. They would keep in touch by secure satcom transmissions at regularly scheduled intervals. When the time came, the guides would be killed and buried, having seen and known too much for their own good.

Barak saw one of his men gesture. The teams were ready to roll. He spilled the dregs of his coffee into the sand, and placed the porcelain cup in the pocket of his fleece-lined sheepskin coat, where for some reason he had carried it throughout most of the journey.

Then he climbed into the Land Rover and gave the signal to move out into the cold desert night.

One after the other, their immense turbofan engines crying out their barbaric songs of naked power, the two Antonov transport planes had roared to safe landings on the hard-packed desert crust. They had been guided to the landing zone by a prepositioned operative, a Kurdish national in the pay of the Russians, who had been paradropped in with a portable radar homing beacon a few days before.

The beacon transmitted course information to the flight decks of the transports, guiding them to within a few meters of the LZ. The man on the ground then used chemical light sticks tossed onto the sands to mark the landing zone, and the planes touched down, between the glowing red, green, and blue dashes that softly lit the night.

No sooner had the planes' landing gear touched earth than the rear ramp of the first Antonov slammed down amid a cloud of swirling dust, and men and machinery spilled onto the desert floor, a process repeated moments later, following the second Antonov's landing.

Before the planes had taxied to a stop, with well-trained precision, the BTR-70 armored personnel carriers and two BRDM armored command vehicles were rolled onto the turf and the Vasaltniki assembled into ranks. As soon as the planes had off-loaded, and with engines still hot, the Antonovs took off again, disappearing into the black night skies.

The transports would return just before dawn the following day to pick up the men and equipment for the return trip, but until then they couldn't afford to sit on the ground, where they would be as vulnerable as beached whales. The Antonovs would fly back across the border, tank up from Ilyushin fuelbirds, and orbit their stations until they were ordered back in for the return leg.

But all of this was still several hours away. Now Nemekov issued final instructions to the reconnaissance unit he was sending toward al-Kabriz as a forward observer team. If what it saw on the ground indicated conditions that were favorable for an attack, then Nemekov's main force would engage the enemy. If not, he would weigh whatever alternative options presented themselves.

Nemekov saluted the commander of the recon team and watched the BRDMs roll off into the night. Once the vehicles were out of sight, he turned toward his aide who was setting up the satcom rig.

"General Potapenko is on the circuit, sir," he told Nemekov, who snatched at the handset.

According to an old Bedouin expression, when Allah created the desert, he laughed. The nomadic tribesmen understand this to mean that the desert is always unpredictable. It can be capricious and cruel. It can be beautiful, bountiful, and life sustaining. But it is always changing, and it never assigns its fidelity to a creature as humble in its eternal eyes as man. With mercurial suddenness, it can change from friend to foe, exposing those it had concealed from enemies and rendering them vulnerable to ambush and destruction.

This it did tonight, before the recon patrol sent out by Nemekov had gotten halfway to its first rally point.

Lieutenant Aksel Trapezhnikov, who had led the scout team, returned with his men to the safety of a ravine on the flank of one of the low, arid hills that began about two klicks from the desert base at al-Kabriz. He at once radioed his superior. He had good news to report.

"Scabbard, this is Saber," he said into the handset. Moments later he heard Nemekov's voice in his ear.

"Say your situation, Scabbard."

"The situation is better than expected. The merchandise is still on the shelves."

"Are there any new buyers?" asked Nemekov, meaning, in their prearranged transmission code, had there been any new negative developments that might abort the mission.

"Negative. No new buyers. Goods are on the shelves and the doors are open, but no interest from any new buyers."

"Excellent news," Nemekov responded, understanding that there was some new development that made attack even likelier to succeed. "Will arrive in time for business. Out." Trapezhnikov would fill Nemekov in when the main force arrived at the hide site.

Nemekov smiled and rubbed his hands, as much in anticipation as for the warmth it would generate in the chilly night air. He turned to his XO.

"It's a go, Baylin," he said to the young lieutenant, attired as he was, in the standard Warsaw Pact variant of the NATO "chocolate chips" desert camouflage pattern fatigues, as popular today on Manhattan streets as they were during the Gulf War months. "Instruct the men that we move out in ten minutes."

"Yes, sir, at once," Baylin replied, saluting smartly. He loped off to transmit his superior officer's order.

• • •

The main contingent of the Iranian ambush force lay in wait amid the rocky landscape of the desert. Colonel Ghazbanpour himself commanded them from the field.

He had sent out patrols, all of them on foot, and all of them naturally adapted to use the desert for concealment and attack. Most had grown up in this environment and called it home. Ghazbanpour's patrols were under orders to report in at half-hour intervals.

The patrols had not seen the landing zone, which was beyond their area of operation, but one of them had spotted the Vasaltniki scout team on its way to the base. Though their running lights were off and though the team navigated by night-vision equipment, the noise of the vehicles carried across the desert, and to well-tuned ears, it was as loud as thunder.

It was not long before Nemekov's advance unit was being watched as it was conducting its own recon of the base.

Now, back at the patrol's hide site, the force was under constant observation by Iranian troops.

Ghazbanpour's orders were to wait and permit the enemy to concentrate its forces, then allow it to launch its attack unhindered. Afterward, it would be counterattacked, encircled, and, if luck held and strategy was sound, completely annihilated.

Nine

Hell Was a Diamond

Dawn was still at least several hours away. Plenty of time to launch a strike that in training exercises had never lasted longer than thirty minutes from start to finish, with an additional forty-odd minutes to make it back to the LZ, and maybe another ten sacrificed to Murphy, which is what even the Russians called the personification of the ancient military law stating that if anything can go wrong, it probably will.

In the case of Nemekov's mission, Murphy would play one of his cruelest jokes ever. But as he issued orders for the team to move into its preattack positions, Nemekov had no inkling of this yet.

As far as the major was concerned, the base was wide open for an unchallenged assault. The approaches had been checked for land mines, perimeter booby traps, and intruder warning devices, and these had been cleared or neutralized where found. Lieutenant Trapezhnikov had been correct in his promising assessment of the odds favoring success. Nemekov had seen this right away. The base was lightly defended, and there was no indication of heavy armor either on the road leading up to it or within the confines of the eight-foot-high chain-link fence surrounding it.

It was not prudent to take matters at face value, of course, and Nemekov was well aware that this could be a deception maneuver on the part of the Iranians. They might have hidden several tanks and APCs in a nearby wadi, ready to provide fire support. But it would have to be close to be effective, and surveillance had detected no sign of any armor on the road or surrounding terrain.

There was a ZSU-123 quad-barreled cannon mounted on an AMX light armored vehicle, but it did not seem operational at the moment. Either it was unmanned or its crew was not paying attention. A lightly armed Hip-H helo sat nearby, also apparently unmanned. Both could be quickly and easily destroyed in place. Ordinarily this would be too good a development to be true, and give grounds for suspicion. But in this case, Nemekov believed that appearances were not at all deceiving.

Nemekov reasoned that in a fight in Europe or in Chechnya, suspicions might be in order, or in the middle of a war practically anywhere else. But this was Iran, and it had been a long time since the American attempt at an airborne rescue that was launched in 1980. His assessment was that the Iranians were simply not expecting a commando raid and did not believe anyone knew that the aircraft was being sequestered at this isolated base. They were simply running true to form—belligerent but careless in critical aspects of warfare.

Nemekov was wrong, however. Appearances here were most deceiving. For this error in judgment his force would pay dearly, and the first installment would be made in a very short while.

Unaware of what was to be, Nemekov issued immediate orders for the assault to proceed.

• • •

The attack commenced swiftly at three hundred eighteen hours, and it continued with clockwork precision after that. Everything came together at once. All the weeks of planning and exercise jelled into a single paroxysm of combat synergies as the assault was put in motion.

There were two attack teams, each striking from the opposite direction. Snipers attached to the teams sighted on ground and tower sentries and took them down with precisely aimed head shots. Guard dogs were fired on if they did not run. Even as the Iranian soldiers dropped, squads of RPG shooters fired shoulder-launched missiles into the base compound.

The HEAT or high-explosive antitank rounds struck one after another, pulsebeat after pulsebeat, producing thunderous reports and blinding strobe flashes of blazing light. Concussion waves shattered glass and pulverized concrete, tore limbs and heads from Iranian soldiers caught in the lethal rain of spinning shrapnel, and reduced military vehicles to burning heaps of twisted wreckage. Cobra heads of flame and tarantula clouds of acrid cordite smoke loomed skyward in the aftermath of the missile hits, and everywhere things had begun to burn.

In the strobing, flashing, splintering light of many high-explosive strikes, hell was a diamond, and each new instant revealed another crystal facet of carnage in monochrome. In jittery, Chaplinesque frames, men died, or were maimed, or burst into flame, or were ripped apart by shrapnel. Only the sounds of battle had continuity.

The screams, the crumps of the initial explosions and the hot whoosh of the fireball, the blunt thudding of the Avtomat Kalashnikov AK rifles ported by both sides, the calls to action and the yells of terror and pain ran out of sync with the flickering images of battle as behind the rocket team the BTR fighting vehicles rushed in, hurling forty-mm cannon fire and hosing down the base with sustained 7.62-mm machine gun bursts.

Minutes after the lightning attack commenced, Lieutenant Trapezhnikov and his team rammed their armored BTR-70 carriers through the wall of the hangar where missiles had blown an opening. Quickly dismounting the BTRs, they charged inside, cradling their weapons. They immediately came under fire.

As they broke for cover or crouched behind the armor, unit members could now clearly see the black stealth plane within the center of the hangar, surrounded by a cocoon of computer and electronic monitoring equipment, worktables and coils of thick power and data conduits.

There were more Iranians within the hangar's recesses manning rifles and machine guns, already set up behind sandbags in prepared defensive fire positions. These troops were better trained, motivated, and equipped than those previously encountered. As soon as they had seen the Russians enter, they opened up with rifle grenades and automatic fire.

Trapezhnikov saw three of his troops take immediate hits as they fired back, and he instinctively knew that these enemy forces were the best troops the Iranians had, ones committed to a final showdown. They could slow the strike up long enough for reinforcements to arrive. Surely that was their purpose, and perhaps there was mechanized armor hidden in the desert after all. But they would not succeed.

"Back! Fall back!" Trapezhnikov hollered, and waved at his men to follow him from the hangar entrance into the flame-drenched night. There they would regroup for a counterattack.

As soon as his men were clustered in a defensive ring behind the armored personnel carriers, Trapezhnikov outlined his plan. The carriers were to storm the hangar again and lay down cover fire while another team set up a typically Russian weapon, the AGS-17 Plamya automatic grenade launcher.

The Plamya cycled belts of fifty thirty-mm high-explosive canister grenades at high speed. It had a range of almost three thousand meters. The Plamya could saturate the hangar with blast and concussion sufficient to kill every living thing inside. The squad carried two Plamyas.

The rest happened extremely rapidly with foreordained consequences.

While the two Plamya teams set up their rigs, small-arms suppressing fire killed those defenders it caught and forced the rest to keep their heads tucked down. Then, when they were ready, the Plamya teams fired off one thirty-round grenade belt after another into the sand-bagged positions in front of the plane, shredding anything living or already dead.

At the same time machine gunners manning the heavy MGs mounted on the APCs raked the steel catwalk running along the top of the hangar on four sides where snipers had been sited. A whirlwind of steel chewed up metal and living flesh without discrimination. The catwalk sections soon broke free at the corners with groans and snaps of shearing metal, and dangled vertically above the hangar floor like Damoclean swords over the heads of the doomed defenders.

"Break fire!" Trapezhnikov shouted at his men. A little more than five minutes had passed from the time the guns had opened up, and thousands of rounds of ammunition had been expended. No answering fire was heard from the emplaced positions. Only corpses now manned the sand-bags. The hangar was secure. The first phase of the assault was now complete.

Trapezhnikov risked standing up and quickly surveyed the smoke-choked interior of the hangar. Lights from his vehicles outside shone through the perforated plate-metal skin of the place, while bodies were slumped over the bullet-riddled sandbags, damasking them with blood.

Above, one of the catwalks had broken from its fastenings and hung at a ninety-degree angle to the hangar floor. On a section of steel platform directly across it that was still intact, a corpse in the olive-drab uniform of an Iraqi regular was slumped over the railing, its arms dangling pendulously.

Lieutenant Trapezhnikov permitted himself a grim smile. They had won the day. The victory had been expected, but what is expected does not always materialize. Trapezhnikov felt that pride was justified by the achievement.

He issued rapid orders for his sappers to place bricks of halvah-textured Semtex high explosive around the plane's fuselage and set the digital detonation timers. While he waited for this action to be completed, he radioed the news back to mission commander Nemekov who was with the team outside the hangar.

"Do nothing until I arrive," Nemekov told the lieutenant. He wanted to make sure the demolition work was carried out to his specifications.

Minutes later Nemekov entered the hangar and noticed the hollow look on his subordinate's face.

"What's wrong?" he asked.

"Sir, the plane, it's, well—"

"Spit it out, what is the problem?"

"It's not the stealth, sir. It is a *maskirovka.* The Iranians have tricked us."

Nemekov pushed the younger man aside and ran toward the plane, to where the sappers had already stood down, their faces grim. At a distance it still looked real enough, and Nemekov willed himself to believe that his subordinate was mistaken, in which case the imbecile would have hell to pay. But up close Nemekov saw that it was he who had been mistaken. Much now seemed amiss with the aircraft.

First, there was the paint job. It was not the characteristic Styrofoam-like coating bonded to a composite metal hull, it was merely flat black paint, sprayed on by an air-powered applicator. The angled surfaces of the wings and fuselage were wrong, too. Through the cockpit window, there was no instrumentation on a crudely fashioned replica of a console. Other than this and the vacant pilot's seat, the cockpit was empty. *Yes,* thought Nemekov, *a replica, and a crude one at that.* Trapezhnikov was right. This was indeed a mock-up, a *maskirovka.*

The Iranians had played them. Played them for suckers.

The white-hot ball of anger that exploded inside Nemekov's stomach and flooded him with a sense of almost maniacal rage forced saner thoughts from his mind. All he knew for the next few seconds was an intense anger at having been conned. His men winced as he raised the AK-47 in his hands and fired off a full clip into the dummy plane, then beat the glass of the phony cockpit to splinters with the rifle's heavy wooden buttstock, and kicked at its flimsy fuselage with his steel-toed boots.

When his rage had been vented, Nemekov stood on the mounting platform set up beside the mock-up, breathing heavily and looking down at his assembled troops. As the rage passed, it allowed the saner realization of what would happen next to come through, and although this realization also caused Nemekov anger, it brought with it as well a sobering sense of caution. If the plane had been a *maskirovka,* then . . .

"Let's get out of here, fast!" Nemekov shouted as he ran down the steps and palmed a fresh clip into his Kalashnikov.

Jumping into the lead command vehicle, Nemekov opened up a satcom link while the column retreated toward the road.

The sky was lightening into the false dawn that comes to the desert before sunrise. A chill wind swept across the land. Nemekov transmitted the bad news to the staging base many kilometers distant.

The Antonovs were on their way to pick them up at the LZ, he was informed. Nemekov only hoped they would live to reach it.

There was no point in striking the misled enemy when he was caught in the trap. At the sham base, the *Shuravi* would have a defensive perimeter to dig in, and it would make his destruction all the more difficult. Ghazbanpour might then have had to call in reinforcements and this would have robbed him of the shining glory of being responsible for his own victory, from start to finish.

Fortunately, the Iranian saw that the Vasaltniki had fallen straight into his trap. He had wanted to decimate their forces and deal them a psychological blow before striking; otherwise he would have chosen to hit them on the way toward the base, well before they'd even reached it.

The purpose of letting them find out that it was a Trojan horse—a kind of inside-out Trojan horse—was to wear them down, whittle away their numbers, cause them to panic, and ultimately to flee.

This, Ghazbanpour seemed to have accomplished. The forces defending the sham base had died shedding the blood of martyrs.

His one great fear, and the single flaw in his plan that he had been able to detect, was that the Russian commander might show the presence of mind and dig his men in at the base, rather than withdraw in panic. From entrenched positions, they might have called in reserve forces.

The transports might have also been able to land closer to the base or even bomb or strafe the Iranian forces. But none of this had happened. The Vasaltniki had panicked as Ghazbanpour had guessed they would, and had fled back into the open desert.

They would have no defenses here, only many kilometers of thirsty sand to soak up their spilled blood. Ghazbanpour owned the desert, and before the sun had risen, he predicted that victory would be his.

Army General Vladimir Illich Potapenko slumped back in his seat. He could not believe what he had just heard. The attack had been carried out against a diversionary mock-up, a phony base and plane, a shrewd *maskirovka.* He listened through his radio link for real-time coverage of the battle.

The shouts of his men, coming to him through the invisible ether of space, filled him with a gnawing dread that seemed to attack his bones with acid. What would happen now? His great victory was tarnished. Soon his political enemies would begin to circle, and bring him down.

He gave no thought whatever to the beleaguered men in the Iranian desert. There was only one ray of hope. If the Antonovs did not reach them in time, the Vasaltniki would be obliterated. The planes would be delayed if the MiG fighters being held in reserve were not sent as escorts. Later, Potapenko could find a way to repair his reputation.

Potapenko picked up a secure phone and began to issue a series of rapid orders in the crisp military tones for which he was famed throughout all of Russia. The Vasaltniki would be sacrificed to his own survival.

Ten
An Ode to Deception

Nemekov realized his double mistake as the Iranian ambush commenced firing on his force. As soon as the opening volley of mortar rounds began to hit with characteristic *crump-crump* sounds, blowing shell craters in the desert and gouging chunks from the wrinkled gray hills of extruded bedrock, Nemekov knew that he should not have given in to his emotions.

Instead he should have dug in and fought, using the wreckage of the destroyed desert base for shooting cover. He could then have called in a cross-border air strike of MiG-29 Fulcrums and decimated the attacking forces, per one of his backup options. The fighter sortie could have bombed and strafed the living hell out of the Iranian bastards who had set them up using the *maskirovka*.

This still could happen, but it would come at a heavy price for his force, and also for his career, once he finally returned home.

But to hell with that. Survival was what counted. Nemekov would return home, and he would take as many of his men along with him as possible.

The Iranian mortar crews out on the desert were sighting in on them, getting their range taped, placing their high-explosive canisters closer and closer to the column with each salvo. Nemekov knew they had to be spotting by light amplification or thermal imaging because it was still predawn twilight, and this would give him precious minutes to deploy to safer ground. There was no substitute for the human eye when it came to calling in mortar strikes. It would be a while yet before they got his range down.

Up ahead, the desert track passed before several immense piles of prehistoric rock that the earth had thrust skyward during its volcanic past. Nemekov told the driver to run hell-bent for leather toward one of the defiles between these rock formations where they would have some cover; pitifully little, but at least some.

The Iranians, he could see, were trying to prevent this with all their might. They were walking their mortar fire toward his force, and getting dangerously close with each successive round they lobbed.

Crump!

Nemekov could now feel the ground shudder as gouts of gravel, dirt, and sand were flung against the sides of the APC, and the clouds of dense cordite smoke grew thicker outside the front slit windows. The armored personnel carriers were not immune to high-explosive strikes, simply more resistant than other vehicles. Their hulls were made of thick plate steel, but not thick enough to withstand a direct HEAT hit.

Nemekov had chosen the BTRs and BRDMs more for their mobility than their armor, forfeiting weight for speed. He hoped the trade-off would not accrue to the destruction of himself and his force as he raced toward the gap in the rocks.

Crump!

Suddenly the light armored vehicle to his right was hit by a near miss. It proved to be close enough.

The BRDM disappeared in a detonation flash and clouds of choking black smoke, reappearing a moment later strangely transformed. It was now a blazing, blackened mass of charred metal wreckage.

The bodies of the five Vasaltniki who had been riding in it were flung here and there, sprawled in death like rag dolls. Nemekov's vehicle was rocked by another brace of mortar shells hitting close by the BTR. He doubted he would live long enough to reach the safety of the defile ahead, or that it was anything but a stopping point before death overtook him.

The pilot and copilot of the lead Antonov transport plane had been in the process of tanking up as the orders to recross the Iranian-Azeri border came over the secure radio circuit. The crew of the Ilyushin fuelbird pumped in the last remaining kilograms of aviation gasoline and pulled up the hose-and-drogue assembly that had been linked to a receptacle at the top rear of the twin-engine transport aircraft, midway between the wings and the tail rudder assembly.

As the Antonov's pilot applied forward thrust, the two huge turbojet engines uniquely mounted at the tops of the swept-back wings, near the fuselage, cycled out thousands of foot-pounds of jet thrust.

From a stationary point below the flight deck of the fuelbird, the Antonov began to move quickly, speeding on a southwesterly course. The second transport plane flew behind it, spaced at approximately one half kilometer.

The planes soon became black specks against the slowly lightening morning sky as the refueling planes returned to base to take on more avgas and then return to fly circles in the air, awaiting a rendezvous with the returning Antonovs on their cross-border flight with their Vasaltniki passengers.

As the fuelbird turned and lumbered back to the base, its pilot noted the white vapor trails of three MiG-29 air superiority fighters at an altitude several thousand feet above them. The Fulcrums were turning in the sky, just as they were, and heading back in the same direction, only at a much greater speed.

The Ilyushin driver supposed that they were no longer deemed necessary. The mission was obviously proceeding according to plan.

Such thoughts would never have crossed his mind had he eavesdropped, only a few minutes before, on the secure channel through which the fighter pilots were linked to the command center on the ground below.

"Talon Leader, this is Scabbard command center," the voice of the ground controller had told the lead pilot.

The fighter pilot acknowledged the transmission and was ordered to return to base. He asked for a repeat and was again told to immediately break formation and head back to the airstrip. The flight leader acknowledged his orders and heeled his plane around.

"What do you make of this?" asked his wingman, whom he could see in the cockpit of the MiG off to his left. "Didn't even ask us to escort the Antonovs."

"Who knows?" the leader returned. "Probably nothing."

"I say let's go have a look," the wingman declared. "Fuck the orders."

"You do anything like that and I'll have you up for court-martial," he said back. "This is a spook operation and I don't want to stick my neck out any further than it is already. Clear, Yevgeny?"

The wingman said that it was clear, but not until after a moment's pause. The fighter pilots picked up no further chatter as the planes made the short run back to base.

So, they were to be made sacrificial lambs, Nemekov thought. He should have seen this coming, too. He and most of his men had safely reached the defile, realizing that they were in fact in a twisting warren of gullies, small wadis, and box canyons cut into the bleak gray folds of the barren desert hills.

He had deployed his vehicles and men along one of the rock galleries, protected by outcroppings and overhangs of weirdly sculpted sandstone. As the sun rose in the sky and it became full daylight, the enemy shelling stopped for a short while. But the lull was all too brief.

Very soon, Nemekov had heard the telltale *thuk-a-thuk* of whirling rotor blades and the banshee whine of powerful diesel-turbine engines.

The soldier was familiar with that particular sound.

Before seeing the choppers appear over the top of the rock galleries, he knew what they were—Mil-24 Hind-F gunships of Russian manufacture, sold to the Iranians in a package deal shortly after the ascent to power of the Khomeini regime in the early eighties.

The Mil-24s were heavily armed with rockets and a thirty-caliber machine gun. The choppers could also carry troops that could be dropped from a low hover to scale the side of the bluffs below which his force was sheltered.

Soon the sound of the rotors and engines swelled to a deafening crescendo in the heat of the desert air.

Nemekov looked up and saw the Hinds just skirting the edge of the defile system, not daring to come overhead in range of his guns.

"Hold your fire," he ordered his men.

Had the helos intended to hit them, they would have swooped in fast, and in formation, firing their rockets and automatic cannons as they converged. Since they weren't doing this, it was something else, probably a surrender ultimatum, that was their objective. Nemekov had no intention of surrendering, but it cost nothing to listen, especially since he needed to buy time until the Antonovs came within rescue range.

The transports couldn't land right on their position, of course, but their pilots might be able to arrange an alternate LZ close enough for at least a contingent to break away and make it back across the border. At this point Nemekov would consider this a token victory.

In the seconds of silence as the Hinds hovered ominously overhead, Nemekov thought back to the events of a few minutes ago, events that now seemed to have taken place at some distant point in another life.

He recalled how, once his men had reached the dubious safety of the defile, he had contacted the mission staging area on satcom, ordering in the MiG fighters that he hoped would neutralize the Iranian ambush. And he recalled how he had been stunned both by what he had heard and by the voice to whom he'd been speaking.

"Negative, the planes have been recalled to base," the ground control officer had told him. It should be Potapenko on this circuit, Nemekov thought. Yet it wasn't. He suspected then that the old bastard had sold him out to save his own neck. That was just now becoming crystal clear. Potapenko didn't want his men to return, dead or alive. Not if they dared fail him.

"What the hell do you mean the planes have been recalled?" Nemekov shouted into the handset's mouthpiece. "And where is Potapenko?"

"The general has instructed me to deal with any further requests for assistance," the voice resumed calmly. "The transport planes are on their way. They should reach their landing zones by seven hundred hours."

"The Antonovs will do us no good if we are all dead, you imbecile," Nemekov shouted again. "I want fighter cover. I want those MiGs sent in!"

"I'm sorry, sir, but as I have said, the fighters have been recalled to base."

"Why?"

"Problems with their communications systems necessitated their abrupt return. We are now working on getting them back into the air. Please have patience."

Nemekov forced himself to keep his voice level, despite his hatred for the nonentity on the other end of the line and the sound of high explosive impacting on the rock faces of the cliffs surrounding them.

"What's your name?"

"First Lieutenant Zotov, sir," the voice said.

"Lieutenant, I want you to find Potapenko and put him on right away," Nemekov said.

"As I said, sir—"

Nemekov cut the other man's voice off.

"Listen here, you maggot," he shouted. "You tell the general that unless he immediately gets on this line, I will order my men to lay down their arms and hoist the white flag of surrender. I will then personally reveal every aspect of this operation to my Iranian interrogators. Have you got that, Zotov?"

"Yes, sir, I—"

"Do it, maggot!"

Nemekov's wait seemed like an eternity, although less than a minute had passed before his mentor was on the line. He had, of course, been right beside Zotov all along, Nemekov knew with sudden certainty.

"Valery Fedorovich, how sorry I am for your predicament," came the old man's mock-soothing voice on the commlink. "Please do not let me down. The Antonovs are on their way."

"I want the MiGs sent over here," Nemekov shouted. "I am told they were recalled? Is this true?"

"I am afraid so," the general replied. "There were some unsolvable problems."

"Liar!" Nemekov shot back. "You've sold us down the river."

"Take care. You are losing control, my young friend."

"I want those planes in here, you stinking old *bizhdenok*!" yelled Nemekov. "Send them in or I will surrender my men."

"If you do that, then I will see to it that your wives and loved ones are severely punished. It's not like the old days, but there are still ways to do such things, if one has the means."

"Fuck you, you bloody murderous bastard," Nemekov shouted, aware that his men were watching him with amazed stares. "If I survive this, I will wring your withered neck. That is a promise."

The general paused a beat. Such a sickening lack of courage in one he had personally raised up by his own strong hand. Besides, the odds strongly disfavored Nemekov ever keeping that particular promise.

Potapenko thought he had been wrong in selecting Nemekov for a protégé. The young man should have been willing to give his life for his superior officer, for the general considered himself the living embodiment of his nation in all its greatness.

"*Do svidahnya, moj' drug.* I hope we shall meet again," was all the old man said before severing radio contact.

In the lead chopper, Colonel Ghazbanpour sat in the copilot's seat and received the nod from the pilot that indicated his lip microphone was patched into the helo's public address system.

Ghazbanpour had not yet decided whether or not he preferred to take the Russian commando forces alive or dead. He could conceive of making excellent capital for his career if it turned out either way. So he could afford to show some measure of mercy. He would let the gods of war decide the outcome.

"Attention, attention." He spoke into the rice-grain mike, hearing his amplified voice thunder even above the sound of the rotors. "This is Colonel Farzaneh Hossein Ghazbanpour of the Iranian People's Army. You are surrounded by superior forces on every side. Escape is impossible. Surrender is your only option—that or death."

He paused for effect, pleased at his command of spoken Russian. "Surrender terms are unconditional. Lay down your arms and leave the enclave with hands raised above your heads. When you reach the road you will be issued further instructions. That is all. You have five minutes to decide."

Nemekov kicked the satcom unit to the ground and faced his men. He had not meant the threat to surrender he had made to Potapenko. It had been a bluff. Still, he thought it only fair that the men should unanimously decide their fate.

"What will it be?" he asked them now. "If we choose to make a stand, our only hope is that some of us can break free and reach the Antonovs by some other route. The defile network we are now within may prove to have other exitways. But many will surely not make it. I therefore leave the choice up to you—surrender or fight."

One by one, the verdict came in. Somebody called out, *"Odin 'ebetsya, druoi draznitsya—kakaya raznitsa?"* and raised a chorus of laughter. The old proverb went, "One fucks, the other teases; what's the difference?" But the point had been made.

The choice was to fight and die rather than surrender.

When the five minutes were up, the Hind pilots saw the Vasaltniki forces begin to disperse along the galleries in the defile complex below them. It would be like shooting fish in a barrel, thought Ghazbanpour, almost too simple. But that was the decision of the trapped commando unit and the Russians would pay a heavy blood price for it.

In the end all would be killed, of this there was no question in Ghazbanpour's mind.

It was impossible to say which side fired the first volley that shattered the brief cease-fire.

As soon as the Vasaltniki's mechanized armor down in the defile started up, shooting broke out. Machine gunners atop the BTRs and on the back of the BRDMs fired up at the Hinds, which dodged and jinked to and fro, loosing high-explosive rockets and automatic cannon bursts in answer.

Men screamed as they were hit and died, and the reek of cordite soon filled the smoke-choked stone galleries as the Vasaltniki scattered for cover.

Nemekov eventually found himself and three other commandos emerging from one of the rock galleries and suddenly out into open sand desert. He could hear bursts of small arms fire and rocket explosions in the distance, but somehow his vehicle had evaded the choppers. This surprise reprieve would not last very long, he knew, but at least for the moment they were out of the maze of death.

Nemekov consulted the portable global positioning unit tethered to the BTR, and saw that they might reach the landing zone in time if they moved quickly and had some luck on their side.

The BTR was dangerously low on fuel, but they had no other choice. Their luck continued to hold, however. The clear blue sky remained free of Iranian gunships.

Now in the distance they heard the sound of the powerful jet engines of the incoming Antonovs.

"We're almost directly below you," Nemekov radioed the crew of the assault transport planes on the preassigned emergency frequency they had kept open for rescue transmissions. "Do you see us?"

The pilot in the lead plane scanned the terrain below.

"Affirm. I see you. Hold steady. Commencing landing approach."

Nemekov breathed a deep sigh of relief. He could see the lead plane begin a landing pattern, and although the BTR's fuel gauge read a little below the empty point, he knew they could probably make it on the fumes. The planes were on their way. Their amazing luck had held.

Then another sound made Nemekov realize that the promise of rescue and safety had been a false one all along.

The Iranian Mil-24 Hind appeared from behind the towers of stone. Either it had been "masking" itself, as pilots used the term—playing a brutal hide-and-seek game of lying in wait for the transports to arrive—or it had just breasted the low desert bluffs on a search path for any stragglers that had not been captured or killed in the fighting. Either case spelled death for Nemekov's small force element.

The lead Antonov saw the Hind gunship and immediately pulled up its nose, trying to claw its way back to the skies and freedom. But that would not happen. The Hind immediately opened up with a rocket salvo and struck the transport aircraft dead center in its unprotected flank.

As the lead plane exploded, whirling pieces of burning wing debris and fuselage fragments, skirling and wheeling outward and downward in a mad tangle of mangled steel, struck the second aircraft that could not turn in time to avoid being hit. It, too, exploded in a second fireball, whose concussive blast front was powerful enough to shake the desert as a pancake of shocked air slammed into the flat ground.

Pieces of burning wreckage and flaming gouts of ignited aviation gasoline poured down onto the rock and sand, turning the desert into a crackling cauldron of flame. Within the amphitheater of fire, the BTR struggled on, a pathetic gray-brown beetle crawling through a flaming brazier of live coals.

Nemekov wasted no time in climbing behind the BTR's 7.62-mm heavy machine gun and pointing it up at the giant steel dragonfly that he saw wavering in the shimmers of heat distortion caused by the superheated air that surrounded him. The metal insect danced and dodged as he cooked off everything in the belt-fed magazine, watching the red tracer bullets that were loaded one to every fourth armor-piercing slug bolt skyward in a stream of crimson dashes.

Suddenly Nemekov saw the Mil-24 dip its nose. A puffball of oily black smoke belched from one of its two side-mounted turbofan engine exhausts. Another followed, and another. The center of each black puff was a blazing yellow.

"I hit the bastard!" he shouted in jubilation as the smoke clouds thickened and the enemy helicopter heeled over sideways, firing a salvo of its remaining rockets at the BTR. It tried righting itself, but failed and began a slow, arcing plunge to the jagged rocks below. Moments before it crashed, the pilot had emptied its rocket racks down on the fighting vehicle.

Nemekov and the two other Vasaltniki who rode with him in the BTR did not live to see the Hind strike an outcropping of stone pillars that towered from the flat desert floor and erupt into a soaring, fifty-foot fireball, as falling wreckage hammered the ground with a shower of blazing steel. The multiple rocket strikes on the BTR reduced Nemekov and his Vasaltnik companions to spinning chunks of charred meat and bone. Seconds later their Iranian enemies were also blown to bits as their helo went up in flames.

Eleven
A Court They Could Play Ball In

The U.S. president wore a light blue *Air Force One* windbreaker emblazoned with the Great Seal of the Republic over a monogrammed golf shirt and blue jeans, his favored attire on longer flights on the executive jet. Dubbed the "Flying Taj Mahal" by some, the mammoth plane contained a plush presidential suite in the nose, two galleys equipped for gourmet cooking, eighty-five telephones, a press room, hospital, two conference rooms, six bathrooms, and enough electronic gear for computing, communications, and defensive electronic warfare to require 238 miles of wiring hidden in its airframe.

Cruising over the midwest at thirty-five thousand feet, en route to the G-5 economic summit in Tokyo, the chief executive's sneakered feet were propped on the edge of the teak conference table as he drank black coffee and faced the large, flat panel display screen. Arrayed around the table of the wide-body 747's conference room were Chief of Staff Lew Baldridge, National Security Advisor

General Oscar E. S. Throckmorton, and Secretary of State Marston Everett Carlysle.

Though there were two other members of his cabinet onboard, the three were the only ones with a need-to-know; nor would Throckmorton have been onboard had the president not decided to hedge his bets against being caught without a knowledgeable staffer close at hand as the C.I.S. commando mission into Iran unfolded. The rest of the traveling presidential entourage, like the group of pool reporters in the aft media cabin accompanying the officials overseas, was occupied elsewhere and thoroughly out of the loop.

As it turned out, and as President Claymore was now learning in detail as the teleconference progressed, the action had turned into even more of a tar baby than had America's 1980 Iran hostage rescue mission. The two-way electronic conference net linked those onboard *Air Force One* with a hastily convened meeting of the National Security Council in the White House Situation Room buried some thirty feet beneath the foundation of the executive mansion. Here the directors of the CIA and NSA, the chairman of the Joint Chiefs, and various other representatives of the U.S. government and military gathered for an emergency crisis management session.

Ordinarily the president would have chosen to remain in Washington until the Russian mission had run its course, but there was no question about missing the Tokyo summit. Fortunately, the president was used to working in the recently refurbished presidential jet. Originally opposed to the jet, which was delivered during the last year of the Bush Administration at a cost of almost $300 million, he now considered it an extension of the Oval Office, where he worked, and the East Wing, where he slept.

Travis Claymore had listened to the briefings from the Pentagon's and intelligence community's representatives that told about the C.I.S. mission's failure. The Russian commando force had been annihilated and the stealth aircraft was still in Iranian hands. This had, to some extent, been expected and Claymore could at least keep a clear conscience, having warned C.I.S. President Grigorenko against the mission. But that was not all. There was a new and unexpected development that overshadowed everything else.

"How can you be telling me those missiles are armed, General?" he asked the JCS chairman, General Parris "Jack" Thibodeaux. "That was the entire point of the mission, wasn't it? To prevent them putting nukes on those things. Am I right or wrong?"

"Mr. President, you're right. Absolutely right." The chairman looked into the camera, aware that all eyes in the Situation Room were on him. "And that should have been what happened, and it didn't. But there is always the possibility of their having outstripped our intelligence, and in this case they did."

"You're sure those are nuclear warheads on those missiles?" the president asked. "How many were there again?"

"Two, with a third possible," the chairman replied. "And we are very sure. The director of the CIA can explain."

"Mr. President."

"Hello, Cliff."

"Mr. President," CIA director Clifford Merrick began, "we know there are nuclear warheads on those Iranian birds because we have watched them being prepared in a manner consistent with procedures for nuclear warfighting. As you know, we have been keeping our eyes on Iran during the last few weeks, with special attention devoted to the missile batteries. In three cases, we noticed conventional warheads being removed and replaced with new warheads bearing markings which indicate they are nuclear devices."

"Could this be some kind of trick?"

"It might be," the DCI replied, "but we don't think it is. We have human intelligence sources, that is, people in there, highly trusted people, who have verified that the Iranians had at least two, and maybe three, nuclear warheads in transit to a test facility at the time of the air strikes, and that they have now placed these on the missiles."

Travis Claymore paused a moment, then asked, "What kind of damage are we talking about here? How big are these nukes?"

The DCI deferred to General Jack for the reply.

"Mr. President," he said, "the best way to answer your question is to put the matter in perspective. We estimate the size of each warhead to be in the three-kiloton range. The burnout zone for such a warhead would be about twenty square miles. Depending on population density and other factors, the casualty rate would be about sixty thousand per warhead. To put it another way, each warhead would have the stopping power of approximately ten Hiroshima bombs."

"Jesus Christ on a fucking raft," the president said.

The DCI added that the missiles appeared to be in a state of readiness for launch. The president then asked for options.

"We have a plan available, Mr. President," said the chairman of the Joint Chiefs, who again held the floor.

The president listened, and then nodded.

"Put it into operation," he told the chairman. "We'll talk again just before I land in Tokyo."

As the big screen blanked, the president picked up the phone and announced to his aides seated at the table that it was time he placed a call to Moscow. This thing had really snowballed.

Army General Potapenko had returned to the Kremlin to brief his political masters on the mission's grave consequences. He knew their displeasure, but he also well knew that they could admit nothing publicly about the matter. He informed them of his decision to retire, further putting himself out of harm's way.

He would escape this fiasco unscathed and withdraw to his dacha on the Moskva River in the unsullied forest country near the Moscow suburb of Archangelskoye.

There he would live out his remaining years in comfort and write the memoirs of his Afghan War exploits. Potapenko had already made arrangements with a Moscow-based literary agent for the rights to his life story. So far, he had heard that publishers in London, Paris, and New York were preparing offers.

Of some of the general's exploits, however, his intended memoirs would never speak, although these were well known to his contemporaries. As the general lay back comfortably in his bed, completely naked, he awaited the evening's enjoyments with growing anticipation.

After this ordeal, in particular, he needed to relax. He was still in perfect health, and though his doctors had advised him to moderate his drinking, he could still comfortably put away more than many a younger man's share of *pertsovka,* the spiced vodka that he, like Stalin, especially favored.

Sipping from his glass, Potapenko now trained his eyes on the doorway to the bathroom, where his guest for the evening was freshening up. He was not too old to enjoy the vigorous pleasures of sex either, and here, too, he had no doubt that he could outlast many a younger man, especially in today's Russia with its so-called new breed.

Disgusting, this current generation! They were weak, like Grigorenko and his bunch of misnamed "modernists," and destined to be overrun by the barbarians of the West in time. This invasion might not be a military one. It could be economic. But it would come. Potapenko was glad he would not be around to see its full development.

But enough of such thoughts. Now was not the time for dark sentiments. As his pretty guest for the evening came out of the bathroom, he smelled the scent of the expensive French cologne he had bought as a gift wafting in his direction.

How sweet it smelled. And how sweet was the appearance of his long-limbed bedroom companion, how beautiful were the sculpted breasts and rounded buttocks. The general cast his eyes across the fetching young body and patted the bed beside him.

"You are a vision, Misha," he said to the muscular young blond man. "Come, sit here beside me."

The old general ran his hands along the youth's body as Potapenko's companion returned his intimate caresses. Potapenko closed his eyes as he lost all track of time.

Long after the rapturous climax that made the air catch in his lungs, however, the general continued to gasp for breath.

This time it resulted from the smothering darkness of the pillow that powerful, unseen hands held down over his face. As he wheezed and panted like a landed fish, Potapenko heard voices above his head, gruff voices that were somehow familiar to him, voices that mocked him bitterly as his lungs strained to inhale the life-giving air that was being denied them.

"This is for the men you sacrificed, traitor," the voices swore.

There was a network, a kind of *nomenklatura* among Afghan veterans, and though Nemekov had not been the keenest of military men, he had belonged to that network nevertheless. It took care of its own, and avenged wrongs done to its own. The betrayal of Nemekov and his Vasaltniki force would be repaid tonight—in full.

On the bed, Potapenko continued to writhe and struggle pathetically. Despite his years he was strong, and he fought hard for his life. But the men holding him down were stronger still. Even Misha had pitched in, for he, too, was one of the *nomenklatura.* The old warrior's last experience as the blackness around him became permanent and he left the scene far sooner than he had ever anticipated, was hearing the sound of his assassins curse his name.

Brigade commander of Iranian Islamic Ground Forces, Western Operational Area Command (field headquarters Karbala), Colonel Farzaneh Hossein Ghazbanpour stood on the catwalk of the underground hangar facility and observed the activity some thirty feet below him. There, in the center of the five-hundred-meter square enclosure, surrounded by technicians and linked by umbilicals of electrical cabling to banks of diagnostic equipment, stood the black plane that had been captured by an incredible stroke of luck.

Ghazbanpour dragged hard on the Marlboro cigarette, one of the twenty he daily smoked, and considered the immense good fortune that had dropped this windfall into Iranian hands. Others, of course, would say that it had been Allah who had been responsible, especially the bothersome Major Meshkati from the Political-Ideological Directorate who was attached to the brigade.

Fortunately, the power of Meshkati and those like him, once so great that the zealots had overridden the commands of competent military leaders during the Iran-Iraq War and sent scores of thousands to needless battlefield deaths, had now waned considerably. Soon such parasites would be gone entirely. For the moment the P-ID's representative still hung on, his duties actually little more than those of a chaplain, although in theory he could go over Ghazbanpour's head directly to the Islamic Revolutionary Court of the Armed Forces should he deem it necessary.

The malignant little parasite watched, but could do nothing. Even in the days of the P-ID's greatest power, chances were he would have had to keep his nose out of the colonel's business. Ghazbanpour's authority came direct from the *faqi* himself, via General Choubak in Tehran. Apart from head of the Majlis, or supreme legislature of Iran, the president was also the country's holiest cleric, who, as master of the Koran and interpreter of the *hadith,* or traditions of the Prophet and the Twelve Imams, determined how the codices of Shia Islamic law were to be realized in the world of living men. By the *faqi*'s decree, Ghazbanpour was to have absolute control of the operation to guard the plane, and he enjoyed a direct channel to the office of the president in Tehran. None could stand in his way.

This, reflected Ghazbanpour, was ironic in the extreme, considering how deeply the colonel loathed the revolution and all it had represented, and how he had lived most of the last two decades with the fear of imminent arrest, trial, and execution. Though a Muslim who believed in Allah and the three pillars of the faith, Ghazbanpour had also loathed fanaticism in any of its manifestations.

At the time the revolution had swept across Iran, he had been a major in one of the northern garrisons, commanding troops riding herd on the Kurdish separatists in the rebellious hill towns. One day he learned that his entire family in Isfahan had been wiped out in one of the political purges that were common during that time.

Fearing for his own safety, and in any case powerless, Ghazbanpour had said and done nothing about it. Somehow, he'd remained untouched by what had happened. It was much later, when his place in the military pecking order was assured, that he had approached the Israelis and offered to spy on his country. A thirst for revenge had tempted him, but he had ultimately changed his mind and recanted.

In the end, the colonel had stayed loyal to Iran, in part because of wise counseling from his friend and mentor General Choubak. He had been able to live with himself these long years, to keep sane and whole, by viewing it all as a global game. Now, after much reflection, Ghazbanpour was certain that he was not far from wrong.

It was indeed a game. One in which lives hung in the balance, but a game for all of that. Ghazbanpour would play his part. As a loyal Iranian, he would see to it that the stealth aircraft was used to benefit his country. But the colonel would continue to provide information, as he had been routinely doing, to his immediate superior, General Katayoon Shadrokh Choubak. And, though close to the ear of the *faqi,* Choubak had for many years been the double agent whom the Israelis knew by the code-name Ahriman.

Book Two

Last-Extremity Solutions

Twelve
A Sierra Oscar in Mind

It had turned out to be a day full of surprises. Major Peace Mitchell still could not believe the VIP treatment he'd pulled. Since leaving Delta's headquarters at Bragg at six hundred hours that morning, it had been one surprise after another, almost like a birthday party.

First off, there was the VC-35A Learjet awaiting him at nearby Pope Air Force Base, tanked up and ready to fly him north and east across the Alleghenies into West Virginia, where a DOD staff car would be waiting to shuttle him to the Pentagon. It's a rare day that the U.S. Army springs for a Lear instead of a rustbucket DC-9 for the sorry likes of a special-forces major. Generals pull rides on those aircraft, other ranks usually take what's left over, which usually means the ghost of *Memphis Belle.*

Were this not surprise enough for Mitchell, there was the spanking-new Lincoln with blue-and-white military tags waiting for him when his plane landed at Washington National Airport less than an hour later. The black government-issue chariot was driven by a helpful young second lieutenant from JCS staff who welcomed Mitchell and even held the door for him. Mitchell considered asking him where the wet bar was, but thought better of it.

Mitchell's driver then chauffeured him the short distance of his journey's remaining leg along the Jefferson Davis Highway through the rolling green countryside of Alexandria, Virginia, confining his respectfully banal remarks to the weather and the colorful autumn foliage.

The lieutenant hadn't even cussed once, hadn't uttered so much as a "damn" throughout the entire half-hour drive. This was another wondrous sign to Mitchell. On previous visits to the Puzzle Palace, Mitchell had either driven himself or pulled a loudmouthed NCO with inevitable obsessions about one or more parts of the female anatomy, who thought the driver's seat of a military staff car was little more than a psychiatrist's couch on wheels.

Not that Mitchell didn't know what underlay today's VIP treatment. He did as surely as the Lord made green apples. It was the downing and capture of the Russian stealth fighter that had taken place weeks before.

The incident had been keeping Mitchell busy around the clock lately since his new boss, Colonel Mike Armbrister, had called him into his office at Delta's home base at Bragg in what had been previously known as Range 19.

This was a secluded, pine-forested area six miles in circumference within the sprawling Bragg military reservation, encircled by a sensor-studded, double-row, razor-ring-topped fence, and patrolled night and day by armed sentries who carried their weapons locked and loaded even in the latrine. Delta had moved out of its original headquarters in the old Bragg Stockade, where "Chargin' Charlie" Beckwith had founded it, and into its new, $75 million Range 19 complex in 1987.

Armbrister had told Peace that the president wanted a mission plan ready to roll in case the White House found a way to co-opt the Russians from going in themselves and trying to retake their lost stealth plane. Unlike the departed Pellegrino, Armbrister was supportive and unafraid to take chances.

The president had tried selling Moscow on the deal, but the former Soviets wouldn't even consider it. It was their aircraft, they'd stonily protested, and they were going to take it back themselves—period. The U.S. was told to butt out, which is precisely what it did.

Nevertheless, the White House still wanted an armed intervention force held in readiness against a possible last-minute change of heart, or some other unforeseen contingency, and the Joint Chiefs had concurred. Delta had been given the job of crafting a credible game plan for a mission into Iran to destroy the Russian aircraft on the ground, and Armbrister had put Mitchell in charge of making the plan take shape. The plan would be for an armed reconnaissance mission, a special recon, as it was called.

Then the Russians had sent a Spetsnaz detachment in with disastrous but—from what the twice-daily intel dumps that came into "Jaysock," the Joint Special Operations Command headquarters at Bragg's neighboring Pope AFB showed—unsurprising results.

Mitchell recalled the morning the Russian operation had commenced, and the amazement he'd experienced when he'd read the intelligence briefings that had come in from the CIA, NSA, and other national and foreign intelligence sources, including British MI6 and Israel's AMAN.

Incredibly, it had not been one of the Spetsnaz companies that had been sent in, but a detachment from one of the GRU's second-string Vasaltniki or assault brigades, which were good at what they did, but simply did not have the training that the mission called for. It was obvious that arcane Kremlin politics, which had changed only superficially since the days of the Communist Politburo's hegemony, had determined the choice. When the mission failed, and failed miserably, Mitchell had felt no surprise, only a numbing shock.

Nor was there much surprise about his being summoned to the Pentagon today in order to be briefed on the role he'd been ordered to play. Mitchell had expected to be called to Joint-Chiefs-of-Staff headquarters the moment he'd learned of the failed Russian operation.

He'd also been certain he would be expected to tell his superiors that his men were good to go for a U.S. mission into the Iranian desert to pull the Russians' chestnuts out of the fire for them.

In the aftermath of the first attempt, the follow-on mission would be twice as impossible to bring off, but that was not Mitchell's lookout. He just went where they sent him.

The headquarters of the Joint Chiefs of Staff, which includes the Pentagon offices of the Joint Special Operations Command, is reached at the Pentagon via the River Entrance, which is also the JCS entrance.

Mitchell's courteous young driver pulled the Lincoln into a numbered bay in the five-sided building's vast north parking lot and saluted smartly as his passenger left, reminding the major to phone the motor pool to arrange for transportation back to the airfield when he was ready.

Once inside the building, Mitchell flashed his military ID, turned right on the E-Ring, and walked a short distance down the bustling corridor, past portraits of several presidents. He recognized Jackson, Grant, and Teddy Roosevelt, but gave up on the others, who glowered at him for neglecting his American history lessons as he crossed beneath their merciless gazes.

Mitchell continued along the hall, passed Corridor Eight, and continued past more portraits and depictions of great nineteenth-century land and sea battles, until he passed the offices of the chairman of the JCS, where he immediately turned left onto Corridor Seven. A few minutes later, after another walk past more noble portraiture, Mitchell reached the closed, unmarked oaken door that opens into the Special Operations Division of the Joint Chiefs of Staff.

Unlike most depictions of the command center of

America's special-forces arm, which includes Army Rangers and Green Berets, Navy SEALs and Delta Force itself, the Pentagon headquarters of the Joint Special Operations Command does not boast a darkened, sunken pit filled with banks of electronic screens and overlooked by enormous television screens. These can be found at NORAD headquarters inside Cheyenne Mountain, Colorado, at Stratcom's underground command post beneath Offut Air Force Base in Nebraska, and some other places, too, but not here.

JSOC's Pentagon headquarters is in reality a warren of meeting rooms and open-plan staff areas sectioned off into modular work zones. The complex also has a few specialized rooms, such as the cipher room, the computer room, which contains a specially made Cray X-2000 hypercube mainframe, and the room with downlinks to real-time and near-real-time satellite imagery, which are all restricted. Otherwise—and with the exception of its many uniformed staffers—the nerve center of America's ultra-secret special-operations capability could pass for the main office of a large insurance company.

It was into one of the large meeting rooms of the JSOC complex that an orderly ushered Mitchell on arrival. As Mitchell entered the bustling enclosure, he saw that he was probably the last person to get there. The massive oval table of dark, polished mahogany was occupied by a half-dozen military brass and as many civilian representatives of the Defense Department, the National Security Council, and the various spook agencies with their cryptic, three-letter names that made up the U.S. "intelligence community."

Mitchell was directed to his place, one duly outfitted with a yellow legal pad, pencil, and nameplate, where he took his seat. He recognized few of the others in the room with him, with the notable exception of Major General Orville B. Childers, who Mitchell knew had been appointed head of the joint task force responsible for the mission and who reported directly to the chairman of the JCS, General Parris "Jack" Thibodeaux. Thibodeaux was

Colonel Mike Armbrister's direct superior, which made him the boss of bosses, as least as far as Mitchell went.

Thibodeaux soon rose and brought the meeting to order. As the general spoke, Mitchell listened with rapt attention. So far, his only source of surprise had been the Pentagon's uncharacteristic travel arrangements. But less than five minutes into Thibodeaux's speech, Mitchell knew that he had gone far beyond mere surprise, into the realm of pure amazement.

The most amazing part of all was that Thibodeaux, who had both airborne and Ranger experience dating back to Vietnam, obviously meant every word he was saying about the sierra oscar, or secret operation, he had in mind.

"Get up!"

The words, barked in Arabic, roused the sleeping men on the cold, hard ground. The two Bedouin guides awoke to find themselves in the middle of a circle of standing men who glared down at them with open menace.

Before they could rise, they were grabbed by the arms and jerked to their feet. The hilts of combat knives were pressed into their hands and the circle around them broadened to give them more room. The Bedouin looked uncomprehendingly at the serrated blades gleaming dully in their hands, then at each other with dawning awareness.

As they traded their wordless glances, a hunk of rope approximately four feet long and knotted at both ends was flung between them, into the center of the circle. Each Bedu knew what was expected of him, and knew why, and both men cursed the need for the few Iranian ehatys that had led them into this trap when they had known better from the first. But there was no turning back, not now.

One man, then the other, stooped and picked up an end of the rope in his free hand. Warily scrutinizing each other, the men placed the knotted ends between their teeth and clamped down hard. Moments later the knives swung and slashed as each man sought an opening through which he could slice up the belly or stab into the heart of his opponent.

Sitting atop the roof of one of the parked Land Rovers, Raful Barak watched the gaunt figures dance their deadly pavane. It was unlikely that either antagonist would survive. But should this happen, the winner would earn the privilege of taking him on next.

Barak unsheathed his Ka-Bar and ran the edge of his thumb along the honed cutting surface of the heavy steel blade, feeling the sharpness of the metal bite the fragile skin. One Bedu had already cut the other in the eye and blood was now pouring from the man's injured face onto his shirt. Barak knew the remainder of the blinded one's life was numbered in seconds.

Then both men went down and Barak could no longer see what was happening above the heads of the men forming the circle that penned them in. More minutes passed, and then one of the Egoz looked his way, holding out two downward-pointing thumbs. Barak nodded and put his knife back in its sheath, then climbed down from the roof of the vehicle. The team would proceed from here on its own, with no outsiders to bear witness.

Sergeant Maggard's beeper went off just as the topless dancer was doing something interesting with the twenty-dollar bill he'd just given her. Various other warbles, trills, and beeps were sounding from the pockets of the four other men sitting on either side. The chorus of electronic noises was already drawing the hostile stares of other dance enthusiasts in the audience.

Although the five men would have had little trouble in cleaning out the bar with their bare hands, they did nothing except switch off their beepers and get up to leave. The paging meant that Delta G-Troop's Blue Team was being assembled for a mission without delay. As Maggard stole a backward glance at the girl on the stage, his one consolation was that, wherever they were and whatever they were doing, the rest of Blue Team had also gotten the same message and, like him, were already on their way back to Bragg.

Thirteen
Boar Hunting in Novosibirsk

Three time zones, two thousand miles, and approximately two hours prior to Mitchell's appointment at the Pentagon, Captain Viktor Arbatov was leaving the center of Russia's military-intelligence-and-special-forces command on the outskirts of Moscow. The Glavnoe Razvedyvatelnoe Upravlenie, or Military Intelligence Agency of the former Soviet Union, is commonly known in the West by its acronym, GRU.

The organization can still be found in the location it occupied during the heyday of the Communist superstate. This is the central building at the old Khodenka Aerodrome, surrounded on three sides by buildings housing the apparatus of several other government service branches of Moscow Center.

While its title might give the impression that the GRU serves the same function as U.S. military intelligence, such as the Army's DIA, the Navy's ONI, or Air-Force Intelligence, this is not the case at all. On hearing the acronym GRU, most Westerners automatically assumed it to be a military counterpart of the KGB. In fact, the GRU has no direct equivalent in the American military force structure, nor is it merely a clone of the better-known Russian KGB.

For one thing, the GRU's functions exceed the mere collection of intelligence, the practice of espionage, and the collection of what the Russians call "cosmic intelligence," that is, intelligence derived from orbital surveillance platforms, including satellites. The GRU is also responsible for active measures, "special" or "tactical" reconnaissance, and other so-called "special assignments."

In order to carry out these varied functions, the GRU also serves as the command center of the former Soviet Union's special forces, including Spetsnaz and Vasaltniki, which are under the control of the Third Department of the GRU's Sixth Directorate.

Viktor Arbatov had just emerged from a briefing given by General Gennady Kirpichenko, and his mind was still spinning out the implications of what he had learned and the orders he'd been handed. All in all, the general's brief had been the culminating moment of an incredible thirty days for Arbatov.

First, there had been the unexpected pardon from the so-called punishment battalion in which he'd languished for the better part of the last month. This was a strange euphemism for a prison, but so it went in Mother Russia. Then there had been the sudden and unexpected death of Army General Potapenko, and now, to cap everything, these new orders he'd received, orders that called for Arbatov to begin training with a troop of American Delta Force commandos for a second mission into Iran.

Arbatov could still hear Kirpichenko's grating voice as it emerged from the round Slavic face of his superior officer, head of the Spetsnaz companies, the elite of all the Russian special-forces units.

Kirpichenko had promised Arbatov everything he required to get the job done—only the job *must* be done, the stealth fighter must be destroyed before the Iranians could make any major strides in copying its advanced systems.

This time, no slipups. The general had made this crystal clear. This time, *khui pinat',* he stressed, slamming his hamhock fist against the top of his desk—asses must be kicked.

Since the abortive first mission, the damned Iranians, the *chernozhopyi,* or "black bottoms," had been increasing their efforts to reverse-engineer the MFI-19 Eclipse's main systems components, and before long it would be too late to deny them the fruits of their research. This time the Americans would have to be directly involved, Kirpichenko added.

First, they had a legitimate stake in the outcome of the mission, both because U.S. planning, targeting, and weaponry had been involved, and also for geostrategic considerations. Second, the C.I.S. needed U.S. bases in the Gulf region from which to stage, because another mission could not be launched from the east—the Iranians were watching their eastern borders like hawks.

Finally, the Americans had sold the Russian president on their plan, and Grigorenko, like any shrewd politician anywhere, had also seen a way to deflect further blame should the second attempt also fail in a joint operation with the U.S.

The damned fools, Arbatov thought as he listened to Kirpichenko's briefing, though he kept his mouth shut. It was nothing short of a suicide mission that the *papakhas,* the big hats, were asking him to now undertake. The Americans were idiots to have become involved in this madness; and so was he, for that matter.

However, Arbatov had little choice but to follow his orders and somehow make it all come together. He had no intention of going back to the cramped, foul-smelling prison cell, with the bad food, the fat rodents, and the sadistic *bugori,* or prison bosses, who had been his companions for many long weeks. Even suicide was preferable to that.

Besides this thought, Arbatov also had the no-doubt-insane notion that there was indeed a way to make the impossible thing work out.

At least Arbatov was guaranteed to have company in this coming fool's crusade.

Kirpichenko had also revealed that Arbatov would doubtless be glad to learn that his old comrade, an American major named Mitchell, would be part of the fusion cell, for the GRU had adopted the American phrase for the mixed special-forces group originally coined during the War in the Gulf when mixed cadres made up of American, British, and French commandos conducted deep-strike missions inside Iraq.

Arbatov would not have used the term "comrade" to describe Mitchell, either in the standard sense of the word or its old, Communist-era sense, but he did think of Mitchell as a kindred spirit. There had been secret liaisons between U.S. special-forces cadres and Spetsnaz since the start of the Yeltsin political era in Russia in December of 1991. Although not openly publicized by either East or West, the special-forces liaison had been ongoing since then.

In the same way that Delta engaged in joint training with European SOF cadres, such as the French GIGN or German GSG-9, it also trained with Spetsnaz, once perhaps the greatest of the adversaries it had been geared up to fight. Arbatov remembered Peace as a real *muzhick,* what Americans would call a "regular guy," and there were not many whom he honored with such a tag. More important, the Russian also respected the American's soldiering skills.

The mission, thought Arbatov, might be doomed to failure, but it was also sure to be an interesting one. Besides, the American Marines weren't the only group of fighting men who held the question "who wants to live forever?" as an article of faith.

With this thought in mind, Arbatov's musings turned to the recent funeral of the coward and traitor Potapenko, who had been buried two days before in Moscow's grand

Ivovkensky Cemetery in the section reserved for military heroes of the Rodina or Motherland. Arbatov knew the truth behind the old *bizhdenok*'s supposed "heart attack" while "boar hunting" in the hills of Novosibirsk.

Boar hunting, indeed! The general had betrayed the Spetsnaz one time too many, and because he no longer wielded the kind of power he once had done, accounts could be settled. Like many another Spetsnaz who had served in the Afghan War and had known Potapenko back then, Arbatov would not have missed the funeral for the world. He had attended not to pay his last respects to the legendary military leader, but to jeer, if silently and with an outward show of respect, one of the most hated scumbags in recent Russian history.

As the Zhiguli MT-40 sedan from the GRU motor pool carrying Arbatov back to the Spetsnaz training site rolled through the wooded suburbs of Moscow, covered with a frosting of one of the last large snowfalls of the receding but still deep Russian winter, Arbatov's mind cast back to the final days in Afghanistan, the days of the desperate Russian retreat back across the border.

It was one of the great retreats of military history, surely the equal of Napoleon's retreat from Moscow or the German withdrawal over the Rhine in World War II. But the history books would never teach it and only a handful would ever know the full story concerning it.

During the war Potapenko had been the supreme commander of all Spetsnaz detachments in the Afghan combat theater. As a chief, he had been capricious, cruel, and arrogant. If not for his commanding officers taking matters into their own hands on more than one occasion, disaster would have befallen many an operation.

But during the pullout Potapenko had sunk to the lowest depth he'd reached in that sorry affair. He had cut a deal with the commander of the Hesb Nasr, the hated Omar Tousek. The Hesb Nasr were not true Mujahideen. They were bandits who infested the rugged mountains of the Panjshir, loyal to no creed but the lust for plunder and following no leader save Tousek. The Hesb Nasr preyed on Afghans and *Shuravi* alike and were hated by both.

The Spetsnaz had occupied the Soviet garrison at Pul-e-Khumri, a fortified hill town that had been built up into a regional command center. The withdrawal was to begin in the morning. But in the dead of night, a Hip transport chopper dusted off, escorted by two heavily armed Hind-F gunships. The Hip carried Potapenko and his retinue to safety.

When they were gone, GAZ trucks appeared at the gate, their drivers bearing military passes. The trucks carried hundreds of Hesb Nasr armed with rifles and rocket launchers. Hundreds more waited in the surrounding hills, ready to storm the base once the shooting started.

The Hesb Nasr had the advantage of surprise and they used it without mercy. Virtually all the occupants of the garrison were slaughtered that night. Thousands of tons of military equipment fell into the hands of the Hesb Nasr as a result. The weapons and hardware formed the nucleus of the arsenal that the fanatic Taliban would use a few years later to enslave the Afghan people, once the Russians had left.

Potapenko had sold the Spetsnaz forces for a handful of gold. They had died for nothing, or as the saying went, *ni za khy sobachy*—for less than a dog's dick. The few Spetsnaz that escaped that night of slaughter found they could not touch the general, legally, politically, or otherwise, until just now. He had been too well connected, first to the Politburo, and then to the corrupt *nomenklatura* that ran the "new" Russia.

Not that Potapenko was alone in his treachery. If he was merely one of the worst, there were still others almost as bad. Still, the old soldier had stood as a glaring symbol, not only of the corruption of the *vlasti* or kingpins of the old regime, but of the apathy and decadence of the new. Arbatov bid him good riddance.

There had been no snow in Jerusalem that winter, although snow was not unknown to that storied city on the Mediterranean coast. But the nights were still cold out in the Judean hills where the *kibbutzim* stood like bastions around the ancient land and where Assaf Gilad had his sprawling farm.

The aging warrior was busy with the winter harvest of Jaffa oranges, winter wheat, and the fruit of his large olive groves, and he carefully took note of the weather, whose capriciousness at this time of year was well known to the *moshavniks,* those perennial soil tillers of the reclaimed desert lands that included Gilad's own family.

This season's early frost could wipe out his entire crop of oranges, the best in all of Israel, and Gilad's personal attention to the harvest was critical to its success. But he had been summoned to the whitewashed building complex on the suburban outskirts of Tel Aviv, and it was a summons that even the lion of the Six Day War was not in a position to ignore, because that summons had been delivered in a phone call from the prime minister himself.

And so, early one morning, farmer Assaf left his harvest in the hands of his sons and hired farm-hands and traveled the narrow blacktop roads that twist and wind their way through the wrinkled, arid hillsides of northeastern Israel, heading toward the warmer, greener, lusher Mediterranean coastal plain.

By late afternoon he had reached his destination—the headquarters of Ha Mossad le Modiyn ve le Tafkidim Mayuhadim or the Institute for Intelligence and Special Operations, most often shorted simply to "the Institute" or Mossad, by which name it is commonly known around the world. The white buildings that house the Mossad stand in plain view of anyone passing them on the A-9 Highway that runs from Tel Aviv to Bethsheba along the Mediterranean coast. In fact, the complex looks like a resort, complete with a large and well-maintained Olympic swimming pool, occupying the palm-topped crest of a hill around which the highway slowly curves.

Unlike the CIA's Langley, Virginia, headquarters, however, there are no road signs conspicuously indicating Mossad's presence to travelers on the highway. In fact, one Israeli intelligence operative was known to have marveled about the sign on the Washington-to-Baltimore ring road that read TO CENTRAL INTELLIGENCE AGENCY, and gave the number of the next turnoff on the highway during a trip to the States. There are no signs that point to the fact that the Mossad headquarters is actually Mossad headquarters and not a country club or hotel set on a hillside amid plantings of date palms. It even boasts a swimming pool.

Unlike a hotel, however, nobody gets through the main gate of the complex without either an invitation or a job at the Mossad complex, and there are even watchers in cars and on foot positioned amid the surrounding neighborhoods whose task is to keep track of suspicious vehicles or pedestrians, especially those with cameras. Such parties find themselves photographed and license-plate numbers are noted. All data is fed into the Mossad's central computer system, nicknamed the "Beast" by those who use it.

But Assaf Gilad was one of the invited few, and on presenting his Israel Defense Forces or IDF ID to the gatekeepers, he was permitted into the Mossad compound, where he parked his car and entered the main building lobby. He was soon on his way up to the fifth and top floor, in the company of an escort and with a name tag pinned to the breast pocket of his sport coat, for a meeting with the head of the Mossad and members of the Israeli cabinet.

Had it been the CIA and Gilad were an American, it would be unlikely that the meeting would be attended by as senior a group as this particular assemblage. But Israel's intelligence, political, and defense establishments are far smaller and much more closely knit than those of its much larger Western counterparts, and the relationships between members of the Israeli elite are far more informal than elsewhere in the world.

Since familiarity can also breed contempt, the meetings between these various branches, when they happen, can also become heated and turn into verbal, and sometimes even physical, brawls. This was close to what took place a few minutes after Gilad entered the secure fifth-floor conference room, whose walls were impervious to electronic listening devices and in which no notes were permitted to be taken.

Gilad soon found himself in a shouting match with the current head of the Mossad, Yitzhak Bar-Illon, an argument that was all the more acrimonious to Gilad since Bar-Illon had served under him during the Yom Kipper War as a lieutenant, and although he had long ago attained the rank of general in the Israeli Defense Forces, Gilad still considered him his underling.

Bar-Illon was also to blame. He had no intention of stroking the Old Man, who he had learned was off on another one of his now infamous cowboying escapades. Who was he to single-handedly write Israeli foreign policy?

The personnel whom Gilad had pulled out of the AMAN and other places had been noticed and little by little the true story of Gilad's operation had leaked out. It wasn't just that the prime minister was livid over Israel's interference in a Russian-American operation, and wanted no part of the stealth plane or confrontation with the Iranians, it was also that Gilad's operation could compromise one of the Mossad's most important espionage assets inside the Iranian military, an agent code-named "Ahriman."

Ahriman, Gilad was told, was a deep-cover mole highly placed in the Iranian defense establishment. Ahriman was already in contact with Israeli intelligence and had reported back on having heard rumors of an Israeli move to retrieve the plane. If so, his life and the precious intelligence he fed the Mossad could be jeopardized. Unfortunately, it was now too late to stop Gilad's mercenaries inside Iran; indeed the moment Gilad had revealed the plane's existence to such men as they, it was already too late to stop them.

But Gilad was informed that he was no longer running the show on his own. He was now working for the Mossad, as a middleman. From now on Bar-Illon would be giving the orders and Gilad would be obeying them. If not, there would be repercussions.

"I built this party with Begin," Gilad had answered. "Ben Gurion, Golda Meir, Moshe Dayan—I knew them all. And now you Johnny-come-lately pishers are shoving me around, threatening me, giving me orders—"

Gilad broke off and stormed out of the meeting, livid with rage. To hell with Bar-Illon and his *minyan* of pishers, he thought. No mere lieutenant was about to tell him what to do, and never would.

Fourteen
Backdoor Recon

Their hulls painted matte black, with the dull white stars and bars of the USAF visible only at close range and invisible in the almost total blackness of the cold, moonless night, the three boxy, rotary-wing aircraft churned northeastward less than one hundred feet above the desert floor.

They were MH53-J Pave Lows, enhanced Block III versions that had been optimized for special-operations missions, with a beefed-up avionics suite and more powerful radars than previous helos of the class. The ships had also been upgunned, with fifty-caliber Browning MG-3 heavy machine guns that could be fired through side windows or the helo's rear ramp in addition to the pintle-mounted door guns, one of which was a 7.62-mm Minigun.

The helos were flying in what their pilots referred to as "turf mode." Others called it NOE, for nap-of-the-earth, or mud-moving. These terms, and others like them, referred to the technique of traversing at extremely low altitude where an aircraft's radar signature is more likely to become lost in the so-called ground clutter, the jumbled reflection of radar echoes bouncing off the terrain.

Helicopters were especially good at exploiting this weakness of radar's ability to see incoming threats, especially those equipped with terrain-following/terrain-avoidance radars. The Pave Low III was especially good at this stunt, because its TF/TA radars, and the computers that controlled them, were the best of the breed.

The same went for the Pave Low's enhanced navigation system, ENAV. As long as its uplink to the suite of global positioning satellites or GPS remained intact, ENAV could bring the bird to within a few feet of its programmed destination point, and do this trick in total darkness with no navigational aids.

This is why the Pave Low is the chopper of choice for special-forces and special-operations missions and why the bird is high on Delta's wish list. But Delta's aviation squadron, added to the force in 1998, doesn't include any Pave Lows yet and probably won't in the future. When Delta needs a Pave Low, it knocks on the door of the USAF's 1st Special Operations Wing, as it did during the Gulf and Kosovo wars, and as it will probably continue to do in future wars and future covert missions.

The Air Force, like the United States' other armed services, likes to keep at least one finger in any given pie, and if its own special operations branch isn't in as great demand as the Navy's SEALs or the Army's Delta, then at least USAF pilots will be in on the action.

The three Pave Lows participating in tonight's mission were owned and operated by the 1st Special Operations Wing's 20th Special Operations Squadron, which was based at al-Jouf, Saudi Arabia, a few dozen miles from the Iraqi border, though the mission would stage out of Kuwait. For the chopper crews, what had at first appeared to be a routine training mission turned out to be the most incredible thing to happen since the hot-shit glory days of the Gulf.

• • •

In the pilot's seat of the lead chopper, Captain Richie Johnson unwrapped a Snickers bar and popped it into his mouth. Chewing the bite-sized junk food snack helped calm his nerves when he flew.

The minute he'd been briefed by his commanding officer, Colonel Marty Applebaum, that the training exercises his squadron element had been flying for the last month were about to go hot and live, Johnson knew it was time to break out the bag of candy he'd been saving for a special occasion.

Now, having just passed his second waypoint ten minutes out of Kuwait and thirty-five miles inside the Iranian border (the first waypoint had been at Kuwait, where the ship's ENAV system had fixed its exact position on the surface of the earth), Johnson still couldn't quite believe that this run wasn't simply another training exercise like all the others.

But the scene in the aft cabin behind the cockpit argued differently. No longer was it empty, except for his flight engineer, Sergeant Sam Williams, who also doubled as tailgunner/backender and his right and left doorgunners, Doug Tallish and Ron Smith. All three also doubled as scanners. As such, they were the chopper's lookouts, regularly calling out the altitude and eyeballing the ground below for obstacles the terrain-avoidance radar didn't pick up.

They also kept their eyes peeled for any Bedouin bands below that might fire a rifle or even a shoulder-launched SAM at the low-flying bird. At the ground-hugging altitude the Pave Low flew, even a single bullet could bring the chopper down by hitting a weak spot in the airframe or penetrating the cockpit window and killing or seriously wounding the pilot.

Bedouin tribesmen roamed all over the deserts of the Middle East, as they had been doing for thousands of years. The sand wastes were their home; moreover, it was their turf. As a general rule, the desert nomads usually minded their own business and kept their noses out of the shifting winds of regional politics. But some bands did not, and many such tribal groups went about their wanderings armed to the teeth.

When driving a flying bungalow only a few-score feet over the heads of potential snipers, it paid to be careful.

As Johnson heard the scanners call out their regular sightings, he also heard the occasional sounds of others in the cabin with them, and the odd creaks of heavy objects shifting as the giant chopper pitched and lunged up and down and left and right above the uneven desert floor. The unfamiliar voices belonged to the team of Delta Force commandos that was webbed down against the sides of the chopper, below the metal "pizza racks" that held the modular component units for the Pave Low's navigational, communications, radar, and other critical onboard systems.

The creaking that from time to time penetrated the steady drone of the chopper's diesel engines belonged to the two fast attack vehicles, or FAVs, that were strapped down to the deck in the center of the bird's vibrating steel belly. Johnson could feel the distinct inertial effects of the additional load, too. The extra few tons of cargo altered the way the chopper handled, making the aircraft feel more sluggish in Johnson's hands.

Although Johnson never let it show in his voice as he called out instructions to his copilot and crew, he was nervous. Johnson was flying a steel house over hostile territory, and it was loaded to the gills with more extra payload than he'd ever carried in his entire career. The only things holding all that matter up were the rotor blades spinning overhead. Suddenly those thirty-foot-long reinforced polycarbon blades seemed as thin and as frail as plastic toothpicks.

Although Johnson had worked out the fuel requirements for the flight to the last pound of avgas, his eyes kept flicking to the chopper's fuel gauge, glowing a dull green in the view field of his night-vision goggles. The flight into Iran would tax every ounce of fuel the chopper carried, even with the extra tanks that the Block III carried and the increased lightness of the helo as the fuel load continually burned off. Mathematics were one thing, but reality could often be another, and usually was a bitch.

Johnson knew that even with the chopper's fuel supply good to the last drop and no unexpected hitches to spoil the party, his bird and the two other Pave Lows trailing behind it would not have enough fuel to make it back over the border to Kuwait. Their returning home depended, in large part, on nonpilot spooks getting all their ducks in line, and this was not a fun thought.

The Army's Intelligence Support Activity or ISA was supposed to have a crew of stay-in-place agents prepare the landing zone. The ISA's assets were native Iranians who had been working undercover since after the abortive Carter-era hostage rescue mission and were considered reliable. ISA's people were supposed to truck two huge bladders of avgas out into the desert for refueling the Pave Lows once they landed.

Supposed, supposed, supposed. That was the scary part. Too many damned supposeds for Johnson's liking.

Johnson had no faith in anyone but himself and his own people. He knew his capabilities and he knew theirs. He did not know the people on the ground from the hole in his rear echelon, and what Johnson didn't know he didn't trust, especially when his life and the lives of his crew depended on somebody else getting it right.

But there it was, and he'd just have to live—or die—with it. Johnson popped another Snickers into his mouth and chewed, scanning the softly glowing readouts on the panel in front of him through the light-amplifying lenses of his NVGs.

The choppers hung and danced, strung like sing-along notes at the bottom of an old-time movie screen, as they rose and fell to the cadence of an inaudible music score. With Johnson's Pave Low in the lead, the sortie flitted through the Zagros mountain range that jutted up along the Iranian border like broken teeth in a bleached donkey's jaw, weaving their way through the tortuous line of serpentine twists and turns between the dark basaltic hills on either side.

The USAF and the Russian Air Force had prepped the invasion on both sides of the Iranian border with a series of near incursions on a daily basis for the last two weeks. Antonovs to the east and F-111s to the west would edge up near Iranian early-warning radar sites to put the Iranians on the defensive, and then abruptly pull back.

After fourteen days of this game of hedge and dodge, the Iranians' edge had been dulled and they would not be as likely to interpret a chance radar contact with the Pave Low fleet with the requisite alarm.

Beyond that, the course flown by the chopper sortie had been planned to exploit a weak spot in Iranian radar coverage shown up by Rhyolite radar satellites and RC-135 electronic intelligence aircraft, both of which had been busily watching the border testing to see where coverage was thin.

The analysts at the National Security Agency's vast computer farm at Fort Belvoir, Virginia, had found a sizable gap in the southwestern sector of the radar shield, an approximate thin spot of five miles where the coverage of two sites didn't quite overlap. That's where the Pave Lows had snuck inside.

From that point on, they had flown through the mountains, lightening somewhat as their extra loads of fuel burned off and handling better in their pilots' hands.

Some forty minutes out of Kuwait, the helo squadron came out of the mountains and skimmed across the open desert of the Dasht-e-Kavir, the great salt pan occupying most of the northern quarter of the country. In the lead chopper Johnson heard the series of warbling tones from ENAV signaling the approach of the third and penultimate waypoint, where a fresh navigational update was taken and minor corrections made to the course.

As the birds passed the waypoint and skirted the last of the brooding, strangely folded hills, they dropped down to fifty feet above the desert floor, their cruising altitude for the remainder of the trip.

As the altimeter showed the drop, and the green-tinted view through Johnson's light-amplifying visor changed from mountains and valleys to the floor of the Dasht rising up all around the cockpit window, he called out to his scanners to keep their eyes peeled and their calls crisp and intelligible.

This was probably the most hazardous leg of the inbound flight, Johnson knew, and he didn't want any mistakes. He could see the desert floor below in detail now, and every boulder, every thornbush and Joshua tree, and every rise and dip in the arid landscape could pose serious hazards for the mission.

He was also picking up some weather, too. Nothing heavy, especially for the deserts of the Middle East in winter, where storms of freezing ice, rain, and sand might appear from out of nowhere, but he could see and hear the pellets of ice and specks of windblown sand strike against the windshield, and he felt the Pave Low rock slightly as it passed through eddies and air pockets.

Johnson turned on his windshield wipers and held back a curse. He didn't need a shitstorm on top of everything else. Fortunately the weather never got much worse than the little bit of hail and soon it stopped altogether. Johnson relaxed a little and ate another Snickers, telling himself that it would work out all right.

It could have been the weather that prevented anyone from seeing a thirty-four-year-old Bedouin tribesman named Hamdi Feroz bin-Tukali who had been sheltering amid the boulders of a sandstone formation about thirty yards abreast of the oncoming path of the choppers. The young Bedu had been awakened from a dream in which his older brother, Achmed, had appeared to him, riding on a donkey and beckoning Hamdi to follow.

Hamdi had pursued his brother across the desert, and stopped to point at a strange rock formation that rose in the distance, shaped something like a woman's naked body yet also something like the body of a poisonous scorpion. Though Achmed had said nothing, only pointed,

Hamdi knew without being told that this rock formation held the key to enormous wealth, somehow even of life itself.

Hamdi was about to ask Achmed why he had shown him this vision when suddenly the rock formation exploded with a thunderous boom, and an immense geyser of black oil gushed forth, spewing high up into the sky. At this point Hamdi awoke with a start, but still heard the thunder in his ears.

Suddenly he realized that the noise was coming from overhead, swelling to a crescendo from out of the west, and that it was made by the huge black forms that swept across the desert.

Helicopters, he thought as the four other members of the band awakened at the sound and stared toward the western horizon. Hamdi was the first to recognize the helicopters as American flying machines.

He had seen many aircraft pass overhead in the desert, including Russian ones, but nothing like this. That meant Americans, or English or French, which to Hamdi were all the same. At the same time he realized that his brother Achmed had warned him of their approach in the dream. Achmed, who had been killed by fire from an American helicopter such as this during the Gulf War, had called him to take vengeance.

Before the others could raise their guns, Hamdi had lifted his AK-7 autorifle and fired off a burst as the dull, bulky black shapes came streaking overhead. In another heartbeat they were gone. Hamdi and the others stared after them as they lowered their weapons, hoping against hope that at least one of the American warplanes would come crashing to the desert floor and explode in a fireball, but nothing happened.

The black shapes disappeared, and soon the thunder of their passage had faded to the nocturnal silence of the desert once again. Only when the birds had returned to Kuwait and the ground crews inspected them and found the places where two of Hamdi's bullets had creased the hull of the second chopper in the sortie, would there be evidence of the helos having been fired upon.

But although Hamdi believed that he had done the American gunships no damage, he had at least not hesitated to shoot. Of this he was proud. And besides this, there was the second part of his dream yet to fulfill. Calling to his comrades, Hamdi mounted his camel and set off in the direction of an Iranian military encampment not far from this place where he had dreamed his dream of wealth and vengeance.

The mission reached its final waypoint and proceeded toward its landing zone unaware that the choppers had been sighted and that the mission was compromised, hitting more weather as the LZ and H-hour both drew closer.

As the lead Pave Low skimmed the desert, Johnson swept his eyes from his instrument panel to the view through the cockpit window.

The moving map display, a circular panel located below and to the right of his altimeter and FLIR or forward-looking infrared displays, and just above his ENAV display screens, showed him that the Pave Low was on course and approaching the LZ.

At the same time the fuel gauges, located on the topmost portion of the control panel, showed him that the fuel supply of his bird was getting dangerously low. The chopper had consumed almost 90 percent of its available avgas load and would be left with less than 10 percent capacity as it approached the landing zone. There was no way short of a miracle rivaling Christ's resurrection for the sortie to make it back to Kuwait if there was no fuel awaiting them at the end of the run.

Yet the creeping, sickening fear that had begun to gnaw at Johnson's entrails and that no amount of Snickers therapy could hope to wipe away (besides, the bag was almost gone by now) was that there never would be any fuel. As the circle representing the helo moved across the dully glowing map display and approached within a mile of the LZ, there was no indication that anybody was down there waiting for them.

By now he should have seen an infrared strobe flashing somewhere below and just ahead, to indicate where the choppers were supposed to land, but there was nothing except the artificially glowing darkness through his light-amplification goggles. Johnson's crew was getting jittery, too. The doorgunners had been craning their heads out into the night, looking for a strobe, and nothing was there except for the wind and the hail and the fine white dust particles that blew into their faces.

"What's up? Where's the fucking strobe?" asked Williams from behind the cockpit.

"Relax. It'll be there," Johnson said, using his calmest tone of voice and hoping nobody sensed the nervousness he, too, felt.

He was also well aware that the flight crews in the two choppers behind him were also just as edgy, but would not break radio silence to express their fears. When another series of warbling tones sounded in the cockpit, announcing that they had reached the LZ, there was still no sign of the ground support team. But by now there was no choice. The chopper's fuel supply was almost totally eaten up.

Johnson was about to announce that they were about to land and fend off any questions about the absence of ground support from his crew, when he saw the flashes dead ahead.

Twice, once, twice—in the prearranged pattern. Johnson took a long, relieved breath and keyed his mike, announcing that the ground crew was waiting and the choppers were about to touch down.

A few minutes later the force was on the ground, the helos' rear access ramps fully lowered, and men and transport rolling out into the darkness.

Fifteen
On a Fast Train

The grounded birds took on avgas from two enormous rubber blivets that slowly deflated on the desert floor as they were emptied of their contents. A perimeter security detail was already walking post, cradling bullpup Kalashnikov AKS-74 autorifles that were standard issue to the cell. Mitchell stood watching the chopper crews refuel and recalibrate their instruments. As soon as the Pave Lows had drunk their fill, they would dust off again. It was still winter in the Dasht and his breath left vapor plumes in the cold night air, whose temperature was a chilly thirty degrees Fahrenheit.

Hundreds of cubic feet per minute of aviation gasoline gushed through the flexible rubber hoses connecting the fuel bladders to the helos' intake receptacles. The chopper crews in their brown nylon jumpsuits had asked for nobody's help in getting their hardware airborne again. They had done their part of the mission and were in a hurry to get out. On the ground they felt vulnerable and exposed, and with good reason; they *were* vulnerable and exposed.

The intelligence support activity or ISA crew that had set up the fuel dump had already melted into the desert. These were local agents in place who for weeks had been storing fuel and equipment smuggled down from U.S. supply depots in Turkey. Having done its part, the advance team was no longer needed. Its continued presence in the operations zone would jeopardize the safety of these nationals, who were all CIA contractors.

As the birds were gassed up, the U.S.-Russian fusion cell checked its weapons and equipment and loaded gear and supplies into the FAVs that had been ramped off the back ends of the choppers. The FAVs were the key to the mission's success, one reason being that there was no reasonable way to march on foot across the hostile desert environment and expect to wind up in any kind of shape to take down a target.

During Desert Storm, the British SAS had been the first ground troops to go into Iraq and clandestinely hunt Scuds, and they did so contrary to CENTCOM's express orders that no ground troops leave Saudi Arabia until the air campaign's conclusion. Britain's special-forces commander, General de la Billiere, had convinced his American opposite number to make a special exception for his SAS, and the Brits had gone in, but they'd paid a heavy price for their boldness.

When the first Anglo-American fusion cells were set up later on in the battle, the SAS warned that between the severe cold, almost lunar terrain, lack of landmarks, and armed Bedouin bands, it was suicide to go into the desert on foot. Ride or fly in, but never walk, they had advised. Walking will get you killed.

The Brits had come up with a solution—LSVs or light strike vehicles. These were essentially Land Rovers stripped down to resemble oversized, heavy-frame dune buggies with a sturdy tubular steel cage welded to the chassis in place of the normal passenger compartment. There was space for two men riding up front, while the frame could be either crammed with gear, carry another team member, or be equipped with a pintle-mounted heavy machine gun, such as a fifty-caliber Browning LM-3 or a forty-mm multiple grenade launcher.

Heavy MGs, thirty-mm cannon, or a variety of surface-to-air and surface-to-surface missiles such as Milan, Dragon, or TOW, could also be mounted up front, over the passenger-side seat, with spare missile tubes, shells, and ammo carried in back within easy reach.

The LSVs quickly became a staple of desert commando warfare and of any special-operations mission requiring high mobility under rugged terrain conditions. Delta later produced LSVs of its own, moving the steering wheel from right to left and rechristening them FAVs, which, with some modifications, were what the fusion cell brought with it into Iran aboard the Pave Lows.

The cell had trained on the FAVs in Kuwait for weeks prior to the mission launch date. By now its members were familiar with every quirk and tick of the machinery. In fact, Mitchell had selected Delta's Blue Team for the mission partly because it was a mobile warfare team that specialized in desert operations on dune buggies.

Delta's policy was to divide its fifteen-to-twenty-one-man troops into four-to-six-man teams, each with a unique MOS or military occupational specialty. Some specialized in sniping, others in counterterrorist ops, but Blue Team's specialty was the one needed for the Iran mission. The team had taught the Spetsnaz everything it knew on the subject, and the Russians were fast learners, devising some new wrinkles of their own that might in the future become part of standard Delta operating procedure.

As the last few kilograms of avgas were pumped from the blivets into the choppers' thirsty storage tanks, Mitchell's glance fell on Arbatov, who was also looking on. Together the two mission commanders watched the refueling of the aircraft and the deployment of the troops. The growls of revving engines, the curses and shouts of busy soldiers, the shrill tones of battlefield communications and computing devices being energized, and the clatter of weapons being loaded and gear being stowed away and lashed down broke the spectral stillness of the desert night.

"They're looking good," Mitchell said to Arbatov, who, like himself, was attired in standard NATO desert camouflage BDUs and U.S. "Fritz" helmet with their black, gray, and white "chocolate chips" patterns. The battle dress had been adopted as standard issue for the cell.

"I would be disappointed if they were not," the Spetsnaz replied. "My men were handpicked, as were yours. They are the best, and the training they received at your Disneyland facility at Bragg is light-years beyond anything we have back home."

The troops' movements communicated a sense of high morale and confidence. There is a difference in the way poorly trained and badly motivated soldiers behave, even when constantly drilled, and commanders can tell at a glance if they have "the right stuff" or not. These guys had it.

It had been agreed that the Delta operators and Spetsnaz company troopers would train in pairs and ride together in the FAVs; otherwise there would wind up being two teams instead of one. Force integration was as important and basic as ammo in small unit operations, and the force would not be a true fusion cell unless it learned to fight, think, and react as a single, cohesive unit.

This was easier said than accomplished, especially at first. Delta and Spetsnaz not only had fundamental differences in doctrine, training, and weaponry, but there were major cultural differences as well. Where the American troopers had been trained to take their own initiative in all situations, the Russians never acted without clear-cut orders, and relied more on brute force than stealth and mobility in their combat style.

The Russians didn't like the American M-16 rifle either, preferring the heavier Kalashnikov AK-47, which had more stopping power than the somewhat underpowered Armalites. A compromise was struck in issuing the lighter, short-barreled AKS-74 Kalashnikov to the fusion cell as its standard assault weapon, which the Americans had already trained on as part of the Delta course. The light machine gun version of the AKS-74, the RPK-74, was also adopted as a squad automatic weapon or SAW, as was the American standard machine gun, the M60A1.

There were many other problems, too, hundreds of them, in fact. But solutions had been found to most of these and compromises worked out for the rest. The men soon formed strong bonds. When H-hour came they had been welded into a fourteen-man squadron under the joint command of Mitchell and Arbatov. By now—Delta's boss, Colonel Armbrister, had acerbically noted during a training review—they even farted in the same key.

They wore the same uniforms, packed the same gear, and shouldered the same rifles. They even cussed alike; most, by now, in two languages. The only noticeable difference in kit between GIs Ivan and Joe were the small shoulder patches high on the right fatigue sleeves—stars and bars for the Americans and the C.I.S. flag for the Russians.

Since Mitchell outranked Arbatov, it had been decided by their respective bosses that while each would cocommand, Mitchell would serve as recognized troop CO and Arbatov as his unofficial "horse handler" or XO. Mitchell would have final say, but both he and Arbatov could issue independent orders applicable to all members of the cell. Neither Spetsnaz nor Delta troopers seemed to have any problems with the arrangement.

Some twenty minutes after the troop had touched down on the sandy floor of the Dasht, the Pave Lows had been refueled for their return journey and all the fusion cell's gear had been broken out and squared away. Mitchell and Arbatov shook hands with Johnson and soon watched the black helos ascend into the even blacker night sky above them.

Within minutes the Pave Lows were swallowed up by mother night, and the final cadenced echoes of their rotor blades had died away completely. An eerie silence descended over the men on the ground, and the clandestine landing zone in the Dasht suddenly felt like a very lonely place to be, and one very far from home. Mitchell gave orders for the cell to mount up, and the six FAVs rolled away from the LZ, heading outbound toward the team's assault positions. The night soon covered over their tracks with a windblown blanket of sand.

The CIA's Langley, Virginia, headquarters are located on 219 wooded acres approximately eight miles from downtown Washington in a campuslike setting envisioned by its first civilian director, Allen W. Dulles, a bas-relief bust of whom can be seen on the marble North Wall of the foyer of the Headquarters Building. This same wall of the central lobby also displays a chevron of silver stars commemorating CIA agents who died in the line of duty. A glass-encased Book of Honor beneath the engraved stars gives the dates of death for all, and the names of a few, of those whom the stars on the memorial wall represent.

It was half-past three in the afternoon when the Director of Central Intelligence, Clifford Merrick, received an urgent call on a secure, scrambled phone line in his seventh-floor office in the one-million-square-foot annex to the Headquarters Building's West Facade that went up in the Orwellian year of 1984. The call originated from Tel Aviv, and Merrick found himself mentally calculating the time difference even as he lifted the handset to his ear.

With seven hours separating the two time zones, it would be about ten-thirty at night in Israel. Merrick braced himself for an unpleasant surprise. His secretary had told him the call was from the head of Israel's Mossad, Yitzhak Bar-Illon, and Merrick knew his opposite number in Israeli intelligence wouldn't be phoning at that hour, local time, if there wasn't some kind of bitch abrew. Merrick didn't turn out to be wrong, either.

As he listened to the voice of what was obviously a very tired man on the other end of the line, Merrick clenched and unclenched his right fist, a nervous habit he had when he was hearing bad news. The worse the news, the more he worked his fist, and he was working it into a white-knuckled ball as the words came out the ear end of the secure phone connection to Tel Aviv.

Some ten minutes later, when Merrick had fired a few questions back at Bar-Illon, and had listened to the Mossad chief's answers, and the conversation was over, Merrick sat at his desk, deep in thought.

We know about the mission to take the plane, the Mossad chief had warned. *Cancel it. There is a leak.*

After a while Merrick picked up the phone and dialed the special direct number to the Joint Chiefs at the Pentagon. It was the chairman himself that he got on the line, after General Thibodeaux was rounded up by his staff members, who could not get the DCI to leave a message. But when he'd finally secured the chairman of the JCS on the wire, Merrick's last shred of hope evaporated.

General Jack informed Merrick that it was too late to recall the Pave Lows. In fact, they had already refueled and dusted off from their desert landing zone. The team was on the ground. The helos were being tracked by satellite at the moment, and were about fifteen minutes away from their point of arrival in Kuwait.

Other measures would have to be taken, the chairman said, and told Merrick to hang in there. The situation on the ground was still salvageable. He'd get back to him. Merrick signed off and telephoned the White House. The chairman's words had not assured him, and the DCI seriously doubted if any part of the mission could be salvaged. Not anymore.

The deserts of the Middle East are not all alike; in fact few deserts are clones of one another, just as few forests are identical. The one thing Middle Eastern deserts do share in common is that they're all arid places without large trees, except for petrified ones. The Dasht-e-Kavir is a case in point.

Unlike its close neighbor, the ar-Rub' al-Khali, or Empty Quarter, of Saudi Arabia a few hundred miles to the west, the north-central desert of Iran is a vast expanse composed of many *sabkahs* or salt flats of alluvially deposited gravel beds, towering rock formations of hard black stone, wadis of varying shapes, sizes, and depths, and some sandy and rocky territory, changing eventually to jagged ranges of low, stickleback mountains that rise up on the distant horizon.

The Dasht is not strictly a sand desert, like the Empty Quarter, the Sahara, or the Sinai farther to the southwest, with sand dunes, barchands, and the other features of the "sea of sand" familiar to anyone who's ever seen a Hollywood epic set in the desert. In winter and early spring, the Dasht can also get extremely cold, with sudden *shamals,* or desert storms, that can rival the oft-capitalized one in severity on a small scale.

As Delta found out on its original mission into Iran in 1980, the topography most characteristic of the Dasht is the Martian crust of sand and gravel that covers most of its flat places. Unlike a true sand desert, which is murder on the tires, suspension, and transmission systems of any wheeled vehicles that have to cross it, the surface crust of the Dasht affords vehicles good traction where the rubber meets the road.

Mitchell had strung out four of the fusion cell's six vehicles in a star formation, with his command vehicle on one starpoint and Arbatov's dune buggy bringing up the rear. The other two FAVs that made the lateral points of the star were spaced out at half klicks from an imaginary centerline running through the lead and rear buggies.

The remaining two vehicles had been sent ahead as scout patrols, leading the main body at a distance of between one and two kilometers and in touch by global-mobile or GloMo communications links. These links incorporated SINCGARS secure radio channels with real-time video transmission and downlinked satellite telemetry, including GPS, all of which could be accessed from portable TRAVLER field units that resembled highly ruggedized laptops, and also from fixed companion units mounted on the FAVs.

The formation was a good way to scope out the area and see oncoming threats before they were right on top of your troops, and it also kept your people from bunching up. Mission data, including a route to the target with multiple waypoints, had been programmed into GPS. The waypoints were spaced approximately ten klicks apart, and when the final one was crossed, the cell would be at the perimeter of the strike zone, which was an imaginary thirty-meter circle drawn around the desert outpost at al-Kabir. It was at this base that Delta's final intel briefing had conclusively pinpointed the missing stealth fighter.

The plan called for the fusion cell to rendezvous at the final waypoint by four hundred forty-five hours, local time, then form up and attack the base in two highly mobile attack formations of three FAVs each, firing Milan antiarmor missiles, fifty-caliber machineguns, and LAW rockets at anything that moved. Once inside, they were to hit the downed Eclipse with more Milan strikes, confirm that the plane was destroyed, and hare out of the burning base before Pasdaran reinforcements had time to arrive.

Before dawn, at around five hundred twenty hours, the returning troopers were to be onboard a Russian Antonov AN-72 all-weather transport aircraft that was tasked with ferrying them out of Iran through the back door—that is, across its eastern border. If the FAVs could not be stowed aboard the Antonovs in time, they were to be left behind at the LZ with five-minute satchel charges tossed in the driver seats.

Mitchell had programmed the dash-mounted GPS on his lead FAV to sound a low-pitched alert tone each time the cell reached its waypoints, at which time he was to make any course corrections necessary and listen in on the secure satcom uplink for any changes in plan. Otherwise the cell was to observe radio silence.

The cell had passed the first GPS waypoint, at Wadi Omar, after under ten minutes of travel, and was midway to the second waypoint at Nay Tabas when the satcom line came to life. Using the keyboard on the dash-mounted comms unit, Mitchell piped the voice transmission through the compact headset he wore while visuals appeared on the TRAVLER unit's color LCD screen. Since the transmissions were accessible over the entire global-mobile communications net, Mitchell knew Arbatov was in on it, too, in the rear FAV. What they both heard was extremely bad news.

It was Colonel Mike back in Kuwait, calling from the Gallant Echo command center. Armbrister was telling them that the mission had been scrubbed. General Yuri Rostovich, the Russian CO for the mission, repeated the orders for Arbatov's benefit. All the general would say was that the intel on the plane's location had turned out wrong, and that the cell was to abort and make for the planned extraction site, where the Russian transport planes would pick them up with an ETA of one hour.

As he spoke to the men out in the Dasht, Armbrister wished he could say more about why the mission had been canked. He also wished he could have gotten word to the team sooner. When CIA Director Merrick had told President Claymore that the Israelis had an agent high up in the Iranian military chain of command who had warned them that the desert base was a trap, he had canceled the mission.

Then Claymore was reminded that he had to act in tandem with the Russian president. It was almost another hour before both leaders reached a mutual decision to pull out the cell, and by that time the Pave Lows had returned to base. The Antonovs, however, were fueled and ready on their Caucasus landing strip, and though not as stealthy as the MH53-Js, they were faster, longer-ranged, and more resistant to bad weather than any helicopter. The planes were also manned by fresh air crews.

Mitchell and Arbatov called a halt and turned the team around. The mission had been scrubbed, they told the troop. All knew they would have to move fast in order to reach the extraction zone by the time the Antonovs came busting in through the back entrance. If the assault had been burned, there could be troops out scouring the desert for them at that moment. Nobody mentioned it, but many in the cell felt like someone had just walked across their graves. Though the feeling was quickly pushed out of mind, it turned out to be prophetic.

• • •

Colonel Ghazbanpour had sent out tripwire patrols as soon as he had received the report from the army outpost located at Khaneh Kvodi garrison, some two hundred kilometers distant. Major Salubesht, the commander of the outpost, was personally known to him, as was the Bedouin band that had warned the major of the presence of American helicopters in the area.

The Bedouin had been on their way to the base, which was one of their regular stops, where they had steady customers for hashish, cigarettes, whiskey, Western porno magazines and videos, and the occasional item of flashy electronics to sell to the bored troops who were stationed on duty there.

Major Salubesht had not told Ghazbanpour about anything except the cigarettes, as he himself was a customer of the other wares sold by the Bedouin. But he did mention to the colonel that he had paid the *mohajer* a reward out of his own pocket amounting to fifty Iranian ehatys. Ghazbanpour assured him that he had done well, and that he would personally reimburse him.

If the report turned out to be accurate, the commander's information would be worth much more than a few ehatys to Ghazbanpour. From the Bedouin's description of the helicopters, he had made a sketch in pencil on the pad in front of him on his desk. After hanging up with the major, Ghazbanpour looked at his drawing.

The sketch looked more like the Pave Low than anything else, and if that were true, it meant that the Americans were inserting their special-forces commandos into his backyard. Which also meant that they had fallen neatly into his waiting hands. It would be too much to expect for the legendary U.S. Delta Force to have been sent in, but the more Ghazbanpour pondered it, the greater the likelihood of this very development became.

Colonel Ghazbanpour lit one of the English Player filter cigarettes he favored, rubbing his hands with glee—what a coup it would be! It would be a second hostage rescue disaster, another embarrassment for a sitting U.S. president. This time there would be no demonstrations outside a captured embassy compound, no mob scenes, no histrionics; the new spirit of détente between the U.S. and Iran would mean that the matter would be handled with far more discretion, indeed, he guessed, in strictest secrecy.

But there would be leaks to the media, and in global political circles, too, and there would be prices that would have to be paid to keep the leaks from widening into common knowledge. Iran would come away the great winner, more powerful than before, while Ghazbanpour would have become the man of the hour, the man who had rubbed the noses of both the Americans and the Russians into the desert stones until they bled.

Ghazbanpour wasted little time in his reverie; he was a doer, not a dreamer. Before his cigarette had half burned to gray ash, he was on the secure line to his troop commanders, ordering out the many patrols. Ghazbanpour didn't have long to wait for results.

The first of the tripwire patrols he had sent into the desert had already reported contact with a formation of fast, military-style commando vehicles moving rapidly in the direction of the Dasht's eastern border.

The patrol had clashed with the formation but was all but wiped out in the flash firefight that ensued. Still, a second, larger contingent of Revolutionary Guard Corps, or Pasdaran, forces had closed with the invaders a few kilometers down their line of advance. They had killed some of these interlopers, forcing the remainder of the foreign commando force to take refuge in the Semnan. This was a region of arid desert broken by low hills and defiles and known for its mineral hot springs and crater-like wadis that marked the flow of underground rivers and streams.

The commando force was presently dug in at one of these naturally fortified areas and under heavy attack by Pasdaran troops. Ghazbanpour knew the region fairly well. He informed his field officers that he would personally oversee the assault, and ordered a helicopter to be ready to shuttle him to the scene of the fighting. Minutes later he was on his way.

Sixteen

Ne Znayu

Petrov's dream was of Vladivostok. Of this he was sure. Yet he couldn't remember another thing about the dream. For a few seconds after jolting awake in the dark, bitterly cold cell, he lay in a semiconscious state, trying to recapture something of the dream vision before he floated back to his bleak reality. It was somehow important that he take something of the dream state back to the waking world with him, though he couldn't say exactly why this should have been.

But after minutes of fishing in the dark lake of his mind, willing himself to recall what he had dreamt, almost nothing would emerge. The only scrap of dreamstuff he could retrieve was incongruous: the sound of a thunderclap or an explosion that had cut short his dream and brought him back to his living hell.

Petrov sat up on the metal slab, set on four poles and bolted to the wall, that served as his bunk. The slab resembled nothing so much as a mortician's gurney, which

Petrov suspected it had once been before being pressed into service in the installation's brig. His first act was to reach for the stinking, louse-infested army blanket that was his sole article of bedding and wrap it around his now gaunt shoulders. The blanket had fallen off when he'd awakened, and he desperately needed the pathetic warmth and meager comfort it would provide.

Not that it could provide much—even the few weeks of starvation rations had weakened him considerably and turned him into an emaciated wretch smelling of sweat, dirt, and urine. In the first hours of his captivity Petrov had demanded better treatment and had been quickly disabused of this approach.

The Iranians had beaten him half-senseless, then spat on the bleeding form they had tossed onto the hard concrete cell floor. One, who could speak a few words of Russian, made it plain to Petrov that he was lucky not to have been lined up against a convenient wall and shot as a spy—in fact, the guard had pointed to a nearby wall outside the cell that was pockmarked with bullet holes and streaked with caked, dried blood, to help make his point.

After a few days of starvation and nights of shivering cold, a new man appeared at his cell door. This one was fluent in Russian. In fact, he spoke with a distinct Moscow accent—and with good reason, Petrov later learned, since the man was a Russian national like himself. The newcomer, whose name was Dikushkin, told Petrov that if he cooperated he would live and receive better rations; ultimately he would be repatriated. If he did not collaborate with the Iranians, then he would be immediately shot without trial as punishment for espionage.

In the beginning Dikushkin stuck to his original cover story of being an Iranian air-force engineer, despite the fact that he was an obvious ringer. What he wanted from Petrov was his assistance in explaining some of the finer points of the MFI-19's advanced stealth and avionics systems. After some show protestation, designed to gain him better treatment, the pilot finally agreed to help. In fact, it was apparent from the first that he really had no other choice. Yet Petrov decided that he would continue giving the Iranians as little aid as possible, and keep an eye out for any opportunity to escape that came his way.

Petrov rubbed his eyes and tried to get his bearings as he drew the filthy, itchy blanket closer against his by now scrawny shoulders, shivering in the cold of the desert night.

Svoboda—freedom. That, he now knew, was the meaning of his dream of home, of Vladivostok; and with that realization something of the dream began filtering back to him. He had been riding on one of the brightly painted tram cars that climb to the Funicular Terminal, and was approaching the hilltop from which one gets one's first view of the bevy of merchant ships riding at anchor in the harbor.

Then there had been—then he had done—what was it? Something wonderful, something . . . he could no longer remember, only that then the dream had ended with a loud and startling noise.

Petrov turned back to his musings. He had been taken from the cell and marched at gunpoint to the large hangar where the multirole fighter was kept under armed guard. It was night, or early morning, just like now, and floodlights lit the interior of the hangar while a contingent of heavily armed Pasdaran soldiers stood their watches. Dikushkin had accompanied Petrov to the cockpit of the plane and immediately began bombarding him with questions.

What was the purpose of this bank of switches? That scope? That readout panel? When putting the plane into a high-g turn, how stable was its angle of attack? Were there any fail-safe devices built into the aircraft to thwart unauthorized tampering, and if so, where were they found and what did they do?

Petrov realized that the Iranians were as much in awe of the aircraft as if a flying saucer had unexpectedly dropped into their laps. They were desperate to learn the secrets of the stealth fighter so they could reverse-engineer the aircraft for their own air force, but they were also totally perplexed by its many technological innovations.

Petrov laughed inwardly. After spending untold millions of dollars since the breakup of the Soviet Union in trying to recruit the best Russian scientists possible, the Iranians still had not gotten themselves a viable brain trust. Or did they know more than they were telling Petrov, trying to confirm what they already guessed?

Whatever the case, the Russian pilot gave them as little assistance and information as possible. *Ne znayu,* I don't know, was his stock reply. The Russian traitor they had used to interrogate him sensed this, though, and there were more beatings. After these, Petrov became somewhat more cooperative, but only as much as traffic would bear. Resisting the bastards was bound up with retaining his last shred of humanity. As long as he could tell himself that he continued to put up a fight, he could stay human. If he capitulated, he might as well slash his wrists, he reckoned.

Then, after nearly two weeks, the pilot sensed a certain urgency about the questions coming from the turncoat, Dikushkin. He was bold enough to ask him why, but Dikushkin's answer was now *ne znayu*. Yet Petrov suspected that something major was in the offing, because among other things the guard detachment protecting the hangar had been doubled, and there were more signs of the base having been put on full alert.

Sirens wailed and searchlights came on at unpredictable hours of the night. Guard dogs barked outside his cell and the engines of mechanized armor coughed and cranked in the shattered desert silence. Although Petrov had been consistently denied any news of home or of current global events, he suspected that a rescue mission had been launched.

Petrov got confirmation of this when he chanced to glimpse a new prisoner being brought into the stockade. A single look told him everything he needed to know.

The prisoner was wearing desert camouflage fatigues of the elite commando forces, Vasaltniki or Spetsnaz from the looks of him. That, and the fact that he himself was still a prisoner, told Petrov that while a rescue mission had been mounted, it had either failed or had been aborted.

The following day his guards boasted of this very thing to him. They laughed and told Petrov that the Russians had been slaughtered like flies as they tried to escape the wrath of Allah's ordained fighters. Only one of his countrymen had survived, and they had him now, too. The Iranians celebrated this event by giving Petrov extra food and cigarettes.

Then had come a small glimmer of hope. When the stench of his cell had become a problem for his guards, Petrov was removed from it long enough for the narrow cubicle to be hosed down. Standing a few feet away, near the door of the adjoining cell of the stockade, was the commando whom Petrov had seen brought in a few days before. A glance told him the man had been injured but not properly treated.

His face bore the signs of a badly healed scar, covered by a dirty bandage. The lone guard in attendance cautioned them not to speak, but for a few moments his attention was diverted by the appearance of an officer who began dressing him down in Farsi. The soldier took the chewing-out like a docile cur, and paid Petrov no attention.

Petrov knew it was to risk a beating, which, in his severely weakened state, might very well kill him, but he was determined to speak to the other man. Though he had no way of knowing it, the captured soldier was Lieutenant Trapezhnikov, second in command of the Vasaltniki team led by Nemekov, and lone survivor of the engagements that had destroyed it.

Petrov sensed the wounded soldier had the same idea as he. When the soldier collapsed in a heap, and suddenly began thrashing as if suffering a seizure, Petrov got ready to act. The officer looked their way, shouted something at the guard, and the guard ran down the corridor to the phone, leaving them momentarily unattended. The officer then followed the soldier and did not return. As Petrov suspected, the Vasaltnik had only put on an act.

"Who are you?" he asked. Petrov told him. "Trapezhnikov," the injured man said back. "I was part of a rescue attempt. All the others were killed. The plane is here?"

"Yes, I have seen it," Petrov said.

"Then it is imperative that we at least attempt to destroy it."

"I agree," replied Petrov.

"Listen," Trapezhnikov went on. "I'll keep my eyes open. If there's a chance to stage an escape, I'll get word to you somehow."

"I shall do the same," Petrov agreed.

"Could you fly the plane out of here if the opportunity presented itself?" Trapezhnikov next asked.

Petrov had long ago thought this over.

"Not unless the plane were fueled and onboard electrical systems powered up, and even then I would need appropriate gear, at least a flight helmet, for comms if nothing else. Still, it would be a closely done thing."

"But you might try given those conditions?"

"Yes," Petrov answered without hesitation. "It's better than rotting in this hell, even though the chances are slim, to say the least. As for the first two points, the electrical systems and the fuel, I believe they may be workable. But I've seen the plane when they brought me for questioning, and the flight gear is nowhere in evidence."

"How much did you tell them?" Trapezhnikov's eyes became gimlets.

"That's my affair," Petrov replied.

The brief conversation ended with the shout of the original Iranian guard, now accompanied by another two new latchkeys and the base medic, who were rushing down the corridor toward the stricken man. Petrov feared that he'd be dragged off and beaten to death for his brazenness, but all he got was a rude shove out of the way as the other men rushed toward the Vasaltnik.

Later Petrov was asked about what he'd been doing near the other prisoner, but his reply that he'd only been attending to an unwell fellow soldier was accepted. Either the Iranians believed him or they didn't care; Petrov assumed the latter.

Now, in the dark confines of his cell just before dawn, Petrov suddenly noticed something new. He had lived in this hell-stricken place so long that every contour of its broken concrete floor and filthy cinderblock walls, even in pitch darkness, was etched in his memory.

Yet something was wrong, he now saw, something was different than usual. But what? What was out of place? In time he perceived that it was a tiny anomaly in the darkness. A section of deeper darkness, like a scab on a body, that should not be there. Slowly, his malnourished body's joints creaking, Petrov heaved himself off the mortician's gurney and warily crossed the cell to the point near the heavy iron door.

There, on the concrete, he saw it, and at first didn't believe it was actually there. But moments of staring down at it convinced him that it was no hallucination. And then, when Petrov had stooped and picked up the key, he knew at least that it was solid, and that it was in fact solid and real.

His heart began to race—there was something else he hadn't noticed about the cell until just now—up close he could detect the absence of a few centimeters of darkness between the iron jamb and the heavy door that meant the bolt was not latched.

What had he to lose, anyway? Only his life, and that was slowly being stolen from him anyway.

Petrov reached forward and gingerly tried the handle of the door. He was only half surprised to see it swing open and the light from the deserted corridor spill into his cell like milk from a ladle. Then, as Petrov stepped hesitantly out into the corridor, he suddenly remembered.

He had dreamed of flying.

Yes, he thought. *That's it.*

Flying!

It was a spot of desolation amid a world of desolation. The desert barrens stretched away on every side, boundless and disorienting. But for the fusion cell, hunkered down like jib rats in the sand, it was a city of refuge. The hide wasn't marked on any of the military maps the team had brought with it, maps supposedly produced from the latest satellite photosurveillance updates. But it was there just the same.

From the looks of the place, it was literally as old as the hills off in the distance—the ruins of a desert fort dating back to the late nineteenth century, the days of what the British called their "Great Game" with the czarist Russian empire for control of the Transcaucasian landmass, a contest of weapons and will that eventually extended from the Khyber Pass in Afghanistan down into the Arabian Peninsula.

One of the scout patrols Mitchell had sent out the previous night had picked the place up on a thermal imaging scan of the terrain through a binocular scope that could be quick-mounted on any of the tubular bars of the FAV's superstructure. The TI scope contained some processor circuitry that also gave estimated range and enhanced the image. The desert floor radiated the solar heat it had accumulated throughout the day back up into the air at its own unique rate. Other objects with their own unique thermal coefficients did the same.

Stone, mud brick, metal, wood, what-have-you, all radiated at different rates. The structure in the distance showed up white against the dull gray of the cooler, less radiant sands. It looked like some kind of run-down adobe building, made of stone, mud brick, and wood beams, part of which had fallen down, with various other smaller and equally dilapidated outbuildings surrounding it. It turned out, under closer inspection, to be a small caravansary—the tactical maps showed two in the region, but none in the general vicinity of the fusion cell. Yet there it was.

Caravansaries dot the deserts of the Middle East, and while they evoke images of camel trains laden with spices and silks, they are the desert equivalent of the lodges found in the world's mountainous regions, from the Alps to the Rockies—places of refuge for wanderers in desolate regions, whoever they may be.

The Mideast's larger and better known caravansaries straddle ancient trading corridors that are well traveled to the present day, and over time many have become small towns and trading posts rather than isolated rest areas. This unknown place wasn't one of these; it lay in the remote desert off the beaten path and was little more than a pile of weather-beaten ruins.

Using secure commo, the patrol had radioed back to the wadi where the main element of the team had set up a hide site. Mitchell and Arbatov checked their maps and decided the caravansary was a better place to hole up than where they were at present. After the firefight, this part of the Dasht was crawling with Iranian patrols, and it was only a matter of time before the game of high-tech hide-go-seek the cell was playing with their hunters ended in capture or annihilation of the force.

The fusion cell was moving cautiously by night, using thermal and low-light imaging, as well as a number of other special technical aids, with which to navigate and avoid detection. These would keep them out of harm's way for an estimated twenty-four to thirty-six hours, but after this, their odds of evading their pursuers diminished steadily down to a flat, bleak zero. The cell either had to extract by then or face the inevitable consequences.

Now, as dawn began to paint the sand, stones, and rock with a wash of yellows, golds, and crimsons, it was satcom time again, the magic moment when Mitchell and Arbatov prepared to give another of their scheduled situation reports to the Gallant Echo command post in Kuwait, which would be satlinked to JSOC operational headquarters at Pope AFB, adjacent to Bragg.

The satcom uplink was a secure, encrypted circuit relayed over military communications satellites using global-mobile protocols. The GloMo links were high bandwidth; the links carried any kind of data, fax, multimedia, not just voice alone. GloMo hardware was a far cry from the walkie-talkies and PRCs used in Korea and 'Nam. The hardware took the form of TRAVLER's shock-resistant laptop unit, equipped with a variety of peripherals including color camera and wireless mikes, and other gear, including SINCGARS frequency-hopping radio units, hard-copy printers, and additional monitors and portable transceivers resembling ruggedized cell phones. Everything was modular and interoperable.

One of the advantages of the TRAVLER portables was their multimedia capability. Mitchell's troop could upload and download more types of data than ever before, including real-time video and still photo imagery from overhead surveillance assets, like the LaCrosse and Keyhole satellites the Pentagon had jockeyed out of their normal orbits to keep an eye on the proceedings below in the Dasht. It was the real-time imagery that Mitchell's crew had been able to view on their TRAVLER screens that had been key to keeping them out of the hands of the Pasdaran search teams combing the desert for them.

Using TRAVLER, they could look down and see their situation from one hundred miles up in geosynchronous orbit, a God's-eye view that showed them precisely where the opposition was searching and—in some ways more important—where it was not. To the Iranians, it was as if the fusion cell had uncorked a djinn from a bottle and cloaked itself in a shield of invisibility. But it was simply that the troopers had eyes that could see in ways the opposition could not. By comparison, the Pasdaran were blindfolded and groping about in the dark.

When the satcom link was operational, Mitchell and Arbatov faced their commanding officers back at the distant command post via two-way teleconferencing. An extraction plan was being put into effect, they were told. But they were ordered to remain in place until given further orders. The political winds had shifted somewhat and new orders were being cut. If there was any possible way to destroy Shadow One, the cell would be ordered to make the attempt, regardless of the risk factor involved.

But the stranded troops might get some extra help in performing this feat, and this was now being worked on.

At the moment new surveillance and tactical assets were the subject of high-level discussions in Washington and elsewhere. The cell was to stand by for further instructions regarding this development. Colonel Mike signed off, and Mitchell shut down the link and put TRAVLER into sleep mode. Next scheduled transmission was in two hours, and he wanted to grab some sack time if he could.

Seventeen
Last-Extremity Solutions

In Washington it was somewhat past three in the afternoon. In the eighteen-by-twelve foot White House Situation Room, which is buried deep beneath the executive mansion, a tense and often acrimonious debate concerning what the cell had just been told was now taking place.

President Travis Claymore was flanked at the large oval table by National Security Advisor Throckmorton, and his secretary of defense, Robert Gooch. The contingent from the Pentagon included the chairman of the JCS, General Jack Thibodeaux, with aides occupying chairs at the rear of the cramped room, ready to wade in with documents and charts when and if their bosses deemed it necessary.

The conclave of mandarins also included two representatives from Israel—the ambassador to the U.S., Shimon Halevi, and Yigael Bar-Zion, of AMAN. Neither wanted to be where he was at the moment, since their inclusion was the result of a last-minute phone call from their Prime Minister Simchoni to President Claymore.

The call had provoked Claymore into one of what the White House staff called his "LBJ blue-streak cussing" attacks after signing off. The president did not like surprises, especially the unpleasant kind, and he found the warnings of moles, cowboy operations, and burned cover distinctly unpleasant.

After some preliminary paper shuffling, the president got the meeting under way and heard situation reports from various staffers. It was now the JCS chairman's turn at bat.

"General Jack," the president began, having dubbed Thibodeaux this to avoid tripping over his last name, which Claymore could not pronounce without a stammer, "we were talking about contingency plans to get this supreme stew of bullshit over with. What have you got for us today?"

"Well, sir, we at JCS have been working to develop a number of options and have prepared three packages for review." The chairman half turned in his seat and gestured to one of his aides, who jumped up and brought over the charts and a stand.

"Package one is what we call the 'Breakfast Special' option. Basically, it calls for tactical strikes using sea-launched cruise missiles from our carrier battlegroup in the Strait of Oman. Once we know the location of the plane, we could pursue this course of action."

"I don't like it," the president avowed. "Too many risks in there. What's package two?"

The chairman motioned at his aide again and a page of the chart was flipped as he explained another option. The president heard out the chairman, but shook his head as he listened. After the chairman had finished his presentation, the president said, "You left something out. How the hell are we gonna know where that plane's at? We don't have any confirmation yet, now do we?"

"No, sir," the chairman admitted. "But we're pursuing various options."

"My information is that you're about as close as a blind

man in a coal hopper to finding his asshole and that the satellites aren't worth a shit, is that right?"

"Well, essentially that's the case," the chairman was forced to concur. "Satellite imaging has its inherent limitations. Normally we would want to rely on surveillance assets that could fly in for a closer look, such as TR-1—"

"That's the spy plane, Mr. President," said Claymore's national security advisor, breaking in.

"Right, that's the spy plane," continued the chairman, "and we'd want to use that type of high-altitude aerial reconnaissance asset in a tactical situation like this, which is what I suggest that we do."

"No can, General Jack," the president told the chairman. "No more pilots getting shot down in Iran this go-round. Had enough of that horse manure over Kosovo. And hell, it's practically raining bodies on the goddamn Iranians by now. What else you got up your sleeve?"

"Well, there is another option, an asset called Tier III—"

"That's a robot surveillance aircraft, Mr. President," said the national security advisor to Claymore, who had glanced his way again for clarification. "But it's supposed to still be under development."

"General, I hear the Tier III's still supposed to be under development," the president said to the chairman without missing a beat.

"Yes, well, technically that's right, sir," Thibodeaux said right back. "Actually, we are at the stage where Global Hawk's roll out is imminent and we at the Pentagon think we can reliably use this UAV, or unmanned aerial vehicle as a solution in the present scenario."

"Global Hawk is what they call Tier III, Mr. President," the national security advisor told his boss, who squinted with annoyance.

The chairman of Joint Chiefs went on to describe the various selling points of using Tier III, such as the fact that it was an unmanned vehicle with a ten-thousand-mile end-to-end range which could fly from the U.S. to Iran transmitting real-time data at any point.

He also pointed out that with its classified cruising altitude—he refrained from stating it was better than ninety-two thousand feet because of the mixed company—it flew too high to be hit by SAMs or even high-performance fighter planes, but that in the unlikely event it ever crashed, there were numerous self-destruct options that would make its falling intact into enemy hands highly unlikely.

The president said he'd consider that while the next speakers had the floor.

"Gentlemen, I believe most of you know Ambassador Shimon Halevi," said the president. "Shimon, please tell us what you've come here at your prime minister's urging to say. And by the way, Shimon, please thank his lovely wife personally for that delicious homemade layer cake she sent over. The first lady and I served it when President Mubarak was at the White House recently and he raved about it."

"Thank you, Mr. President," Halevi began. "I will personally convey your thanks to the prime minister. Now"—he glanced at the briefing papers in front of him on the table, having permanently forgotten about the cake—"as you but nobody else in this room is aware, there are some aspects to the situation that bear on what has just been discussed."

He proceeded to tell the NSC about the cell of highly trained Israeli commandos that was now operational in the Iranian Dasht-e-Kavir, but that they were working for Assaf Gilad, who was staging what was basically a one-man operation. At the cussing that followed this revelation, Halevi tried to blunt some of the rancor by making comparisons with Oliver North's White House basement operation during the Reagan presidency, which in foreign policy terms was practically a shadow White House, but these didn't go over well.

Still, he'd made his point. Nobody's skirts were clean. America had had its Nixon-era Plumbers and its Colonel North and Israel had its Assaf Gilad. As different as they were in other outward aspects, both men were cut from the same cloth.

This point having been made, Halevi dropped his next and even more devastating bombshell. The Israelis had an agent in place, a HUMINT or human intelligence asset who was close to the action on the ground in Iran and in a position to contribute high-level intelligence on the location of the aircraft and perhaps even assist with an extraction plan for the fusion cell on the ground.

There was more cussing and commotion after this news, and the chairman of Joint Chiefs asked why the Israelis hadn't told anybody about this until just now. Halevi brought up the Eilts Affair, which took place during the Carter era. This involved the last-minute exposure of an American intelligence agent in Libya in order to protect then U.S. Ambassador Herman Eilts from a Qaddafi-sanctioned assassination plot, burning the covert U.S. agent in the process.

Halevi, who also hinted that there were other, more secret examples he could also cite, had again made his point, and he'd done his homework.

Now it was the president's turn.

"General Jack," he told the JCS chairman, "you go ahead and use that bird of yours—"

"Global Hawk, Mr. President," said the national security advisor.

"Global Hawk, right," said Travis Claymore. "You get that Hawk in gear, General, until we know more about the location of that sumbitchin' Russian plane. This meeting's adjourned, gentlemen. Same time, same place tomorrow, unless some more shit hits the fan, and we'll see what happens."

President Travis Claymore rose and straightened his jacket, and left the Situation Room. Attended by his entourage, he strode in his trademark cowboy boots toward the private elevator that would whisk him several stories to the White House above where he had a taped address to make to the nation, defending himself against a fresh round of charges by the opposition party.

By now, President Claymore had already forgotten the events in the Mideast and his mind was focusing on concerns of a more personal nature, involving a financial killing he'd made in pork-belly futures trades, some of which had wound up in the coffers of his recent campaign's slush fund, though he suspected that all that was going to change in a very short time. San Antonio's favorite son knew the lumber was about ready to hit the spinning buzzsaw blade, and when it did, Katy, bar the door . . . —Iranian nukes would blow pork bellies clean off the media's anti-Claymore playlist. Maybe for good.

Petrov felt alive for the first time in weeks. Every nerve tingled with heightened awareness—awareness of risk, of danger, but also of the tantalizing promise of *svoboda.* The pilot's hope was far more than a state of mind. It was something tangible, as real as the sharp scent of moisture on the wind that heralded the approach of a cleansing rain.

The fatigue, hunger, and despair of his imprisonment faded away as Petrov stole down the deserted cellblock corridor as quietly as possible, praying one of the Iranian turnkeys from the checkpoint around the corridor's L-shaped bend would not choose this moment to begin his late-night rounds. These were seldom predictable, he had found, from many nights of listening and watching.

But no one came to challenge his escape. Not so far, anyway. His pulse racing, he passed one, then two, then three steel cell doors. Outside the fourth door in the queue, he drew up and gave two short raps with his knuckles.

It opened in a flash and a strong hand pulled him quickly inside, into pitch darkness.

"Shhh," he heard a gruff voice in his ear.

Petrov nodded. The warning hadn't been necessary. He had no intention of crying out. Why should he?

The hand released his arm and the commando gestured toward the bunk at the far end of the cell. Petrov sat beside him in the dark.

"You, too, have been freed, I see," he said.

"Yes, it seems we have a friend on the inside."

"Or an enemy who is manipulating us for purposes of his own," the Vasaltnik added.

"You want to stay and rot here, then be my guest," Petrov angrily replied in a loud whisper. "For myself, I have other plans."

He held up the key he'd found on the floor of his prison cell and showed it to the soldier in the semidarkness. "I've seen the storeroom where my flight gear is stored. I'm betting my life that this key fits its lock."

"It's not digital?"

"You're joking, aren't you?" Petrov shot back, having grown tired of the man's posturing. "Here camel dung is used for cologne and you think they have cipher locks?"

"What are the chances?" the commando asked, still unperturbed.

"Maybe thirty percent," Petrov answered. "You want better?"

"Yes, I do," he answered, nodding. "Though I suspect we will have to live with thirty percent odds."

"Or die."

"Yes," the Vasaltnik said.

"By the way, Trapezhnikov, what is your first name?"

"Call me Aksel," the Vasaltnik told Petrov.

"I am called—"

"I already know," said Aksel. "Let's get started."

The two men soon were moving stealthily toward the door of the darkened cell.

Minutes later they had acquired the olive-drab uniforms of two Iranian regulars who had been subdued by Aksel. The first soldier had been the unluckier of the two. Aksel had been forced to take him down without benefit of a weapon, which meant he had to hit him, and hard—sleeper holds and arcane kung fu pressure points are as much the stuff of fiction as related techniques from the planet Vulcan, unless, of course, you prefer running the risk of having to hit your opponent a second time as he comes back at you, mad as a hornet.

A roundhouse right with plenty of steam behind it to the solar plexus, or a swift kick in the groin with a steel-toed combat boot, followed up quickly with a forearm or elbow smash across the bridge of the nose is the best prescription for sending an opponent to dreamland in a hurry—providing, of course, that the element of surprise lies in your favor.

In the case of the hapless Iranian soldier, who'd been grabbed as he passed Aksel's cell a few moments after he and the pilot concluded their escape plan, this was certainly the case. Before the guard could pass the cell door, it was flung open, two powerful hands caught him by the tunic, and he was hauled inside into darkness, where he was soon put to sleep by the generous application of pummeling fists to the appropriate soft spots.

After Aksel had changed into the guard's uniform, which was fortunately loose enough to fit his somewhat larger frame, he left the cell in search of a surrogate for the pilot. He found the second soldier having a smoke against the side of the tunnel wall that was part of the base's underground bunker system. This soldier, too, paid the price for relaxing his vigilance while on watch.

Aksel used two of the phrases he recalled from his premission refresher courses in conversational Farsi. He, like many an Afghanistan veteran, had become fluent in Farsi, which was a lingua franca during the days of Soviet involvement there, and also in Dari, Farsi's Afghan dialect.

The first phrase was *ta kan na khor,* meaning "don't move," which was used in tandem with the application of the muzzle of his commandeered AKS-74 autorifle against his captive's chest as he stripped him of sidearm and rifle. The other was *man koja hastam,* which meant "walk this way," and preceded the guard's being frog-marched down the brig's tunnel toward the cell where the other guard was now bound tightly with strips of the lice-infested blanket that Petrov had cut into thongs with the bayonet of the captured rifle.

With a change of clothes and the other guard now joining his comrade on the filthy floor of the murky cell, Petrov and Aksel made their way toward the storage room on the installation's ground level. The key fit the lock as Petrov had predicted, and the pilot's flight gear was soon retrieved with Aksel's help.

They also found some spare ammo clips and a case of antipersonnel grenades, which they stuffed into a musette bag along with the spare AKS taken from the second downed guard. Perhaps more important, they found food, in the form of canned rations. They scarfed down what they could and carried as much of the rest as they could cram into their pockets. Almost instantly they felt new energy flowing through their bloodstreams and into their starved cells.

Minutes later Aksel was marching Petrov at rifle point toward the hangar where the stealth plane was being fueled.

"This one is wanted by the eggheads again," Aksel said in Farsi to the Iranian guards stationed outside the cellblock.

"What happened to Hossein?" asked the head latchkey, a lieutenant seated at a desk.

"His syphilis is acting up again. He's off vomiting somewhere."

"His what? You say he has syphilis?" The guard stopped chewing his kebab and rice balls in midsentence.

"Yes, didn't you know? Hossein has had it for years. It acts up every now and then. Don't worry, he'll be back as good as new as soon as he's finished puking out his guts. It's the mercury they give him for it. Fucks up the whole system. Gives him fierce spasms sometimes."

The guard eyed Aksel, openly skeptical. The look on his face said, Is this man joking? But there was not even a hint of a smile. The Vasaltnik's face was completely deadpan. Here was a man who was as serious as an imam at the muezzin's evening chant. But this story he was telling . . .

"What is your name, Sergeant?"

"Nateghi, sir."

"Papers, please, Nateghi."

His hand was already reaching across the desk.

"I have no papers. You see, I don't need papers with my brother on the People's Islamic Revolutionary Council, close to the ear of the *faqi* himself." Aksel leaned in close and glared at the seated man. "Maybe you want to speak to him concerning my papers, eh, Lieutenant?" Trapezhnikov picked up the phone and offered the handset to the seated man. "Go ahead. Call my brother and ask him about my papers. He'll tell you all you want to know."

The guard stared at Aksel's deadpan face and then at the receiver in his outstretched hand. Tense moments passed. Finally, the guard took the handset from Aksel and gently placed it back in its cradle.

"That won't be necessary, Sergeant. You may proceed. Of what concern is this prisoner to me, anyway? Take him away, Nateghi."

The head guard waved them through the checkpoint dismissively. They walked toward the door set in the cinderblock wall at the corridor's end. Aksel reached to pull it open, when the lieutenant at the desk shouted for them to stop.

"Just a moment, Nateghi," he called out.

Aksel turned, his finger tightening on the trigger of the rifle in his hands. His heart pounded, but neither his eyes nor his expression betrayed his wariness.

"Yes," he said evenly. "What is it?"

The head guard stood up and slowly walked toward them. He stood abreast of Trapezhnikov and stared hard into his eyes.

"Your brother, Nateghi," he said. "He is a big shot in Tehran, you say?"

Though tensed for action, the Vasaltnik remained outwardly calm. He dared not look at the pilot, but prayed that Petrov would not betray them with a show of panic. Trapezhnikov kept his eyes on the Iranian's as he answered.

"One of the biggest shots," he told the guard.

The sergeant nodded and gestured at one of the armed soldiers stationed nearby. The Pasdaran walked over. Trapezhnikov could almost hear Petrov's heart thud in his chest. He tensed his muscles for action and got ready to take both men down with a burst of autofire.

"Private Razouk here has a wife in Tehran," the sergeant said. "She's with child, but our commander won't give him maternity leave. Think you might have a word with your brother about this for a brother in the ranks? Maybe he can pull some strings?"

Trapezhnikov instantly relaxed, though the lieutenant didn't know it.

"You can be sure that I will," he answered with feigned outrage. "You have my promise, Razouk, that matters will be fixed. I'll let you know by tomorrow."

"Good man, Nateghi," the lieutenant said, and gestured for Private Razouk to return to his post. "I'll not forget this."

"My pleasure," Traphezhnikov said. "Anything for a *baradar*—a brother in arms."

They mounted a flight of concrete stairs behind the door without incident as the head latchkey returned to his desk and his dinner. So Hossein had this disease? the lieutenant thought as he began to knead the moist rice in the bowl before him into a tight ball. Well, that was certainly news. He put the rice ball into his mouth, followed it with a piece of kebab, and resumed reading the newspaper on which the bowl sat while he chewed his meal.

"You damned fool! What was the meaning of that stunt? You could have gotten us killed!" Petrov took the opportunity to whisper to the commando, whose expression remained as flat and unperturbed as ever. "Had that guard seen even the smallest trace of a smile, and had luck not been on our side this once, it would have been all over!"

"I *was* smiling," Aksel said, his expression grim. "But

on the inside. And our luck held, didn't it? Now shut up and don't play Jesus with me—your halo's covered with shit. Do what I say if you want to fly your precious black plane out of here."

Eighteen

The Hammer and the Anvil

They emerged from the passageway and found themselves standing in a corner of the hangar. Suddenly the two escapees caught a good look at Shadow One. It was only a few hundred meters away, though as Petrov had found before, it was the center of attention for numerous military and technical personnel.

Petrov noted mentally that the Eclipse looked ready for takeoff. It was connected to an auxiliary power supply unit and its cockpit canopy was canted up and back from the fuselage, as if the plane awaited a pilot. Were the Iranians planning a test flight in the dead of night? Possible, very possible, he decided. Now he also realized the hangar door was open. It had never been so before when he had been summoned to the plane.

Then, without a chance to turn his face aside, Petrov spotted the turncoat Dikushkin across the hangar, seated at a worktable. The engineer had been crouched over a sheaf of printouts, talking to two other men in Pasdaran khakis and red berets. The table was piled with waveform generators, oscilloscopes, high-speed raster printers, and other electronic gear. Dikushkin did a double-take and stared at the newcomers for a shocked, lingering moment.

"Quickly—the traitorous bastard's seen us!" Petrov stage-whispered to Aksel out of the corner of his mouth, while Aksel slipped him the second AKS he'd kept hidden in a large musette bag. The bullpup autorifle was cocked and locked, and a 5.45-mm blunt-nosed round was already cranked into the firing chamber, its safety catch set to automatic burstfire.

A second or two passed, and then Dikushkin unfroze. Jumping to his feet and dropping his papers, he hailed the nearest soldiers in his vicinity. Petrov and Aksel couldn't hear what he was blustering at them, but Dikushkin was gesticulating wildly, pointing their way, and shouting toward the khaki-clad Iranians who'd run up to him. The soldiers immediately rushed the duo. Other troops dropped down and aimed their rifles.

"Go!" shouted Aksel. "Don't stop for anything!"

He whipped the bullpup Kalashnikov to navel height and squeezed off a multiround burst. Flame erupted from the lateral vents in the weapon's muzzle brake as he wrenched the barrel to and fro. Bullets sprayed the running Pasdaran before the soldiers could return fire. The wounded Iranians staggered and hit the concrete bleeding, but the troops who had already taken cover had begun to shoot. The hangar had come alive with crisscrossing steel.

Petrov reached the stealth unharmed. But as he grabbed for the railing of the access platform whose steps ascended to the cockpit, he heard the whine and spang of ricocheting bullets. Pivoting reflexively, he fired back from a half crouch, his index finger tightening on the trigger before he even thought to sight the weapon.

Answering with a panic burst had saved his life. His bullets tore into the midsection of an Iranian army major who'd been leveling a mean-looking, long-barreled Magnum at the back of Petrov's head. Petrov had beaten death by a trigger squeeze and a split second. Now it was the major who struggled to push his digestive organs back into his abdomen. As Petrov looked on, his knees buckled and he collapsed in a heap, his intestines uncoiling in a bath of blood.

Petrov whirled and remounted the steps of the platform. Now level with the stealth fighter's cockpit, he turned to see Aksel hurl two canister-type antipersonnel grenades. The grenades exploded as airbursts, raining shrapnel down on everything within a thirty-foot splinter radius. Aksel reloaded his AKS with a second banana clip, then cut loose with a sustained burst of autofire as a trio of soldiers tried to rush him, forcing them to hit the deck. In the momentary lull that followed, Aksel turned toward the plane.

"Cover me!" he shouted to the pilot.

Petrov propped the muzzle of the AKS on the iron bars that surrounded the platform. He dropped to a crouch, the most natural firing position, and got off a long, steady burst.

Too many bullets, Petrov thought as Aksel ran for the aircraft. They had taught him in the survival course always to fire many short bursts instead of a few long ones, but his fear had made him forget his training.

He wondered how many bullets were left in the magazine. Petrov had forgotten the number this weapon's clip could hold. *Is it thirty? Forty? Fifty, perhaps?* But what did it matter now?

Petrov continued to fire, but went to shorter bursts to conserve ammo as Aksel closed the distance to the plane, bullets sniping close at his heels as he sprinted a broken-field run.

"Inside!" the Vasaltnik shouted, taking the platform's metal steps double time. "I'll cover you." He reached out his free left hand. "The weapon," he demanded. Petrov's AKS was soon in Aksel's practiced grip.

Aksel turned and fired sweeping, side-to-side bursts of autofire from the twin Kalishnikovs while Petrov hustled into the stealth's cockpit. Quickly plugging into Shadow One's oxygen supply and comms, he fired up the engines and energized the avionics, relieved that both were functional. He then turned to Aksel and gestured for him to get into the plane. There was enough room between the pilot's seat and the bulkhead, if Aksel was prepared for a very bumpy ride. If necessary, he could breathe from the backup oxygen supply. The Vasaltnik shook his head.

"Get going!" he shouted. "That's an order!"

Petrov was about to shout back in protest when a three-round burst struck Aksel in the side. Part of his rib cage dissolved in an aerosol of blood and bone that spattered the black flank of the aircraft's hull, christening it with martyr's blood. Though he was dying, Aksel found the strength to throw two more grenades and continue cranking out steel, thereby slowing the determined advance of the Iranian force that was pressing in on the plane.

"Go, Vassily," he shouted. "Dammit—go now!"

Petrov couldn't bear the sight of the stricken man who was expiring before his eyes. Filled with emotions he could not name, the stealth driver turned his head and tugged back on the throttle, feeling the black plane's engines roar to brute wakefulness. A moment later he saw Aksel shudder as more bullets riddled his body, the two weapons he'd clutched clattering to the concrete a moment before his corpse hit the bloodstained concrete.

Now! Petrov screamed inwardly. *Go now!* A paralyzing fear had overcome him. Yet he had to summon the nerve. *Now!* the inner voice continued to demand. *It will work!*

Yet Petrov knew it would be futile in the end. There was surely no time to get the plane airborne before they cut him down. Even so, at least Shadow One would be destroyed in the process. The Iranians would still lose. Then Petrov realized that they weren't shooting any longer and risked a look out the cockpit canopy window.

He saw an Iranian officer with arms in the air, ordering the troops to break fire. They clearly weren't prepared to risk hitting the valuable plane. At the same time red hazard lights flashed and sirens klaxoned. The hangar's steel plate door had begun to slide closed again. It was now or never, the pilot realized. In minutes he might as well open the canopy and give himself up.

Petrov advanced the throttle to its middle power stop and the twin turbojet engines roared more loudly than before. The jet leapt forward with a savage lurch, pulling away from its access platform and sending tables supporting diagnostic equipment crashing to the hangar's concrete floor. Like a once captive bird of prey, Shadow One shrugged off its fetters and bolted for the freedom of the night, which was its natural element, screaming out its yearning for the sky.

Petrov's total attention was focused on the moving hangar door that loomed up ahead of the plane, slowly shearing off the night beyond. It wasn't that far from the nose of the aircraft—less than thirty meters if he estimated correctly—but the gap was quickly shrinking. He knew he had only a matter of seconds to reach it before it had rolled shut to a point where he would be caught like a moth in a sparrow's beak. Even the most minor damage to the fuselage could abort his flight, and if the hangar door closed too far before he reached the entrance, it would be the same as striking a steel wall at high speed.

Yet he was committed now.

Live or die, there was no turning back.

Petrov advanced the throttle forward again. Centrifugal forces slammed him back in his molded seat. Twin plumes of burning cxhaust gases seethed from the plane's thundering turbofans, setting men and equipment afire. As the black arrowhead streaked toward the hangar door, two-legged torches did a flailing, screaming dance in its wake, like human sacrifices set afire to appease some ancient god of death.

Petrov saw the edge of the armored guillotine rushing toward the fragile glass bubble of the cockpit, coming so close it almost scraped the thin transparent skin. And then he had crossed the threshold between light and darkness, then he was hurtling across the flat pancake of the desert sands, gaining velocity and greater lift with each elapsed second and already feeling the landing gear begin to elevate off the ground as the black spearpoint he rode shot through the air at fantastic speed.

But now, above the roar of the turbofans, Petrov could also hear the staccato chattering of automatic weapons fire. The sound was like a choir from purgatory, mixed with high voices and low, the alto voices belonging to scores of carbine rifles and light machine guns hurling glowing red-and-green tracers at the hurtling plane, the basso-profundo voices belonging to the heavy, vehicle-mounted machine guns loaded with armor-piercing slugs that sought his range.

Personnel carriers, Jeeps, trucks—anything and everything that rolled and could carry troops and weapons—sped toward the plane from the four corners of the airstrip. Shadowy man-figures behind the big guns triggered off a vortex of steel at the escaping prisoner and the coveted prize he was about to snatch from their grasp. Petrov saw they meant to stop him on the ground if they could, and were throwing everything at him but the kitchen sink in order to do it.

Pulling out all the stops, Petrov shoved the throttle forward to the hilt, applying full military power, and yanked back on the stick, feeling the plane gain immediate lift and its belly turn at a sharp angle toward the sky.

Built for stealth and not speed, the MFI did not have the thrust-to-weight ratio of a MiG-29 or an F-16—its engines weren't powerful enough for Petrov to stand the plane on its tail and shoot into an almost vertical ascent trajectory, and its wafered airframe was far too fragile for any kind of hotdog stunt like that.

But Petrov pushed the stealth's airframe to its design limits, feeling its bulkheads, control panels, and the stick in his hands shudder and buck like the whole plane was about to come apart around him. His mind was intent on gaining as much altitude in the shortest possible time, on putting the earth and the death and madness that infested it like crawling lice as far below him as possible, on escaping the hellhole in which he'd rotted and stunk and suffered for end-to-end weeks.

The moments passed as the numbers ascended on his digital altimeter gauge and his rate of climb increased. Soon all indications of firing had stopped, and even the yellow puffballs of Triple-A the Iranians were sending up were many meters below his ceiling. He was alone with the sound of the stealth's engines now, and he knew he was out of range of anything they could throw at him from the ground except their longest-range SAMs.

Petrov leveled off at sixty thousand feet, near the top of his envelope. The aircraft was stable now, and the stick no longer bucked in his gloved fist. Below, night mantled the earth and he was all but invisible to radars, including those of the Russian-built SA-10s with which the Iranians would even now be trying to pinpoint the runaway plane.

The Iranians would be scrambling their fighters, too, and these would also pose a significant threat, because although they couldn't see him, the planes could concentrate in the approximate area of his flight path and have a better chance of making visual contact, from which point they could effectively attack.

Petrov plotted an evasive course vector that would bring him within range of the northeastern border while he scrolled through the satcom frequencies. The Iranians, who had forced him to give them the encryption keys to the frequencies during his captivity, would be listening on all channels, but that couldn't be helped. He'd have to get off a message, or even if he made it across the border, there would be no refueling aircraft waiting for him and his tanks would run dry.

Someone would be listening. Someone *had* to be listening. If they were not . . . he pushed the thought from his mind and continued to transmit. But as his pleas for acknowledgment went unanswered, even this hope began to fade. He had less than a half hour of fuel reserves, according to his readouts, and after that, he would drop to earth like a stone.

And then—

"Shadow One, this is Whiskey Bravo Delta control. Say your situation."

The signal had been faint at first, but electronic warfare officers aboard a Mainstay airborne warning-and-control aircraft flying a figure-eight track above the Caucasus had picked it up at the very edge of airspace identification range. Now the crew dogs had a lock on the signal and could pull it in clearly.

"Am airborne and proceeding on flight vector delta eight-point-zero-zero-seven." The course coordinates were coded and the Iranians had no reason to have asked Petrov for them. Even if his transmissions were intercepted, it would do the opposition no good. "Fuel reserves are critical. Will require immediate AAR. Can you provide?"

"Affirmative, Shadow One," the Russian voice answered. "We have a bird with plenty of fuel waiting to RV with you at coordinates six-zero-niner-point-gamma-six. Can you make it?"

Petrov consulted his fuel gauge and did a fast and dirty course plot on the keypad linked to the plane's flight computer.

"Roger, Whiskey Bravo Delta," he said. "I can just make it. With a little luck."

"We will cross our fingers, Shadow One. May lady luck crouch between your legs the rest of the way. Out."

Petrov smiled, and corrected his course as he made for the refuel RV point. But as he flew his plot, he began to have fresh doubts that he would reach it. As his heartbeat slowed and his adrenaline rush subsided, he realized that an intermittent sluggishness of the flight controls that he'd noticed earlier was now noticeably worsening.

The inertial navigation system that controlled the ungainly, angular aircraft was malfunctioning, he knew that now with certainty, and it had begun to destabilize. Petrov flipped switches and punched buttons on the console, shunting to redundant systems, but the backups didn't fix his problems.

He surmised that either the plane had been hit by gunfire in a vulnerable spot on takeoff, or that the Iranians had tampered with the electronics—a loose connection header, an IC zapped by static, any number of small glitches of that order could damage the delicate, interconnected systems that controlled the aircraft in flight.

Seconds later the plane had become almost too unstable to handle, a black Icarus burned by the heat of the night, its waxen wings beginning to melt. Dropping from his cruising altitude of sixty thousand feet—a ceiling proof against SAM launches—Petrov descended down to lower altitudes, risking the chance of visual contact, or even contact with enemy tracking radars, against the hope of gaining greater control in the heavier air closer to the ground. The maneuver helped somewhat, but not enough. The plane's controls had begun bucking again in Petrov's hands, and this inability worsened by the minute.

The plane shuddered and began drifting off course, and then suddenly, the pilot felt the sickening lurch he had been half expecting as the stealth's left engine flamed out. Then came a second, more severe jolt as the condition pilots called "infectious flameout" made the second engine sputter and die as well.

Pushing the lighted restart button did nothing—the stealth's avionics were now behaving the way the electrical system of an automobile with a dying alternator behaves on the road—the illuminated dials and buttons on his console blinked off and on, flashing to an epileptic rhythm. His tactical displays froze, and then kaleidoscoped into sheets of electronic noise. His systems were shutting down all around him, sliding into shock, crashing like plates from a cupboard.

No doubt about it.

His plane was going down.

On the four-lane highway below the emergency landing approach of the stricken stealth fighter, its amber running lights aglow, a diesel truck hitched to a long, low trailer called a HET, or heavy equipment transporter, was making the dreary northbound return run from Masshad in the east to Tehran.

Behind the wheel of the slow-moving lorry was a tired man named Omid Farzaneh, who had spent the last five hours on the desolate desert road and was anxious to complete the final leg of his trip back to his home in the outlying suburb of Kaf Amal. Not long before, Omid had trucked his cargo—a medium-sized crane—to a construction company in Masshad, and was now highballing it back home with a signed manifest.

It was just shy of four o'clock in the morning and the long, straight blacktop highway was devoid of traffic, as it had been for many uneventful kilometers. Farzaneh hadn't seen a headlight for what seemed like ages. He was feeling mentally drained and physically fatigued, but that went with the territory, and besides, the radio was keeping him from dozing off behind the wheel. He'd make it all right—he'd made this run often enough to almost do it in his sleep. There was no point in pulling over, not for a while yet. He could go at least another fifteen klicks before he was too dazed to drive without a nap, he reckoned.

But tonight's run would be considerably different from any Farzaneh had ever made before in his lengthy career as a long-haul trucker. It was as he lit the end of his bogarted cigarette with a plastic butane lighter that Farzaneh saw something in the sky that seemed to blot out the stars. As the lighter flame snapped off, leaving the cab in total darkness, Farzaneh saw that he was not hallucinating.

A large, black, saucer-shaped object—some sort of plane, maybe even a UFO, it seemed to the startled driver—was hurtling down, directly in the path of his truck. In a heartbeat he would collide head-on with the thing.

The trucker panicked and acted without thinking. Had he been more alert and less frightened, he might have averted the disaster to come, but that wasn't to be. Acting from blind hysteria, Farzaneh violently jerked the steering wheel to the left, hoping by this maneuver to evade the path of the oncoming airborne object.

It proved to be a fatal mistake.

Had he turned the wheel to the right instead, the truck

and its long trailer might have fishtailed onto the flat gravel surface that was graded level with the road and probably stopped without further incident.

But to the left of the highway was an incline—not a steep one, even for the desert, but steep enough to send the mammoth rig careening nose-first onto the sands below the level of the highway. In the process, Farzaneh was catapulted from his seat, over the steering wheel, across the top of the dashboard, and squarely into the windshield with enough force to shatter the small vertebrae of the upper neck, killing him almost instantly. The truck was not equipped with an airbag.

As the black, discoid shape passed only a few scant feet overhead, the truck continued rolling for several minutes longer, until it plowed headlong into a rock outcropping, crushing part of its front end. Then it came to a full, juddering stop, with the body of its deceased driver flung half out the shattered window to wind up sprawled across the hood.

Petrov's landing was not much smoother, but fortunately for him it did not prove fatal. The stealth plane set down on the flat desert pan with its landing gear extended, and for a minute its nose dipped sharply downward and almost plowed into the soft, dark sands. But then, still rolling, it straightened up, and with wing flaps distended, Petrov managed to slide to a shaky stop only a few hundred meters from the disabled HET.

The stealth driver undid his harness webbing, unbuttoned the cockpit canopy, and pulled himself out from under it onto the boxy left air scoop. He checked his watch, or rather the Japanese watch he had taken from one of the Iranians they had bushwhacked for fatigues in place of the flight suit his captors had stolen from him, reading the time from its backlit LCD dial.

The black numerals on the glowing green display showed the time was precisely four A.M.

Only half of Vassily Petrov's dream had come true. He had lived to fly. But he had flown to nowhere.

Nineteen
The Falcon and the Falconer

At Nellis Air Force Base, which sits just southeast of the hotel and casino towers of downtown Las Vegas, a HET roughly twice as long and considerably wider than the hapless Farzaneh's had arrived in the dead of night. It carried a cargo in a special formfitted container.

Civilian employees of the U.S. Defense Department with high security clearances had been expecting the delivery and quickly got to work unpacking it from its crate, once the HET had driven into a security-screened hangar facility, a facility in the heart of Nellis that is the headquarters of the USAF's 11th Reconnaissance Squadron, the first operational unit formed to fly long-endurance unmanned aerial vehicles to distant regions of the globe.

The personnel who surrounded the HET were employees of DARO, the Defense Airborne Reconnaissance Office, a department of the larger organization known as DARPA, which stood for Defense Advanced Research Projects Agency. DARO had been involved in the initial development of the UAV or unmanned aerial vehicle programs for the Air Force, and it had recently finished conducting its final ACTD or advanced concept testing and development trials of the Tier program's advanced UAVs some months before.

Hours later, when they had uncrated the delivery, Global Hawk was rolled into a section of the enormous hangar where the process of programming the UAV and fitting it out for its clandestine mission commenced. The long-range remote airborne surveillance system was a thirteen-ton aircraft the size of a single-engine plane with a 116-foot wingspan. Its fuselage blended seamlessly into a huge ramjet intake at the rear and flared into a rounded sensor bulge at the front, with long, slightly backswept glider wings sprouting from the hull's midsection.

The combination of design elements gave the robot plane the look of a winged monster blindworm imbued with cold, sinister intelligence—which is not very far from what it was. In addition to downloading digital maps into its memory, the preflight maintenance process, which would take several hours, would upgrade Global Hawk's hardware and ROM software and comprehensively test all its systems, including its classified imaging payload.

Global Hawk was built to fly long endurance missions that required it to stay airborne—or, as it's said in military parlance, "loiter"—for as much as twenty-five hours before returning to base. During that time it could aerially survey approximately forty thousand square nautical miles, a target area equivalent to the state of Illinois, with a resolution of objects as small as three feet in diameter. Utilizing spot-mode scanning, it could surveil a much smaller area with a resolution of objects down to one foot in size, if necessary.

The UAV was also equipped to carry EO, or electro-optical, and SAR, synthetic aperture radar, imaging payloads as well as a third infrared (IR) system simultaneously while operating at altitudes of greater than sixty thousand feet. The UAV could be crammed with up to a ton of cameras, radars, and other sensors. Global

Hawk could also transmit real/near-real-time data via line-of-sight datalink and satcom relay. As already stated, it could also be armed, which this bird most definitely was, with both air-to-air and air-to-ground capabilities.

As the crew of technicians worked on the plane, another crew labored to set up a command-and-control area for the remote operation team that would be responsible for the flight of the Hawk. A series of tall Plexiglas screens had been set up to cordon off an area about thirty feet square. Behind this soundproof, and indeed bulletproof, glass barrier, banks of rack-mounted communications equipment and miles of thick power and data cables were being installed to enable long-range control of Tier III Minus.

A portable stereo sound system was also being set up, including a CD changer stocked with two hundred of the loudest rock albums ever recorded.

But that was for the Hawkman.

Petrov gave up on the plane's satcom unit. He'd wasted precious time in trying every conceivable combination of settings, but nothing but static repaid his struggles. He surmised that the antenna element had been damaged during the forced landing, but couldn't be sure.

Whatever the case, his communications link was down for the present. Nor were there now any means available to him to destroy the aircraft. This time Petrov had not hesitated to trigger the MFI-19's autodestruct sequence, but nothing happened. The Iranians had either removed the explosive charge or pulled out the circuit modules that controlled the detonation sequence. It was now either destroy the plane with his bare hands or leave it alone. Petrov decided to leave it alone.

He stood looking around him, at the desert on all sides, at the pale white skull face of the leering moon that seemed to mock him from its perch in the black, star-filled sky above, at the asphalt highway that ran ruler straight across the sand desert to the distant line of the faraway horizon, at the two black skidmarks of peeled tire rubber, illuminated by pale moonlight, that skewed off the roadbed and into the dark, and the metal behemoth that had made those tracks now motionless in the distance against a jumbled heap of strangely twisted and deformed rocks.

Petrov was suddenly overwhelmed by the alien weirdness of it all; he felt he was living a moment in hell caught in amber. He thought that if ever there were a perfect time for a man to lose his sanity, this was it. He seemed to have been catapulted through Alice's looking glass into a surreal world where nothing made sense anymore and where all his bearings on reality had been stolen from him.

The profound disorientation he experienced, Petrov knew, was the combined effects of stress, sleep deprivation, hunger, and probably illness, too, and he also knew that in order to survive he would have to turn off all parts of his mind that weren't directly connected to his military training and instincts for survival. He knew also that he had to move, to get away from where he was, and to do so before sunrise. He'd already wasted too much time in his futile efforts to phone home.

But what to do? And where to go? Petrov needed to admit to himself that he'd been defeated. He was as good as dead. In a few more hours it would be fully light, and with each continuing hour of daylight, his hours of freedom steadily dwindled down to the zero mark. Before the next day was out, he was certain of recapture. This time the Iranians would have no more use for him and would give him no quarter.

He would be executed on the spot and the plane retaken, and when the final reckoning came, his death would be reported as an "accident" to his wife and children back home in the port city of Vladivostok. It now dawned on Vassily Petrov that his own personal survival was bound up with the survival of the plane he'd piloted.

If he could only find some way to hide the aircraft from discovery, he would have gained a bargaining chip, might even be able to work a deal in exchange for his freedom.

But how would he do such a thing? Lift the damned machine on his back? Plow up the desert crust and bury it in a huge hole? Maybe even summon some sleeping djinn from a magic lamp to pry apart the crust of the earth and swallow the plane in its hidden depths.

In anger, Petrov picked up a handful of small stones from the desert scree and hurled them at the side of the plane, hearing them go *plonk, tink, plonk, tink* as they struck the composite-material fuselage with hollow thuds. What was the use? He was through, and that was a no-shit judgment call. Petrov might as well admit it to himself. There was no way to hide a plane in this flat, almost featureless desert country. He might as well try to draw water from one of those rocks in the distance, the way Moses had done in the Bible.

He reared back to hurl the last of his handful of stones at the half-buried monster cockroach when he got hit with what they call a BFO at the Pentagon—a blazing flash of the obvious. Petrov simply called it *nomskaya,* intuition. By whatever name, its effect was to stop him cold and spin him around, as he suddenly recalled an image of the area from his descent and forced landing that matched something else he had seen on his flight into Iran.

The stone that he'd been about to hurl in impotent rage thumped instead to the sandy desert floor as Petrov ran toward the higher ground of the roadbed and surveyed the encompassing terrain by the electric blue wash of ghost-pale light from the shining lunar skull.

It was amazing, he thought. But yes, there it was. Right in front of him all the time. Time and the odds both ran against him, because the darkness would soon give way to the rising sun. But with a little luck, he might just be able to pull it off. Dear God, how he prayed that he might!

The black Camaro, with blue federal tags and a huge bird of prey with outspread wings painted on its hood, that pulled up to the guard post at 11th Recon's gate at Nellis wasn't new, but it had seen a lot of the detailer's shop. The air scoop protruding from the front of the hood bespoke a heavier, more powerful engine than the car had come off the assembly line with. The tinted windows weren't standard either. Sergeant Everett Loomis, who'd been watching the car pull up, was instantly on the alert.

This wasn't the usual type of vehicle that came and went through the portals he guarded. That was good by him. Loomis was in a shit mood. His wife had found out about his affair with a waitress in Reno. She'd already taken the kids and left for her mother's in Tempe, Arizona. Then the waitress had dumped him for a Mexican dishwasher. Doing a number on some smart-ass punk would make his day. He hoped the driver gave him an attitude. He really hoped the driver was high. That might give him an excuse to point his rifle at the car and maybe shoot it up some, after which he'd see the motherfucker handcuffed and arrested by the base MPs.

Please, let me beat the shit out of this guy, he prayed silently as he stepped from his booth.

Loomis glowered down at the Camaro's driver's side as the electric window slid down into its recess in the door. One look at the driver told Loomis that his ship had come in. Long, lanky black hair, those kind of Ray•Bans with round lenses, and fingerless driving gloves. Loomis inhaled, hoping for a whiff of pot to go with the rest, but was disappointed. The car interior smelled like new leather. He bet the guy used one of those bullshit fake leather sprays to make it smell like that. Never the fuck mind. At least he could tell the punk to turn down that loud rock music that was blasting out of the car stereo. What the fuck was that shit? Definitely not music, that's for sure.

Before the MP could say a word, though, the driver hit a button on the dash and the music dropped several decibels in a heartbeat. Undaunted, Loomis fixed the driver with his most daunting scowl and asked him to state his business at the base.

"My business? Guess you'd have to call it saving the world from its own bad karma," is what he answered.

"What was that?" Loomis asked, with tightening jaw,

omitting the "sir," with which he normally concluded questions to visitors. This dude did not rate a "sir," not from Loomis.

"Check this out, my man," replied the driver, and shoved a base pass into his hand.

Sergeant Loomis's frown deepened as he read the name on the pass—Bartholomew Simpson. What was this, some kind of joke? Man, he was going to kick old Bart Simpson's smart ass if that name didn't match his manifest, which Loomis was sure it wouldn't.

Except, there it was. Bartholomew Simpson. In black-and-white. Still, this had to be some kind of bullshit. It had to be. Somebody was pulling Everett Loomis's chain. Just to make sure, Loomis told the visitor to wait. He was going to check it out. Take his sweet fucking time doing it, too. But a phone call convinced Loomis that he was to pass the car through immediately, and Loomis was smart enough to know that he'd been wrong about the profile—this guy was some kind of spook.

"Sorry to keep you waiting, Mr. Simpson," Loomis said to the driver, who simply grinned at him in response and stuck out his hand for his pass.

Loomis handed back the base pass and saw the window roll up, failing to keep the sound of thudding bass from infecting the hot desert air with its mad vibrations as the muscle car rolled into the parking lot of Nellis's high-security Section Three.

"Oh, one thing," the driver said, rolling his window down again.

Loomis turned to listen.

"Go fuck yourself, asshole."

Everett Loomis was soon enveloped by clouds of exhaust fumes as the sound of peeling tires screeched in his ears.

Loomis didn't know it, but the Hawkman had just arrived.

It was better than Petrov had dared to expect as he neared the place he had reconnoitered from the air and spotted from the road. It was far enough from his landing site not to be overly obvious to pursuers, yet close enough to have allowed him to reach it on foot in a relatively short time.

As it was, he had made it with bare minutes to spare. The false dawn had already arrived, and with each passing minute the deep black sky lightened by half tones to shades of gray and blue and the air temperature imperceptibly climbed. Petrov crept closer, past the ubiquitous camel thornbushes and rock outcrops dotting the landscape, examining this place of refuge in every detail, while part of his mind replayed the events of the past few hours.

After his flash of inspiration, the pilot had climbed down the embankment and ran toward the crashed truck that had come to rest nearby. It became obvious that the big rig's engine was still kicking over as the winking amber running lights along the sides of the cab and flatbed grew nearer.

The faint sound that Petrov had heard in the distance was fast becoming the deep, throbbing idle sound of a powerful diesel engine. The plume of exhaust seeping from the tailpipe confirmed this to Petrov as he finally reached the truck, out of breath from the desert jog in his weakened state, and saw Omid Farzaneh's mangled corpse sprawled across the hood through the shattered windshield.

He would need to turn off the engine, probably, which would entail pulling the cadaver's legs free of the cab and rolling it onto the desert floor, but this ghoulish task would have to wait until Petrov had satisfied himself that the truck met his needs. Convinced that the rig was in no danger of rolling away from him after chocking its rear wheels with large rocks, Petrov walked around to the back of the HET and lifted himself onto its steel-plated deck. As he paced it with arms outstretched to measure its length and girth, he estimated that it was wide enough for his purposes, though barely.

At the front of the trailer, just behind the cab, was a heavy-duty electric winch that was operated by a pushbutton remote-control unit. Petrov switched on the remote, and tested out the winch, which moved up, down, left, and right, paying out and reeling in the heavy woven steel cable with flawless efficiency. The duty ratings of the winch were printed on the remote unit in English and Arabic. Petrov knew enough of the former to understand that the maximum load the winch could safely handle roughly matched his specifications. From this end, at least, the job seemed doable.

Petrov next went around to the front of the cab to see about the feasibility of the rest of his plan, but this would involve removing the driver's already rigor-mortis-stiffened cadaver so that Petrov could check the fuel gauge and move the truck.

With the door swung open and one foot perched on the running board, he paused to consider the best way of accomplishing this task. A few test pokes at the body told Petrov that it had become too stiff to easily force back down into the seat and be dumped out the door, so the best approach would be to drag it from the cab. This proved to be much harder than he had anticipated.

Rigor mortis was advanced, and the jackknifed posture of the corpse around the dashboard meant that Farzaneh's bloating legs kept catching on the steering column, brake pedals, shift, and bottom of the dash. Extracting Farzaneh's mortal coil was really a two-man job. Petrov had alternately to pull from the front of the truck and push from inside the cab, working back and forth like a dog worrying a large bone, until the legs of the dead driver finally came free of the cab's interior.

At least another hour was to pass before Petrov succeeded in freeing the corpse from the cab. By this time he was badly winded, but he knew he couldn't stop to rest more than a moment. He also knew that apart from concealing the body as best as he was able, he needed to take its papers. He didn't want anything to lead back to him.

Now, seated behind the wheel, Petrov restarted the truck's diesel engine, backed away from the boulders, and drove the juddering semi across the uneven desert landscape toward the squat black shape that loomed in the ebbing darkness.

It took him almost another hour to winch the stealth plane up onto the bed of the carrier and lash it down in a way that was secure and as unobtrusive as he could make it. There was plenty of tarp in a storage locker on the back of the carrier, and tie-downs of various kinds. Petrov was able to cover enough of the plane with tarp before lashing it deckside to make it reasonably hard to spot. It would take more than a single glance in the dark of night from a passing vehicle to identify the new cargo.

Now, back behind the wheel of truck, he shifted into first gear and juddered his way again across the desert floor until he found a low part of the embankment where he thought it reasonably safe to pull up onto the flat surface of the highway. Praying that the plane would not snap loose from its cables or that the truck wouldn't overturn under the uneven load it carried, he applied power, felt the triple rows of wheels find purchase, and moments later was crawling onto the highway in growling low gear.

From there, on the level roadbed, the remaining ride was smoother and considerably faster. Petrov pushed the rig for as much speed as he dared squeeze from it, because it was getting close to dawn. He could see the horizon faintly lighten to a blue hairline toward the east, in the direction he was heading, and the once bright stars begin to grow dim. With no traffic on the remote stretch of desert road, he made good time, and found a shallow-graded turnoff onto the spot he'd seen from a few kilometers' distance.

He took another shallow-graded turnoff and heard the tires splash in the brackish water of the mud through which he rolled, watched the steep concrete walls towering up on either side of him. He could kiss those high walls, because they would hide him from the light of day, and from the sun, and he knew the place would provide even better hiding places as he pushed deeper into it.

This place to which Petrov had driven the truck was a

huge concrete culvert built to funnel the precious seasonal outflow from the distant mountains to the parched cities to the north of the Iranian plateau. The culvert was part of a system that fed the taps of Tehran, Yazd, and smaller towns in between. In some places, the watercourse dove underground, but here the form it took was a deep, square-bottom channel, in the form of an exaggerated *U*, reinforced with poured concrete, and dug into the desert floor by foreign engineers in the 1970s.

The walls of the main channel were honeycombed with side tunnels for the inflow from other water sources, including seasonal rains, and the huge ditch was entirely covered over in places to prevent evaporation by steel plates that had become buried underneath sand through the years.

Culverts like this one had been used successfully by Iraqi Scud crews during Desert Storm to hide Saddam's missiles from satellite and aircraft surveillance. The culverts had made ideal hiding places for the Scuds for a number of reasons. For one, they were wide enough to easily accommodate the Scuds' transporter-erector-launchers or TELs, and their shape, construction, and proximity to water meant that they combined a mix of temperature gradients that radiated a kind of thermal stealth, making the TELs hard to spot on IR or TI scans.

Petrov hoped this culvert on the edge of the Dasht would offer him a similar sanctuary. He had no other choice, in any case. The winter sun had already risen, a leprous orange blotch on the far horizon, wavering in the thermals that had begun to rise from the desert floor—another day in the Dasht-e-Kavir had begun.

In the distance, the pilot thought he could hear the wavering thud and drone of attack-and-surveillance helicopters, but that might be his imagination, he knew. Fatigue and hunger played tricks with the mind, and he was suffering from both. As the sun parted from the horizon line and swam toward the center of the brightening blue sky to become a yellow Cyclops eye, Petrov fell asleep in the cab of the truck, and dreamed of nothing.

• • •

Several hours after Petrov had found the culvert in which to hide the truck, and many kilometers distant from his hiding place, Barak and his squad of Israeli Egoz renegades were changing into the uniforms of the Iranian regulars they had ambushed and killed. As a result, some of the uniforms were bloodstained and bullet-riddled, but that couldn't be helped. To make an omelette, one always had to break some eggs.

He and his men needed the uniforms, just as they needed the BTR-70 armored personnel carrier that the troops had been riding in when they'd been summoned, in flawless Farsi, by radio to a remote spot where Barak's commandos had set up a crude but effective rock trap designed to immobilize the vehicle without damaging it too much.

The rock trap was one used a lot by the Afghan guerrillas in their brief but bloody war against the Soviets during the 1980s, and it was a trap they had developed to perfection. As soon as the armored BTR had plowed across a trip wire invisibly strung across the road, tons of boulders perched atop a desert promontory tumbled onto the APC, trapping it like a huge, steel-plated rhinoceros beetle.

Before the shocked crew could react, flashbang grenades were shoved through the BTR's gunports at front and rear, immobilizing the troops inside, who were killed by the application of automatic nine-mm Uzi fire through the same gunports. With the bodies of the Iranians joining the boulders cleared from the BTR at the bottom of the wadi below the roadbed, Barak's crew changed uniforms and climbed into the carrier.

Barak now had fresh orders, which had just come in via secure satellite communications direct from Tel Aviv. His orders came straight from the prime minister, by way of a now somewhat more contrite Assaf Gilad. His team was to make contact with the U.S.-Russian fusion cell. The cell was pinned down some distance away at a caravansary. Barak's force was to assist it as a unit in reserve.

Under no circumstances were the Egoz to intervene directly or to do anything to the downed stealth aircraft. They were only to offer assistance, and then pull out. That was all. Assist and withdraw, but under no circumstances become embroiled in the worsening international conflict.

Barak acknowledged these orders. Then he promptly forgot about them and invented new ones of his own. In his rule book, orders were among the many things in the world that were made to be broken.

"Flash just came over VLF, sir."

"Let's have it," Gustavsen said back, his eyes on the map on the table in front of him.

The *Teaneck*'s communications officer handed the captain the sheet of paper that had just come off the secure satcom teleprinter. Normally, transmissions to the Los Angeles–class nuclear attack submarine were received at periscope depth during scheduled surfacings along its patrol route. An array of antennas on the fairwater would be raised to receive satcom, ground station, and airborne radio signals. Then the sub would resurface and be on its way.

Flash-coded messages were transmitted using very low-frequency radio waves or VLF, which penetrated the water and could be picked up by the nuclear boat's towed sensor array. Using the new HAARP antenna farm in Alaska, however, VLF signals could now travel across even greater distances, and over the earth's horizon. These could pass through water and be received below periscope depth, but were reserved for high-priority messages due to their relative slowness, bandwidth limitations, and the need to trail a long wire antenna behind the cruising submarine.

Gustavsen scanned the transmission sheet. The message, which had been decrypted by the sub's computers before being printed, read:

FLASH
FROM: CINCLANTFLT ELMSWORTH ADM

TO: SSBN 1889-YYN TEANECK// J3 NMCC//
AIG 931
TOP SECRET U M B R A
FG0284//OPREP-3 PINNACLE COMMAND ASSESSMENT//
001//021950Z MAR 21 02//

(TS/SI) ALL EVIDENCE IS THAT IRANIAN MRBMS LOCATED AT AGHA JARI HAVE BEEN BROUGHT TO STATE OF LAUNCH READINESS. MISSILES ARE THOUGHT TO BE TARGETED ON STRATEGIC NATO TARGETS IN SOUTHERN EUROPE. YOU ARE TO SET COURSE FOR GRID COORDINATES 0027BF-96W61 AND REACH THIS POSITION BY 0600 HOURS TOMORROW. AT THAT TIME YOU WILL RECEIVE GO/NO-GO CONFIRMATION FOR TLAM STRIKE ON MISSILE TARGETS IN IRAN VIA SATCOM.

END MESSAGE.

"What's up, Skipper?" asked Gustavsen's exec, who had seen the look on his face as he scanned the message. Gustavsen wordlessly handed him the sheet. The exec nodded and handed it back.

"Gonna be a bitch," he told the captain.

"Tell me about it, Danny."

Gustavsen fed the orders to the shredder beneath his desk. While it consumed its snack with a low growl of meshing corkscrew gears, Gustavsen picked up the handset beside him and punched in the exchange number of the boat's navigator. While relaying his instructions for a new course plot, Gustavsen was already scanning one of the bathymetric charts that his exec had brought over.

The chart showed that the coordinates related to a spot in the Mideast a few nautical miles from the mouth of the Gulf of Oman.

The exec then drew a grease-pencil plotline across a clear acetate plotting sheet.

Where he made a circle was where the sub had to be in a day's time. From the sub's present position in the

Indian Ocean, that was more than eight hundred nautical miles—a long haul at the sub's maximum thirty-knot submerged cruising speed. But, hell, thought Gustavsen. This was the Navy, wasn't it? Same business, different day.

Twenty
Dogs in the Manger

Nominally, the Hawkman worked for DARO, which made him a civilian employee of DARPA, which in turn made him an employee of DARPA's controlling organization, the Department of Defense or DOD. This was technically true but not, as they say, completely true. Although the Hawkman did in fact technically work for DOD, he really worked for NSA, an acronym that stood for the supersecret intelligence organization officially called the National Security Agency, and less officially called No Such Agency or Never Say Anything by many in government and politics familiar with its superclandestine methods of operation.

Since NSA is, according to the U.S. Government Manual, part of the Department of Defense, the partial truth was given some shred of credibility and the Hawkman's cover as a technical engineer with a high security clearance employed by DARPA was able to hold up under scrutiny. If anyone was interested in checking the Hawkman out more thoroughly, they could contact the appropriate offices at DOD and pull his file jacket, which described him as a skilled expert in computers and robotic systems who had worked on government projects at IBM, McDonnell Douglas, and various other major defense contractors.

Personal data on the Hawkman would include information on his age, educational background, personal habits, marital status, and finances, all of which would depict him as a highly competent if slightly eccentric and belligerent whiz kid who enjoyed playing with high-tech toys for his Uncle Sam, and being well paid for it in the bargain. He had even written a few paperback spy and military novels for Berkley books and other publishers. Some of these even sold.

All of this would be convincing, but it would also be a complete fabrication and a carefully stage-managed lie devised to conceal the real truth concerning who and what the Hawkman actually was, because these truths were bound up with the covert history of America in the years since the Korean War and covert history and true nature of the NSA itself.

The NSA was formed in 1952 by executive order of President Harry S. Truman, an order so secret that it remained classified for over thirty years; even today its text has never been publicly divulged.

Unlike the CIA, which was created by act of Congress, the NSA has never openly revealed its exact nature, the identities of its staff, or precisely what it is empowered to do, only that it has something to do with a vaguely defined state of affairs dubbed "national security."

In fact, it's believed by some that the CIA is no more than a front for the NSA, and that the operations of the CIA are often little better than a cover for the much deeper and blacker operations conducted by the NSA. It has been estimated that the director of central intelligence controls less than 10 percent of the combined national and tactical intelligence efforts of the United States; the NSA controls the other 90 percent.

Even the Hawkman, who had worked for the NSA since the secret wars in Laos and Cambodia at the close of the Vietnam era, and possessed a coveted NSA security clearance of top-secret Category Three, Cryptographic Code Word Two, did not have a handle on the big picture. The NSA is obsessed with the concept of need-to-know.

Thc organization's stock-in-tradc is information, which to its nameless, faceless personnel, is the very essence of power. Every scrap of information is compartmentalized and controlled through codes, as identities are controlled through aliases and code names. Within the agency, power and rank are denoted solely by security clearances and the codes a person has the ability to read and understand. Within the pyramidal structure of the NSA, access to information leads to promotion and power, lack of access leads to failure and ostracism.

The Hawkman's orders were passed on to him in a secure area within a deep underground facility outside of Washington, D.C., known as a Space-Three facility. He never came within miles of the NSA's supposed headquarters at Fort George G. Meade, as these so-called headquarters are actually a vast computer farm and a control center for the less covert satellites that the NSA orbits around the earth. Contrary to well-cultivated popular belief, the true nerve centers of the NSA lie deep within the earth, in a series of ultrasecret facilities. These are easily the most secure areas on the planet, impregnable even to a nuclear strike at ground zero and capable of sustaining the lives of occupants for up to a year.

After passing through an elaborate security screen and several cipher-locked guillotine gates, where his identity was checked and verified at each point, the Hawkman had entered Space Three. There he met an NSA briefer who gave him his orders.

The briefer, whom the Hawkman had never met before and would never meet again, did not understand the words he spoke to the operative whom he was briefing. Most of the words were in arcane codes, and the briefer merely passed these on to others in the chain of command. The

Hawkman, cleared for the codes, understood the meaning fully. The briefer comprehended nothing.

On completion, the Hawkman left and began his mission. He would return to be debriefed in the same Space Three facility, and repeat the process in reverse, passing on a string of incomprehensible code words that would in turn be passed on by his debriefer until they reached someone in the NSA hierarchy who possessed enough clearance to understand their meaning.

The Hawkman's real name was no longer real to him, so he never used it. It had been lost, with his original identity, in the disarray of the Indochina misadventure. After that, his name became whatever name the mission demanded; his identity became the self that the job called for to get done. Those names, identities, and jobs had varied with the years between his loss of operational virginity and the present day. In the beginning they had comprised a string of covert rescue-and-assassination missions inside the triple-canopy jungles of Southeast Asia. After that, the focus of the Hawkman's efforts had shifted to Eastern Europe, then Latin America, and then into Russia and the Balkans before, during, and after the Soviet breakup.

Throughout his career, the Hawkman's genius for remote weaponry and robotics had involved him with cutting-edge operations. He had been the architect of several of the most ambitious ever attempted, including the secret mission to fly a refurbished SR-71 spy plane over the Soviet Union following the mysterious blinding of United States surveillance satellites almost a decade before and an attempt by a cabal of rogue military officers to provoke a limited nuclear war between East and West.

It had been on the Hawkman's orders that veteran SR-71 Blackbird pilot Dan Cox had been selected to fly the mission. The Hawkman had known Cox in his early Indochina days and had been behind the CIA's ferreting him out to fly the once mothballed SR-71. Cox's mission had averted a nuclear exchange between the superpowers and had paved the way for the shaky but so far unbroken peace that was to follow. The Hawkman, using a pen name, had written the story as fiction and published it under the title *Bandit*.

But this peace was only a by-product, a reflection in the real world of politics and people of the hidden world in which he was a player. In the true world of intelligence, the only thing that counted was the game; playing it, staying in it, winning a round as often as possible. The highest aspiration for winning was this and this only: you got to play again.

The Hawkman was playing another game today.

As usual, unlike the majority of the other players, he was one of the few who knew it.

Twenty minutes before, a powerful rocket engine had executed a multisecond booster burn, propelling Global Hawk into an angular climb to twenty thousand feet above the barbecue-hot sands of southern Nevada. The ascent of Global Hawk was visible to anyone peering from the window of one of the high-rise casinos on the Vegas strip, but there were so many flights out of Nellis every day that few—even the sober ones—would have noticed.

Once the UAV had reached its ceiling, the now useless booster rocket engine was jettisoned and the vehicle's single jet turbofan ignited. The specially built ramjet engine would carry Tier III Minus to its destination and back again, consuming the minimum amounts of fuel to keep the bird aloft and enable it to perform its intelligence-gathering routines from high- and low-altitude surveillance envelopes.

In the control center in the cordoned-off area of 11th Recon's ultrasecure hangar at Nellis, the Hawkman was monitoring the progress of the UAV from his instrumentation console. A large, fifty-inch, flat-panel display screen showed near-real-time imagery from Global Hawk's array of cameras and sensors of various kinds: the god screen.

At a mouse click, the god screen could switch from a single zoom view from any one of the UAV's cameras or sensors to display multiple windows from some or all of the drone's imaging suite. There were backup screens that showed real-time satellite imagery from orbiting Keyhole satellites so the UAV itself could be kept in direct view at all times.

Beside the keyboard, there was an elaborate joystick that could be used to control the bird while in flight, aim its imaging sensors, or activate its autodestruct mechanisms in case the mission had to be aborted. As the Hawkman chewed on the crust of a double-cheese pepperoni pizza his staff had brought from the surprisingly well-stocked Nellis canteen, and listened to the Cream's "White Room" on the nearby stereo system, he used his free right hand to pilot the UAV on the first leg of its long flight, which took it on an easterly course across the lower third of the continental U.S. and then out to sea.

At the moment the Hawkman's interest was in checking out the way the drone handled and running a few in-flight diagnostics. In a few minutes, he would put the UAV on autopilot and kick back and just keep a weather eye on the god screen. There would be another ten hours of flight time until the drone reached its operational envelope, and then things would start getting hairy. Until then, he could relax, listen to the music, and watch the in-flight movie that only Zeus normally gets to scope.

Colonel Ghazbanpour waited tensely for the report from the field. He needed results. The rear-echelon generals in Tehran were frantic. First the damned stealth plane disappears, then a foreign commando unit operating in Iranian territory can't be found—vanishes right off the goddamned map. Finally, an Iranian patrol has gone missing, complete with APC, weapons, and radio. Something had better be done, and quickly, they had told him, or he would be held responsible.

Ghazbanpour received a report that a helicopter crew had noticed signs of suspicious activity in the northeastern quadrant of the desert. This was in Sector Hamadi, one of six sectors into which his staff had divided the overall search area. This new sighting was far from where the last reports of the commando force had put the likely position of the American special-forces unit, but that did not necessarily mean the sighting was in error. Ghazbanpour had ordered a mobile detachment to encircle the area and be prepared to attack if necessary.

Many kilometers away from Ghazbanpour's desk, two companies of Iranian regulars, with APC and helicopter support, were closing in on a group of men in a desolate region of decaying ruins. The men within the enclave did not see the troops approach. Their orders had been to take the commando force alive, if possible. But then automatic fire had started up, and the assault force responded with every available gun. The helicopters targeted their missiles on the ruins and fired salvo after salvo of high-explosive rounds down into the rubble.

Minutes later nothing moved within the smoking bomb crater gouged from the earth. The attacking force sent a detachment into the blasted ruins with rifles at the ready and bayonets fixed. As they mounted the heaps of shattered rubble through clouds of acrid cordite smoke that stung their eyes, nothing moved. The only sign of human presence was the scattered body parts of those who had sheltered within. The denizens of the ruins had been blown to pieces by the sustained barrage of bullets and explosives. None still lived.

The company's leader, a Captain Hammoudi, immediately debriefed the detachment and radioed back to the colonel. Ghazbanpour tensed as he heard the news and hung up the telephone, clenching his fists.

Hashish smugglers! The U.S. commando assault force was still at large, and each day brought his career closer to a halt.

Sergeant Wayne Tollier hunched over the militarized TRAVLER unit, the laptop's shockproof metal case perched atop a small, flat-topped boulder that served as his desk. Tollier had gotten to kind of like it by now. For a rock, it made a neat desk. He had been attempting to install the upgrade package he had just downloaded via high-speed satcom transmission, but the OS or operating system of the wireless adaptive mobile information system or WAMIS node continued to reject the new program. Without the upgrade, TRAVLER would not be able to receive telemetry from the unmanned aerial vehicle whose ETA put it at less than an hour from the edge of its performance envelope.

Due to issues of fuel consumption, the time that Tier III Minus could loiter overhead was limited, and every spare minute counted for two. Tollier, the fusion cell's communications specialist, had been on the team's Hammer Lane secure satcom link to Nellis, where a DARO computer systems specialist was talking him through the install, so far without success. The OS was telling him the drivers were loaded, but when he restarted TRAVLER, they vanished back into the electronic ether. Tollier was pissed. This was one fuckup you couldn't blame on Bill Gates.

While Tollier worked to establish a reliable downlink to the arriving Tier III Minus, the three-man patrol that Mitchell had dispatched to conduct a recon mission reported in via secure SINCGARS radio transmission. The position of the U.S.-Russian team was pinpointed on a TRAVLER map display of the region. Hanes, Judson, Vishinsky, and Nazarov had been conducting a long-range patrol that had taken them in a fifty-kilometer arc to the southwest of the base. They had moved by night only in their FAVs, holing up during the hours of daylight in shallow wadis deepened with entrenchment tools.

So far they had spotted a few patrols and some itinerant groups of desert Bedouin, but the Iranians didn't seem to have a clue to the cell's whereabouts. The patrol had reported that they had quit the ruins of a desert outpost only a few hours before, when they soon heard the sounds of firing. Reconnoitering from the vantage point of a desert promontory, they saw that the outpost was under fierce attack by Iranian ground forces backed up by heavily armed Hip attack helicopters. The "black bottoms" were gunning for bear.

Mitchell ordered the patrol to immediately return to the caravansary. He knew the team could not remain there for longer than a dozen hours or so. They would have to move soon or risk an unevenly matched confrontation.

"Got it!" Mitchell suddenly heard Tollier say behind him as the program finally loaded, and this time stuck. The next fifteen minutes were spent waiting for the UAV to come within range, at least three of them on a round robin of high fives. Tollier even kissed his rock.

The Hawkman slipped an old Guns N' Roses CD into the changer and pulled on a special pair of gloves. This phase of the operation called for detailed work and he needed the right music for the job. The gloves, which were fastened around his wrists with Velcro quick-tabs, were wired and pumped full of air. Tiny sensors embedded in the spun nylon fabric were capable of detecting even the most subtle movements and pressures of his fingers.

The force-feedback gloves, as they were called, were linked to the high-speed computer processing system that controlled Global Hawk, which had now reached a point thirty thousand feet above the surface of the earth and more than three thousand miles from where the Hawkman sat. Before putting on the gloves, the Hawkman had strapped on a compact and lightweight head-mounted display or HMD.

The HMD design had come a long way since the first VCASS helmet was introduced in the early eighties. The VCASS, which quickly became known as the "Darth Vader" because it wrapped around the head like a strange, bug-eyed metal mask, used a primitive head-tracking system and arrays of cathode-ray tubes or CRTs to beam its imagery at the wearer's eyeballs. Although they were marvels of miniaturization for the era, the CRTs were huge, energy-intensive, and contributed to the sense of disorientating "simulator sickness" that testers of the Darth Vader reported after sessions.

By contrast, the HMD that the Hawkman wore as he listened to the opening guitar chords of "Welcome to the

Jungle" was about the same size and weight as a pair of safety goggles and flashed its imagery onto the human retina by means of a flat, semitransparant display film that gave a sharp, realistic wraparound view. The head tracker unit was no larger than a silicon chip, and as sensitive to movements of the Hawkman's head as the datagloves were to those of his hands. The ultra-fast computer processor and software suite insured that he maintained real-time control of the UAV.

What the Hawkman now saw in his visual field was the view he would have had if he were actually ensconced inside the cockpit of Global Hawk instead of thousands of miles away. There was a bank of virtual display screens in front of him, keyed to the various image sensors that studded the UAV's bottom and sides, as well as computer-aided radar imaging.

Within reach of his "hands" was an aircraft-style steering yoke with additional controls mounted on its surface. He could use the yoke to control the flight path of the drone in any direction he wanted. None of this was real. It was all computer-generated imagery, including the life-like firmness of the yoke in the Hawkman's fists. He would be piloting Global Hawk in cyberspace.

We got fun and games, he thought as the music played.

Mitchell and Tollier studied the screen of the TRAVLER field unit in front of them. The ruggedized laptop's ten-by-twelve-inch flat-panel display gave them a view of the op zone from twenty thousand feet in the air, downlinked from the several electro-optical sensors embedded in Global Hawk's sleek airframe.

With their multiband communications links to the UAV now securely established, the cell was able to see what the Hawkman saw on the god screen back at Nellis. Although the fusion cell had no direct control over Tier III Minus, they were now able to act as backseat Hawk drivers, telling the Hawkman about terrain features at which they wanted a better look.

Hours had passed already, and although the remote,

low-altitude reconnaissance of the desert had been thorough, it had also proven to be monotonous—and ultimately fruitless—going. So far the search hadn't turned up any solid leads regarding the location of the downed stealth plane.

"Wait one." It was Tollier who piped up.

He had noticed what looked like a possible man-made object at the bottom of a dry canal or culvert. *A wing section, maybe?* he thought.

No, he corrected himself, it was the *shadow* of a wing assembly's leading edge. No mistaking the object's angular contours. He'd been over this culvert area earlier, too, remembering the lessons from Iraq, but the sun's angle had been too high then. Now, though . . .

"What's your take on this, boss?" he asked Mitchell over his shoulder. "Think it's maybe our missing stealth plane?"

"Could be," Mitchell said back, watching the screen and drawing the same conclusion as Tollier. "Get in closer."

"Good to go, boss."

Tollier clicked the magnification factor up to 200, then 300, then 500 percent. This time he thought he also saw the trailing edge of an actual wing that protruded from just beyond the overhang of a road bridge spanning the culvert.

"Hawk One, please swing your bird around for another look," he said into the lip mike of the headset he wore. Consulting the search grid he'd clicked over the real-time active matrix display, Tollier continued, "Make altitude ten thousand feet and heading thirty-point-six degrees north-northeast."

"Your wish be my command, dude," said the Hawkman's voice in his ear, adjusting course and altitude and pointing the nose of his Hawk down toward the line of highway that stretched toward a culvert system that bordered a line of high-tension cables.

As he did, the Hawkman punched up a moving map display on one of the virtual screens in his HMD field of view. The map showed that this was an oil-producing region called Gur Qudair, a foul-smelling wasteland of pipes, vats, bubbling tar pits, and humming, crackling electrical power cables lying between the southern industrial centers and Tehran many klicks farther to the north.

Now the Hawkman could see what Tollier had been pointing at.

There, down below, was a black rectangular patch that he had at first mistaken for a shadow cast by one of the tall, pointed pyramidal structures that supported the elevated high-tension cables that ran across the desert floor and disappeared over the horizon. The Hawkman sharpened the image resolution and was left with no doubt that what was being looked at was a man-made object.

"Eenie meenie meinie mo. Gonna see how low this sucker can go," he told Tollier, and executed a ninety-degree turn, aiming the nose camera of the Hawk down from another angle, one that pointed away from the disk of the afternoon sun.

Minutes later, as the UAV returned for another overflight at fifty thousand feet, its cameras picked up the characteristic swallowtail rudder assembly of the Russian stealth plane. No other aircraft, save the F-117A that it had been cloned from, could produce that telltale design signature. The computer agreed, matching the imagery with a profile stored on disk.

The cell had found its thus-far-elusive quarry, and not a moment too soon—a virtual fuel gauge and warning icon had popped up on the god screen, showing that Global Hawk was now flying on its reserves. The UAV could not loiter over the area any longer.

"Gotta hop back into my magic lamp now, guys," the Hawkman told Tollier and Mitchell. "But—to quote the immortal Arnold—I'll be back."

The Hawkman wasted no time in turning the bird around, ascending the UAV to its SAM-resistant high-altitude flight ceiling, and plotting a return course.

Twenty-One

Zero-Sum

Even the flattest of deserts—and the Dasht is among the world's flattest—has subtle depressions and elevations, rifts and hollows, folds and inclines, into which men and vehicles can disappear and from which they can unexpectedly emerge to evade or engage enemy forces.

Desert warriors speak of needing to develop a so-called feel for the desert in order to operate successfully in its stark environs, in acquiring the habit of memorizing the location of every wadi, rock formation, and thornbush they encounter, in interpreting the sights, sounds, and smells that might warn of danger or herald safety from attack, and in honing the instincts necessary to survive and thrive in one of the planet's most forbidding natural environments.

The Israelis are no exception to this iron law of necessity; in fact, they are pioneers in this particular sphere of land warfare. Developing a feel for the desert is an essential facet of Israel's military doctrine and especially applies to commando troops, who are trained in the fine art of SERE—search, evasion, rescue, and escape—as it relates to the intricacies of desert combat.

For days, Barak's team had been using the desert topography to their advantage, as part of their *taboula,* Hebrew for "battle strategy" back in Joshua's day, as now. Although the commandeered Iranian APC was roughly the size of two pachyderms yoked in tandem, Barak's team exploited wadis, roadbeds, rises, and hollows in the landscape, and other natural terrain features, to keep itself well hidden from view.

This was the same basic strategy described in what the IDF calls Plan Ashdod. This secret contingency plan, prepared in the event that Israel should ever find herself faced with waging another ground war against her Arab neighbors to east, south, and north, calls for Egoz forces to stage wasting actions against the flanks and rear of Syrian and/or Egyptian armor while air and ground elements conduct a more conventional military campaign.

During the reign of the shah, Israel had conducted secret liaison exercises in the Iranian desert, where a core group of experts on special warfare in the Dasht had been formed. Barak had been one of these experts. Such were the intricacies of Middle Eastern power politics that even after the ascent of the Ayatollah Khomeini in 1979, and the turbulent wave of extremist Islamic fundamentalism that followed, the Israel-Iran special relationship continued. Later on, as relations thawed, Israeli agents could again be infiltrated into the remote fastnesses of the Iranian sand desert, to study and familiarize themselves with its unique ground truths.

Most of Barak's commando team possessed firsthand experience with the complexities of land navigation and land combat in the Dasht-e-Kavir. By this time Barak knew the desert almost as well as the Bedouin Arabs, Kurds, and other nomadic tribesmen, or *mohajer* in Farsi, who plied its arid wastes.

This knowledge of the desert was far more intimate and complete than anything that American high technology could duplicate, try as it might. No matter how good Global Hawk's sensor imaging suite, or how adept at interpreting the data was the crew at Nellis or the Deltas in Iran, the Israeli team knew the Dasht's secrets better than any Westerners without hands-on knowledge could ever hope to equal, even on their best day.

And so it was that as Barak's crew monitored wireless communications frequencies using their land-mobile radio equipment, they discovered a vital clue to the location of the missing stealth. On a civil band channel they heard a police report in Farsi concerning the unexplained disappearance of a heavy trailer truck in the Gur Qudair region. The truck, and its driver, had disappeared without leaving so much as a tire track behind. Something about the report rang a bell in Barak's mind. Particularly something about Gur Qudair. But what, exactly?

Asking one of his men to fetch him a map, Barak laid it out on the sand and propped its edges with a few rocks to keep it flat against the cold, steady wind. Crouching on the balls of his feet, he studied the empty terrain of the Gur. As soon as his eyes fixed on the culvert, he smelled pay dirt.

Barak mentally went over the image of the culvert, which had been built during the last year of the shah's reign with the help of the Israeli army engineer corps. He had chanced to have an opportunity to visit the building site near its completion in 1978 as part of Assaf Gilad's entourage. As he recalled, the plan had been to divert the course of an underground river that flowed beneath the northwestern part of the Dasht and spanned the major wadis, a project requiring the emplacement of a network of massive siphons and culverts of poured concrete. Would one such culvert be large enough to hide a stealth fighter with the rough dimensions of an American F-117A?

Assuming the plane could somehow be gotten down into the place, yes, definitely. Though it was unlikely that one battered pilot, acting on his own, could accomplish this feat, Barak had to admit it was technically possible. There was one other thing, too, that Barak noticed as he scanned the map—the location of the culvert put it athwart the flight path that Shadow One was projected to have flown to its initial ordnance release point, according to his premission briefing by AMAN personnel.

"Piss call is over," Barak shouted as he rolled up the map and stood erect. "We're moving out."

"Where?" asked one of his men as he flung a cigarette into the sand.

"You'll see," Barak said, and climbed in beside the APC's driver.

The plane sat there on the trailer, baking in the cold desert sun. Petrov was baking, too, the sun sucking the moisture out of his body. Odd how it could do this even in the cool of winter, but the place was so damned dry . . .

Petrov didn't finish the thought. It didn't matter. The point was that neither he nor the aircraft could remain here much longer. Neither was designed for these conditions. The plane needed a hangar and regular maintenance. Even exposure to the extremely fine particles of windblown desert dust for any length of time could damage its avionics and propulsion systems—a few stray particles in the wrong places and the engines would not even start.

He'd covered the engine intake ducts and other avenues of ingress as best he could, but who could be sure? Petrov was tired, cold, hungry, thirsty, lost, and alone. He estimated that he could hold out here for another twenty-four hours—at the very most. Then he would have to break cover or begin to starve; his rations would be gone.

Petrov's only hope lay in flying Shadow One out and back across the border, and he had been working on this option ever since it had gotten light enough for him to see. Shivering in the early-morning chill, refreshing himself as best he could by drinking brackish water that he had scooped in the hollow of his palm from the muddy bottom of the culvert, the pilot struggled to make repairs to the MFI's critical flight systems.

The most critical of all these had been the plane's INS or inertial navigation system, and here he had gotten lucky. He had believed that the Iranian techs had tampered with the VHSIC modules that comprised INS, and since he had no spares, this would have meant he could not reliably get the plane airborne again.

But, as Petrov carefully removed each module and inspected the ICs that were socketed on the printed circuit boards, he discovered that nothing was missing, every chip, circuit trace, and pin jumper was where it should normally be found. After detaching and reinserting each of the four VHSIC modules, Petrov started up the Shadow's avionics from the cockpit and ran through diagnostics again. In the absence of a sweep oscilloscope and other diagnostic tools, merely repositioning components on a board was a crude fix, but it often worked.

To his immense relief, Shadow One's systems now reported that INS was performing perfectly, even after running diagnostics again and again to confirm their integrity. Petrov surmised that one of two things had happened. The first was that something foreign, maybe even something as small as a few dust-fine sand particles, had shorted a passive backplane connection and screwed up his system—not an uncommon occurrence where high-technology military systems meet the ancient, windblown Mideastern deserts. The second was that the Iranians had pulled some of the modules just as he'd done but had not reinserted them just right, which might have had the same net effect. Then, too, there had been the multiple shocks of the initial landing and his recent narrow escape.

After several hours of work, Petrov was sure that Shadow One was flight capable. Now it was time to grab whatever sleep he could, because once night fell he would have to roll the HET back up onto the highway, single-handedly winch the stealth back off the end of the huge flatbed, and take off, using the highway as a runway.

Making himself as comfortable as possible beneath the flat underbelly of the plane—there was no room beneath the low-slung HET trailer itself—Petrov closed his eyes, thinking about how to block oncoming traffic later that night in place of counting sheep. Soon he slept fitfully, though deeply enough not to notice the tread of eight tiny feet.

These belonged to the scorpion that was slowly making its way up along his arm and inching toward his face, as the tip of its tail stinger gleamed with a clear drop of poison.

Skimming low across the arid, lunar surface, its mantis shadow stretching and twisting like elastic smoke as it passed across the high and low places in the desert crust, the Mi-8AMTSh variant of the Hip-H attack/transport helicopter hunted the night for an elusive prey.

The Hip's A suffix stood for *ataka,* indicating that it was equipped for automatic gun and rocket attack on ground targets, and its MT designation, standing for *modifitsirovanye transportnoi,* indicated that it could ferry a platoon of troops to any battle zone within its four-hundred-kilometer combat radius.

Colonel Ghazbanpour had both increased mobile ground patrols and aerial search missions as well as placed all his forces on round-the-clock alert status. He was under increasing pressure to locate and destroy the commando cell that had infiltrated the desert. He needed to locate the missing aircraft before they reached it and destroyed it, for such was surely their mission. Another twenty-four hours without results and Ghazbanpour would be relieved of command, of this he had been assured.

Yet it was pure luck that accounted for the first success against the invaders that Ghazbanpour could boast so far. The Mi-8's pilot had made a chance sighting of one of the cell's patrols as it was returning to the caravansary just before first light on the final day of the mission.

Flying conditions were excellent, and this was the primary reason for the break in Ghazbanpour's long streak of bad luck. The darkness was pellucidly clear, the moon not quite full, yet bright enough to blanket the barren desert expanse far below with a milk-white lunar radiance. Here and there the landscape glistened where dew had frozen into fragile patches of thin ice, and a mild night wind swept across the moonlit sands.

The chopper crew was about to swing back for base, when suddenly, in the distance, off to the west in an area that the helo's crew had not yet searched, something seemed to move against the hairline blue glow of the far horizon, making a band of stars low on the inverted bowl of the sky wink on and off in a straight line.

"Did you see that, Massoud?" the pilot asked his copilot via helmet commo.

"Yes, Adnan. Think it's anything?"

"Try to put it on TI," the pilot suggested.

There was nothing on the thermal imagining screen except open desert and the forms of night predators. Their fuel reserves precariously low, the Hip crew decided that they'd seen a mirage and proceeded to turn again, when suddenly the dust trail raised by a small, highly mobile vehicle crossing the desert was caught on the thermal scope.

Normally, such dust trails are dead giveaways, and during daylight hours are visible for miles around, which is one reason why the fusion cell's patrols moved only at night.

"Zoom to highest resolution factor," the pilot ordered, his voice now tense and without any trace of his former casualness.

The copilot punched buttons and there it was—the scout patrol's FAV caught rolling across the open desert. The pilot smiled triumphantly. He knew he had them now. If he watched his fuel gauge carefully, he would be able to make it back all right. Dropping low to mask the chopper behind terrain features, the pilot vectored in for the kill.

The two FAVs composing the long-range scout detachment were on their way back to the caravansary. They had little more than another six kilometers to cross before they reached the relative safety of the ruins. They were not to make it.

The Mi-8 Hip loomed up from behind the rise they were about to cross, cutting into the face of the moon like an apparition sprouting from the grave. The Hip driver was slick. He had positioned the chopper just beneath the lip of a deep wadi, unmasking the helo at exactly the right moment. To the patrol, it seemed to have popped right out of the earth like a jack-in-the-box.

The crew of the first FAV opened up immediately with automatic fire from the fifty-caliber MAG heavy machine guns mounted atop the roll bars of the vehicles. At the same time Sergeant Munnion Higgs, team leader, keyed his lip mike and got off an alert to Blue Corner.

"We're taking fire," he reported to the main body of the force at the caravansary.

"I copy that, White Corner. We are making arrangements." The communications watch officer consulted the orbital imaging from an Iridium satellite equipped for infrared photoimaging of the earth below it. "I have one helo on you. Repeat, only one helo."

"Affirmative," Higgs replied. "One—"

The transmission was abruptly cut off.

The satellite imaging was technically real-time, but in fact it was near real-time; there was a two-to-three-second delay in the video feed.

Two seconds after Higgs's voice stopped in midsentence, the watch officer saw a bright flash of light and a boiling fireball that ballooned high off the desert floor, all of it captured in the blacks, whites, and grayscales of thermal imaging sensors. The FAV was gone from view. It had been disintegrated by a rocket strike from the Hip.

Fragments of the disintegrated vehicle and the mangled human remains of the patrol lay burning in scattered heaps across a fifty-foot blast radius. Above the shattered, incinerated flesh and metal hovered the Mi-8. The watch officer stared in helpless shock into the screen showing satellite imaging as the helo rose and darted off toward the west, leaving the zone of destruction devoid of any living thing.

"Goddammit," Mitchell cursed as Arbatov looked on

and shook his head. Those men had been friends and comrades, closer in many ways even than family. Now they were gone, their lives snuffed out in an instant of contact with the remorseless certainties of pushbutton warfare.

Mitchell heard a beep in his communicator headset. The Hawkman's face appeared in a window of the global mobile field unit's LCD screen. By now the team had nicknamed him "God" from the way he kept watch on them all this time.

"I saw what happened on satellite feed, and I'm sorry about it," the Hawkman said, "but there's more shit on the way. Take a look."

Back at 11th Recon, the Hawkman moved a mouse cursor and clicked on one of the radio buttons above his windowed screen, duplicating the image on the remote unit several thousand kilometers away in the Iranian Dasht. The window that popped into being depicted a radar image from a Rhyolite satellite in low earth orbit. The Rhyolite had only minutes before reached an orbital trajectory that put it over most of northern Iran.

The Rhyolite's synthetic aperture radar or SAR is of photographic quality. Mitchell and Arbatov could clearly discern the wing of heavily armed Hips flying out from al-Munir Airbase about two hundred klicks southward, while armor and infantry was mobilized from local garrisons in the desert. Waves of hunters were spreading out toward them, and contact was inevitable.

"Wait one," Mitchell told the Hawkman as the Russian communications officer gestured for him and Arbatov to come over to his position. With Arbatov translating for Mitchell, the comms operator informed them that the Antonov An-72 "Coaler" medium-range STOL—or short takeoff and landing—transport was at an estimated range from their position of 620 kilometers, which would give it an ETA of two A.M. local time, depending on the RV zone selected.

The fusion cell's two leaders consulted their tactical maps and checked their watches. A single rendezvous point, given any chance of taking down the aircraft at the culvert with enough time to spare for a getaway, presented itself. The two-lane blacktop highway adjacent to the culvert could also be used as a landing zone for the cell's Antonov transport back into C.I.S. airspace. Alternatively, the Antonov could also land on the flat desert, if the terrain were properly cleared and marked with chemlights. The aircraft was built for rough-field capability and short takeoffs that other planes in its class, including the American C-135 Galaxy, would have a hard time handling.

Arbatov relayed the RV point's map grid coordinates to the comms operator and he transmitted it to the Antonov's crew. The decision whether to use the highway or the desert as a landing site would be put off until a few minutes before landing and depend on the tactical picture at that time. Otherwise, the plane was on schedule.

The cell's travel arrangements out of Iran having been taken care of, Mitchell turned back to TRAVLER's display screen, where the Hawkman was waiting for his feedback.

"While you were away . . . I worked up a rough plan for getting to the MFI," the Hawkman said. "Check it out."

The screen now displayed a color map of the surrounding terrain with a projected line of advance toward the Antonov's landing zone boxed in green. The threat envelopes of helos and Iranian ground forces were represented by icons of varying shapes denoting aircraft and ground vehicles. The path to the LZ wound and snaked between the threat balloons, changing position as the balloons marched across the desert terrain.

"As you can see, I project about an hour's ETA to the culvert if you move out now," the Hawkman summed up. "But I mean *now* like in *yesterday, capisce?*"

Mitchell and Arbatov studied the picture. What could they say? God had spoken.

Twenty-Two
Introductions Are Made

Gustavsen had done it with time to spare.

At five hundred forty hours, zulu, SSBN *Teaneck* reached her assigned station coordinates, having completed the more than thousand-kilometer passage in just under twenty-three hours. Maybe not a record for the Navy, but a record for Gustavsen's boat for sure.

Cruising at periscope depth, *Teaneck* was now making a leisurely seven knots. Before surfacing, its skipper and crew had run through a precautionary checklist of procedures to scan for hostile, and potentially hostile, underwater and surface sonar contacts. Even commercial vessels posed grave dangers. Since the sub had little positive buoyancy, being rammed by a large surface ship could break her up and quickly send her to the bottom.

In her combat information center or CIC, the electronic environment in the air above the sub was scanned for traffic that might present a threat. Then Gustavsen raised the periscope mast and made a sweep of the surface. Only after the skipper had visual confirmation of the absence of surface threats from three full periscope circuits, did he give the order to surface.

While the sub proceeded on its course, encrypted satcom transmissions from one of the array of FLTSATCOM satellites in geosynchronous earth orbit was beaming telemetry into the *Teaneck*'s BSY-1 weapons control system. Under the watchful eye of the boat's chief torpedoman, the coded signals were downloading updated targeting data into the electronic guidance systems of six of the twelve Tomahawk Block III cruise missiles that the *Teaneck* carried in vertical launch tubes arrayed along its hull.

BSY-1's decryption processors decoded the telemetry into trajectory information that would enable the Tomahawks to fly stealthy overland routes into Iran to destroy the missiles on their launchers. The missiles would rely on their TERCOM and DSMAC navigational systems to reach their destinations. Using high-speed digital communications, the entire update would require less than fifteen minutes at periscope depth, yet Gustavsen counted every minute that passed.

He knew how vulnerable his boat was near the surface, and how little it would take to sink her. The Iranian navy, or IRIN, was perhaps the best equipped in the Gulf, and his latest situation reports had shown that IRIN surface vessels and subs were heavily patrolling the sea lanes.

Gustavsen's worst worry were the Kilo-class diesel-electric boats that the Iranians had bought from the C.I.S. The subs were arguably the best nonnuclear boats in the world. They were fast, stealthy (their hulls were lined with sonar-absorbent anechoic rubber tiles), and formidably armed. They had damn good sonar, too. Gustavsen knew he would have to be ready to deal with them once inside the Gulf—evade them if he could, kill them if that's what it came to.

Mounted on five surviving FAVs, the Delta-Spetsnaz fusion cell made for its rally point through the cold desert night. To preserve stealth, the headlights of the FAVs were damped and none but essential communications between crew personnel were permitted.

All instrumentation controls, including buttons, switches, and dials, were lit by a dim blue-green electroluminescent glow. Invisible to distant observers, it was readily seen by passengers wearing night-vision goggles or NVGs. All members of the fusion cell were equipped with NVGs using advanced GEN-III light-amplification tubes.

A TRAVLER mobile terminal secured to each vehicle was uplinked to an array of satellites that constantly updated navigational data. These data were fused in a multispectral display that showed the team's projected safe route toward the RV point superimposed over a moving map display.

Along the line of advance, which shifted somewhat as TRAVLER updated the route with minor course corrections, line-of-sight data, such as GPS waypoints, elapsed time to RV, and time till daybreak, were also displayed in the form of numerical readouts.

The scheduled route was navigated without incident. A little before daybreak, the fusion cell had reached its rally point at Gur Qudair and was within unaided visual range of the culvert.

A high-low warble preceded the Hawkman's voice in Mitchell's earbud.

"I have the plane on my screen again," he said. "I can see a piece of the tail assembly jutting out from beneath one of the overpasses about a half klick to your left. The walls are steep, but if you jog right a tad, you'll reach some kind of access or maintenance ramp."

The Hawkman threw the revised projected path on the TRAVLER display in red, to overlay the green wire-grid diagram of the original route of advance.

"Roger, I copy that," Mitchell said back. He informed his men via the lightweight headsets the team wore that they were following the course update.

Under fifteen minutes later the cell reached the access gradient that sloped away from the desert roadbed. This was a ramp that graded down to the poured concrete floor of the culvert. Mitchell's FAV took the point, with three of the other five dune buggies rolling down the incline after it. A perimeter security detail was left on the flanks of the culvert to scout for trouble.

As the lead vehicle rolled slowly down the wet, muddy centerline of the concrete-walled ditch, they quickly spotted the HET with the aircraft strapped to its back. The cell quickly dismounted its vehicles and fanned out across the middle of the trough, weapons kept at the ready, eyes alert.

"Maggard, sitrep." Mitchell asked the scout team leader over headset comms. "Any action up top?"

"Negative. Lizards are fucking the snakes. That's all."

"Don't ever teach biology, Maggard," Mitchell told the sergeant. "Sitrep in five."

"Gotcha, boss."

The cell element at the bottom immediately got to work checking out the aircraft and searching for the pilot, who hadn't put in an appearance and was nowhere to be seen.

"Over here," Mitchell heard in his headphone while Arbatov heard the same in Russian from one of his Spetsnaz.

They ran toward a corner of the culvert where the cell's Russian medical officer was ministering to a prone man. Mitchell listened to the byplay in Russian between the doctor—he was a fully trained physician, not a corpsman—and the man on the culvert floor.

"This our pilot?" asked Mitchell.

"Yes," said the doctor, switching to English. "His name is Petrov."

Mitchell looked down at the injured Russian, and then at the HET with its ungainly cargo.

"He loaded the plane on that flatbed and got it down here all by himself?" Mitchell asked.

"Yes," translated the doctor. "And he says he would have tried to fly it out, too, had he not been poisoned by the scorpion's sting while he slept."

"Tell him he's nuts, but he's a hero," Mitchell said, adding, "and that we'll be taking him out with us."

"He's also lucky the scorpions in this desert have weak venom," the doctor added. "A North African scorpion would have finished him."

Mitchell left the doctor to his patient and walked over to the HET, where Arbatov was supervising the demolition of the aircraft. Plastic explosive, det cord, and electronic timers were being unshipped by cell personnel working all around the HET.

"Maggard, sitrep," Mitchell said into his lipmike.

"All is cool, boss. Was just about to call you."

"In five, Maggard."

"Yo, boss. Five."

Arbatov hailed Mitchell over.

"We can have the plane done in ten minutes. We'll set it for remote detonation. We can blow it up as the Antonovs land, with a five-minute delay as a fail-safe in case it doesn't take."

Mitchell regarded the stealth fighter and the large flatbed truck.

"That'll about do it," he agreed.

"Boss, the pilot wants to tell you something," one of the American personnel said in Mitchell's earbud.

"Be right there."

Arbatov came along, too. It turned out that Petrov was better now. Moreover, he felt well enough to finish what he had come to the culvert to do in the first place.

"I can fly this plane out of here," he told them. "It's got enough fuel to make the trip back. I'm well enough."

Petrov explained that he had checked the plane out. There had been problems with the inertial navigation system that he'd first attributed to tampering by the Iranians, but later discovered were due only to a loose integrated circuit chip on one of the controller boards. The plane worked perfectly. He could make it.

"No can do," Mitchell said. "We can't take the risk. That plane's a shit magnet."

Arbatov agreed. It was better to blow the stealth aircraft

on the ground than risk an attempt at flying it out. Too much bad luck had attended the flight of this particular plane, and soldiers could be superstitious, especially of any man, unit, or piece of equipment that seemed to have acted as a lightning rod for trouble. To the cell's leaders, if not Petrov, this plane had brought trouble in spades. Besides, they had their orders—blow the plane and get out.

The demolition prep work continued.

Barak's team spotted the cell's security detail on the perimeter of the culvert long before they were aware of the Israeli commando unit's presence. In part, it was because luck happened to be on Barak's side.

The Rhyolite had since moved out of position and they were in a transmission gap between it and the Keyhole that was moving into an overhead surveillance window as they approached. Trained to move soundlessly across the desert's surface, a detachment left the BTR with orders to kill only if necessary and to disarm if possible.

The watch detail's first intimation that they were in trouble came when they felt the barrels of captured Iranian AKS autorifles jammed against the sides of their heads. The detachment was quickly subdued with cable ties and made to lie facedown on the ground under armed guard.

With the cell's ground-level security screen down, the main body of the Israeli team rappelled down the sides of the culvert, avoiding the ramp that they suspected the fusion cell had used, and possibly mined with claymores. They reached their target just as the demo charges around Shadow One were being armed.

Barak, preparing to follow them to the channel floor, took the headset from one of the captured cell members. He heard a voice speak faintly from it.

"Maggard, sitrep," Barak now heard the voice say clearly, as he placed it over his head.

The double click over Barak's handheld radio transceiver was the signal for the BTR crew to turn its powerful hundred-kilowatt spotlight down into the culvert. Caught unaware, the light blinded the fusion-cell personnel, who were quickly herded into a compact unit by Barak's crew already inside the culvert. Most were no longer wearing NVGs, but those who did experienced severe blooming effects when the light came on. By the time their vision had adjusted, the surprised soldiers were prisoners, and Barak's technical people were going over the aircraft.

"Let me introduce myself," Barak announced, and proceeded to do just that, informing his captives of how he had been fully briefed on their mission and instructed by the Israeli prime minister on behalf of the U.S. and C.I.S. to offer the fusion cell every assistance possible.

"But," Barak added, a harlequin's smile contorting his damaged face as he lit a cigarette and swept his eyes across the faces of the cell members, "I don't give a crap about the prime minister or anybody else, including the great nations you represent. I care only about number one." He jabbed a thumb at his chest. "And I mean to have this plane if I can, gentlemen. It will make me rich."

Barak called out to his technical crew.

"What's her condition?"

"She's flyable," he was told. "All systems check out. All we have to do is drive this HET onto the roadbed, winch the stealth onto the highway, and take off. There's enough fuel to cross the border."

Barak nodded, understanding the reference to crossing the border to mean the Israeli border, with the added implication that there would be sufficient fuel reserves to enable the aircraft to land on the many kilometers of fenced-off Negev land owned by Assaf Gilad.

Barak still had the long-range burst transmitter that Gilad had given him. He could send a satcom message with reasonable security once the plane was airborne. Gilad would have an airstrip lit by infrared landing lights ready. It could be done.

"Chayim," Barak called out to another of his technical officers, who was punching the keys on one of the mobile

TRAVLER terminals, "what can you tell me about this contraption?"

"I would call this device a high-bit-rate, point-to-point, wireless multibandwidth link with multihop capability," the team's technical officer answered.

"You would call it that, eh?"

"Yes, I would," Chayim affirmed smugly.

"Then I would call you a putz with an enlarged vocabulary," Barak answered. "In plain Hebrew, what is this fucking thing?"

"It's a sophisticated communications and navigational computer," a chastened Chayim answered. "We're working on something like it."

"And what does this contraption tell you?"

"Something is on the way," Chayim reported, working TRAVLER's integrated mouse and clicking at the keys, his eyes on the screen. "I think . . . yes, it's a transport, a Russian transport . . . ETA less than one half hour."

"Then we'd better move fast," Barak declared.

"You're the one who gives the orders," Chayim replied testily.

Barak turned. He issued instructions to his crew to dismantle the demo charges around Shadow One and roll the HET up the ramp to the highway above.

Twenty-Three

A Takeoff Run

A warble in the earphone of the Antonov pilot's helmet radio preceded a secure transmission from the operation's command post in Kuwait.

"One-Zero-Foxtail to Big Bear. Do you copy?"

"Affirmative, One-Zero-Foxtail. What can I do for you?"

"There has been a change in plans. Your LZ has been moved to map references seven-zero-three-dash-four-zero,-slash-zero-niner-zero-dash-five-zero-six. That is a section of Highway 32 running north-south about thirty kilometers from your original LZ."

"Wait one, please," the pilot said into his helmet mike.

The Antonov's navigator had already entered the map reference coordinates into the aircraft's navigational computer and was now consulting a printed map of northern Iran that was propped open in front of him.

"I have it," he told the pilot over the aircraft interphone. "A level stretch of roadway. Straight as a damned ruler."

"Can we land on it?"

"I suppose we'll be finding out, Fedor."

The pilot keyed his throat mike and said back to the distant command post, "That's affirm on the revised LZ. We copy the nav update. Estimate time to the LZ at approximately fifteen minutes. Advise that traffic on the highway could present a problem on landing."

"Affirmative. Forces on the ground will be advised. Good luck."

The pilot broke squelch and executed a thirty-degree turn. The new heading put the Antonov on a course for the revised LZ.

"What do you make of that?" he asked the copilot.

"What do I make of it?" he repeated. "I suppose we'll find out soon enough, Fedor."

"Is that all you can say, Nikolai?" asked the pilot.

"What, Fedor?"

"Never mind, Nikolai," the pilot replied, and flew his new black line.

A numerical readout showing zulu, or Greenwich Mean Time, flashed across the bottom of the god screen set up at 11th Recon. The view was downward, from a geostationary Keyhole satellite positioned over the Persian Gulf. Resolution was at a medium zoom factor, looking down through the thin, striated clouds meteorologists call nimbostratus, showing a three-hundred-mile swath of the earth's blue-green surface, with the Gulf glittering off to the extreme left and the Iranian coastal regions occupying the center of the picture.

The Hawkman's gray eyes were fixed on the god screen as he munched honey-roasted peanuts from a cellophane bag and sipped at a Diet Pepsi through a striped plastic straw.

"Bingo," he said. "Make that mah-jongg."

Suddenly the bulbous forward assembly of Tier III Plus popped into view from high on the left, soon followed by the razor-shaped, swept-back wings, and aft section of the reconnaissance drone. The second, armed version of Global Hawk that had lifted off some ten hours before had just been acquired by the overhead surveillance platform.

Craning back in his chair, the Hawkman emptied the last of his peanuts into his mouth and chucked the balled-up bag into a nearby trash receptacle, one that had been steadily gathering an assortment of other junk-food packaging and dented aluminum soda cans over the last several hours. He then proceeded to keystroke data into the keyboard resting on his lap as he propped his sneakered feet up on the edge of the trestle table piled with equipment. The commands he'd entered had just told the Keyhole to begin tracking Tier III Plus and change to a higher magnification setting.

The computer had calculated an estimated time of arrival to the attack coordinates of about twenty minutes. While Global Hawk was en route, the Hawkman deflowered another bag of honey-roasted nuts and ran a diagnostic check on the flying arsenal's weapons systems. It never hurt to be careful. And how come you never got a flex-o-straw with a can of soda anymore?

They had rolled the HET onto the tarmac, parked the lumbering metal brontosaur, and extended the four stabilizing pylons on the vehicle's sides to keep it steady during the off-loading process. Barak supervised the work crew, looking on and issuing orders while Shadow One was stripped of its tarp coverings and its tie-downs, then slowly and carefully winched off the back end of the low-rise flatbed.

After all three landing gear were secure on the tarmac, the HET was driven a few meters down the highway and ditched on the side of the road. The MFI now stood on its own like a newborn black monster insect, drinking in the darkness that was its natural element. The Israelis had cheered spontaneously, and Barak had permitted them a moment of jubilation, despite the fact that sound carried far and clearly in the desert, and Iranian forces might be in the vicinity. Yet, if ever there was a moment to break the rules, this was it.

By the spectral light cast by vehicle-mounted spotlights and headlamps, Barak watched the ground crew maneuver the aircraft onto the blacktop and disengage the HET's motorized winch cable from the tie-downs that made the tarp fast around the plane. Once these were gone, Barak studied the plane for a moment, drinking in the stark black beauty of its angular airframe.

A great prize had come into their possession, of this there was no doubt. Barak's cut of the plane's realized value, once it was safely back in Israel and in the hands of Gilad's affiliates in the defense industry, would amount to millions of dollars. He could retire for life on the proceeds of this one deal alone.

Each of the plane's subsystems was, almost literally, worth its weight in gold. The advanced stealth and avionics technologies could be back-engineered and repackaged in a variety of new ways, then sold to various global clients for a huge return on the original investment. For Raful Barak, the term "black gold" had just taken on an entirely new meaning.

The Old Man in the Negev would fix the political end of things. He'd always managed to succeed at this in the past.

Gilad was a survivor of three regional wars and scores of political battles. He had come through the War for Independence, the Six Day War, and the war in Lebanon with few physical injuries. His worst defeat was at the hands of his friend and political mentor Menachem Begin, who had been in on the frame for the Sabra and Shatilla massacres that had blackened Gilad's name.

But the wily old campaigner had outlived Begin, as he had survived so much else. Barak had no doubt that Gilad would find creative ways to turn this operation into something that had never happened.

"Zamir," Barak called out as his thoughts returned to the present. He gestured at one of his men who had climbed into Petrov's flight suit on Barak's orders while the stealth was being off-loaded from the HET.

"Can you do this?" Barak asked, his eyes on the plane as the soldier came over.

"*Magneev*—no problem," Zamir told him. "Stop worrying, Raful. I've already told you three times I can handle this aircraft." He clapped his hand on Barak's shoulder.

"If I don't worry, who will?" Barak shot back.

"My mother in Tel Aviv," Zamir said. "She worries enough for all of us."

Despite the tension, both men laughed at the crack.

The Israeli pilot was the veteran of numerous air combat missions, overt and covert. He had participated in the air war over Lebanon, which so far holds the record for the biggest aerial dogfight in air-warfare history.

"I've talked with the Russian pilot," Zamir explained. "It will be simple. There should by rights be an auxiliary-power supply unit hooked up to the aircraft prior to take-off, but this can be done without. The electrical system seems fully stoked."

Zamir Amroni had retired with an Israeli air-force colonel's full pension, but it had not been enough to pay his gambling debts, alimony, and the lavish lifestyle to which he had become addicted during his years at the top.

"Let me know when you're ready to take off," Barak told him.

Amroni nodded and loped off toward the plane. Moments later he had undogged the canopy and climbed into the cockpit, which was soon illuminated by the soft blue glow of the instrumentation console. Barak smoked a Marlboro and watched Amroni as he began running down a preflight checklist of all systems. The whine of electrical systems and turbines was soon bansheeing through the desert night. *Not good, all that noise,* Barak thought. *But it can't be helped.*

Barak turned away from the plane and flicked his cigarette into the darkness amid a brief spray of orange sparks. His glance now fell on the captive members of the U.S.–Soviet fusion cell.

Now to other matters, he thought. His lighter flared, and he soon dragged hard on a fresh smoke.

Colonel Ghazbanpour removed his glasses and rubbed his burning eyes and the pinched bridge of his aquiline Persian nose. He glanced at his wristwatch. It was one hundred twenty hours—again. He had been awake for almost four straight days, grabbing fitful snatches of sleep on the wobbly cot in his cramped office. He couldn't go on this way much longer. He would need a few hours of real sleep, in a real bed soon, or he would be incapable of thinking clearly.

But he could not yet afford himself this luxury. As long as the plane remained out there—Ghazbanpour replaced his glasses and stared at the wall map—likely somewhere in the Dasht, he had to remain awake, had to stay in constant touch with his forces on the ground. The troops were well trained and many were dedicated, but he had no illusions about their capabilities, especially in the face of a new commando offensive to retake the plane.

Where had it gone? Where? The desert was a big place, true. Yet the aircraft had simply disappeared, as thoroughly as if the ground had opened up and swallowed it. It had never crossed the border. Even a stealth could not have slipped past the alert following the Russian's escape. Of course, he thought, there was the story of a derailed diesel locomotive that had been buried in the Dasht, hidden from the eyes of the shah, who was arriving for an inspection tour of a new railway line. But it had taken a full crew with a backhoe to accomplish this feat.

Ghazbanpour turned from the map and reached for the pitcher of ice water on his desk. Suddenly his mind fell into sync, and he saw a connection that had escaped him before. His head jerked back to the map. This time the dead eyes were alive, the sleep-hungering mind keen and alert from a quickening rush of adrenaline.

He stared at the water, and then at the map.

"As if the earth had swallowed it . . . *swallowed* it . . ." he muttered.

Yes, of course. That was it. Had to be. Everything had suddenly crystallized and become whole, where before there were only pieces. Amazing how that happened under pressure sometimes.

The culvert system. Large and deep enough and . . . what else? Something in the back of his mind still gnawed at him.

Setting down the pitcher, Ghazbanpour was rifling through sheaves of intelligence reports strewing his desk, and—yes! There it was. He pulled a page from the stack of Teletypes and faxes that had come in since the night the plane had been retaken by the escaped Russian pilot.

The report cited a missing trailer truck, one used to haul heavy equipment over great distances. In this case it had been a construction crane that had gone to a building site in Tehran. Again Ghazbanpour consulted his wall map. He saw that the truck could indeed have passed close to the culvert on its route through the Gur Qudair. Any truck that could have hauled such a huge piece of equipment could also easily accommodate a fighter plane.

But the Gur Qudair was no-man's-land. The last place on earth anyone would willingly venture. Yet such a place was the perfect earth for foxes. And this pilot had been a fox, hadn't he? One being chased by hounds, in fact.

Ghazbanpour stared into the blackness outside the window of his office. The full moon shone with a limpid light, but it had sunk lower in the sky since he had last looked. Time was fast running out. The colonel picked up the phone and dialed his adjutant, ordering a helicopter readied for immediate dust-off. This time he would personally lead the operation. There would be no more foul-ups. The plane was hidden in that culvert. He would stake his life on it!

The second Global Hawk variant, Tier III Plus, had reached its operational envelope sixty thousand feet above the northeastern desert of Iran. Its onboard processor activated the array of imaging sensors located on the underside of its forward fuselage, and these shifted into spot scanning mode. Within a matter of seconds the imaging array had detected the movement of an Iranian armored column in the direction of the culvert.

The Hawkman had by now donned his HMD and force-feedback gloves and was in control of the second Hawk. Minutes later the robot aircraft was within sensor range of the culvert and the Hawkman had a good picture of what was taking place on the ground.

He could clearly see the stealth plane being prepared for takeoff. Its hot engines, cowled and baffled as they were, gave off a telltale IR signature and its avionic systems were emitting tempest energies, the leakage of radio emissions from energized electronic circuitry that produced a signature as distinct as that of other forms of radiant energy, such as heat or light.

The Hawkman could also see something still more disquieting. The fusion cell was being held captive by an armed commando force. He would have to do something about that. Moving his hands across a virtual control panel that occupied a corner of his visual field, the Hawkman dragged the gun-shaped icon across the screen, activating the weapons package of the Hawk.

Barak faced Mitchell and Arbatov across the tarmac. They, along with the plane, had been brought from the culvert to the level of the highway above. In a pool of light cast by magnesium arc lamps mounted on the captured FAVs, he sized up both men, pondering their fates. There was, of course, only one way to end this, and no reason whatever to hesitate.

The two commando leaders had to be taken out. This went for the entire fusion cell, for that matter. It would not do to have any witnesses to what was about to take place.

"We seem to have come to the end of the road, literally and figuratively," Barak told the American and the Russian. "The plane is in my hands and my pilot is about to fly it out to safety. Your involvement leaves me with a problem. But also, I think, with an opportunity."

The short-barreled AKS assault rifle in the Israeli's grip was locked and loaded with a thirty-round magazine jacked into its receiver. Barak held the rifle casually in his right hand, its muzzle pointing at the ground. But his index finger was lightly curled around the trigger, and when he brought the AKS up and into play, he could squeeze off a burst in a fraction of a second.

"You see," he went on, "a few American and Russian corpses left behind after the plane takes off could prove advantageous. They might divert attention from the involvement of, shall we say, a 'third force.' "

Barak paused and studied the faces of the men he was about to shoot down at point-blank range. "Yes, that's how we'll do it."

He jerked the rifle up from his hip, leveling its business end at his captives. As always, Barak wore a sardonic smile frozen on his face. This time, though, the graveyard grin was genuine.

"Like, extreme close-up!"

The Hawkman zoomed in the video on three figures near the fringes of the activity on the road. At a magnification factor of three hundred, the image resolved into a man in Pasdaran-issue olive-drab fatigues and red beret facing two other men in NATO chocolate-chips BDUs. The man in ODs held a baby Kalashnikov. The other two were unarmed.

"Got a bad moon rising here," the Hawkman said, enlarging the image still further so he could get a clear shot of their faces.

Once he had them, the Hawkman used a scissor tool to outline each face and dragged the images into the database icon on the floating palette bar. Seconds later the computer gave him two matches out of three: the dude with the rifle was unknown, but the other two were the fusion-cell commanders, Mitchell and Arbatov.

Suddenly the unidentified man in the Iranian ODs raised his weapon. The Hawkman knew he'd fire in a split instant.

"Bummer," he said to himself, pushing a mouse cursor across the display.

The men stood too close together to target any of them accurately by one of the kinetic energy rounds that the Hawk fired, but the Hawkman could come pretty close. He had already put Tier III Plus into a steep dive with its thermal gun cameras trained on the area in focus. Before the shooter had a chance to pop some caps, the Hawkman triggered a salvo of kinetic-energy fléchettes from the swooping Hawk's electromagnetic coil gun.

The burst struck the edge of the blacktop close to the APC. The three-inch darts of depleted uranium alloyed with tungsten contained no explosive, but the sheer velocity released tremendous energies on impact. The fléchettes tore sizable chunks out of the roadbed and produced a sound similar to that of a mortar round hitting.

"Yeah, we bad," shouted the Hawkman. "We baddddd!"

Tier III Plus now swung around for a second attack run, this time tearing into the machine gunner atop the APC and ripping off half the top of the vehicle, which quickly exploded and burst into a fireball.

The Hawkman circled his bird around one more time and came in for another final strafing run. Then he got the hell out of there. He had other things to do. A high-low warble had sounded in his ear. The Antonov was getting in touch. The transport was about to commence its approach and landing on the highway.

Teaneck was less than three nautical miles to her Tomahawk launch coordinates when she caught a whiff of trouble.

"Skipper, I have two transient contacts at bearing zero-seven-six-zero and zero-seven-eight-five," the chief sonarman called out to the helm. "Cavitation noises . . . I make them Kilo boats. Textbook sonar signatures."

Gustavsen didn't want a fight, and though he could outrun the Kilos, he could well find himself flying into the teeth of the Iranian navy by doing so.

If possible, he would opt to hide from the Kilos. Their sonar suite was good, he knew, but not as good as all that, and the *Teaneck* had a lot of stealth technology—including sonar-absorbent anechoic tiles that lined her hull—built into her design. Plus, his charts told him that the thermal makeup of the Gulf waters and the topography of its floor would help to conceal his boat from sonar detection if he played his cards right.

"Full stop," Gustavsen said to his exec, who relayed the orders to the chief diving officer, who in turn commanded his planesmen. The crisp, clear chain of spoken commands left no room for misinterpretation during combat. The *Teaneck* stopped dead in the water, her propeller still.

The crew in the control room was silent. Minutes ticked by as the sonarmen listened through their headphones and intently monitored the waterfall displays linked by high-speed computers to the sensitive hydrophones at bow and stern, including the new BQR-24 conformal array of hundreds of three-inch sensors that made up the sub's passive sonar sensor system.

"Contacts are moving off," the chief sonar operator reported after several minutes had passed. "I don't think they've seen us. Distance is increasing. Contacts have now passed beyond passive sonar range. We've lost them, Skipper."

Gustavsen hoped the sonar operator was right. He waited an extra five minutes to make sure neither of the Kilos had doubled back, then resumed *Teaneck*'s course to her missile launch point off the coast of Iran.

Twenty-Four

Outbreak of Peace

Mitchell prepared himself. He knew he was about to take a burst in the heart. There would be a moment of pain, then some drifting, then a forever of nothing. He'd never let the idea that he might die in combat trouble him. It went with the territory. Mitchell was ready for it, when and if it came. He was ready for it now.

But when the explosions struck, it was not the cycling of automatic fire that Mitchell heard. It was the lightning crack of high explosive. Gouts of rock fragments, geysers of sand, and spouts of upflung asphalt rubble erupted in all directions. It seemed like somebody was dropping mortar rounds on his position, but that wasn't exactly right, either.

They definitely weren't being shelled. There was no telltale ripping-silk sound of inbound mortar or artillery rounds, no acrid stink of cordite. They had certainly come under attack. But from where? And from what?

Barak had turned, too, as alarmed and as perplexed as

Mitchell and Arbatov beside him. Barak also asked himself the same questions as Mitchell. More important from Mitchell's standpoint was that the barrel of the Israeli's AKS was now temporarily turned away from himself and the Russian.

Without hesitation both men jumped Barak, but the Israeli was fast on his feet. He reacted like a cornered cougar, lashing out savagely with the weapon. A side slash of the AKS's buttstock to the side of Arbatov's head knocked him over, felling him like an axed tree. Barak spun on the follow-through and went for Mitchell, but before he could connect, Mitchell sidekicked him with a spinning geri that ripped the rifle from Barak's hands and sent it clattering to the sands.

The Israeli recovered quickly from the lightning foot blow. Now unarmed, he whipped around and delivered a flurry of karate-style front kicks that sent Mitchell dodging and ducking to avoid being tagged. The Egoz was a good fighter, strong and fast, sharp and cool. He would not go down easy, if at all, Mitchell knew. Closing with Barak, Mitchell blocked another flurry of kicks, and lunged at Barak with a series of hand blows using fists and elbows to the face and upper chest.

Both men were aware of more nearby explosions and the clamor of shouting and sporadic small arms fire. Glimpsed scenes of the firefight now taking place all around them reached them in a detached, abstract way as each man fought for survival. Mitchell and Barak were locked together in a death struggle, in a tunnel where time moved like burning magma. Neither had a decisive edge over his opponent, and a moment's lapse in concentration could translate into sudden death for either one of them.

Mitchell parried a series of kicks and closed-fist blows delivered by Barak with a flurry of blocks and kicks of his own, which sent the other man whirling backward. Then Barak's foot struck a rock and he lost his balance. Barak pitched sideways. A second later his own momentum had brought him down, and he hit the sand, sliding on his face. His head struck a sharp stone and blood spurted from a cut above his left eye.

Barak felt himself start to black out, but the dull glint of moonlight on gunmetal brought him back to his senses with a sudden rush of adrenaline. His dropped rifle, he saw, was only inches from his outstretched hand. A desperate lunge, and the gun was in his grasp once again.

Before Mitchell could rush him, Barak was back up on his feet, leveling the weapon into firing position from a half crouch.

Barak was breathing hard and blood streamed down his face from the deep cut above his left eye. But before pulling the trigger, he permitted himself a grin. All that mattered in the end was who came out on top. To a soldier, it was one of battle's timeless truths.

"You lose," Barak said, and pulled the bullpup's trigger, wasting no more time on banter. The air was suddenly rent by an earsplitting report.

The stricken man felt a hammer blow in his upper torso, was lifted off his feet, and fell to earth in a bloody sprawl. Half his right chest was suddenly gone, and in its place was a raw mass of butchered organ matter and gore-streaked blood.

Mitchell rose from the dust and ran over to where Barak lay in the shell hole blown by the Iranian mortar round that had landed within inches of the Israeli commando. Both men had heard the telltale whistling of the incoming round and Mitchell had dropped prone in a fast hunker. Nothing Barak could have done would have saved him. The round had had his name written on it. It had been almost a direct hit, with Barak standing right on the bull's-eye.

Amazingly, Barak was still alive, though Mitchell didn't need a medic to tell him that he wouldn't be for long. The Israeli's life was draining away, soaking into the dark, cold sands on which he'd fallen. Mitchell crouched beside the dying man, feeling bloody fingers pulling at his arm with demonic power.

Barak wanted to tell him something. His hand closed

on Mitchell's arm and gripped it with amazing pressure and force. Mitchell was irresistibly drawn down toward the face that was already somehow skeletal, as a death pallor spread across the gaunt features. Barak's thin lips moved and he tried to croak out his final words. He struggled with every last ounce of strength he possessed to mouth them . . . and ultimately he succeeded.

"Tizdayen . . ." was all Barak said.

Then he expired, his macabre harlequin smile still frozen on his cadaverous face. Peace, who didn't know Barak's native language, heard something that sounded like " 'tis dyin' " and wondered what the Israeli had meant. Some philosophical statement about death, maybe? Who knew?

But Mitchell had no time to reflect on this. He struggled to pry loose the fingers of the corpse that were locked like a vise of muscle and bone around his arm. He finally worked them loose and struggled to his feet, Barak's dropped AKS cradled in a combat grip.

Standing, Peace tried to reorient himself to his immediate surroundings. How much time had passed since the moment before his imminent execution? It seemed like hours, but time telescopes in a fight.

Where was Arbatov? Mitchell caught sight of the Russian over by the stealth. He then recognized his exec, Sergeant Martinez, and called him over. Just then a mortar round came whistling in—this time it was unmistakable—and Mitchell went prone, crabbing in the sand. When he came back up, amid acrid cordite clouds and a fog of airborne dust particles lit by explosive flashes, Martinez was at his side.

"Taking mortar fire, boss, in case you didn't just figure that out yourself," Martinez explained. "An Iranian column's on the way in. We got aerial surveillance again, by the way."

"What about the Antonov?"

"ETA ten minutes, maybe less," Martinez answered. "Even money whether the Iranians beat the plane into the

LZ or whether it can't land because of the shelling. We're standing by, either way."

"What about the stealth?"

"Change of plan, boss," Martinez replied. "Arbatov wants to brief you. He's over by the aircraft right now."

Martinez added that "God" was back on the screen. He had sent down some thunderbolts in the nick of time. That had been the first "attack." The fléchettes explained what Mitchell had originally thought was a mortar strike. Using the diversion, the fusion cell had turned the tables on the rogue Israelis and a brief but intense firefight had ensued. The four Israeli survivors were now prisoners, but it had cost. There had been casualties on both sides.

Pausing to take cover as another Iranian mortar round whistled in and exploded with a loud *crump!* in a geyser of flame, noise, cordite stink, and choking desert dust, Mitchell made his way across the highway blacktop to where the Spetsnaz commander was speaking to a pilot wearing a flight suit.

This time it wasn't the Israeli pilot, but Vassily Petrov, who was suited up and ready to climb into the MFI's cockpit.

"Change in plans, my friend," Arbatov told Mitchell as soon as he was in earshot. "Petrov flies her out."

"Why not blow her up?" Petrov noted that Arbatov's head was bandaged and taped on one side, the gauze caked with dried blood. Barak had landed a solid shot.

"Too risky now," Arbatov answered with a shake of his head. "We have no time to guarantee that the charges will be properly placed. The Antonov is now minutes away. What happens if there's a foul-up?"

"Yeah, this has been one goat rope after another."

"*Da.* A real *pizdetz,* as we say; a flaming fuckup."

"What about the Hawk?"

"Our friend 'God' says he's out of lightning bolts for the moment," Arbatov replied. "Check for yourself if you've any doubts."

Arbatov nodded at one of his men, who handed Mitchell a wireless headset keyed to the TRAVLER ground station. A brief conversation with the Hawkman settled Mitchell's residual doubts. Mitchell signed off and turned back to Arbatov.

"You're right about that. He used up his ammo reserves pulling our asses out of a sling before."

"It doesn't matter," said Arbatov. "The Iranians seem to have loaded two new Addax missiles from their inventory in the stealth's missile bay. Petrov thinks they were about to make a test flight using live ordnance. We can use our newfound plane on our way out of this mess to ride the stagecoach, as you say."

"Ride shotgun," Mitchell corrected. "We'll have to—"

An earsplitting din drowned out his words. This time it wasn't another incoming mortar salvo. The roar belonged to the immense wing-mounted turbofans of the AN-72 Coaler as the huge transport plane appeared out of thin air like a flying mountain and approached for a landing, its mammoth engines whipping up a minisandstorm in the process.

The transport had its landing gear extended, but before the plane touched down, another mechanical scream split the night. This one was the sound of Shadow One's engines firing up to full power. Mitchell and virtually everyone else in the vicinity watched the black stealth plane begin to roll along the highway—which had been turned into a makeshift illuminated runway by the placement of chemlights along its flanks—picking up speed until it began to lift into the air. The stealth finally nosed up and disappeared into the night, its rectangular exhausts glowing with yellow-blue flame.

Once the plane was out of sight, the crew on the ground sprang into action. FAVs were driven off the roadbed, which was a simple task since the highway was no more than a layer of asphalt steamrolled across the flat pancake crust of the Dasht. The commandeered Iranian BTR was trundled out of the way while the HET was driven off the shoulder and onto the desert.

Now the Antonov touched down, its immense girth filling the highway as its outsized nose gear bit into the tarmac with a deafening screech. Then its rear landing gear and tail assembly descended to earth. The screaming engines changed pitch suddenly as the pilot applied reverse thrust, and the plane began rolling to a full stop. The aircraft was stationary no longer than a few seconds when the top of its rear fuselage canted upward on pneumatic actuators, exposing its yawning cargo bay to the night, wind, and clouds of blowing sand.

As the plane continued to roll slowly along the highway, the FAVs and men were hustled into the rear of the cargo area. The AN-72's pilots kept the plane's engines hot as more mortar rounds came whistling in and exploded with an earsplitting tumult, coming thicker and faster as the Iranian mechanized column advanced.

In a matter of minutes all personnel and vehicles were onboard the Antonov, and the pilot reapplied thrust, rolling forward along the blacktop with gathering speed. The assault transport aircraft was quickly airborne again, and flying eastward at its maximum speed and ceiling. By the time the advancing Iranian armored column reached the rally point, the LZ was stone-cold.

The MiG-29 Fulcrums were first-line fighters, and the best planes the Iranian air force had in its inventory. The Fulcrums' pilots were the cream of the Iranian top-gun academy. A sortie of two planes was scrambled and ordered to intercept the Antonov. They already had its rough heading and position punched into the MiGs' navigation computers.

Much faster than the transport, the agile, powerful fighter aircraft closed with the lumbering jet heavy-lifter before it had gone very far on its transit to the border.

"There she is." The flight leader heard his wingman's voice in his headset. "I have radar contact with the transport."

"I copy that," the flight leader said. "This should be child's play, but be careful—we don't know what we're up against. Missiles from standoff range."

"Come on, Nabil"—the wingman's voice came back in

his helmet radio—"we don't have to do that. Let's have some fun with that fucking dinosaur of a plane. We can fill her full of holes with our nose cannons and watch her break apart. With a missile kill it's a fireball and then—*poof!* That's it."

The flight leader considered a moment. He had not received any orders that would preclude simply strafing the transport. The Antonov was armed, of course, and it was equipped with antimissile countermeasures, but that would only put some more sport into the game.

Hell, why not? he thought. It would be good for his pilots' morale, instill more of a thirst for blood in them that might come in handy during a real dogfight, say with the Israelis or Americans one fine day.

"Okay, Ibrahim," he answered after a pause, "we'll have it your way. Gun cannons it is. But if there's any trouble, we'll finish her with missiles."

"Affirmative," the wingman answered, the relish in his voice plain to hear.

"Tracking radar emissions," the copilot of the Antonov announced as he scanned the symbols on his scope. "MiG-29 tracking radars. Six hundred meters and closing."

Now the pilot saw the threat symbols appear on his main scope. The Antonov's avionics suite came equipped with the best radars and antijamming and electronic countermeasures the Russians had available. The bogies were identified as MiG-29 fighters.

"Activate ECM," the pilot ordered.

"Activating countermeasures," he heard the copilot say.

Switches were flipped and dials turned on rack-mounted ECM black boxes. Podded transmitters on the underside of the plane emitted intense signal noise across multiple bandwidths, returning false radar echoes to the search and tracking modulators aboard the MiGs.

The countermeasures worked, but only temporarily.

"They're burning through our jamming," the copilot warned after a few minutes and several score more kilometers had passed.

"I'll try to ditch the bogies," the pilot said, and put the large plane through a series of jinks, dives, and S-turns in an effort to throw off the Fulcrums' tracking radars.

"Still closing, closing. Five hundred meters. Continuing to close," the copilot declared in stages. "Less than two hundred meters now . . . one hundred meters . . . still closing . . ."

"Why haven't they launched a bird?" the pilot wondered out loud.

"I don't know," the copilot replied. "There's nothing so far. No missile homing radar. No indication of a launch signature."

"Check your—"

A MiG suddenly burst into view from below, crossing directly in front of the AN-72's flight deck. The warplane did not fire, but the larger, slower transport aircraft was buffeted by a sudden, fierce shock wave. In a heartbeat, another MiG passed beneath the Antonov's underfuselage, so close to the plane's underside that the shock front of compressed air it generated at Mach one velocity almost sent the Antonov into a flameout.

"*Ebat-kopat!* The bastards are toying with us like cats with a fat mouse," the copilot cursed.

Suddenly another MiG appeared. For a fraction of an instant before they heard the telltale stuttering of the thirty-mm nose cannon, the Antonov crew saw the rotoring belches of yellow-white flame that indicated they were taking cannon fire. A heartbeat later they felt the thud of the armor-piercing rounds punching through the aircraft's thin metal skin.

Fire licked and smoke belched from the Antonov's control panel and bulkheads. The copilot jumped up and unclipped a fire extinguisher from one of the racks, spraying the panel where a section of gauges had shorted and burst into flame.

Suddenly the pilot noticed he'd been hit. Blood welled from his arm and his flight suit had begun to sop with it. The pilot called for a medic, and the cell's doctor rushed forward from the aft cabin with his first-aid kit and began to apply a sterile dressing. Suddenly another MiG appeared athwart the Antonov, and more bullets rotored out, stitching a line across the plane's underfuselage.

Now the AN-72's left engine was trailing smoke, and flames sporadically erupted from the damaged turbine nacelle. The system diagnostics readouts were flashing on the plane's instrument console, dire warnings appeared on all of the displays and readouts. It was clear to the aircrew that after another such salvo they would likely break apart.

But neither the crew of the Antonov, nor the sortie of MiGs that attacked the transport, was aware that twelve thousand feet above them, Shadow One's fire-control system had already made its final calculations on a solution for the two Addax air-to-air missiles the stealth carried, or that Petrov had opened the conformal ordnance bay to lower the missiles into firing position from beneath the belly of the stealth.

Roughly equivalent to the AIM-190X AMRAAM of the U.S. inventory, the Addaxes were heat-seeking missiles that were resistant to countermeasures, including flare and chaff clouds. Shadow One's fire-control system was capable of tracking nine targets simultaneously and plotting firing solutions on four of them.

The MiGs could not see the stealth on their radars, but scope icons had popped up telling them that they had been acquired by an unidentified aircraft. Petrov already had a firing solution on both Iranian fighters, but the planes were spaced too close to the Antonov to risk Shadow One's missiles breaking lock and striking the transport instead in error. Petrov kept his eyes on his scopes, waiting for his chance.

The minutes ticked by. And then his patience paid off. Petrov saw the transport begin to pull away from her attackers, yet the MiGs did not pursue. Petrov knew what was about to happen. The flight leader had called for missile strikes against the transport to finish her off. They had grown tired of their cat-and-mouse game and were about to loose the killing stroke. First the MiGs would deploy to standoff range. Then they would fire.

Petrov calculated the maximum time he could wait to launch his own birds against the distance the Antonov had gained on the MiGs, and watched the gap between the MiGs and the Antonov continue to widen. At the last possible moment before he judged the MiGs would fire, he pickled off the Addaxes, feeling the MFI shudder and restabilize as the missiles left their conformal racks and sped forward, their glowing exhausts shrinking to pinpricks in the night.

As the rounds disappeared, Petrov switched to his remote nose-camera scope that relayed real-time data from the missiles' warhead assemblies. The missiles could be set to auto or manually overridden. He had programmed them for auto but had flipped the protective shrouds off the lighted manual detonation buttons for each round. As his eyes scanned the realtime gun-camera feed, he was ready to press the buttons at any moment.

Petrov continued monitoring the video feed. The cluster of MiGs grew in his scope until they seemed to be right on top of him. By this time the two Iranian fighters' own threat radars had picked up the incoming missile rounds. But it was now too late.

At the instant the MiGs took evasive action, Petrov pushed the remote detonate button to the side of the main scope and a bright flash filled the thermal imaging window on the stealth's console display. Outside Shadow One's cockpit canopy window, multiple detonations pulsed in the heavens, lighting up the black sky for microinstants with throbbing, booming fireballs and pinwheels as the sortie of MiG-29 Fulcrums exploded into supernovas of vaporized metal, spinning debris, and burning fuel.

Moments later the night sky was cleared of MiGs. Petrov applied full thrust and shot ahead of the Antonov. As he passed it, letting it have a taste of his own pressure wave, he jinked Shadow One's wings back and forth in a farewell salute.

The AN-72's pilot and copilot saw the MFI through their flight-deck windows, and then the stealth plane was gone, becoming invisible to their eyes and their radars. This time, Petrov told himself, there would be no more mishaps. If nothing else, God and the dues he had paid would see to that. He would return to Vladivostok again, he knew this in his marrow. His dream had not lied. He would fly to freedom, just as it had foretold.

Petrov didn't know it, but "God" was watching him. The Hawkman had been cruising his bird high above the action. At seventy thousand feet, he had a good view not only of the situation in the air, but of the situation on the ground as well.

He had loitered the Hawk until the Antonov had gotten clear of Dasht airspace and was flying over the eastern mountain range, making fast for the border, satisfied that nothing else was in the air that could find it or harm it on its way back into the Caucasus.

On his own way home, the Hawkman couldn't resist dropping down to fifty thousand feet and getting some close-up imagery of the Iranian armor on the ground. Apparently there was some new stuff in the mix of tanks and APCs that the Pentagon would want to know about—looked Chinese, but the analysts would figure out the nuts and bolts. Now the Hawk was at the top of its envelope, cruising westward at its flight ceiling of eighty thousand feet. The Hawkman slipped off his HMD and pulled off his force-feedback gloves. Autopilot could take his bird the rest of the way.

It was time to change the music.

"Hendrix at Woodstock," he called out. As he reached for the last cold soda can in the cooler nearby, the strains of an electrified fuzz guitar playing "The Star-Spangled Banner" began to blare from the boombox.

"Louder, man," he said, taking a slug and working the stereo remote.

"Much louder."

Tomahawk launch depth was fifteen meters, a little below periscope depth. With the sub stopped dead, Gustavsen scanned his final orders from CINCLANTFLT. The launch order was still a go. It was time the fat lady sang.

"BSY-1 systems report full readiness. Targeting data are loaded. Ready for missile launch on your command," was the status report from the torpedo room.

"Open launch-capsule hatches one through six," Gustavsen said to his exec, who echoed the order to the torp room over the boat's interphone circuit.

"Launch-capsule hatches are open," the exec said back less than a minute later.

Now only a thin plastic membrane separated the missiles from the surrounding seawater, the pressurized atmosphere in the launch capsules preventing water pressure from flooding the tubes.

"Launch on my mark," Gustavsen said back to his exec. "Three, two, one—mark!"

"Launch the birds. Now, now, now!" the exec echoed to the chief torpedoman.

At the bottom of capsule one, an explosive charge detonated, thrusting the first Tomahawk through the membrane and catapulting it away from the launch tube. Under a second later, at approximately eight meters from the *Teaneck*'s hull, the missile's booster stage ignited, shotgunning it up through the surface and into the air, where its tail fins popped out to stabilize its upward flight.

The Tomahawk climbed to a 304-meter altitude, where its booster burned out and dropped away, and then the missile began its transition to level flight. Stub wings slid from grooves in the fuselage and a rear air scoop deployed, forcing air into the missile's turbofan engine, which spooled up and began to deliver thrust as the round went horizontal and began flying its programmed track.

Before the first Tomahawk had leveled off, the second cruise missile was repeating the initial phase of the firing sequence, roiling the water around *Teaneck* as it streaked toward the surface. In a blur of sound and fury, fire and steam, the sea above the submarine would erupt four more times, as *Teaneck* launched the rest of her missile load at her land-based targets.

As far as her skipper was concerned, he had just telegraphed the boat's position to the entire Iranian navy. He would need all his skill and a mortgage on his luck to make it to the safety of the Arabian Sea, where the carrier battlegroup *Strickland* had steamed at flank speed to forestall action by the Iranian navy. Gustavsen made his chances as one in three of his crew surviving the next hour in the water. But anything was better than staying where he was currently.

"Diving Officer, make my depth sixty-five feet. Prepare to dive," Gustavsen ordered, and the command was echoed down the line.

Though their targets were a group of launchers clustered together, the Tomahawks did not fly identical tracks to reach them. To maximize their chances of survivability, and to confuse the tracking radars of Iranian early warning and SAM installations, each cruise was programmed to fly a slightly different, looping, snaking track to the target zone and to detonate at varying altitudes once there.

Guided to the shoreline by their inertial navigation systems, the missiles switched on their TERCOM maps once they'd crossed the sea-land boundary of the Iranian littoral. Radar returns of the terrain below were digitized by onboard altimeters and compared against digital terrain maps stored in memory that were composed of grids of contoured squares.

From this first TERCOM map, the Tomahawks took their preliminary course readings and made initial corrections. Farther inland, TERCOM switched on to repeat this process over a series of increasingly smaller grids as the missiles flew their tracks, until each Tomahawk had advanced to within a few kilometers of its designated target. At this point the DSMAC system switched to active mode to provide terminal guidance via infrared imaging of the terrain and landmarks below.

With a CEP or circular error probability assured to less than ten feet, all six Tomahawks reached their impact points within minutes of launch. Some missiles popped up from low-trajectory flight paths to explode in airbursts that hammered their target sets with concussive wavefronts and gouts of broiling flame. Others plowed straight into the missile launchers, detonating at the moment of impact. The net result was a firestorm so intense, as it fused metal and incinerated fissionable warhead materials, that the light could be seen and the sound could be heard as far inland as Tehran.

This time, nothing humanly possible had been left to chance.

Onboard the AN-72 Coaler, Mitchell went across to where one of his men stood guard over the sullen group of captive Israeli commandos. Mitchell suspected their ultimate fate would be repatriation to Israel, where they would either be put on trial to draw heat off other guilty parties too politically well connected to touch, or to simply fade into the woodwork. Right now, though, he had a question to ask of them. Peace had been turning over the words Barak had uttered just before he'd expired. Mitchell wondered what " 'tis dyin' " meant. With the fighting over, Barak's last words gnawed at him.

Mitchell could not get the look in the doomed man's eyes out of his mind. Could he have been asking him to pray for his eternal soul? he wondered. Barak had been an enemy. Yet Mitchell would still not feel right about denying him his last rites. Barak had been a soldier, and a brave one. Despite his twisted value system, there was a shared commonalty between them.

Since all of the Israelis spoke fairly good English, Mitchell had no trouble learning the answer. In fact, they were all too eager to tell him what he wanted to know.

"Tizdayen?" one of the prisoners replied, dragging on a cigarette, the price of his knowledge, and glancing over to the pile of zippered mortuary bags lashed down in a corner of the plane that contained their leader's mortal remains. "Ah yes, a very good Hebrew word.

"It's very simple, my American friend," he went on as smoke curled from his nostrils. "With his last breath, Raful was telling you something in Hebrew. He was telling you—*to go fuck yourself.*"

Gouts of pent-up laughter erupted from the throats of the captive Israelis. Somewhere, they all felt, Barak was laughing, too. To the surprise of all, the laughter proved infectious, and Mitchell, too, got caught up in it. Soon it had spread to the entire plane. The psychs had a name for it. They called it postcombat euphoria and both Mitchell and Arbatov knew what was happening.

But fuck it, they thought.

It was a gift.

"Bradley, are you there?"

"Yes, Scott."

"Bradley, can you still see the fires in the distance?"

"Scott, I can not only still see them, but I can still hear some secondary explosions, which, they tell me, are the result of ammunition depots blowing up in the wake of what was apparently a preemptive air strike by Tomahawk missiles on Iranian missile targets."

"Now, for the benefit of viewers who have recently tuned in, these are suspected to have been nuclear-tipped missiles, weren't they?"

"That's right, Scott. Pentagon spokesmen claim that a preemptive strike was launched just an hour ago to prevent Iran from firing those missiles on targets as far away as Turkey or Greece."

"Both members of NATO."

"That's right, Scott. The Iranians confirm that missile installations were hit, but deny that any of the missiles had nuclear capability or for that matter anything like the range which the Pentagon claims. They insist the missiles are for defense only."

"Okay, Bradley. We need to pause for a commercial break right now, but we'll return to you shortly, so please stay with us." The split screen dissolved and the camera pulled in close on the newsanchor's familiar, craggy face. "Again, for the benefit of those who have just tuned in, U.S. missiles have hit what are claimed to have been nuclear missile sites in Iran. All Iranian missiles are reportedly destroyed. More when we come back in just a few minutes with up-to-the-minute reporting on this breaking news story."

The newsanchor held his expression steady as the camera stayed tight on his face. Two seconds later the television screens of millions of dinnertime viewers switched to a multicolor animated logo that read TENSION IN THE GULF. Drumrolls and brassy horns sounded in the background. Then a commercial for a new luxury sedan filled the airwaves. For a few minutes more the world was safe again, and business went on as usual.

Prologue

How did it ever come to this? thought eighteen-year-old Pvt. Stephanie Roberts as she stared at the dusty roadblock that marked the new boundary carved into America.

Stephie, the youngest infantryman in the squad of nine and one of only two women, climbed aboard the truck. "I don't trust you," the hulking Animal said to her. At five-seven and 125 pounds, Stephie and her rifle were security for the lone machine gun attached to her squad. Attached to the machine gun was a 250-pound asshole who sank onto the bench seat beside Stephie. The white, former junior college football lineman was nineteen, but he had an emotional age of six. "I don't trust split tails," he whispered with breath that made Stephie wince, "so just stay the hell outa the way of my gun, or I might have to kill you to kill Chinese." Her squadmates ignored her clash.

"Suits me fine," Stephie replied. "And you stink."

It was a hot day. Throngs of refugees crowded the border of the Exclusion Zone two hundred miles north of the

Alabama Gulf Coast. Two hundred miles north of her home. On the northern side, all seemed normal. Laundry hung on clotheslines within a stone's throw of the sand-bagged guard post. Stores were open. Towns were busy. People went about their lives. Had it not been for the concealed machine guns, tanks, and missile batteries, the casual eye wouldn't have detected much change. Even the evacuee relocation center—tents pitched amid motor homes and barbeques—looked like a national park campground in summer.

The mixed team of MPs and state highway patrolmen raised the barrier and waved the dozen-vehicle convoy through. The diesels growled and belched noxious fumes, but Stephie was glad even for that breeze on the sweltering day. Their truck passed the sentries, and Stephie got the distinct impression that they were leaving America.

The sandbagged walls that rose up the road's shoulders parted, and the pavement began to flash by. They were in disputed territory. The no-man's-land between two great armies. Barren of life. Still and quiet and empty as if braced for the violence to come.

No maps had been redrawn to show the dashed lines that now carved into the southeastern United States, but the CO had shown everybody in their infantry company maps, stained with blood, that had been captured from Chinese reconnaissance teams. The American teenagers had passed them around in silence while seated on helmets and packs at the end of a week-long field-training exercise. They were 110 brand-new infantrymen—only one month removed from the shocking rigors of boot camp, and four from cocoons of middle-class comfort. All now were grimy, sunburned, sweaty, mosquito-bitten, scraped, and bruised. Exhaustion was evident in their slumped reposes.

But as the maps were handed from soldier to soldier, anger crackled. It burned in squinted eyes. It swelled from rhythmically clenching jaws. The maps had made the circuit by the time the trucks had arrived to return them to their makeshift barracks in a nearby Holiday Inn, but no one rose from the big circle in which they sat. The rides meant back to a semiprivate room shared with nineteen-year-old Becky Marsh from Oregon, the other woman in Stephie's squad. It meant showers, air conditioning, soft beds. But the bone-weary teenagers refused to leave the field. Lieutenant Ackerman, their platoon leader, feigned annoyance while hiding a grin. Staff Sergeant Kurth, their platoon sergeant, and his noncoms never smiled.

That day, troops led their officers back into the woods. They spent another week digging holes, chopping brush, firing at trees, and assaulting a charred hump of dirt. The names of the Alabama towns that were shown on the captured enemy maps were already printed in Chinese.

"Lock 'n load," Sergeant Collins, their squad leader, barked as the trucks picked up speed. The first deployment of their newly-formed unit was a combat patrol of the exposed Gulf Coast beaches. Metallic clacks of magazines and snaps of breech covers pierced the steady *whoosh* of the wind of the road. They had cinched up the truck's canvas sides to get a breeze, and Stephie began to point out the familiar landmarks of her native state. She knew the cracked two-lane highway like the back from her hand. They passed the Stuckeys where Stephie's stepfather had always stopped for peanut brittle on the way home from football games in Tuscaloosa. She recognized the service station where they had waited one long, hot day for their leaking radiator to be repaired. And there was the stand that her mom had always insisted carried the freshest watermelons of any place on earth. All were now boarded up. Abandoned. Forlorn.

Her squadmates, for their parts, pointed out the road's new attractions. A billboard with the image of a famous actress, who always played the high school slut in the slasher flicks, pressing her index finger to ruby red lips. The seductive image drew lewd comments and gestures from the boys, who overlooked entirely the point of the message. "Loose Lips Sink Ships," read the legend at the top. Stephie wondered at how bad the actress's career must have turned.

Concrete bunkers with periscopes and electronics mastheads—facing south—had been dug out of the banked earth of highway overpasses. Bridges had been marked with orange signs that read, "Warning! Wired for demolition!" In the distance, open farm land—potential landing zones if aircraft suicidally flew at their missile defenses—had been pitted with black craters by preregistered artillery. And along the side of the road, ubiquitous triangular markers lined the roadside warning not to stray from the pavement onto shoulders already dotted with landmines. The regularly spaced triangles—black skulls and crossbones on yellow signs—flashed by as the convoy drew ever nearer the dangerous sea.

Every so often they passed small towns still being stripped by engineers. Tractor trailers were being loaded with everything militarily useful: portable generators, backhoes, transformers, propane tanks. What the engineers couldn't move, they destroyed. Columns of black smoke rose from all points of the compass. The convoy was stopped periodically by the demolition. Hoops and hollers rose from the parked convoy as charges toppled a metal water tower. Painted on the falling tank's side was a weathered, "Go Wildcats! Division II Basketball Champs 2001–02." After the great crash, the agitated male and female infantrymen reenacted the stupendous sight with hand gestures and special effects sounds. All were on their feet, agitated. Excited. *Scared out of their fucking skins*, Stephie thought with a quiver as if cold on the hot, hot day.

Over the next half hour, the thunderous booms that rolled across the landscape from unseen engineers near and far eventually had the opposite effect of that big steel crash. The thumps of high explosives on their bodies soon quieted the anxious chatter in the truck. War hadn't yet come to America, but the thudding jolts that rattled their insides frayed their nerves with portents of death. The teenagers looked inward. Peer pressure demanded it. No one contemplated what loomed ahead out loud, except Becky. Stephie's roommate spent two weeks at the Holiday Inn imagining doom to all hours of the morning despite Stephie's pleas for sleep.

The convoy resumed their journey toward the Gulf at about 0800 hours and soon plunged into a thick, low-hanging haze. Some covered their mouths and noses with handkerchiefs against the choking smell. Stephie remembered. The Canadian Rocky Mountains, summer vacation, when she was eight. Her first smell of a forest fire.

The conflagration that consumed the Alabama woods was nowhere in sight, but the trees that lined the highway were now nothing more than charred hulks, brittle limbs, and pointed black fingers. The Chinese would find no wood for shelter or for campfires when the nights grew cold. There would be no brush to provide concealment from killing American fire. They would find nothing but death and devastation, Stephie thought with boiling hatred. Her face twitched and she fought back tears. Anger always made her cry.

Only PFC John Burns, seated beside her, noticed. He glanced her way, cracked a half-smile from one side of his mouth, then closed his eyes to resume his slumber.

At first, he was the only one among the almost two dozen soldiers in the truck who seemed to be resting comfortably. The two squads and weapons teams were packed shoulder-to-shoulder. Everyone other than Burns stared out in sullen silence at the cloud-shrouded, desolate scenery. They clutched their weapons as if for psychological comfort.

One-by-one, however, they began to drift off. Soon—miraculously, Stephie thought as she looked all around—every last one of her comrades had fallen sound asleep, including Animal, the beef eater next to her, who slumped her way. The huge guy created quite a stir when he shouted after Stephie knocked his leaning machine gun back against his helmet. Animal's eyes opened wide. For a heartbeat that Animal clearly believed would be his last, he thought that he'd been hit. He was so happy to be alive that he grinned at Stephie instead of punching her, then went back to sleep in seconds.

Stephie felt the same pull toward slumber. The warm

breeze stifled conversation, forcing thoughts inward. The clicks from the tires as they crossed the regularly spaced seams in the aging concrete were almost hypnotic. The old truck's stiff suspension rocked steadily from side to side and front to back. But Stephie could never rest while on the road. She had never felt comfortable enough to relax in a moving vehicle.

John Burns flashed Stephie another encouraging smile before again closing his eyes and leaning his helmet back against the metal frame that held the canvas. Stephie had smiled back at the boy—the man, really, for the dark-haired Burns was a little older than the others in their platoon—out of a habit bred in high school. *High school,* she thought. *High school!* Four months earlier, she had walked across the stage and been handed her diploma. The night of the prom she and Conner Reilly, her boyfriend, on leave from his unit, had hopped until dawn from one party to the next in the rented limousine. *Four months ago.*

She felt depressed, on edge, dispirited, and suddenly totally unprepared. In the balmy silence of the late-summer morning, a single question dominated the eighteen-year-old's thoughts: *How did it ever come to this?*

Scenes of a distant war flickered across the television screen. Ten-year-old Stephie Roberts watched though her mother ignored the grainy pictures of combat on the nightly news. "The addition of Thai army forces to the war in Vietnam has done little to slow the advancing Chinese." When the news moved on to some boring ceremony in Korea, Stephie returned to her journal. "Sally H. said today that we'll look really hot when we get our braces off, but that Gloria W. needs a nose job. I told Judy, who told The Evil James Thurmond, who told Gloria, who got really, REALLY pissed at *me,*" she underlined, "for some totally warped reason!" U.S. troops, the reporter explained, had been withdrawn as a condition to reunification of the North and South. On the eve of a nationwide free election, the North Korean government had collapsed as its leaders—fearing retribution—had fled the country. China and South Korea had both stepped into the void to quell the violence. Their armies had clashed, and China had occupied the entire Korean Peninsula: North and South. The Chinese-backed puppet government was now celebrating the long-awaited reunion. "Must destroy James Thurmond!" Stephie wrote as she muted the boring program. "Hey, hey!" her stepdad said, grabbing the remote. They listened to a report that affected the company where he worked. Despite falling defense appropriations, Congress was authorizing billions of dollars for an antimissile shield. Her stepdad was beaming. Her mother said, "Now, finally, maybe you'll get the guts to ask for a raise." Stephie went outside and took a walk down the beach barefoot in the fading Alabama sun, plotting the total social demise of The Evil One.

The blue water of the Gulf didn't look the same as it had in Stephie Roberts's youth. Nothing was the same as it had been before. "First Squad, *out*!" shouted Sergeant Collins. "Stay off the beach! It's mined! Look *alive*!" The six other men and two women of Stephie's squad climbed down from the green, canvas-covered truck with their weapons and combat loads. Tony Massera, a private from Philadelphia, stood on the pavement squinting into the midday sunshine before donning his army shades. "Is it *always* this fuckin' hot in Alabama, Roberts?"

"*Puh*-ssy," Animal coughed into his fist. His fit of faux hacking ended with, "Puh-, puh-, *pussy*!" and a smile at Massera to ensure that he'd heard it correctly. Had the insult come from anyone else, the wiry and tough Massera—Animal's assistant machine gunner—would clearly have faced the man down or pummeled him to the ground with a flurry of blows. But the hulking machine gunner they all called Animal—who was semi-permanently attached to their squad—was a would-be offensive lineman for Ohio State. He dwarfed everyone else. Massera let it drop. Animal cleared his throat. "Sorry. *Shit!* Must be comin' down with somethin' Antonio."

"Tony," Massera corrected for about the hundredth time since the crew-served weapons had been handed down to the platoons. No one else had anything to say.

By age twelve, Stephie was even less interested in world events. But she remembered the day her class was watching the big screen in the Internet Lab of her Mobile, Alabama middle school. A grown man—India's prime minister—stood crying on a dock in Bombay. The sight riveted the darkened room filled with seventh graders. All were still young enough to take their cues from distraught adults, but not yet old enough to fully understand the reason for their shared distress. Indian civilians and soldiers were hastily boarding an overcrowded gray destroyer. "Does anyone know why the Indian prime minister didn't get on that ship?" the hyperstrict teacher asked the class. When no one answered, she said, "With Pakistani and Chinese troops just outside the city?" Again, no one ventured a guess. "Because the ship is *British*," the teacher explained with a sigh. It was a class for the gifted and talented. Stephie felt they were letting her down. "He was too proud to leave his country on a foreign ship." Everybody stared at the crying man. Stephie raised her hand and, when called upon, politely asked what had happened to him. "He was executed," came the teacher's reply. "Shot." All Stephie could think to say was, "Thanks."

"Shut up and shoulder yer loads!" snapped their squad leader despite the fact that no one standing at the back of the truck was talking. At twenty, Sergeant Collins was the oldest among them, and he was nervous. "This is the *coast*, in case you morons missed it!"

No one *had* missed the fact, of course. The nearer their convoy had come to the water, the flatter the terrain had grown. The Corps of Engineers had over a month before completed its work on the ghost towns outside Mobile. Peter Scott had commented that the blackened rubble of hospitals, schools, and courthouses already looked like the aftermath of heavy fighting. But Stephie had scrutinized the pictures of war's total devastation on the covers of news magazines. The selective demolition of public buildings paled when compared to the moonscapes left in Yokohama, Singapore, and Bombay. *And Tel Aviv,* she thought with a shiver.

Their first sight of the Gulf had come as a shock. The azure horizon visible in gaps between the tall pines had caused Stephie's stomach to begin to turn flips. After they had taken the coast road, some of the soldiers had stared at the shore as if to confront their inner demons. Others had rested their helmets against the raised front sights of their army surplus M-16s, focusing instead on their boots.

At thirteen, Stephie's soccer team won the state championship. Stephie played all ninety minutes at midfield. Although she got no goals or assists in the one-nil victory, she ran her heart out from penalty area to penalty area, challenged every header, made crisp passes despite legs that ached from the week-long tournament. Her crowning achievement in life to that time came in the waning moments of the game when she cleanly tackled the ball away from their opponent's greatest scoring threat. When the whistle blew, the entire team slid on their bellies into a pile on the rain-soaked pitch and hugged, cheered, and cried in equally shared, maximum celebration. At the beginning of the season, the coach had promised them that if they won state—and they had a chance—they would go as a team to soccer camp the following summer . . . in the south of France! They had practiced five days a week. Played regular season games, then driven to faraway tournaments and played again later the same day. Before the quarterfinals in the statewide, all had agreed not to talk about the trip for fear of jinxing it. As they left the pitch after the semis, however, a muddy Sally Hampton into Stephie's ear, "We're going to *France*!"

And she was right. They had won the state championship.

Over the squeals of excitement, all heard their coach's voice. "Sorry, girls!" he shouted apologetically. They all looked up at him. "We're not going to be able to go." There were a couple of cries of "*What?*" but a half-dozen cries of "*Why?*" He replied that because of the war in the Indian Ocean, the French had canceled the soccer camp. "Can't we just go *anyway*?" objected Gloria Wilson, their goalkeeper. "Your parents don't think it's safe," replied their frowning coach. The girls, still lying prone rose to their cleats and descended upon the gathering of parents, employing every conceivable argument. "We're not going by boat, we're *flying* over!" tried one. "The war is, like, a thousand miles away!" came another attempt. "You *promised*!" was the last, plaintive gasp. Their coach held out his hands to quell the uprising. "Everybody's really sorry, girls, but after the battle Europe lost to China in the Indian Ocean, it's just not safe to go overseas anymore. Nobody really knows what's gonna happen next." The girls were crushed. Some of the holdouts cried and argued their way to the car. The only thing that prevented Stephie from doing the same was that she spotted her father—her real father—still sitting in the stands. Stephie's mother rolled her eyes on seeing him and seethed at his mere presence.

Stephie ran to him. He held out his arms and threw them around her, holding her tight. "I'm so proud of you!" he said into her hair as she grinned and pressed her face flat against his chest. "You ran so hard! You won so many headers! Your passes were all right on target! And that steal at the end from the other team's best player was what won the game!" Stephie raised her face to beam at him, but had to stifle the grin with lips that she curled over her teeth. "You can smile now, Stephie," her father said, gently grasping her chin and raising her face. "You're not wearing braces anymore. You have always been, and are now, the most beautiful thing in heaven or on earth." She laughed. He tenderly cupped her mud-flaked cheeks in his hands. "I love you with all my heart," he said. At the team cookout, Stephie's angry mother had groused incessantly about her ex-husband ruining Stephie's wonderful day, and her sullen teammates had vented their ire on their parents about the canceled trip with a pre-agreed wall of silence. But behind her wall, Stephie had been euphoric. Absolutely euphoric. All was right with the world. Things were great.

Stephie backed up to her heavy field pack, which stood upright on the truck's tailgate. "You want me to carry some of your gear?" John Burns asked in a low voice. He was stooped forward under the weight of his own eighty-pound pack, and he wasn't even in Stephie's squad. Animal wagged his tongue obscenely up and down in the air. Her squadmates snickered at the machine gunner's crude mockery of John's offer. "I can handle it," Stephie said, hoisting the pack onto her back with a grunt. Her legs almost buckled but she clenched her teeth and tried to continue breathing while tightening the harness across her chest and stomach. She then grabbed her M-16, which came with an M-249. The 40-mm grenade launcher mounted underneath the barrel looked like a toy. The stubby, bullet-shaped projectiles bulged from sleeves on bandoliers crossed over her torso, making her look like some large-caliber *pistollero.*

Becky Marsh watched John join the ranks on the road without once offering her his assistance. She winced and grunted as she shouldered her own massive pack. "No, *I* don't need any help," she muttered sarcastically, "but thanks for fucking asking!" Becky glared at Stephie, who chose not to notice.

Third platoon consisted of thirty-one soldiers. Lieutenant Ackerman and his commo and Platoon Sergeant Kurth stood in front of four, nine-man squads of infantry, which formed ranks for inspection. Of the twenty-seven infantrymen in the four numbered squads, nineteen were men and eight were women. Each squad had two fire teams, and the eight women were evenly distributed: one in each fire team. The squad leaders—three buck sergeants and a corporal—stood at the far right with their squads stretched at arm's-length to their left. The soldiers in the formation raised their left arms for proper, parade-ground spacing. The formation extended longer than normal because of the four soldiers added to the end of each squad's rank. A two-man machine gun crew and a two-man all-threat missile crew from the company's weapons platoon had been attached to each squad. With the four medics from the battalion medical detachment in the rear, Third Platoon today fielded fifty.

At fourteen, Stephie became obsessed with the opposite sex. And the latest in a series of the-cutest-boys-she'd-*ever*-seen was at an interdenominational prayer servicc for the victims of the Second Jewish Holocaust. He looked to be older—sixteen—and had shiny black hair, dark eyes, and smooth skin as white as paper. *He must have dermatologists for parents,* she marveled. Then, all of the sudden, Stephie realized that he must be Jewish. As the prayers wore on—some familiar, others in Hebrew—an imagined romance blossomed in Stephie's mind until her stepdad leaned over and whispered, "They brought it on *themselves*, you know. China *warned* Israel not to use nukes." Stephie's mom crushed her stepdad's toe in embarrassment. When he hissed in pain, Stephie's imaginary boyfriend looked back and shocked Stephie straight to the core. Tears flowed from "radiant pools," she wrote in her journal, down the mysterious boy's porcelain skin. That night, Stephie got on the Internet and read news reports about Tel Aviv. It turned out that China *had* warned Israel against using nuclear weapons to try to stop their invasion. In retaliation, China had destroyed Tel Aviv with its population trapped inside. Stephie watched the video over and over. She couldn't read the Chinese characters in the lower righthand corner, but the countdown on the clock was universal. When the clock struck zero, half a dozen blinding flashes swallowed the city's skyline.

"First, second, and third squads and attached crews," the tall and angular Ackerman, newly commissioned officer and platoon leader, announced, "will come with me and Platoon Sergeant Kurth for a patrol of the beach! Fourth Squad will guard the trucks!"

"Knock it off!" Staff Sergeant Kurth boomed, although

Stephie had heard nothing from the troops. His stare menaced fourth squad in the rank behind Stephie. The squad that had drawn easy duty.

"Everybody patrolling the beach, keep your eyes open!" continued Ackerman. "West Point" is what most called him behind his back. "If you see any tracks, call 'em out! This is a free-fire zone! Watch for mines on both sides of the road. The mines underneath the pavement are under positive control and are currently safed. Weapons loaded. Rounds chambered. Safeties *on*." There was a steady clacking of metal as men and women pointed their weapons away from their buddies and checked their selector switches. Stephie ejected a curved, thirty-round magazine. The brass cartridges shone from atop their double stack. She reloaded the full mag into her assault rifle and loaded a 40-mm fragmentation grenade into the breach of her launcher. She slid the launcher shut with a snap like a pump shotgun and confirmed that the selector switches on both weapons were on "safe."

"Pursuant to the Coastal Defense Act," Lieutenant Ack Ack announced officiously, "this area is under martial law! We have orders to arrest any civilians we come across, and we are authorized to use deadly force! If we come into contact with any Chinese forces, we are to report in, engage, and destroy! Single file! Corporal Higgins, you're wired for the point! Take the lead! Let's *move* out!"

Fifteen was a time of questioning for Stephie. "Why'd those people in New Zealand throw garbage at our ship?" With his mouth still full, her stepfather said they were ungrateful 'cause we didn't defend 'em. Stephie's mom cleared her throat at her husband's table manners. "Why didn't we defend them?" Stephie asked. 'Cause it wasn't worth World War Three, 'specially right before the new, second-generation missile shield's in place. "Who's stronger—us or the Chinese?" Us. "Then how come we let 'em rape Manila?" Don't use that *word*, her mom said. Stephie's stepfather replied that the Chinese had used Korean shipyards that previously had built super*tankers* to build their new super*carriers*. They're five times bigger than our carriers and hold three times as many planes. Some are transports that can carry twenty thousand troops at a time. "How big is their army?" Stephie asked. Thirty, forty million, give or take. "How big is *ours*?" Dunno. A few hundred thousand. "Then how can you say *we're* stronger than *them*?" 'Cause of the missile shield his company was helping build. "But aren't *they* building one, *too*? Isn't *everybody* building one?" Her stepfather grew tired of Stephie's incessant questions.

One by one the ranks headed down the highway parallel to the shore, straight toward Stephie's house. Her squad was third and last in line. With a ten-meter spread, the point man was over 300 meters ahead, but Stephie could see what Higgins saw from the point—an empty ribbon of road that swayed with the point man's every step—on a one-inch LCD screen suspended on a slender boom before her face. The old-style Kevlar helmets had been retrofitted with a strap-on electronics suite. It consisted of the screen and a microphone on the boom, headphones under the armored ear flaps, and a wire running to a battery and receiver on the shoulder of the webbing. To that ensemble, the point man added a tiny pen-sized camera and transmitter.

The electronics system of the newly raised 41st Infantry Division was, however, basically just a hodgepodge. It wasn't nearly as advanced as the equipment of the lower-numbered divisions of America's regular, standing army. The system used by the professionals was fully integrated into their newer and lighter ceramic helmets.

Stephie scanned the dunes on the left and beaches on the right, but saw nothing save the litter common to any roadside. Candy wrappers. Coke cans. Yellowed newspapers half buried in sand.

"Lookie *here*!" Stephon Johnson said from ahead. His voice broke in and out on her balky left earphone. Johnson—a corporal—was a grenadier from Washington, DC, and the leader of Stephie's fire team alpha. He kicked at a used condom with his combat boot. "Looks like you had yourself some good *times* down here on the Redneck Riviera, *Roberts*." Men laughed and commented in turn as they passed the wilted prophylactic.

"Cut the shit!" Sergeant Collins finally snapped. They marched on in silence, skirting a fresh crater in the cracked pavement that was half-filled with brackish green water. It must have been from a practice bombing run, Stephie thought, or an Air Force attack on a Chinese probe.

Stephie's thighs and lungs began to burn. Her lower back and shoulders grew to ache from the heavy "existence load." Sweat showed through the men's thick, woodlands-camouflage battle dress as they marched farther and farther from the trucks. Closer and closer to her house. The only contact they had with the outside world came in the form of an occasional crackle over the commo's audio/video gear, which carried on the ocean breeze from the middle of the formation where Ackerman and the commo were. Two other platoons in their company were on different stretches of the empty shoreline, and the company commander was with one of them. Although they weren't in range now, when they were within a four-mile radius of the transmitters, the CO could watch video from any of his four platoons.

Or so it was supposed to work. No one really had any idea what to expect. Their unit—the 41st Infantry Division—had first unfurled its colors at a ceremony at Fort Benning, Georgia, only one month earlier. The six hundred men and women of Stephie's 3rd of the 519th Infantry Regiment were in one of the division's fifteen infantry battalions. Charlie Company of the 3/519 had been given orders for this—their first mission—only the day before.

Stephie had wondered about the mission's real purpose ever since. During a semisleepless night, she had reasoned that they could reconnoiter the coast by air. But she knew they were sending units south every day. Maybe it was to give them tactical training on the theater's terrain. A chance to get a feel for the ground on which they would fight. Or maybe it was a purely symbolic act. Going down to the water's edge one last time to assert U.S. sovereignty over territory that would soon be the property of the Chinese. But even if symbolic, their combat patrol was dangerous. There were skirmishes practically every day. The coast was alive with Chinese scouts, pathfinders, patrols, and raiding parties. *But*, she decided, *we've gotta get blooded some time. Better now—against a recon team that we outnumber ten-to-one—than when we match up against the Chinese one-to-ten.*

Third platoon's Caucasians, Hispanics, African-Americans, and "Others" came from all parts of the country. There were practically no deferments from the draft, so they came from every socioeconomic class. But the representatives of their generation were more alike than any other soldiers that America had fielded in its history. In an interconnected world they had melded into a uniform blend. And one attribute shared by the forty-odd teenagers was that none had ever killed a living thing. There was not a single hunter or outdoorsman among the teenage urban-and suburbanites.

Stephie had her first beer and smoked her first pot on her sixteenth birthday. On a walk down the beach she ran into some juniors from her high school, who were drunk on the six-pack they'd bought at a nearby convenience store. Conner Reilly, the coolest of the cool, finally offered her a beer.

"You know they're out there," said Conner Reilly, nodding at the Gulf, as soundless coughs still wracked Stephie's chest. Conner was tanned and tall—on the basketball team—but had green eyes and long eyelashes like a fashion model. He also dated the best looking girl in school, Stephie reminded herself, who would crush Stephie, socially, if she perceived any threat, which she couldn't possibly. "Bullshit," replied Walter Ames. Walter's father was black, and his mother was white. Walter defined the word cool. Stephie felt cool just being around him, and she wondered if any of the boys would acknowledge her Monday when they went back to school.

"They're too busy invadin' Japan," Walter insisted, but Conner was unswayed. "China's got bases," he said, rocking forward in the circle and drawing a map in the sand, "on those islands up and down the coast of Africa!" Conner's islands looked like freckles on his hand-drawn sea. With her finger, she completed the sea's smiley face.

They marched about a mile down the beach before they came upon a body. It had washed up on the shore and was covered in seaweed. You couldn't tell much more than that from the road. They took a break as the LT checked his map showing minefields, then sent two men out onto the beach. The soldiers recoiled in disgust and returned to report to the LT, who called a report in to the CO. Word quickly spread that it was a U.S. sailor who'd been in the water a long, long time. Men returned to the corpse, sunk a piece of driftwood into the sand, and tied a white towel to the upright marker.

"Must've been from the Straits of Havana," Animal said. He was sweating profusely and rested his heavy, vintage M-60 in his lap as he mopped his face with a towel. He and Massera were from weapons platoon—not a numbered platoon—thus they, like the missile team, were outsiders.

The ultimate insider was Stephon Johnson, who knew everybody in every unit. He had advance word of just about everything important because of the network of contacts that he always touted. "I hear there was 30,000 squids 'n jarheads on those ships. That Chinese wolfpack had a hun'erd subs in it, just waitin'. Bodies been washin' up all the way over to Texas."

"And there are five million Chinese soldiers in Cuba," Stephie said in the low tones everyone else had assumed. Nobody said a word in reply.